PENGUIN
PICTURE IM

Saradindu Bandyopadhyay wa[...]
Jaunpur, Uttar Pradesh. His first [...]
poems published in 1919. At t[...]
Vidyasagar College, Calcutta, and lived in a mess on Harrison
Road (now Mahatma Gandhi Road). His room at the mess was
later to become a model for Byomkesh Bakshi's famous first
residence. While still a student, he married his wife Parul in
1918. Subsequently he studied law, and then dedicated himself
to writing. By 1932, when the first Byomkesh mystery appeared,
he was already an established writer.

In 1938, Saradindu moved to Bombay to work on screenplays
for Bombay Talkies and later for other banners. He worked in
Bombay till 1952, when he gave up his ties with cinema and
moved to Pune to concentrate on his writing. He went on to
become a popular and renowned writer of ghost stories,
historical romances and children's fiction in Bengali. But the
Byomkesh series remains his most cherished contribution to the
world of contemporary Bengali fiction.

Saradindu Bandyopadhyay was a recipient of the Rabindra
Purashkar in 1967 for his novel *Tunghabhadrar Tirey*. He was also
awarded the Sarat Smriti Purashkar by Calcutta University in
the same year. The latter part of his life was spent in Pune where
he passed away on 22 September 1970.

*

Sreejata Guha has a BA in Comparative Literature with a First
Class First from Jadavpur University, Calcutta, and an MA in
the same subject from State University of New York at Stony
Brook. She is currently working on a Ph.D. dissertation on
translation theory which studies texts that have travelled in
translation from the original Bengali. She has worked as a
translator and editor with Stree Publishers and Seagull Books,
Calcutta, and written extensively on theatre, popular culture
and the environment for various national publications. She lives
in Pittsburgh, USA.

Saradindu Bandyopadhyay

Picture Imperfect

and Other Byomkesh Bakshi Mysteries

Translated from the Bengali by
Sreejata Guha

PENGUIN BOOKS

An imprint of Penguin Random House

PENGUIN BOOKS

USA | Canada | UK | Ireland | Australia
New Zealand | India | South Africa | China | Singapore

Penguin Books is part of the Penguin Random House group of companies
whose addresses can be found at global.penguinrandomhouse.com

Published by Penguin Random House India Pvt. Ltd
4th Floor, Capital Tower 1, MG Road,
Gurugram 122 002, Haryana, India

First published in English by Penguin Books India 1999

Copyright © The Estate of Saradendu Bandyopadhyay 1999
This translation copyright © Penguin Books India 1999

ISBN 9780140287103

Typeset in Palatino by Digital Technologies and Printing Solutions, New Delhi

Printed at Repro India Limited

www.penguin.co.in

MIX
Paper from
responsible sources
FSC® C047271

Contents

Contents

I still remember that evening when, as a nine-year-old on a vacation to a remote hill station with my parents, I had my first encounter with Byomkesh. It was a lazy evening with no special recreation to speak of, and in response to my clamours for a story, my mother picked out a Byomkesh mystery and, in the evocative candlelight occasioned by a power cut, entertained me for several hours. The experience has stuck in my mind because since then, I have read and re-read these stories many times at different stages of adolescence and adulthood, and that is exactly what they have always done—entertained.

The beginning of Byomkesh's journey dates back to 1932 when Saradindu Bandyopadhyay, already an established author, decided to try his hand at detective fiction. The first story, 'Pather Kanta' ('The Gramophone Pin Mystery') was published in the monthly magazine *Basumati* and was an immediate success. After another story was published, the author decided to make a series out of the exploits of Byomkesh and with 'Satyanweshi' ('The Inquisitor', written in 1933) began the series involving Byomkesh and Ajit. Over the next thirty-seven years, right to his dying days, Saradindu Bandyopadhyay wrote a total of thirty-two Byomkesh mysteries, including several novels. Over time, the cases of Byomkesh Bakshi have become some of the most enduringly popular stories in Bangla literature. Recently, when some stories were adapted for a television serial shown on the national network, Byomkesh acquired a new legion of fans nationwide. 1999 marks Saradindu Bandyopadhyay's birth centenary, and it seems a fitting tribute to the author's art to publish this first volume of Byomkesh stories in English to coincide with the centenary celebrations.

What set Saradindu Bandyopadhyay apart as a writer of

detective fiction were his inimitable writing style and his exceptionally sophisticated character portrayals. In early twentieth century Bengal, writers and readers alike had looked down upon crime thrillers as a genre. It was Saradindu's Byomkesh Bakshi mysteries that gave the detective story its place of pride in the corpus of Bangla literature. This was partly due to the fact that while Saradindu, like his predecessors Panchkori De and Dinendrakumar Ray, was doubtless influenced by the detective fiction written by Arthur Conan Doyle, Edgar Allan Poe, G.K. Chesterton and Agatha Christie, his characters and locales, unlike those of any other mystery writer of the time, were rooted unmistakably in the Indian context. But what put Saradindu's writings in a class of its own was his ability to bring characters and situations alive, and the inimitable humour that permeated through his narratives. The Byomkesh oeuvre is not only superb as detective fiction, but has stood the test of time in its appeal to a wide cross-section of readers, young and old alike, as a collection of stories one enjoys re-reading for the sake of the narrative alone, even when the resolution is known. This is a remarkable achievement for any popular fiction, and it is this everlasting appeal that makes Saradindu's Byomkesh Bakshi series—along with Satyajit Ray's Feluda adventures—a classic of our times.

Byomkesh's iconic status owes a great deal to the fact that, for a protagonist working within the norms of a specific literary genre, his is a remarkably well-etched persona. To start with, both Byomkesh and Ajit are characters drawn from quintessential types of pre-Independence Bengali educated youth, and as such are familiar and immediately identifiable representatives of the middle class. There is no aura of the exotic about Byomkesh, except perhaps his name. As we trace his personal history through the stories, we see him meeting and courting his future wife and later marrying her and settling down to domesticity. The only thing that makes Byomkesh unusual is his intellect, which he uses to good effect in the professional arena. Even professionally, however, Byomkesh is a self-styled *satyanweshi* or inquisitor, not a private investigator. His job does not end with solving the case and pocketing the fee. His quest is the intellectually—and sometimes philosophically—charged activity of truth-seeking, a morally defined pursuit that has won him the admiration of generations of readers.

The character of Ajit is just as remarkable. Unlike most chronicler/assistants found commonly in detective fiction, Ajit is a professional writer who has dedicated himself to narrating his friend's extraordinary exploits. This explains the literary flourishes that appear periodically in his accounts of Byomkesh's cases. Unlike Watson and Holmes or Hastings and Poirot, Ajit and Byomkesh are contemporaries, partners in each and every one of Byomkesh's investigations, and cohabitors of the same apartment for the longest time, even after Byomkesh is married. There is a sense of a rooted relationship between the two, which elevates Ajit from the status of the customary satellite to that of an associate. Ajit understands Byomkesh as few others do; he works as Byomkesh's sounding board and sometimes—though not very often—offers insights that expedite the deduction processes of his friend.

This collection contains seven of the first eleven Byomkesh Bakshi stories written by Saradindu Bandyopadhyay, starting with 'The Inquisitor' and proceeding in chronological order. The first six stories included here were all written between 1932 and 1936. After writing 'Upasanhar' ('An Encore for Byomkesh') Saradindu decided he had had enough of Byomkesh for the time. Soon afterwards, he moved to Bombay and became a full-time screenplay writer for Hindi films. Sixteen years later, in 1952, just before his retirement from the world of cinema, he bowed to popular demand and revived the Byomkesh series with 'Chitrachor' ('Picture Imperfect'). This story marks the beginning of the second long innings of the inquisitor's escapades, written for the post-Independence reader, and therefore forms a fitting finale to this first volume of Byomkesh stories available in English.

As a translator, my primary concern was to capture and replicate the attraction these stories have had for generations of readers in original Bangla. What grips me in these stories every time is the prospect of the protagonist's razor-sharp intelligence being pitted against the wiles of a worthy opponent, and the fact of this contest being set against the backdrop of a near-perfect representation of the Bengali middle class milieu. In order to keep these laudable qualities of Saradindu's writing intact, I have often had to make choices that either preserve the cultural flavour and topical references of the original, or recreate a corresponding echo in the English language that nevertheless retains a neutral cultural space for the original. In the intricate, didactic and theoretical domain of translation theory, the validity and 'justifications' for such choices are still the subject of much contention and the 'task of the translator' is still under debate. But in the world where this 'task' is actually performed, one has to make one choice or another in transferring a narrative from one culturally coded context to another, and some 'losses' are inevitable. I have followed a pragmatic methodology, which serves to bridge the gap between two languages and their respective socio-cultural concomitants to the best of its capacity. The success of these modes and methods of translation lies in the ability of the final product to engage and absorb, to thrill and delight as many readers (preferably more) as did the original Bangla series.

The traditional conception of a translation is that it should 'travel' well from the source language to the target language. Just like any journey, this wasn't an easy one and neither was it solitary. I am thankful to Udayan Mitra, Sudeshna Shome Ghosh and Anjana Ramakrishnan, my editors at Penguin India, Ravi Singh for thinking up a superb cover, and David Davidar for expressing an interest in publishing the Byomkesh stories in the first place. For his help in locating key points of contention in the source text I am indebted to Dr Shibaji Bandyopadhyay, my mentor and my advisor on my doctoral project. To my friend Debjani Banerjee I owe a special word of thanks for her help with some of the finer points of the text. I would like to take this opportunity to also thank the various members of my family and the many friends who expressed eager anticipation for the publication of this volume—their interest made a difference to me. Finally, a word of immense gratitude for my most ardent critic and admirer, my dearest friend, Dipankar Ganguly: without his constant encouragement, this journey would have seemed much longer and more desolate. The frailties and flaws of the translated text, of course, are entirely my responsibility.

Pittsburgh, USA   Sreejata Guha
January 1999

The Inquisitor

M y first meeting with Byomkesh Bakshi took place in the
spring of 1925.

I was fresh out of the university. There was no pressing
need to try and earn my keep. The money that my father had
left in the bank generated an interest decent enough to cover
the expenses of a single person living in a boarding-house in
Calcutta. I had decided to remain a bachelor all my life and to
spend my time practising the literary arts. The first flush of
youthful enthusiasm had led me to believe that a serious
dedication to the literary muse would enable me to change the
face of literature in Bengal. At this point in life it is not
uncommon for Bengalis to dream of greatness—and it usually
doesn't take very long for these dreams to shatter.

However, let me continue with the story about my first
encounter with Byomkesh.

Even those who are deeply familiar with Calcutta are
perhaps unaware that there is an area in the very heart of the
city which is flanked on one side by dwellings of badly-off
non-Bengalis, on another by a degenerate slum, and on the
third by hutments of the pale-skinned Chinese. In the centre of
this mélange is a delta which by daylight does not seem
unusual in any way. But after sundown, the locality is
completely transformed. At the stroke of eight all businesses
down their shutters and the entire place becomes shrouded in
a deathly silence; just a few paan or cigarette stands remain
open. Only shadowy figures flit across these streets after that
hour. If a stranger happens to stray into the area at night, he
quickens his pace and vacates the locality as soon as he can.

It would be pointless to discuss in detail how I happened
to land up in a boarding-house in a neighbourhood such as this.
Suffice it to say that in the light of day the surroundings had
not aroused any suspicions in me and since I was getting a

large, airy room on the first floor of the mess for a very reasonable price, I moved in without further ado. It was only later that I came to know that every month two or three mutilated corpses were discovered on the streets here, and a police raid was a common occurrence at least once a week. But by then I had come to feel a certain attachment to my dwelling and the thought of shifting bag and baggage did not appeal to me. I usually stayed in after dark, concentrating on my literary activities; the fear of personal injury was therefore practically non-existent.

On the first floor of the house there were five rooms in all, each occupied by a single gentleman. They were all middle-aged and employed in regular jobs. Every weekend they went home and returned to their respective jobs on Monday. All of them had been living in this mess for quite a while. Recently one of them had retired and gone back to his hometown; the room that was thus vacated was assigned to me. In the evenings the inhabitants settled down to sessions of bridge or poker—complete with the raised voices and aggressiveness that these games occasioned. Ashwinibabu was a veteran at these games and his chief opponent was Ghanashyambabu. The latter would kick up a ruckus every time he lost. At nine o'clock sharp the cook would announce dinner and everyone would proceed peaceably to eat and subsequently retire to their respective rooms. The days at the mess passed in this fashion with unvarying routine. I too had fallen into the comfortable rut of this serene lifestyle quite willingly.

The landlord Anukulbabu occupied the rooms on the ground floor. A homeopath by profession, he was a simple, amiable man. Possibly he was a bachelor too since there was no family in the house. He looked after the daily needs of the tenants and also supervised the meals. He did it all with such finesse that there was no scope for complaints—once the sum of twenty-five rupees was deposited in his hands on the first of the month, one could be assured of every comfort for the next thirty days.

The doctor had a good patronage among the poorer

sections of the local people. Both in the mornings and in the evenings patients queued up in front of his office. He distributed medications at a negligible cost. He seldom made house calls; even if he had to, he did not charge for these. As a result the doctor was well respected by everyone in the neighbourhood. I too became a great admirer of his within a very short time. Every day, by about ten in the morning, everyone in the house left for work and just the two of us remained at home. We often had lunch together and the afternoons passed in light conversations and analyses of the day's newspaper headlines. Although the doctor was a mild-mannered man, he had the gift of the gab. He was under forty and had no university degree to his name; but sitting right at home, he had amassed such a vast amount of knowledge about everything under the sun that I felt a growing sense of wonderment listening to him. If I expressed my admiration he would shyly say, 'There is hardly anything else to do; so I just sit at home and read. All my knowledge is garnered from books.'

I had been in the boarding-house for a couple of months when one morning, around ten, I was sitting in Anukulbabu's room, glancing through the newspaper. Ashwinibabu left for work, chewing on his daily paan. He was followed by Ghanashyambabu who asked the doctor for some medication to soothe his toothache and then departed officewards. The other two gentlemen also left in due course. The house was empty for the day.

A couple of patients still awaited the doctor's attention. After sending them on their way with the requisite medication, he pushed his spectacles up over his forehead and asked, 'Is there anything interesting in the news today?'

'There was a police raid in our neighbourhood again last night.'

'That is a daily affair,' Anukulbabu smiled. 'Where was this?'

'Quite close actually, at number thirty-six; the house of one Sheikh Abdul Gaffoor.'

'Really! I know the man. He comes to me often for

treatment. Have they mentioned what the raid was for?'

'Cocaine. Here, read this!' I handed the *Daily Kalketu* to him.

Anukulbabu brought the spectacles back upon his nose and began to read:

'Last night there was a police raid in —— at the house of Sheikh Abdul Gaffoor, a leather merchant residing at number thirty-six, —— Street. However, no contraband material was found. The police is convinced that there is a secret hideout in this area, which supports the illegal trafficking in cocaine in the neighbourhood and elsewhere. A canny gang has continued to fox the police and conduct its illegal activities for some time now. It is indeed a matter of shame that the den of these miscreants has not been discovered yet, and that the identity of their leader still remains a mystery.'

Anukulbabu paused and then remarked, 'It is true. I too have been feeling that there is a huge distribution centre for illegal drugs in this area. I have received some indications of it sometimes. You know how it is, with so many patients coming in to see me. Whatever he may do, a cocaine addict cannot hide his symptoms from a medical man. But—that Abdul Gaffoor didn't seem like one to me. In fact, I can vouch for the fact that he is an opium addict. He said so himself.'

'Anukulbabu, what do you think is the reason for so many murders being committed in this neighbourhood?' I asked him.

'There is a simple explanation. Those who break the law by trafficking in illegal drugs are always apprehensive that they'll be caught. Hence, if someone happens to stumble onto one of their secrets, they have no choice but to kill him. Look at it this way: if I am dealing in cocaine and you come to know about it, will it be safe for me to let you live? If you open your mouth to the authorities, not only would I go to prison, but my huge business would also sink. Goods worth millions would be confiscated. Could I allow that to happen?' He began to laugh.

I said, 'It appears that you have made quite a study of the criminal psyche.'

'Yes—that is one of my interests,' he stretched himself and stood up.

I too was preparing to leave when suddenly a man entered

the room. He looked to be about twenty-three or twenty-four. His demeanour was that of an educated person. He was fair, well-built and handsome, and his face radiated intelligence. But he seemed to have fallen on bad times lately; his dress was in dishabille, his hair was uncombed, his shirt looked frayed and his shoes too had taken on a rough hue for lack of polishing. He had an expression of anxious eagerness on his face. He looked from me to Anukulbabu and said, 'I heard that this is a boarding-house—are there any rooms available?'

Both of us looked at him, a little surprised. Anukulbabu shook his head and said, 'No. What do you do for a living, sir?'

The man sank onto the patients' bench wearily and said, 'Right now I'm barely managing to keep myself alive—applying for jobs and looking for a roof over my head. But in this hapless city, even finding a decent boarding-house is next to impossible—every place is chock-full.'

Sympathetically, Anukulbabu said, 'It is rather difficult finding a vacancy in mid-season. What is your name, sir?'

'Atul Chandra Mitra. Ever since I arrived in Calcutta I have been doing the rounds for a job. The meagre funds that I had brought with me after closing up my place in the country and selling the last of my possessions are about to run out too—I hardly have twenty-five or thirty rupees left. That won't last much longer either if I have to eat at hotels twice a day. That is why I am looking for a decent mess—not for long . . . just a month or so; if I just get two square meals a day and a place to stay, I would manage.'

Anukulbabu said, 'I am extremely sorry Atulbabu, but all my rooms are taken.'

Atul gave a great sigh and said, 'Well then, there is nothing to be done—I shall have to set off again. Maybe I'll go and try the Oriya neighbourhood; my only concern is that at night all my money may be stolen. May I have a glass of water, please?'

The doctor went to get it for him. I was feeling very sorry for this helpless man. After some hesitation, I said, 'My room is quite large—it can easily accommodate two people. If you have no objections . . .'

Atul jumped up and said, 'Objections? What are you

saying, sir, I shall consider myself extremely fortunate.' Quickly he fished out a bundle of notes from his pocket and asked, 'How much do I have to pay? It will be kind of you to accept the money in advance. You see, I am not exactly . . .'

His eagerness amused me. I laughed and said,' It's all right, you can pay me later, there is no hurry.' Anukulbabu had returned with the water and I told him, 'This man is in a fix, so he can stay in my room at present—I shall not be inconvenienced.'

Overwhelmed with gratitude, Atul said, 'He has been very kind. But I shall not bother you for long—if I can make alternative arrangements in the meantime, I shall leave immediately.' He emptied his glass and put it down.

Anukulbabu looked at me in astonishment and said, 'In your room? Well—all right. Since you have no objections, I have nothing to say. It will be good for you too—the room rent will be split in half.'

I hastened to say, 'No, that is not why . . . he seems to be in a fix—'

The doctor laughed and said, 'Yes, that is true. Well then, Atulbabu, why don't you go and get your things? You are most welcome here.'

'Yes, certainly. I don't have too much to bring—just a bedding and a canvas bag. I left them with the watchman in a hotel. I shall go and get them right now.'

I added, 'Yes, and do join us for lunch.'

'That would be excellent indeed.' Atul threw a grateful glance in my direction and left.

After he left, we were silent for a few minutes. Anukulbabu was absent-mindedly cleaning his glasses with the end of his dhoti. I asked, 'What are you thinking, Anukulbabu?'

He started and replied, 'Nothing. It is charitable to assist someone in distress and you have done the right thing. But as you know, we have a saying about harbouring persons of unknown credentials . . . Anyway, I hope there will be no trouble.' He rose and left the room.

Atul Mitra started staying in my room. Anukulbabu had an

extra cot which he sent upstairs for him to use. Atul wasn't around during much of the day. He left early in the morning, looking for jobs, and returned around eleven. He would go out again after lunch. But the little time that he spent in the house was enough for him to build up a camaraderie with all the other inmates. He was eagerly sought for in the common room every evening. But since he had no knowledge of cards, he would leave quietly after a while and slip off downstairs to chat with the doctor. I struck up a rapport with him very quickly. We were the same age and room-mates to boot. So it wasn't long before we became quite informal with each other.

After Atul's arrival, a week passed by quite peacefully. Then some strange things started happening at the mess.

Atul and I were sitting and chatting with Anukulbabu one evening. The crowd of patients had thinned considerably. A few of them were still drifting in, describing their symptoms and collecting their medicines. Anukulbabu was handing them the medicine and keeping the cash in a box at hand, conversing with us all the while. There was some commotion in the area about a murder that had been committed right in front of our house the night before, the body being discovered in the morning. That was the topic of our discussion too. The main reason for the excitement was that although the victim appeared to be from the poorer sections of the non-Bengali community, his waistband had contained a bunch of hundred-rupee notes.

The doctor said, 'All this is related to the cocaine smuggling. Just think about it: if the murder was committed for money, the man wouldn't still have a thousand rupees tucked away in his belt. My guess is that this man was a buyer of cocaine; he had come to purchase some and had perhaps discovered some secret about the traffickers. Maybe he had threatened to go to the police or to blackmail them. And then—'

Atul said, 'I don't know, sir, I am pretty scared. How do you manage to live in this area? If I had known about all this—'

The doctor laughed and said, 'Then you would rather have gone to the Oriya neighbourhood, wouldn't you? But you see, we are not scared. I have been living here for the last ten years or so, but since I do not poke my nose into anybody's business, I never get into trouble.'

Atul said in a hushed tone, 'Anukulbabu, I am sure you know some secrets too, don't you?'

Suddenly we heard a sound behind us and turned around to find that Ashwinibabu was peeping from behind the door and eavesdropping on us. His face looked inordinately pale. I asked, 'What is the matter, Ashwinibabu, what are you doing downstairs at this hour?'

Ashwinibabu stuttered in confusion and replied, 'No . . . it's nothing, er . . . just . . . I wanted some *beedis*—' Still muttering, he climbed back up the stairs.

All of us looked at each other in turn. Everyone had a lot of respect for the elderly, sombre Ashwinibabu—but what was he doing tip-toeing downstairs and listening in on our conversation?

When we sat down to dinner we heard that Ashwinibabu had already eaten. After the meal, I lit a cheroot as always and returned to my bedroom. There I found Atul sprawled on the floor with only a pillow beneath his head. I was a little taken aback because it wasn't warm enough yet to warrant sleeping on the floor. The room was in darkness and Atul wasn't stirring either—so I presumed he was tired and had fallen asleep. I was still nowhere close to feeling sleepy, but since a light in the room would have woken Atul, I started pacing the floor barefoot instead of trying to read or write.

After a while of doing this, I suddenly felt I should go and check on Ashwinibabu, in case he wasn't feeling well. His room was two rooms down from mine. The door was open and no one answered when I called out. Curious, I entered the room. The light switch was beside the door. I switched it on to find the room empty. I peeped out of the window that overlooked the street, but he wasn't to be seen there either.

Well, really! Where could the man have gone at this hour of the night? Suddenly it occurred to me that perhaps he had gone down to the doctor for some medication. Quickly, I went downstairs. The doctor's door was locked from within. He was probably asleep at this hour. I stood before the door, hesitating, for a few minutes. I was just about to turn back when I heard voices from within. It was Ashwinibabu speaking in a very excited whisper.

For a minute I was tempted to eavesdrop. But the next instant I controlled myself. Perhaps Ashwinibabu was discussing some illness—I should not listen in on it. Soundlessly, I came back upstairs.

On returning, I found Atul lying in the same position on the floor. He turned his head when he saw me and asked, 'Ashwinibabu is not in his room, is he?'

Amazed, I said, 'No. Are you awake?'

'Yes. Ashwinibabu is with the doctor downstairs.'

'How did *you* know that?'

'All you have to do to gain that knowledge is put your head upon this pillow and lie on the floor.'

'What? Have you lost your mind?'

'My mind is fine. Just try it.'

Compelled by curiosity, I rested my head beside Atul's on the pillow. After I few moments of lying still I could hear indistinct voices and snatches of conversation. And then I clearly heard Anukulbabu's voice. He was saying, 'You are far too agitated. That was nothing but a figment of your imagination. It is quite common when you are deep in sleep. I am giving you some medicine, please take it and go to sleep. If you still feel the same way when you wake up in the morning, you may do as you please.'

Ashwinibabu's reply was rather indistinct. From the sound of chairs scraping the floor, I could make out that both of them had stood up. I abandoned my supine position and sat up, saying, 'I had forgotten that the doctor's room is right below ours. But what do you think is the matter? What is wrong with Ashwinibabu?'

Atul gave a great big yawn and said, 'Who knows? It is quite late. Let us sleep.'

Suspiciously, I queried, 'Why were you lying on the ground?'

Atul replied, 'I was tired after roaming the streets for the best part of the day and the floor seemed rather cool; before I knew it, I had dozed off. Their voices woke me up.'

I heard Ashwinibabu's footsteps on the stairs. He entered his own room and slammed the door shut.

I checked my watch—it said eleven. Atul had gone to sleep and the mess too was completely silent. I lay on the bed and started thinking about Ashwinibabu. Somewhere along the way, I fell asleep.

It was Atul who shook me awake. It was seven o'clock in the morning. He said, 'Hey, you'd better get up. There's something wrong.'

'Why? What's the matter?'

'Ashwinibabu is not opening the door. He isn't even answering our calls.'

'What is the matter with him?'

'Nobody knows. Come along—' and he hastily left the room.

I followed him and saw that everyone had gathered in front of Ashwinibabu's room. Many excited speculations and much pushing at the door were in progress. Anukulbabu had also joined us from downstairs. Everyone was getting quite anxious because Ashwinibabu was not in the habit of sleeping so late. Moreover, even if he were asleep, wouldn't such a clamour be enough to wake him up?

Atul approached Anukulbabu and said, 'Look, let's just break the door down. I have a funny feeling about this.'

Anukulbabu replied, 'Yes, yes, that goes without saying! Perhaps the man is unconscious, otherwise why isn't he answering? Let's not wait any longer. Atulbabu, please break the door open.'

It was a wooden door, about an inch and a half in thickness and locked by an Yale latch-lock. But when Atul and a couple of other people threw themselves at it forcefully, the British lock fell to pieces noisily and the door burst open. The sight that greeted us through the open doorway drew our breath away in fear and horror. Ashwinibabu was lying on his back just inside the room—his throat was slit from one end to the other. The blood had congealed on the floor beneath his head and shoulder, resembling a velvety rug. In his extended right fist, a bloody razor blade still seemed to be jeering at us viciously.

We stood rooted to the spot as if bereft of all will to move. Then Atul and the doctor entered the room simultaneously.

Anukulbabu gazed in appalled bewilderment at the grotesque sight and said in an unsteady voice, 'How terrible—Ashwinibabu took his own life!'

But Atul's gaze was not on the body. His eyes were flicking around each and every corner of the room with the sharpness of a rapier. He looked at the bed first, peeped out through the open window overlooking the street, then returned to us and calmly declared, 'Not suicide, Anukulbabu, this is homicide—a heinous murder. I am going to inform the police. Please, none of you should touch anything here.'

Anukulbabu said, 'What are you saying Atulbabu—murder! But the door was locked from within—and then that—' He pointed to the bloodstained weapon.

Atul shook his head and said, 'That may be so, but this is murder. All of you stay here—I shall bring the police immediately.' He went out hurriedly.

Anukulbabu sat down with his head in his hands and said, 'My God, this had to happen in my house!'

The police interrogated each and every one of us, including the servants and the cook at the boarding-house. We disclosed whatever we knew. But none of our statements shed any light on the mystery behind Ashwinibabu's death. He was an amicable person; he had no friends other than those at the office and the mess. He went home every Saturday. Without an exception, that had been his routine for the last ten or twelve years. For a while now he had been suffering from diabetes. Only a few general facts like these came to light.

The doctor also gave his testimony. What he said only served to make the matter of Ashwinibabu's death more complicated.

'Ashwinibabu had been living in my house for the last twelve years. His home was in the village of Hariharpur in the district of Burdwan. He worked in a mercantile firm and drew a salary of approximately one hundred and twenty rupees. On such a small income it was inconvenient to stay with his family in Calcutta and so he lived alone in the mess.

'As far as I know, Ashwinibabu was a simple and responsible man. He did not believe in owing anyone any money and so he didn't have a single debt. To my knowledge, he had no nasty habits or addictions. Everyone else in the mess can vouch for that.

'In all this time I had never noticed anything unusual or suspicious about him. He has been suffering from diabetes for the last few months and so I was treating him. But I had never received any indications of his mental illness. For the first time yesterday, I noticed an abnormality in his conduct.

'Yesterday at about nine forty-five in the morning I was sitting in my office when suddenly Ashwinibabu came in and said, "Doctor, I need to discuss something with you in private." A little surprised, I looked at him. He seemed extremely distraught. I asked, "What is it?" He looked about and said in a hushed tone, "Not now. Some other time." He left for work in a hurry.

'In the evening Ajitbabu, Atulbabu and I were chatting in my room when suddenly Ajitbabu noticed that Ashwinibabu was eavesdropping on our conversation from behind the door. When we called out to him, he mumbled some excuse or the other and hurried away. All of us were taken aback, wondering what the matter was with him.

'Then, at about ten in the night he came to my room stealthily. From the look on his face it was obvious that his mental state was not at its best. He shut the door and rambled on for quite a while. First he said that he was having terrible nightmares, then that he had come to know some dreadful secret. I tried to calm him down but he went on and on in a frenzy. Eventually I handed him a dose of tranquilizer and said, "Why don't you go to sleep tonight and tomorrow I shall listen to you again." He took the medicine and went upstairs.

'That was the last I saw him—and then this happens in the morning! I had my misgivings about his mental balance then, but never in my wildest dreams could I think that a momentary anxiety would drive him to take his life.'

When Anukulbabu stopped, the inspector asked, 'So you are of the opinion that this is a suicide?'

Anukulbabu replied, 'What else can it be? Still, Atulbabu was saying that this isn't suicide—it is something else. Perhaps he knows more than me on this subject. He would be able to tell you about that.'

The inspector turned to Atul and said, 'You are Atulbabu, aren't you? Do you have any reason to believe that this is not a suicide?'

'I do. No man can slit his own throat in that macabre fashion. You have seen the body. Just think about it—it is impossible.'

The inspector ruminated for a few moments and then asked, 'Do you have any idea who the murderer may be?'

'No.'

'Can you think of a possible motive for murder?'

Atul pointed to the window that overlooked the streets and said, 'That window is the cause for the murder.'

Suddenly alert, the inspector asked, 'The window is the cause? You mean to say that the killer entered through the window?'

'No. The killer used the door.'

The inspector suppressed a smile and said, 'Perhaps you do not remember that the door was locked from the inside.'

'I do remember that.'

A trifle mockingly, the inspector said, 'So did Ashwinibabu lock the door after being killed?'

'No, the killer locked the door from the outside on his way out.'

'How is that possible?'

Atul smiled and said, 'Very simple, just think about it and you'll understand.'

All this while, Anukulbabu was scrutinizing the door and he exclaimed, 'It's true! Very true! The door can easily be locked from the outside as well as from the inside. We just hadn't thought of it. Don't you see, it has a Yale lock on it.'

Atul said, 'The door locks itself when you shut it from the

outside. Then there is no way to open it except from within.'

The inspector was a veteran. Stroking his chin meditatively, he said, 'That may be so. But one uncertainty still remains. Is there any proof that Ashwinibabu had left his door open at night?'

Atul said, 'No. In fact, there is evidence to the contrary. I know he had locked his door.'

I added, 'True. I heard him lock his door.'

The inspector said, 'Well, then? It isn't very likely that Ashwinibabu would get up and open the door for his murderer to come in, is it?'

Atul said, 'No. But perhaps you remember that Ashwinibabu was suffering from a particular disease for the last few months.'

'Disease? Oh! You are absolutely right, Atulbabu! That fact had nearly slipped my mind.' Rather smugly, the inspector continued, 'I see you are an intelligent man. Why don't you join the force? You would do well in this profession. But meanwhile, the matter grows more complex here. If this is indeed a murder, then there is no doubt that the killer is an extremely shrewd individual. Do you have your suspicions on someone?' He looked around at everyone.

All of us shook our heads in silence. Anukulbabu said, 'Look sir, you are perhaps aware that this locality witnesses more than its fair share of murders. In fact just the day before yesterday one took place right in front of this house. My guess is that all these killings are linked to one another—if one is solved, all the others would be too. That is, of course, if we accept that Ashwinibabu has been murdered!'

The inspector said, 'That may indeed be true. But if one is to wait for the other crimes to be solved, I am afraid it might turn out to be an eternal wait.'

Atul said, 'Sir, if you want to get to the bottom of this murder, please ponder over that window.'

Wearily, the inspector replied, 'We shall have to ponder over each and every thing, Atulbabu. Now I shall have to search your rooms.'

All the rooms, both downstairs and upstairs, came under

the most vigilant scrutiny—but none of them revealed anything that went towards clearing up the mystery of the sudden death. Ashwinibabu's room was duly inspected too, but it yielded nothing more than a few ordinary letters. The empty case of the razor lay beside the bed. We all knew that Ashwinibabu had been in the habit of doing his own shaving and it wasn't difficult to identify the case either. The body had already been removed. Now his room was locked and sealed off. Having done his bit, the inspector left the premises at around one-thirty in the afternoon.

Ashwinibabu's family had been informed of the tragedy by telegram. In the evening his sons and other close relatives arrived. They were all in a complete state of shock. Although we were not related to Ashwinibabu, each of us was deeply affected by his death as well. Moreover, there was some concern for our own lives too. If such a thing could happen right next door, what was to prevent it from happening to us? The distressing, unfortunate day passed in a haze of ragged, apprehensive gloom.

At night, before going to bed, I dropped in on the doctor and found him sitting still with a sombre look on his face. The events of the day had etched deep grooves on his usually calm, unruffled countenance. I took a seat beside him and said, 'I believe everyone in the mess is planning to shift somewhere else.'

With a wan smile Anukulbabu said, 'They are not to blame, Ajitbabu! Who wishes to stay in a place where such incidents take place? But what I am wondering is whether this is really a murder or not. For, if it is indeed one, it couldn't have been committed by someone from outside the boarding-house. First, how would the killer reach the first floor? You are all aware that the staircase door remains locked at night. Even if we assume that the man accomplished the impossible and reached upstairs, how did he come to lay his hands on Ashwinibabu's razor to slit the poor man's throat? Isn't that too much of a coincidence? So, it is evident that the crime wasn't committed by an outsider. Then who could it be but someone who lives in the mess? Is there anyone among us who could kill

Ashwinibabu? Of course, Atulbabu has joined us very recently—we do not know much about him . . .'

I started in alarm, 'Atul? Oh no, no, that is not possible. Why would Atul kill Ashwinibabu?'

The doctor said, 'There you are, your reaction makes it quite clear that it couldn't have been someone from the mess. What is the other option? Only the possibility that he took his own life, isn't it?'

'But there should be a motive for suicide as well.'

'I too have wondered about that. Do you remember, a few days ago I had told you that there is a secret web of cocaine-traffickers in this area? That nobody knows who the leader of the gang is?'

'Yes, I remember.'

Slowly, the doctor continued, 'Now suppose, if it was Ashwinibabu who was the ringleader?'

I exclaimed in astonishment, 'What? How can that be?'

He said, 'Ajitbabu, nothing in this world is impossible. On the contrary, my suspicions in this regard deepen when I consider all that Ashwinibabu was telling me last night—he seemed to be scared out of his wits. When a man is that terrified, he often loses his mental balance. Who knows, perhaps it was this that drove him to suicide! Just think about it—doesn't this seem like a possible explanation?'

My brains were addled by this ingenious theory. I said, 'I don't know Anukulbabu, I cannot really make anything out of all this. Perhaps you should talk about your suspicions to the police.'

The doctor stood up and said, 'I shall do that tomorrow. I am unable to rest until this matter is resolved.'

Two or three days passed after this. The endless comings and goings of the various members of the CID and their repeated interrogations added to our already distressed state of mind and made life a living hell. Almost everyone in the boarding-house couldn't wait to move out bag and baggage. But then again, no one wanted to be the first to leave. After all, a hasty departure might cause the police to suspect foul play on the part of the evacuee.

It was becoming quite clear that the noose of suspicion was tightening gradually around one individual in the mess. But we were unable to guess who that person might be. Sometimes a sudden fear made the heart skip a beat—they weren't suspecting me, were they?

One morning Atul and I were going through the newspaper in the doctor's office. Some medicines had arrived for Anukulbabu in a mid-sized packing case. He was unpacking them and carefully arranging them on the shelf. The case bore American stamps. The doctor never used Indian-made drugs—whenever he needed a new stock, he had them shipped from America or Germany. Nearly every month he would receive a shipment of drugs.

Atul folded his newspaper, put it down and said, 'Anukulbabu, why do you import your medicines from abroad? Aren't the domestic ones any good?' He picked up a large bottle of sugar-of-milk and read the manufacturer's name on the label, 'Eric and Havell—are these the best in the market?'

'Yes.'

'Tell me, does homeopathy truly cure diseases? I am a bit sceptical. How can a drop of water cure an ailment?'

Smiling, the doctor said, 'I suppose all these people who come for treatment are merely playing at being sick?'

Atul replied, 'Perhaps the cure is natural while they ascribe it to the drugs. Faith can be a great healer.'

The doctor merely smiled and did not deign to respond. After a while he inquired, 'Have they mentioned anything about our house in the daily?'

'They have.' I began to read aloud: 'The murder of the unfortunate Mr Ashwinikumar Chowdhury remains unsolved as yet. The CID has now taken on this case. Certain facts have reportedly been uncovered. It is expected that the criminal will soon be apprehended.'

'My foot he will! They can go on expecting for as long as they like.' The doctor turned his head and exclaimed, 'Oh, it is the inspector—'

The inspector entered the room, followed by two

constables. It was the same inspector as before. Without any
preamble, he went straight up to Atul and said, 'There is a
warrant in your name. You'll have to come to the police station
with us. Please do not try to resist; it will be useless. Ramdhani
Singh, handcuff him.' One of the constables immediately
obeyed the order with deft and well-practised movements.

We were on our feet in consternation. Atul exclaimed,
'What is all this?'

The inspector said, 'Here is the warrant. Atul Chandra
Mitra is to be taken into custody on the charge of murdering
Ashwinikumar Chowdhury. Can you both identify this man
as Atul Chandra Mitra?'

Stupefied, we nodded in silence.

Atul smiled a little and said, 'So your suspicions homed in
on me eventually. All right, I'll come with you to the police
station. Ajit, don't be worried— I'm innocent.'

A police van had arrived in front of the house. The
policemen hauled Atul into it and drove off. Deathly pale, the
doctor said, 'So it was Atulbabu—how terrible! How terrible!
It is impossible to tell one's nature from one's face.'

I was unable to utter a word. Atul, a murderer! Over the
days that I had shared a room with him, I had become quite
attached to Atul. His pleasant nature had won me over
completely. And this same Atul was a murderer! I was beside
myself with shock.

Anukulbabu continued, 'This is why they tell you to think
twice before giving shelter to complete strangers. But who
would have guessed that the man was such a—'

My agitation was mounting and I marched off to my room,
slammed the door shut and lay down. I had no inclination to
wash up or to eat. Atul's things lay strewn on the other side of
the room. I looked at them and tears came to my eyes. I realized
just how fond I had grown of Atul.

Before being taken away, Atul had said that he was
innocent. Could the police be making a mistake? I sat up on the
bed and tried to recollect each and every detail from the night
when Ashwinibabu was killed. Atul was lying on the floor
listening in on the conversation between the doctor and

Ashwinibabu. Why was he doing that? To what end? I had fallen asleep at about eleven o'clock—I did not wake until the morning. What if Atul had, in the meantime—

But it was Atul who had insisted from the very beginning that this was murder and not suicide. If he was the killer, would he say something like that and tighten the noose around his own neck? Or was it possible that he had said it precisely to ward off suspicion from himself, so that the police would think that since he himself insisted on it being a murder, he could not be the killer?

I racked my brain for hours, tossing and turning on my bed and sometimes getting up to pace the floor. It was afternoon now. The clock struck three. Suddenly it occurred to me to go and seek the advice of a lawyer. I had no idea what was to be done in a situation such as this and neither did I know any lawyers. But be that as it may, I figured it would not be difficult locating one. So I began to put my clothes on, preparing to leave, when there was a knock at my door. I opened it and—it was Atul!

'Atul, it's you!' I threw my arms around him, nearly crushing him in my delight. All controversy regarding whether he was guilty or not disappeared from my mind without a trace.

Hair unkempt, face drawn, Atul smiled and said, 'Yes Ajit, it is me. They harassed me no end. With great difficulty I got someone to bail me out—otherwise I was in for a stint in jail today. Where were you off to?'

A little abashed, I said, 'To a lawyer's.'

Atul pressed my arm warmly and said, 'For me? That isn't necessary any more; but thanks anyway. I have received a temporary reprieve for now.'

We went inside the room and sat down. As he took off his shirt, Atul said, 'Uff, my head is close to bursting. I haven't eaten all day. It looks like you haven't eaten either. Poor thing! Come on then, let's have a quick bath and then go have some lunch. My insides are clawing at me.'

I tried to overcome my uncertainty and blurted out, 'Atul, you—have you . . .'

'Have I what? Killed Ashwinibabu or not?' Atul gave a soft laugh, 'We can have that discussion later. Right now we need to eat something. My head really hurts. But there's nothing that a quick shower cannot fix.'

The doctor walked in. Atul looked at him and said, 'Anukulbabu, like the proverbial prodigal, I am back. The English have a saying about a "bad penny"—my situation is something similar; even the police tossed me right back.'

The doctor's face was grave as he said, 'Atulbabu, it is good to see that you are back. I hope the police have found you innocent and therefore let you go. But over here, you cannot—not anymore—I hope you understand, it's a matter for everyone's concern. As it is, everybody wants to leave the mess. To add to that if you—I mean—please do not get me wrong; I have nothing against you personally, but—'

Atul replied, 'Oh no, certainly! I am now a branded criminal. Why should you get into trouble in the process of sheltering me? You never can tell, the police may bring a charge of aiding and abetting against you for it . . . so, do you wish me to leave today?'

The doctor was silent for a while and then, reluctantly, he said, 'Well, you can stay the night, but tomorrow morning—'

Atul said, 'Most certainly. I shall not trouble you tomorrow. I shall find myself a new place, wherever that is. As the last resort, there is always the Oriya hotel.' He laughed.

Anukulbabu asked him about what had happened at the police station. Atul gave some vague replies and went for a bath. The doctor said to me, 'I can see that I have offended Atulbabu—but what choice do I have? The mess has already earned a bad reputation. If I add to that by harbouring someone with a criminal record, would it be very safe—you tell me?'

In truth, nobody could be blamed for this little bit of caution and self-preservation. I nodded cheerlessly and said, 'Well, the mess belongs to you, so you have to do what you think is best.' I slung a towel over my shoulder and proceeded towards the bathroom. The doctor sat there, looking contrite and forlorn.

As Atul and I were coming back to our room after lunch, we saw Ghanashyambabu returning from work. He jumped out of his skin on seeing Atul. Blanching, he said, 'Atulbabu, you—is that really—'

Atul smiled a little and said, 'Yes, it really is me, Ghanashyambabu. Are you having trouble believing your eyes?'

Ghanashyambabu said, 'But I thought the police had . . .' He gulped twice, said no more and darted into his room.

Atul's eyes twinkled with merriment as he remarked softly, 'Once a criminal, always a criminal, eh? Ghanashyambabu seems to be quite shocked to see me.'

That evening Atul remarked, 'Hey, the lock on our door appears to be broken.'

I checked and found that the foreign-made lock was not functioning properly. We informed Anukulbabu. He also took a look at it and said, 'That is the problem with locks from abroad—when they are fine, there is nothing to worry about, but once they start acting up, no one but an engineer can fix them. Our indigenous bolt is better than this. Anyway, I shall have it fixed first thing tomorrow morning.' He went back downstairs.

At night, before going to bed, Atul said, 'Ajit, my headache is getting worse—can you suggest a remedy?'

I said, 'Why don't you take some medicine from Anukulbabu?'

Atul said, 'Homeopathy? Will it work? Well, all right, let us see what some little waterdrops can do!'

I said, 'I'll go along with you—I am not feeling too well either.'

The doctor was almost closing shop at the time and he looked at us inquiringly. Atul said, 'We have come for a taste of your medicine. I have a horrible headache—can you help?'

The doctor replied gladly, 'Sure. I most certainly can. It is nothing but a little indigestion that is causing the headache. Take a seat—I shall get you a dosage in a moment.' He fetched some fresh medications from the shelf, wrapped it up and handed it to Atul, saying, 'Go on, have this and go to sleep—tomorrow you'll never know you had a headache. Ajitbabu, you don't look too well either. It must be the exhaustion catching up with you after all the excitement, right? Are you feeling out of sorts? Why don't you let me give you some medicine too—you'll be fit as a fiddle in the morning.'

As we were leaving with the medicine, Atul said, 'Anukulbabu, do you know someone called Byomkesh Bakshi?'

A little startled, the doctor replied, 'No. Who is he?'

Atul said, 'I do not know. I heard his name at the police station today. I believe he is in charge of solving this case.'

The doctor shook his head again and said, 'No, I've never heard of him.'

After coming back to our room, I said, 'Atul, now you have to tell me everything.'

'What should I tell you?'

'You are hiding something from me. But that won't do, you will have to tell me all about it.'

Atul remained silent for a while, then he took one glance at the door and said, 'All right, I'll tell you. Come, sit here on my bed. I was beginning to feel that it's time you were told something.'

I sat down on his bed. Atul came and took a seat beside me after shutting the door. I still held the pouch of medication in my hand and I thought perhaps I should take it and then listen to the story in peace. But as I was about to open the pouch and pour the contents into my mouth, Atul reached out and said, 'Let that be for now. Listen to my story and then you can have it.'

He switched off the lights, brought his mouth close to my ear and began to whisper his tale into it. I listened to him in speechless wonder, shivering in terror and awe from time to time.

About a quarter of an hour later, after completing his account in brief, Atul said, 'That is enough for today. The rest can wait until tomorrow.' He checked the phosphorescent dial of his watch and said, 'There is time yet. Nothing will happen before two in the night. Why don't you take a nap in the meantime? I shall wake you when it is time.'

At about one-thirty, I lay awake in my bed. My aural senses

were so heightened that I could feel the tremors of my body as it drew breath. In my clenched fist I held onto the object which Atul had given me.

Suddenly, in the dark, although there was no sound, I felt Atul's light touch on my arm. It was a pre-determined signal and I began to breathe heavily, like a person fast asleep. I could tell that the time had come. I was not aware when the door opened, but suddenly there was a thudding sound upon Atul's bed and immediately the lights came on. I leaped up on my bed, holding the iron rod in my hand. I found Atul standing with a revolver in one hand and the other on the light switch. Beside Atul's bed, on his knees, glowering at Atul like the mortally wounded tiger does at the hunter—was Anukulbabu!

Atul said, 'It is very unfortunate indeed, Anukulbabu, that a veteran like you finally ended up stabbing a pillow! That's it—don't move. Please drop the dagger. You move an inch and I shall fire. Ajit, please open the window. The police is waiting outside. Hey—watch it—'

The doctor lunged at the door but immediately Atul's iron fist landed on his jaw like a sledgehammer and knocked him down.

The doctor sat up and said, 'All right, I won't try to escape. But pray tell me, what may my offence be?'

'It will take too long to list them all, doctor. The police have drawn up a comprehensive chargesheet—it will be revealed in due course of time. But for now—'

The inspector walked in with a few constables in tow.

Atul continued, 'For now, I am handing you over to the police for assaulting and attempting to murder Byomkesh Bakshi, the Inquisitor. Inspector, this is the culprit.'

Wordlessly the inspector handcuffed Anukulbabu. The doctor looked vicious and said, 'This is a conspiracy! The police and this Byomkesh Bakshi have colluded to frame me falsely. But I shall not let you off. There is a legal system in the country and I have plenty of money too.'

Atul said, 'That you most certainly do. After all, cocaine fetches good value in the market.'

With a distorted expression the doctor said, 'Is there any

proof that I sell cocaine?'

'There certainly is, Anukulbabu. How about those bottles of sugar-of-milk?'

The doctor recoiled as if he had stepped on a snake. He did not say a single word after that; his steady gaze rained flames of futile anger on Atul. This was not the amiable, peaceable Anukulbabu I knew; a homicidal desperado had emerged from within his shell of gentility. I shuddered to think that I had spent the past few months in perfect amity with this man.

Atul inquired, 'Now tell me, doctor, what medication was it that you offered us last night? Was it powdered morphia? You won't tell? Suits me fine—the chemical tests will tell us everything.' He lit a cheroot and reclined on the bed, saying, 'Inspector, now please take my statement.'

After the First Information Report was lodged, the doctor's room was searched and it yielded two large bottles of cocaine. The doctor continued to hold his tongue. It was almost dawn before we sent him off to the police station along with the booty. Atul said, 'This whole place is in a turmoil now, why don't you come along home with me and have a cup of tea there?'

We arrived at a three-storeyed house on Harrison Road. A brass-inscripted plate beside the door read:

Byomkesh Bakshi
Inquisitor

Byomkesh said, 'Welcome! Please do me the honour of setting foot in my humble abode.'

I asked, 'What is this "Inquisitor" business?'

'That is my identity. I don't like the sound of the word "detective"; "investigator" is even worse. So I call myself an Inquisitor, a Seeker of Truth. What's the matter—don't you like it?'

Byomkesh had the entire second floor to himself—there were four or five rooms in all, quite decently kept. I asked, 'Do you live alone?'

'Yes. My only companion is Putiram, the domestic.'

I gave a sigh and said, 'It is a very nice place. How long have you been living here?'

'Almost a year now; I was away for just a short period in between when I had moved temporarily to your boarding-house.'

Putiram had quickly lit the stove and prepared some tea. Byomkesh took a sip of the hot liquid, 'Aah! I must say these few days in disguise passed quite pleasantly indeed at your mess. But the doctor had caught me out towards the end. Of course, I was to blame for that.'

'How was that?'

'It was my mention of the window to the police that gave me away—can't you figure it out? It was through the window that Ashwinibabu—'

'Oh no, please begin at the beginning.'

Byomkesh took another sip from the cup and said, 'All right, I will. Some of it I have already told you last night. Now listen to the rest. The police authorities were beginning to get quite worked up about the series of murders that were being committed in your neighbourhood every month. There was also a lot of pressure on the police from the government as well as the press, who didn't miss a dig at them. Since this was the case, I sought an interview with the Commissioner of Police and said, "I am a private detective and I believe I can solve the mystery behind these crimes." After much deliberation the Commissioner granted me permission to pursue my investigations. The only condition was that this was to remain strictly between him and me.

'I landed up at your mess. In order to conduct an inquiry it is necessary to have a base of operations which is close to the situation at hand; it was for this purpose that I chose your mess. At the time I had no idea that the opposition's "base of operations" was located in that very boarding-house!

'From the very beginning the doctor struck me as excessively nice. It also occurred to me that it would be only too convenient to have a homeopathic practice to camouflage an illegal drug-trafficking setup. But I hadn't yet arrived at the conclusion that it was he who was the ringleader.

'I suspected the doctor for the first time on the day before Ashwinibabu died. Perhaps you remember, that day an impoverished non-Bengali's corpse had been found on the road right in front of the mess. When the doctor heard that the dead man had been carrying a thousand rupees in a pouch tied to his waist, an expression of thwarted greed crossed his face for an instant. Immediately all my suspicions were directed at him.

'Then there was that incident of Ashwinibabu eavesdropping on us. Actually he hadn't come there to listen in on our conversation, but to speak to the doctor. But when he found us there, he dished out some lame excuse and hastened away.

'Ashwinibabu's behaviour threw me in a quandary again and for a while I considered the possibility that *he* might be the culprit. When I overheard his conversation with Anukulbabu that night, things still weren't any clearer. But I did sense that Ashwinibabu had witnessed something terrible. Then when he was murdered that night, everything became crystal clear to me.

'Can you figure it out now? The doctor used to traffic in illegal drugs, but maintained complete secrecy about his role as the leader of the gang. If anyone stumbled onto his secret, he did away with them immediately. That is how he had remained unscathed for all this time.

'The man who was murdered on the street was perhaps Anukulbabu's broker or maybe it was he who supplied the drugs into the market. This is my assumption and I may be wrong. That night he came to the doctor and they had a fallout. Perhaps the man tried to blackmail Anukulbabu or threaten him about going to the police. And then—when he left the house, Anukulbabu followed him and finished him off.

'Ashwinibabu happened to observe this from his window and some misguided notion made him go to the doctor with his story. I do not know what his intentions were. He was indebted to Anukulbabu and perhaps he wanted to caution him. But the result was the exact opposite. In the eyes of the doctor Ashwinibabu had just forfeited his right to live. That very night, at some point when he got up to go to the bathroom, he was murdered brutally.

'I cannot say whether the doctor had suspected me initially, but when I mentioned to the police that the window was the cause of Ashwinibabu's death, the doctor concluded that I was on to something. So I too earned the right to quit my mortal body! But I was not the least bit eager to comply. Hence my days began to pass in great caution and watchfulness.

'It was then that the police committed a blunder and arrested me. Anyway, the Commissioner came and released me, and I returned to the mess. That was when Anukulbabu became convinced that I was an investigator. But he hid his emotions and magnanimously allowed me to stay the night. This benevolence masked a single purpose—to put me to death at some point in the night. Perhaps nobody else knew as much about him as I did.

'Until then there really was no proof against the doctor. An inspection of his room at this point would have produced some cocaine and it would be enough to send him to jail. But it would have been impossible to prove in a court of law that he was a cold-blooded murderer too. So I had to try and trap him. It was I who jammed the lock by putting a nail into it. When the doctor heard about this, he was thrilled—our door would have to stay unlocked that night. Finally, when we sought him out for some medication, he couldn't believe his luck. He handed us a dosage of morphia each and figured that we would be as good as unconscious by the time he came in to put us to eternal sleep.

'And then—the tiger stepped into the trap. What else?'

I said, 'It is time I left. I don't suppose you would be going that way in the near future?'

'No. Are you going back to the mess?'

'Yes.'

'Why?'

'What do you mean—why. Don't I have to go back?'

'I was thinking that since you'll have to leave that house anyway, how about coming and living over here? This is a pretty decent place.'

After a few moments' silence I said, 'Are you returning the favour?'

Byomkesh placed his arm on my shoulder and said, 'Oh no—not at all. I am beginning to feel that I shall miss you. I have got used to your presence in the past few weeks.'

'Are you serious?'

'Never more.'

'In that case, why don't you stay here while I go and get my things?'

With a smile, Byomkesh said, 'Don't forget to bring my things along too.'

The Gramophone Pin Mystery

Byomkesh folded the morning's newspaper neatly and put it aside. Then he leaned back in his chair and looked out of the window abstractedly.

The sun was shining brightly outside. It was a fogless February morning. There wasn't even a cloud in the sky. We had the second floor of the house all to ourselves. The window in the drawing room provided a nice view of a part of the city and the sky. Down below, the sounds of the city coming awake had already begun; there was no end to the rush of traffic and activity on Harrison Road. Some of this bustle seemed to have carried over to the sky. Sparrows were flying around, filling the air with their uncalled-for chirps; way above them, a flock of pigeons were soaring, as if hoping to circle the sun. It was nearly eight o'clock. The two of us had just finished breakfast and were lazily turning the pages of the newspaper, looking for interesting news from the world outside.

Byomkesh turned away from the window and said, 'Have you noticed that a strange advertisement has been appearing in the newspaper for the last few days?'

I said, 'No. I do not read advertisements.'

Raising an incredulous eyebrow, Byomkesh said, 'You don't read advertisements? Then what *do* you read?'

'Just what everyone reads in a newspaper—news.'

'In other words, stories about someone in Manchuria who has a bleeding finger, or somebody who has had triplets in Brazil—that's what you read! What's the point of reading that? If you are looking for genuine, relevant news, look to the advertisements.'

Byomkesh was a strange man, as will soon be evident. On the surface, from his looks or even his conversation, one wouldn't judge him to be extraordinary in any way. But if he was confronted or taunted into a state of agitation, his real self emerged from within its shell. In general he was a reserved person. But once he was jeered or ridiculed and lost his cool, his inherent razor-sharp intelligence ripped apart all modicum of uncertainty or restraint and then his conversation was truly something worth listening to.

I could not resist the temptation to needle him a little. 'Oh, is that so?' I said. 'But then these newspapermen are real scoundrels, aren't they? Instead of filling the newspapers with lots of advertisements, they waste the space by printing pages of meaningless news.'

Byomkesh's eyes grew sharp. 'They are not to blame,' he replied. 'Since their newspapers would not sell unless people like you are entertained, the poor souls have to come up with all that rubbish. But the real meaty news lies in the personals. If you want to know all kinds of important things like what is happening around you, who is using what ruse to rob whom in broad daylight, what new schemes are being hatched to smuggle contraband goods etc., you have to read the personal columns. Reuters' telegrams do not carry that stuff.'

I laughed and said, 'That may be so, but—anyway, perhaps I *shall* read only the advertisements from now on. But you still haven't told me which was the one you found strange.'

Byomkesh threw the newspaper at me and said, 'Read it—I have marked it.'

I turned the pages and came upon a tiny, three-line classified. I managed to find it only because it was highlighted with a red pencil, or it would have been difficult to spot.

Thorn-in-the-Flesh

If desirous of getting rid of a thorn-in-the-flesh, please wait on Saturday at five-thirty with your arm resting against the lamp-post on the south-western corner of Whiteway Laidlaw.

I could make no sense of this message, even after going over it a couple of times; so I asked, 'What is he trying to say? Will the thorn-in-the-flesh disappear magically if someone stands at the crossroad, leaning on the lamp-post? What does this advertisement mean? And what or who exactly *is* a thorn-in-the-flesh?'

Byomkesh answered, 'That is what I haven't been able to figure out yet. If you go through the old newspapers, you'll find that this insertion has been appearing every Friday without fail for the last three months.'

I said, 'But what is the purpose of this message? Usually people have a purpose behind placing an advertisement. This one makes no sense at all.'

Byomkesh said, 'At first glance there seems to be no apparent purpose, but that doesn't mean that there isn't one. Nobody spends their hard-earned money to place a pointless advertisement. When you read it though, one thing attracts your attention instantly.'

'And what is that?'

'The advertiser's desire to conceal his identity. First, note that there is no name on the message. Often, an advertisement may not contain a name, but the newspaper office holds all the details. In such cases there is a box number, which, also, this advertisement doesn't have. As you know, when someone places an advertisement, he usually wishes to negotiate something with the people out there. This one is no different, only this man wishes to remain incognito while doing so.'

'I don't quite follow you.'

'All right, I'll explain—listen carefully. The man who is placing this advertisement is calling out to people and saying, "Hey, if you wish to rid yourself of a thorn-in-the-flesh, wait for me in such-and-such place at so-and-so time—wait in such a manner that I am able to spot you." Let's not get into what exactly a thorn-in-the-flesh is right now, but let's assume that you wish to get rid of one. What do you have to do? Go to the assigned spot and stand there, leaning against the lamp-post. Suppose you do go there at the appointed time and wait. What happens next?'

'What?'

'I don't have to tell you about the kind of crowd that gathers there on a Saturday evening. There is Whiteway Laidlaw on one side and New Market on the other and several cinema halls all around the place. You wait there, holding on to the lamp-post for half an hour and get jostled by passing pedestrians, but the purpose with which you had gone there does not get accomplished—nobody arrives with a magic cure for your thorn-in-the-flesh. You are disgusted and come away thinking the whole thing was a hoax. Then suddenly you find a note that someone in the crowd has dropped into your pocket.'

'And then?'

'What then? The patient and the medicine-man do not meet and yet the cure to the anathema is found. A contact is established between you and the advertiser but you have no idea of who he is or what he looks like.'

I remained quiet for a while and then said, 'Even if I were to accept your line of thinking as the right one, what does it prove?'

'Just this, that the thorn-in-the-flesh peddler wishes to retain anonymity badly—and someone who is that reluctant to expose his identity may be a modest person, but he certainly isn't a straightforward one.'

I shook my head and said, 'That is just your assumption—there is no proof that what you are saying is true.'

Byomkesh rose and began to pace the floor. 'Listen,' he said, 'a correct assumption is the best proof. When you look closely into what you call empirical evidence, you'll see that it consists of nothing but a sequence of assumptions. What else is circumstantial evidence if not an educated guess? Yet, these have formed the basis for sentencing so many to life-terms.'

I remained silent, but could not accept this logic from my heart. It is not easy to grant that an assumption can be as good as evidence. But neither was it easy to refute Byomkesh's reasoning. Hence I decided that my best bet was to make no comments. I knew that this silence would drive Byomkesh to greater heights of restiveness and before long he would present me with more irrefutable logic.

A sparrow flew onto the window ledge and perched itself there, with a straw in its mouth. It stared at us with its tiny, sparkling eyes. Suddenly Byomkesh stopped pacing and, pointing to the bird, asked, 'Can you tell me what that bird is trying to do?'

Startled, I replied, 'What is it trying to—oh, I suppose it's looking for a place to build its nest.'

'Do you know that for sure? Beyond a doubt?'

'Yes, I think so—beyond a doubt.'

Byomkesh crossed his arms behind himself and said, smiling gently, 'How did you figure that out? What is the proof?'

'Proof . . . well, the straw in its mouth—'

'Does a straw in its mouth necessarily indicate that it is trying to build a nest?'

I realized that I had fallen into the trap of Byomkesh's logic. I said, 'No—but—'

'Assumption. Now you are talking. Why were you vacillating for so long then?'

'Not vacillating, really. You mean to say that the assumption that works for a sparrow would work for a human being too?'

'Why not?'

'If you were to perch on someone's ledge with a straw in your mouth, would it prove that you wish to build a nest?'

'No. It would prove that I am a raving lunatic.'

'Does that need any proving?'

Byomkesh began to laugh. He said, 'You shall not exasperate me. Come on, you'll have to accept this—empirical proof may be fallible, but a logical assumption is failproof. It can't go wrong.'

I too was adamant, and said, 'But I am not able to believe all those wild conjectures which you just made about that insertion.'

Byomkesh said, 'That only shows how weak your mind is—even faith needs a strong will. Anyway, for people like you, empirical evidence is the best way. Tomorrow is a Saturday and we don't have anything to do in the evening either. I shall demonstrate to you tomorrow that my assumption is right.'

'How would you do that?'

We heard footsteps on our stairway. Byomkesh strained his ears and said, 'Stranger . . . middle aged . . . heavy-set, maybe even rotund . . . carries a walking-stick—who could it be? He certainly wants to make *our* acquaintance, because nobody else lives on the second floor.' He smiled to himself.

There was a knock on the door. Byomkesh called out, 'Come in, the door is open.'

A middle-aged, portly man pushed the door open and walked in. He held a thick, Malaccan bamboo walking-stick with a silver knob, wore a buttoned-up black coat made of alpaca wool and a well-pleated dhoti. He was fair and good looking, clean-shaven and balding. The climb up the three flights of stairs had winded him and he was unable to speak at first upon entering the room. He fished out a handkerchief from his pocket and began to wipe his face.

Byomkesh muttered to me under his breath, 'Assumption! Assumption!'

I had to digest this gibe in silence since there was no doubt that in this case Byomkesh's hypothesis about the stranger's appearance was right on target.

The gentleman got his breath back and asked, 'Which one of you is detective Byomkeshbabu?'

Byomkesh turned on the fan, indicated a chair and said, 'Do take a seat. I am Byomkesh Bakshi. But I do not like that word "detective". I am an Inquisitor, a Seeker of Truth. Anyway, I can see that you are quite distraught. Do rest for a while and then I shall hear all about your gramophone pin mystery.'

The gentleman sat down and continued to stare at Byomkesh in bemused stupefication. There was no end to my amazement either. I failed to understand how Byomkesh had managed to connect a middle-aged stranger to the infamous gramophone pin mystery by taking just one look at him. I had witnessed several instances of Byomkesh's remarkable powers, but this seemed to be in the realm of magic.

With great effort the gentleman controlled his emotions and asked, 'You—how did you know?'

Byomkesh laughed and replied, 'Mere assumption. First, you are middle-aged; second, you are well off; third, you have been having a problem recently, and finally—you have come to me for assistance. Hence . . .' Byomkesh left the sentence incomplete and waved his hands as if to indicate that given all this, deducing the reason for his arrival was mere child's play.

It would be worth mentioning at this point that in the last few weeks some strange incidents had taken place in the city; the tabloids had christened these occurrences 'the gramophone pin mystery' and reported its details with bold headlines emblazoned across their front pages. There was no end to the curiosity, excitement and terror these reports had generated in the minds of the people of Calcutta. After reading the spine-tingling accounts in the newspapers, the conjectures at the local tea stalls had got increasingly out of hand. Now there wasn't a Calcuttan who didn't feel a shiver run down his spine when he stepped onto the streets.

This is what had happened: about a month and a half ago Mr Jayhari Sanyal, an inhabitant of Sukiya Street, was walking down Cornwallis Street in the morning. As he stepped onto the road to cross to the opposite pavement, he suddenly fell flat on his face. There was no dearth of people on the street at that hour of the morning; when they carried Mr Sanyal to one side of the road, they found that he had expired. On enquiring into the cause for this sudden death, they found a drop of blood on the dead man's chest—there were no marks anywhere else indicating any wounds. The police suspected it to be an unnatural death and sent the corpse to the hospital. The post-mortem revealed a strange fact. Apparently, the cause of death was a tiny gramophone pin that was embedded in the heart. Questioned as to how this pin had pierced the heart, the weapon-specialist judged that it was fired through a gun or a similar instrument from the front, penetrating the victim's skin and flesh and going straight into his heart, thus causing instantaneous death.

There was considerable commotion in the newspapers over this incident; they even came out with a brief biography of the dead man. Many analyses were published discussing whether this was murder or not and, if so, how it came to be executed. But the one thing that nobody was able to figure out was the motive for the murder and what the killer stood to gain from it. The papers also wrote that the police had started investigations on the case. The tea-stall veterans pronounced that there was nothing to it, the man had had a heart failure and for the lack of any sensational news, the newspersons had come up with this new hoax, making a mountain out of a molehill.

About eight days later, the news that hit the headlines, in print one and a half inches tall, made the entire genteel community of Calcutta sit up and take notice. Even the all-knowing veterans of the tea stalls were stunned. Rumour, conjecture and speculation ran rife, sprouting as freely as mushrooms in the monsoon.

The *Daily Kalketu* reported:

GRAMOPHONE PIN STRIKES AGAIN
STRANGE AND MYSTERIOUS HAPPENINGS
Streets of Calcutta are No Longer Safe

The readers of *Kalketu* will remember that a few days ago Mr Jayhari Sanyal met with sudden death as he was crossing a street. Examinations revealed that a gramophone pin had pierced his heart and the doctor pronounced this to be the cause of death. At the time we suspected that this was no ordinary matter and that there was a grave conspiracy hidden behind this. Our suspicions have been confirmed. Yesterday the same strange incident has repeated itself. The famous, wealthy businessman Kailashchandra Moulik was driving around the Maidan area at about five o'clock last evening. On Red Road, he stopped the car and got out to take a short walk. All of a sudden, he emitted a cry of pain and fell to the ground. His chauffeur and the other people nearby assisted in bringing him back to the car quickly—but he had already passed away. This sudden tragedy unnerved everyone who was present, but fortunately the police arrived very soon. Kailashbabu had a silk kurta on and the police noticed a drop of blood on his chest. Fearing it to be another unnatural death, they sent the body to the hospital immediately. According to the doctor's report after the post-mortem, there was a gramophone pin embedded in his heart and this pin had been shot into his heart from the front.

It is clear that this is not an unpremeditated crime and that a group of nefarious assassins have arrived in town. It is difficult to say who they are and what might be the purpose behind their killings of these acclaimed citizens of Calcutta. But what is truly bizarre is their mode of assassination; the weapon and the means being used in these murders remain shrouded in mystery.

Kailashbabu was an extremely generous and amicable gentleman and it is unthinkable that anyone would wish him ill. At the time of his death, he was only forty-eight years old. Kailashbabu was a widower. He is succeeded by his daughter who inherits his property. We convey our deepest sympathies to Kailashbabu's daughter and son-in-law, who mourn him deeply.

The police are proceeding with their investigations. At present, Kailashbabu's chauffeur Kali Singh has been detained on grounds of suspicion.

After this, there was a considerable amount of excitement in the newspapers for about two weeks. The police went ahead full steam in their search for the criminal, and soon began to sweat under their collars as a result of the wild-goose chase. But let alone apprehending the culprit, they were unable to shed any light at all on the dark mystery of the gramophone pin murders.

And then, after some fifteen days, the gramophone pin appeared again. This time its victim was a rich moneylender called Krishnadayal Laha. He collapsed on the road while crossing the intersection between Dharmatolla and Wellington Street, and never rose again. The bedlam that broke loose in the media now defied description. The editorial comments about the ineffectiveness of the police department grew sharper and more critical. A terror gripped the city of Calcutta, reigning over the mind of every citizen. There was no other topic of discussion in *addas*, tea stalls, restaurants or drawing rooms across the city.

Two similar deaths followed in quick succession. The city was numbed by shock, not knowing how to defend itself against this unknown tormentor.

Needless to say, Byomkesh was deeply drawn to this

mystery. Catching wrong-doers was his profession and he had gained some renown in the field as well. Much as he hated the term 'detective', he was well aware that for all intents and purposes he was nothing but a private investigator. So, this ingenious carnage had fired all his mental faculties. We went to each of the various scenes of crime, and took a good look around. I do not know if that helped Byomkesh in discovering anything—even if it did, he did not share his discoveries with me. But he meticulously made a note of the tiniest bit of information on this case in his notebook. Perhaps he believed, deep down inside, that someday a loose thread of this mystery would fall into his hands.

Therefore on this day, when such a thread finally came within his reach, I realized that despite his calm exterior, he was quite excited and restless within.

The gentleman said, 'I came because I had heard about you—I see now that it wasn't a mistake. The incredible skill that you have just shown makes me feel that only you may be able to save me. The police wouldn't be able to do anything and so I haven't gone to them. Just see how no less than five of these murders took place right under their noses in broad daylight—could they do anything? And today, they nearly got me too!' His voice faltered and trailed off, as beads of perspiration stood out on his temple.

Byomkesh tried to calm him, saying, 'Please have faith. It's a good thing you came to me instead of going to the police. If anyone can solve this mystery, it certainly isn't the police. Please tell me everything from the very beginning. Don't leave anything out as unimportant. No information is redundant to me.'

The gentleman seemed to regain some of his composure and said, 'My name is Ashutosh Mitra. I live close by, in Nebutola. Since I was eighteen, my business has kept me on the move—I haven't had the time to settle down with a family. Besides, I am not very fond of children scrambling about and hence I have never had any desire to marry. I am a man of strong likes and dislikes, and I prefer my own company. The years have gone by—I shall be fifty-one next January. I retired from work about two years ago. I have my lifetime's savings, a lakh-and-a-half or so, in the bank. The interest from this money is enough for my needs. I do not even have to pay rent since I own the house I live in. Music is the only hobby I have. All things considered, I have had nothing to complain about.'

Byomkesh asked, 'But do you have any dependents?'

Ashubabu shook his head, 'No. There aren't any relatives to speak of and so I don't have that burden. I have one good-for-nothing nephew who used to bother me for money sometimes. But that young lad is a drunkard and a gambler to boot—so I do not let him into the house any more.'

Byomkesh asked, 'Where is this nephew now?'

With visible satisfaction Ashubabu replied, 'At present he's in prison. He was sentenced to two months' imprisonment for public misconduct and for getting into a fracas with the police.'

'I see. Please continue with what you were saying.'

'After that rascal Binod—my nephew—went into prison, life was quite peaceful for the next few days. I do not have any friends, but neither have I ever harmed anyone on purpose—so it is quite unthinkable to me that I may have enemies. But suddenly yesterday, there was a bolt from the blue. I would not have imagined that such a thing were possible. I had read in the newspapers about the gramophone pin mystery, but I didn't believe it; I thought it was all made up. But I have been proved wrong, and how!

'Last evening I had gone out, in keeping with my daily routine. There is a musical soirée near Jorasanko where I spend the evening and return home at around nine or thereabouts. Usually I walk there and back since it does me good, at my age. Last night, on my way back, when I reached the crossing of Harrison Road and Amherst Street, the clock there said nine-fifteen. The streets were quite crowded even at that hour. I waited on the pavement for a while, letting two trams go by. Then, when there was a lull in the traffic, I started to cross the road. When I had gone halfway, I suddenly felt a tremendous jolt on my chest. It felt as if someone had punched me hard on my ribs, nearabouts my breast-pocket, which held my pocket watch. At the same time, I felt a pain as if a sharp, thorny object had pierced my breast. I nearly fell over from the impact of the blow, but somehow managed to regain my balance and reach the other side of the road.

'I felt dizzy and could not figure out what had happened. When I tried to get my watch out of my pocket, I found it was stuck. Carefully I extracted it from my pocket and found that the glass had shattered completely and . . . and this gramophone pin had pierced it right through.' Ashubabu had broken out into a sweat again. He wiped his brow and with a shaking hand, took out a box from his pocket and handed it to Byomkesh, saying, 'See, this is the watch.'

Byomkesh opened the box and took out a pocket watch made of gun metal. The glass cover was missing and the watch had stopped at twenty minutes past nine; a gramophone pin was jammed viciously into the centre of the watch. Byomkesh examined the watch at great length and then put it back in the case. He placed the box on the table and said, 'Go on.'

Ashubabu continued, 'God alone knows how I managed to get back home after that. I could not sleep a wink the entire night, from worry and tension. Thank goodness for the watch in my pocket—or else I too would have wound up on the post-mortem table in the hospital by now . . .' Ashubabu shuddered. 'In one night I have lost ten years of my life, Byomkeshbabu. The entire night I was pondering over what to do, where to run, how to defend my life. Towards dawn, your name came to my mind. I had heard about your extraordinary competence and so I came to you at the earliest possible moment. I came in a closed taxi—I didn't have the courage to walk—what if . . .'

Byomkesh went up to Ashubabu and placed his hand on his shoulder, 'You can relax now. I am giving you my word that no harm shall come your way. It is true that yesterday you had a very narrow escape. But henceforth, if you follow my advice, your life will be at no risk.'

Ashubabu took Byomkesh's hands in his own and said, 'Byomkeshbabu, please rescue me from this predicament; save my life and I shall reward you with one thousand rupees.'

Byomkesh returned to his chair and said with a brief smile,

'That is very generous indeed. That makes it a total of three thousand. Hasn't the government also announced a reward of two thousand rupees? But that comes later—first answer some of my questions. Yesterday, just at the moment when you were hit, did you hear any sound?'

'What kind of sound?'

'Anything. Say, for example, something that sounded like the bursting of car tires?'

Ashubabu replied confidently, 'No.'

Byomkesh asked, 'Any other kind of sound?'

'Nothing that I can remember.'

'Think carefully.'

After ruminating for a while, Ashubabu said, 'I heard the same kind of traffic noises that one hears on a crowded street. You know, cars, trams, rickshaws. And I think—at the exact moment when I got the jolt, I heard the ring of a bicycle bell.'

'No unusual kinds of sounds?'

'None.'

Byomkesh was silent for a few seconds and then asked, 'Do you have any foes who may want you dead?'

'No. At least none that I know of.'

'You haven't married and so there are no children. I suppose your nephew is your beneficiary?'

Ashubabu hesitated a little and then said, 'No.'

'Have you drawn up your will?'

'Yes.'

'Who is your beneficiary?'

Ashubabu was blushing slowly. He remained silent for a few moments and then replied falteringly, 'You may ask me any question except that one. That is a very personal matter—private . . .' And he halted abruptly in confusion.

Byomkesh cast a piercing glance at Ashubabu and finally said, 'All right. But is your future beneficiary—whoever that may be—aware of your will?'

'No. It is strictly between me and my lawyer.'

'Do you meet your beneficiary often?'

Ashubabu looked away as he said, 'Yes.'

'How long is it since your nephew has gone to prison?'

Ashubabu did some mental calculations and said, 'About three weeks now.'

Byomkesh sat still with a frown on his face for a little while. Eventually he sighed and stood up, 'You may leave for now. Please leave the watch and your address with me. If I need any further information, I shall contact you.'

Ashubabu grew quite anxious as he asked, 'But you didn't make any arrangements for me. What if again . . .'

Byomkesh said, 'The only precaution you have to take is that you must not venture out of your house.'

Ashen-faced, Ashubabu said, 'I live alone in the house— what if . . .'

Byomkesh said, 'No, you are quite safe inside the house. But if you wish, you may employ a watchman.'

Ashubabu asked, 'Am I not to leave the house at all?'

Byomkesh gave it a moment's thought and said, 'If you must go out in the streets for some reason, always keep to the pavement. Under no circumstances should you step onto the road. If you do that, I shall not be responsible for your safety.'

After Ashubabu left, Byomkesh knitted his brows in a frown and remained deep in thought. There was no doubt that he had received enough material to keep his mind occupied for a while. So I did not get in his way. After half an hour had elapsed thus, he suddenly looked up and said, 'You are wondering why I asked Ashubabu to refrain from stepping onto the road and how I came to be so sure that he was safe within the house?'

Startled, I said, 'Yes.'

Byomkesh said, 'In the gramophone pin case, if you notice, all the deaths have occurred on the street. Not even at the kerbside but in the middle of the road. Have you thought about why this may be so?'

'No. What is the reason?'

'There could be two reasons for this. First, it might be easier to get away with murder on the street—though, on the face of it, that doesn't seem very feasible. Second, the murder weapon might be such that it can only be used in the street.'

I was curious, 'What kind of a weapon could that be?'

Byomkesh said, 'When I find that out, the mystery of the gramophone pin will not be a mystery any longer.'

An idea was burgeoning in my head and I said, 'Well, is it possible for someone to manufacture a pistol or a gun which would use gramophone pins instead of bullets?'

Byomkesh looked at me approvingly, 'That's quite an idea, but there are a few snags in it. Why would a person who wishes to use a gun or a pistol look out for crowded streets? Logically, he would prefer secluded spots. Besides, even a pistol shot, not to mention a gunshot, is too loud to be camouflaged by the noises in the street. Then there is the smell of gunpowder. Isn't there a saying: one sound masks another, but what can cover a smell?'

I said, 'Suppose it is an airgun?'

Byomkesh laughed out loud, 'I suppose there is novelty in the idea of setting off to commit a murder with an airgun slung over your shoulder, but it is not a very practical one. No, my dear, this is not so simple. The point to be considered here is that whatever the weapon is, it is bound to make a sound at the time of shooting—how then is that sound concealed?'

I said, 'Weren't you just saying—one sound masks another . . .'

Suddenly Byomkesh sat up straight and stared at me with eyes wide open, muttering to himself, 'That's right—that's right—'

Taken aback, I asked, 'What is it?'

Byomkesh shook his head and said, 'Nothing. The more I think about this gramophone pin mystery, the more I feel as if all the deaths are linked in some way. There is a peculiar similarity running through all of them, although it doesn't seem apparent at first.'

'How is that?'

Byomkesh began to tick the points off on his fingers, 'To begin with, all the victims were in their middle age. Ashubabu—who was saved by the watch—is also middle-aged. Second, all of them were well-to-do. Some may have been richer than others, but no one was badly off. Third, each one was killed in the middle of the road, before hundreds of witnesses. And finally—and most importantly—they were all childless.'

I said, 'Then your guess is . . .'

Byomkesh said, 'I have not yet made any assumptions. All of these are the foundations for my yet-to-be-formulated assumption—you might call them premises.'

I said, 'But to catch the murderers from just these few premises . . .'

Byomkesh interrupted me, 'Not murderers, Ajit, *the* murderer. The plural is completely superfluous here, except to add eminence. Much as the newsmen are clamouring about a "murderous gang", this gang consists of a single individual. He is the sole patron, high-priest and executor of this human massacre. He is the one and only.'

I could not help sounding a little doubtful, 'How can you be so sure of that? Do you have any proof?'

Byomkesh replied, 'Proofs there are many; but at present one will suffice. Is it possible for five people to have this same incredible skill of hitting the bull's-eye every time? Each of the pins have pierced the victim right through the heart, and not hit him a shade below or above it. Take Ashubabu's case, for example. But for the watch, where do you think that pin would have landed? How many persons do you think can have such perfect aim? This is like looking at the shadow of the wooden fish in the water and shooting it in the eye through the spokes of a rotating wheel—I suppose you do remember Draupadi's *swayamvara*? Just think, that was something that Arjun alone could accomplish—even in the days of the Mahabharata such infallible precision was unique to one person.' Byomkesh was laughing as he stood up.

There was a room next to the drawing room which was Byomkesh's den. He didn't even let *me* in there at all times. In effect this room was his library, laboratory, museum and dressing-room, all in one. He picked up Ashubahu's watch and proceeded towards that room now, saying, 'There will be enough time after lunch to ponder over the patterns of this case. Now it is time for a bath.'

Byomkesh went out at around three-thirty in the afternoon. I had no idea where he went, or why. It was dark when he returned. I was waiting for him and so was the tea. As soon as he came in, Putiram brought in some snacks. We ate in complete silence. By force of habit, it didn't feel right if we didn't have our evening tea together.

Leaning back in his chair and lighting a cheroot, Byomkesh broke the silence first, 'What kind of person did Ashubabu strike you as?'

A trifle surprised, I said, 'Why do you ask? I thought he was a decent man—quite mild and amicable—'

Byomkesh said, 'And his moral character?'

I replied, 'From his animosity towards his nephew, the alcoholic, I would say he is quite upright. Moreover, he is aging. He isn't married. He may have sown his wild oats in his youth, but this is hardly the right age for all that.'

Byomkesh smirked, 'It may not be the right age, but that doesn't seem to have prevented him. The house in Jorasanko where Ashubabu goes every day for some musical soirée happens to be a woman's house. Actually, it would be wrong to say that it is her house because it is Ashubabu who pays the rent. It is also probably incorrect to call it a musical soirée—surely it takes more than two people to make a soirée.'

'What are you saying! So the old man is quite a colourful character, eh?'

'There's more. Ashubabu has been supporting this lady for the last twelve or thirteen years and so there is no doubt about his fidelity. And apparently it is reciprocated because other than Ashubabu, no other music-lover is allowed admittance there—the door is strictly guarded.'

I was all agog, 'Really! Were you trying to sneak in as a music aficionado? Did you see the lady? What does she look like?'

Byomkesh said, 'I caught a fleeting glimpse of her. But I shall not deprive a die-hard bachelor like you of your precious night's sleep by describing her beauty to you. In a word, she is stunning. She is perhaps twenty-six or twenty-seven years old, but doesn't look a day over twenty. I cannot help being impressed by Ashubabu's discriminating taste.'

I laughed as I said, 'I can quite see that. But why have you developed this sudden interest in Ashubabu's personal life?'

Byomkesh said, 'Uncontrollable curiosity is one of my weak points. Besides, the question of Ashubabu's beneficiary was bothering me.'

'So *this* is Ashubabu's beneficiary?'

'That is my assumption. I also saw another gentleman there—in his mid-thirties—quite a dandy. He walked up to the guard, hastily tucked a letter into his hands and disappeared with equal speed. But let that be. The topic may be appetizing but is not of much use right now.'

Byomkesh stood up and began pacing the floor.

I realized that he didn't let the discussion go any further for fear that these redundant deliberations about Ashubabu's personal life might distract his mind from the more basic path of inquiry that was concerned with the safety of his client. I too was aware that this was how the human mind was inclined to prioritize the insignificant and consequently, unknown to itself, lose sight of the main objective. So I moved on, 'Did you discover anything from the watch?'

Byomkesh stopped in front of me and said with a short laugh, 'My examination of the watch has yielded three pieces of information: first, that the gramophone pin is of an ordinary Edison brand; second, that it weighs exactly two grams; and third, that Ashubabu's watch is an irreparable loss—it is beyond repair.'

I said, 'Which means you have reached no material conclusions.'

Byomkesh pulled up a chair and sat down, saying, 'That I cannot agree with. Firstly, I have figured out that at the time of shooting the pin the distance between the killer and his victim could not have been more than seven or eight feet. A gramophone pin is so lightweight that any distance greater than that would not ensure such an accurate bull's-eye. And you have seen what an excellent marksman the killer is. Every time the missile has hit the target without fail.'

Incredulous, I asked, 'He has killed from such close quarters and yet no one has been able to catch him red-handed?'

Byomkesh said, 'That is what poses the greatest conundrum. Just think, after committing the act, the man may have stood among the bystanders, may even have lent a hand in moving the body; and yet nobody has been able to figure out how he has managed to conceal his identity so well.'

I contemplated for a while and then remarked, 'Well, how about if the killer has an instrument in his pocket which can fire a gramophone pin. When he approaches the victim, he fires it without taking it out of his pocket. A lot of people walk with their hands in their pockets and it doesn't arouse any suspicions.'

Byomkesh said, 'If that was the case, he could have accomplished the task on the pavement. Why would he need the victim to get onto the road? Besides, I don't know of any instrument which can fire noiselessly and yet shoot a projectile through a man's skin and muscles and hit his heart directly. Have you thought about the kind of force needed for that?'

I remained silent. Byomkesh propped his elbows on his knees, sank his chin into his palms and remained deep in thought for a considerable length of time; at last he said, 'I can feel that a simple solution to this is close at hand, but it is eluding me. The more I try to grasp it, I feel it slipping away.'

There was no further conversation over this that night. Until he went to sleep, Byomkesh continued to be abstracted and unmindful. Realizing that he was in close pursuit of the solution to the problem, which was near and yet refusing to reveal itself to him, I too didn't disturb his train of thought.

The following morning he woke with the same withdrawn look on his face and after washing quickly and gulping down a cup of tea, rushed out of the house. When he returned about three hours later, I asked, 'Where were you?'

Untying his shoelaces, Byomkesh replied absent-mindedly, 'At the lawyer's.' Since he was so preoccupied, I didn't press him any further.

Towards afternoon he looked a little more light-hearted. He spent the entire afternoon working in his room, behind closed doors; once I heard him speaking to someone on the phone. At about four-thirty he opened the door and stuck out his neck saying, 'Hey there, have you forgotten about what we decided yesterday? It is nearly time to furnish indubitable proof on the thorn-in-the-flesh issue.'

Truly, the matter of the thorn-in-the-flesh had completely slipped my mind. Byomkesh laughed and said, 'Come on then, let's get you dressed up a little. We cannot just go as we are.'

I entered his room and asked, 'Why can't we go as we are?'

Byomkesh opened a wooden almirah and took out a tin box from within. He picked out some crepe, scissors, etc. Applying spirit-gum to my face with a brush, he said, 'It is not unknown to many a gentleman that Ajit Bandyo is a friend to Byomkesh Bakshi—hence the slight precaution.'

A quarter of an hour later when Byomkesh finished with me, I went to the mirror and—oh lord! This was no Ajit Bandyo, it was a complete stranger. Ajit Bandyo had never grown a French-cut beard or a pointed moustache. The man seemed older too, by about ten years, and darker by a few shades. I quavered and asked, 'Do I have to step out dressed like this? What if the police pick me up?'

Byomkesh chuckled and said, 'Have no fear! The best of the police doesn't have the remotest chance of recognizing you. If you don't believe me, go downstairs and speak to one of your acquaintances. Ask him—where does Ajitbabu live?'

My panic mounted and I said, 'No, no, that won't be necessary. I shall go as I am.'

As I was leaving Byomkesh said, 'You know what you are to do—just be careful on your way back; you may be followed.'

'Is there a chance of that happening too?'

'It isn't unlikely. I shall be at home—try to come back as soon as possible.'

After stepping out of the house, I felt very ill at ease at first. But when I realized that my disguise wasn't drawing any attention, I felt a little relieved and also a bit bolder. I was a regular customer at a paan shop at the end of the road and the north-Indian paanwallah always gave me a salute when he saw me. I went up to him and asked for a paan. The man nonchalantly handed it to me and took the money without even taking a good look at me.

It was nearly five o'clock and so there was no more time to be lost. I boarded a tram, got off at Esplanade and sauntered over to the suggested spot. Although it was no romantic tryst and my state of mind was far from that of a lover, I began to feel a growing sense of curiosity and excitement.

But the excitement was short-lived. It wasn't an easy task standing like a rooted column on a road where throngs of people rushed to and fro like the tides of an overflowing river. I took a few jabs and digs from unidentified elbows, without demur. There was another predicament in standing by the lamp-post for no apparent reason. A sergeant stood at the crossroad and he looked me over inquiringly a few times—at any moment he would come over and ask me why I was loitering. With no other option before me, I fixed a steady, admiring stare at the shop window of the Whiteway Laidlaw, which was attractively decorated with various foreign merchandise. I thought to myself, there's no harm in being taken for an ignorant bumpkin, as long as it keeps the policeman from taking me for a pickpocket and slipping the handcuffs onto my wrists.

I checked my watch which said ten minutes to six. Another ten minutes and I would be off the hook. I began to wait with growing impatience; all my concentration was focused on the pockets of my kurta. A few times I felt around in my pockets too, but my fingers found nothing new.

Eventually, at the stroke of six I gave a great sigh of relief and abandoned the lamp-post. I checked my pockets once again, carefully. There was no sign of any missive. Along with the disappointment, there was a spiteful sense of joy as well—now I had at least one example of an instance where Byomkesh's assumption was not necessarily the right one. So I would be able to mock him to my satisfaction. With that happy thought in my head, I began to walk towards the tram depot at Esplanade.

'Want some pictures, babu?'

The words, spoken right in my ear, made me jump out of my skin. I turned around to find a shady-looking Muslim man in a lungi offering me an envelope. Puzzled, I opened it and an obscene picture fell out. I was aware that such trash was peddled on the streets of Calcutta and so I stretched out my hand in disgust, meaning to return it. But the man had vanished. I looked ahead, behind and all around me; but the man in the lungi was nowhere to be seen.

In great bewilderment, I was wondering what I should do next when a suppressed chuckle broke through my reverie. An elderly Englishman was standing beside me. Without looking at me, he spoke in flawless Bangla in a very familiar voice, 'I see that you have received the note. So now go on home. Take a roundabout route. Go upto Bowbazar by tram and then take a bus to Howrah crossing; from there, take a taxi home.'

A tram bound for Circular Road materialized before us; the gentleman jumped aboard.

When I reached home after dragging my feet through half of Calcutta, Byomkesh was stretched out in his armchair smoking a cheroot. I pulled up a chair and said, 'So sahib, when did you get back?'

Byomkesh exhaled some smoke and said, 'About twenty minutes or so.'

I said, 'Why did you follow me?'

Byomkesh sat up straight and said, 'The purpose behind my doing so happens to have failed by a few minutes' delay. When you were leaning against the lamp-post, I was behind the glass-window of Laidlaw's, selecting some silk socks. Perhaps the peddler of thorn-in-the-flesh suspected something, and he had good reason to—from the way you were inspecting your pockets once every two minutes and fidgeting endlessly. Hence he did not hand you the letter then. I must have walked out of the store a couple of minutes after you left, but that was enough time for our man to slip you the envelope. When I reached there, you were standing like some what-you-may-call-it holding the envelope in your hands. How did you come to receive it?'

When I described to him how I got the envelope, Byomkesh asked, 'Did you get a good look at the man? Do you remember anything about him?'

I pondered over it and said, 'No. Only, I think, he had a huge mole by his nose.'

Disappointed, Byomkesh shook his head and said, 'That was fake—not real. Just like your beard and whiskers. Anyway, now let me see the letter; you can go and take your disguise off in the meantime.'

When I returned after getting rid of my hirsute excesses, Byomkesh's demeanour had changed completely. He was pacing the floor agitatedly, with both his hands behind him. His face was glowing with exultation. My heart leaped up in expectation. Eagerly I asked, 'What did you find in the letter? Are you on to something?'

With suppressed elation Byomkesh patted my back and said, 'Just one thing Ajit, just one tiny thing. But I shall not tell you anything yet. Have you ever seen the Howrah Bridge when it is open to let the ships through? My mind was in a similar state—two ends came from two sides, but left a slight gap in the middle—the pontoon was open. Today that gap has been bridged.'

'How did that happen? What does the letter say?'

'Read it for yourself.' Byomkesh handed me a sheet of paper.

I had noticed earlier that there was another piece of paper in the envelope, besides the obscene photograph; but I hadn't had a chance to read it. Now I read it; it was written in a clear, bold script:

Who is the thorn in your flesh? What is his name and address? Put down what you want clearly on a sheet of paper. Do not conceal anything. There is no need to sign your name. Seal the note in an envelope and proceed with it to the Kidderpore racecourse on Sunday, 10th March, at midnight. Walk westwards along the road adjoining the racecourse. You will see a man approaching you from the other end of the road on a bicycle. You will know him from the goggles he will be wearing. As soon as you spot him, hold the note out towards him. The man on the bicycle will take the letter from your hands. You shall be contacted in due course.

Please come alone and on foot. If you are accompanied by anyone else, the rendezvous will be called off.

Carefully, I went over it two or three times. Admittedly, it was very unusual and terribly fanciful too—there was no doubt about that. But I failed to discover the cause for Byomkesh's unbridled jubilance. So I asked, 'Do tell me what this is all about. I mean, I don't see anything . . .'

'You cannot see *anything*?'

'Of course, whatever you had prophesied yesterday has undoubtedly come true to the last detail. There may even be some unseemly intent behind the man's desire to conceal his own identity. But I do not see anything beyond that.'

'God help the blind one! How could you miss it when it is staring you in the face?' Suddenly Byomkesh stopped as we heard steps on the stairs outside. He listened to it attentively for a few seconds and then declared, 'It's Ashubabu. There is no need to tell him about all this . . .' He took the letter from my hands and slipped it into his pocket.

When Ashubabu entered the room, his appearance was a sight to behold. It was beyond my imagination that a man's countenance could change so drastically in one single day. His dress was in disarray, his hair dishevelled, his cheeks sunken. There were dark circles under his eyes. It looked as if he had suddenly received a great blow and been shattered by the trauma. Yesterday, even after his narrow escape from near-death, I had not found him looking quite so disconsolate and distraught. He threw himself tiredly into a chair and said, 'There is some bad news, Byomkeshbabu. My lawyer, Bilash Mullick, has absconded.'

In a sombre, yet sympathetic tone Byomkesh replied, 'I knew he would. I suppose you have also come to know that your friend from Jorasanko has gone along with him?'

Ashubabu sat there dumbfounded for a few seconds and then said, 'You—you know everything?'

Calmly, Byomkesh said, 'All of it. Yesterday I had gone to Jorasanko and I also saw Bilash Mullick. It's been a while now since the lady of that house and Bilashbabu have been conspiring against you—you had no knowledge of this, of course. Right after drawing up your will, Bilashbabu had gone to look up your beneficiary. Initially perhaps the only motivation was curiosity, and then—you know how it is. They were just waiting for an opportunity all these years. Ashubabu, you must not lose heart. You are much better off now—free of the schemings of a dishonest woman and a deceiving friend. Your life is no longer in danger—you can walk down the middle of the road fearlessly.'

Ashubabu cast a troubled glance at him and asked, 'Meaning?'

Byomkesh replied, 'Meaning, the suspicions that are gnawing at your heart but which you are loath to utter, are absolutely true. It was these two who conspired to kill you; but not with their own hands. In this very city lives a man—no one know who he is or what he looks like, but his relentless weapon has silently removed five innocent, harmless men from the face of this earth. You too would have followed in their footsteps, had your karma not come to your rescue.'

For several minutes Ashubabu sat with his face buried deep in his hands. Finally he gave a morose sigh and began to speak, 'I am paying for my own sins in my old age, so I have no one else to blame. My character was impeccable until the age of thirty-eight and then, suddenly, I slipped. I had gone to visit Deoghar. There my eyes fell upon an incredibly beautiful girl and—I lost my senses. I had always been averse to marriage, but suddenly I was desperate to marry her. Eventually, one day, I came to know that she was a courtesan's daughter. So there was no question of marriage, but neither could I leave her. I brought her to Calcutta and rented a place for her. Since then, for all of these twelve years, I have looked upon her as my wife. You already know that I made out everything that I possessed in her name. I thought she also loved me in return—as her husband—there was never any doubts in my mind. What I did not realize was that a woman conceived in sin could not possibly be capable of fidelity. Anyway, perhaps I shall benefit from this lesson learnt in my old age, in another lifetime.' After a short pause, he asked in a ragged voice,

'They—the two of them—do you have any idea where they have gone?'

Byomkesh said, 'No. And there is no use in knowing that either. You would not be able to follow them on the path to which destiny is dragging them. Ashubabu, your transgression may be censured by society, but please rest assured that in my eyes you will be revered always. Your heart is in the right place; even after wading through murk, you have retained your sincerity and that is what is praiseworthy. Right now you are deeply wounded, and who wouldn't be in the face of such betrayal? But gradually you will come to understand that a better fate could not have befallen you.'

In a voice brimming with emotion, Ashubabu said, 'Byomkeshbabu, you are much younger to me in age, but the solace you have given me is beyond my expectations. When someone pays the price for his own shameful sins, nobody sympathizes with him. That is what makes his repentance so much more difficult. Your commiseration has lifted half the weight off my shoulders. What more can I say—I shall remain indebted to you for the rest of my life.'

After Ashubabu took his leave, his tragic tale left me depressed for the rest of the evening. Before going to sleep, I asked Byomkesh one question, 'When did you find out that the woman and Bilashbabu were behind Ashubabu's attempted murder?'

Byomkesh took his eyes off the beams overhead and replied, 'Last evening.'

'Then why didn't you catch them before they escaped?'

'It would have been useless. Their crime cannot be proved in any court of law.'

'But they could have led us to the real killer behind the gramophone pin mystery.'

Byomkesh hid a smile as he said, 'If that were possible, then I wouldn't have personally induced them to flee.'

'You made them abscond?'

'Yes. Since Ashubabu had had his fortunate escape, they were on the verge of fleeing anyway. I went to Bilashbabu's house this morning and implied through oblique hints that I already know a lot and if they didn't make their escape soon, they'd be behind bars. Bilashbabu is an intelligent man. He took off in the evening train along with his companion.'

'But what did you gain out of making them disappear?'

Byomkesh gave a huge yawn and said, 'I didn't gain much, except putting a small spoke in a wheel of evil. Bilashbabu was not one to disappear empty-handed. He took with him all the money belonging to his clients that he could lay his hands on. By now I presume the police have arrested him at Burdwan—they had prior information, you see. Anyway, nothing will stop him from serving a two-year sentence at the very least. His rightful penalty would be death, of course, but since that is not possible under the circumstances, I suppose two years is better than nothing.'

The following morning a stranger dropped in on us.

I had just finished my tea and was about to open the morning paper when there was a knock on the door.

Byomkesh looked up attentively and called out, 'Who is it? Please come on in.'

A decently dressed youth came in. He was clean-shaven, slim in build and looked to be on the right side of thirty. There was something athletic about the way he carried himself. Walking in, he smiled pleasantly at us and joined his hands in greeting, saying, 'I hope you do not mind my coming to bother you at this early hour. My name is Prafulla Roy; I am an insurance agent.' He dropped into a chair uninvited.

Byomkesh said disinterestedly, 'We do not have the money to take out a life insurance policy.'

Prafulla Roy laughed out loud. There is a breed of people who look quite presentable otherwise, but when they laugh, they become quite unsightly. Prafulla Roy belonged to that category. He was probably a chronic paan-chewer because his teeth were heavily stained by the betel-leaf juice. I was intrigued seeing how a handsome face could be thus distorted.

Prafulla Roy continued to laugh as he said, 'I may be an insurance agent, but that isn't exactly what has brought me here. Of course, these days even our near and dear ones have taken to slamming the door shut on our faces even before we can speak; and I can't say I blame them either. But you may rest assured that right now I do not have any such nefarious intent. You, I presume, are Byomkeshbabu—the famous detective? I have come to take some advice from you on a private matter, sir—if you have no objections . . .'

Byomkesh's lips curled in irritation as he said, 'There has to be some advance payment for a consultation.'

Prafulla Roy immediately took a ten-rupee note out of his wallet and placed it on the table, saying, 'What I have to say is not exactly classified, but . . .' he glanced at me inquiringly. I made as if to leave, but Byomkesh said, quite sternly, 'He is my associate and friend. You may say whatever you have to say in front of him.'

Prafulla Roy said, 'Certainly, certainly. Since he is your associate, I have no objections at all. You are—? Oh, forgive me, Ajitbabu, I did not realize that you are Byomkeshbabu's friend. You are a fortunate man indeed, working so closely with such a famous detective, helping crack so many strange cases and crimes—it is no small matter. You probably do not have a dull moment in your life. I sometimes wish I could quit this boring life of an insurance agent and lead a life like yours.' He took out a case of paan from his pocket and put one in his mouth.

Byomkesh was growing increasingly restless and he said, 'I think it would be nice if you now state your case on which you need my advice.'

Prafulla Roy hastily turned towards him and said, 'Yes, I was coming to that, sir. As I have already told you, I am an insurance agent. I work for Bombay's Jewel Insurance Company. I have raised nearly ten to twelve lakhs of rupees for the company and so, as a reward, they have sent me to Calcutta, entrusting the office here to my charge. For the last eight months I have been in this city on a permanent basis.

'The first few months were fine on the work front. Then suddenly there was an unexpected problem. I do not want to take names, but an employee of a rival firm was the cause. I do not handle the smaller commissions. Those that are worth a few thousand rupees are taken care of by my subordinates. I come in only for the big cases. Now, this man began to steal my bigger clients—major policies—from me. He would turn up after me wherever I went, berate my company by carrying tales to the clients, and take away my business. Eventually things came to such a pass that these bigger life policies began to slip out of my hands.

'Four or five months went by in this fashion. I began to receive pressures from above, but I had no idea about how I could retrieve my business from this man's hands. A legal suit was not the solution—it would damage the company name. And yet, I would have to shake this bloodsucking leech off somehow. A couple more months passed, without any solution coming to my mind. Then . . .'

Furtively, Prafulla Roy pulled out two chits from his wallet and handed the smaller one to Byomkesh, saying, 'About a fortnight ago this advertisement caught my eye. You, perhaps, haven't noticed it; there was no reason for you to do so. But sir, although it is a small classified, as soon as I read it, my heart leaped up! Is my case a thorn-in-the-flesh or what? I thought, let me see if my thorn-in-the-flesh can indeed be extricated! The state I was in, I think I would not even have objected to exotic talismans.'

I craned my neck and saw that it was a cutting of the same thorn-in-the-flesh insert. Prafulla Roy went on, 'Have you read it? Isn't it peculiar? Anyway, on the appointed day, that is, the Saturday before last, I went and stood by the lamp-post, like a Santa under a Christmas tree. Oh, nothing can describe that ordeal. My legs went to sleep, but it was all in vain—nobody came. Utterly disgusted, I was coming back when I suddenly realized that this letter was in my pocket.'

He handed the second piece of paper to Byomkesh and said, 'Take a look—this is the one.'

Byomkesh opened the letter and began to read it; I came and stood behind his chair and read it over his shoulder—it was an exact replica of the letter I, too, had received, except that the date for the rendezvous was not Sunday, but Monday the eleventh of March.

After a brief pause when Prafulla Roy gave us time to scan

the letter, he continued, 'For one thing, I have no idea how the letter came into my pocket. Moreover, a strange fear gripped me after reading it. I am not very fond of mysteries, sir, and this letter is precisely that from beginning to end. It is as if a sinister motive is concealed within it. Why else would there be so much secrecy? I know nothing about who this person is, what he is—I have never even set eyes upon him and he is asking me to walk down a lonely road at midnight. Isn't it cause for grave suspicion? Don't you agree with me?' He looked directly at me.

Before I could answer, Byomkesh said, 'Whether he does or not is completely irrelevant. Please tell me what you need my advice for.'

A trifle aggrieved, Prafulla Roy said, 'That is what I am asking. I do not know the author of this letter, but his intentions seem far from honourable. In light of this, would it be right for me to go there with an answer to this note? I have pondered over this for the past two weeks and come up with nothing; but, if I have to do it, there is only one more day to go. So, not being able to decide upon a course of action, I have come to ask for your help.'

Byomkesh gave it some thought and then said, 'I am sorry, but I shall not be able to give you any help today. Why don't you leave these two chits here; there is still plenty of time. I shall give it the necessary consideration and come up with a solution for you, first thing tomorrow morning.'

Prafulla Roy said, 'But I cannot come tomorrow; I have to attend to some business. How about if I dropped by tonight, say around eight or nine o'clock—would that be inconvenient?'

Byomkesh shook his head, 'No, I am busy tonight—I have some business to attend to . . . ' Realizing that this had slipped out, Byomkesh stole a glance at Prafulla Roy and changed the subject, 'But you have no reason to worry yet; even if you come tomorrow evening at four o'clock or thereabouts, it will do.'

'All right, then, that is what I shall do.' He pulled out the case from his pocket again, put two paans in his mouth and offered it to us, 'Do you take paan? No! There are some habits that we humans just cannot quit; I can go without a meal, but not my paan. Well, then—I shall see you later. Namaskar.'

We returned his greeting. He went upto the door and then turned around, 'How about informing the police about this? I feel they may be able to investigate and get the details of this man's identity.'

All of a sudden Byomkesh lost his temper and said, 'If you want to go to the police, do not expect any help from me. I have not worked with the police ever, and do not intend to start now. Here—take your money back.' He indicated the ten-rupee note that lay on the table.

'No, oh no, I simply wanted your opinion on it. Since you are so opposed to it . . . well, then, I shall be going.' Prafulla Roy made a hasty exit.

After he left, Byomkesh picked up the note from the table and went into his library, slamming the door shut behind him. I was aware that, although he grew irritable at times, the phase passed after a few hours' solitude. So, in spite of the barbs of curiosity pricking my mind, I picked up the unread newspaper and tried to immerse myself in it.

A few minutes later I could hear Byomkesh speaking in the other room. I figured he was making a telephone call. A few English phrases came to my ears; but I couldn't make out who he was talking to. The conversation lasted for about an hour and then, eventually, Byomkesh came out of the room. I looked at him and saw that he was back to his usual cheerful self.

I asked, 'Who did you call?'

Without answering my question, he said, 'Did you know that you were being followed on your way back from Esplanade yesterday?'

Startled, I said, 'No. Was I?'

Byomkesh said, 'Yes, beyond a doubt. But what amazes me is the extreme audacity of the man.' He began to laugh quietly to himself.

I could not fathom what was so audacious about following me; but sometimes Byomkesh's remarks were so baffling that it was a futile exercise trying to comprehand them. There was also no point in questioning him about it because he wouldn't

say a word until the right moment arrived. So, without wasting
my breath, I went in to have my shower.

Byomkesh spent the afternoon and evening sitting around,
doing nothing. I asked a couple of questions about Prafulla
Roy, but he continued to lie there with his eyes closed, as if he
didn't hear a thing. Finally, he looked up with a start and said,
'Prafulla Roy? Oh, you mean the man who came in this
morning? No, I haven't got around to thinking about him yet.'

At night, after dinner, we were smoking in silence. At the
stroke of half past ten, Byomkesh jumped up, saying, 'Awake
and arise, O supine one—it is time to start getting dressed or
the time for the tryst would be past.'

Surprised, I said, 'What do you mean?'

Byomkesh said, 'Come on, we have to honour the
thorn-in-the-flesh rendezvous, remember?'

I stood up apprehensively and said, 'I am sorry—at this late
hour, I refuse to go there all by myself. If you wish, you may
go yourself.'

'I shall certainly go, but you must come too.'

'But must we go? What is this undue interest in the
thorn-in-the-flesh affair? Instead, if you concentrated upon the
gramophone pin mystery a bit, things may actually begin to
look up.'

'Perhaps they would. But in the meantime what's the harm
in satisfying one stray curiosity? The gramophone pin case isn't
running away. Besides, Prafulla Roy will come back tomorrow
for advice and we should have some information for him.'

'But it won't do for both of us to go. The letter insisted that
only one person should show up.'

'I have made arrangements for that. Now please come to
the other room—time is running out.'

Once inside the library, Byomkesh deftly changed my
visage. I took a peek at the tall mirror hanging on the wall and
saw that, as if by magic, the old moustache and French-cut
beard had made a comeback. He let me go and then began work
on his own disguise. He made no changes to his face; he simply
took a black suit from his cupboard along with black shoes with
rubber soles and donned these. Then he made me stand five or

six feet away from the mirror, took up his position right behind me and asked, 'Can you see me in the mirror?'

'No.'

'Fine. Now walk on ahead—can you see me now?'

'No.'

'Well, then it's done. Now just one item remains to be put on.'

'What now?'

When I entered the room, I had noticed that Byomkesh had two oval-shaped ceramic plates set on the table—the kind in which they serve you mutton chops in restaurants. He took up one of these plates now, tied it onto my chest with a broad piece of cloth and said, 'Careful, it shouldn't slip. Now if you pull on a coat over this, nothing will show.'

In great bewilderment, I asked, 'What's all this?'

Byomkesh laughed and replied, 'Oh, we have to have the armour—don't we? Don't worry, I am wearing one as well.'

Byomkesh slipped the second plate under his waistcoat and buttoned it up; there was no need for him to tie it in place.

After thus completing our peculiar disguises, we left our home at twenty minutes past eleven. As he was taking a few final things from the cupboard and putting them in his pocket, Byomkesh asked, 'Have you taken the letter? Oh no, hurry up and get it ready—quick, slip a blank sheet of paper into an envelope . . .'

We managed to find a taxi at the Sealdah crossing and got into it. The roads were empty and most of the shops had closed for the day. Our taxi sped through the empty streets, as per our instructions, towards Chowringhee.

We got off at the point where the tram-lines for Kalighat and Kidderpore parted ways. The taxi driver collected his fare and drove away, honking pointlessly. As I glanced around me, I realized that there wasn't a single soul anywhere on the road. The light from the countless streetlamps all around cast a ghostly tinge on the desolate cityscape. My watch said there were still ten minutes to midnight.

We had already discussed our course of action in the taxi, so there was no need for further conversation. I walked on ahead and Byomkesh silently merged with the shadows behind me. His black garb and inaudible footfall made him seem like an apparition, even to me. He matched his steps with mine and followed me at a distance of exactly six inches, and yet I felt as though I was alone. The streetlights illuminating the wide expanse of the road were not very bright. If there had been buildings along the roadside, they would have served to reflect the lights and brighten the surroundings. In this case, the barren lands all around simply engulfed half the strength of the lights. Under the circumstances, nobody approaching me from the opposite direction would be able to tell that I wasn't alone, that a shadowy figure was silently trailing in my footsteps.

The tram-lines running on one side of the road had been in disuse for a while. On the other side the white railings of the racecourse ran without a break. I began to walk down the middle of the road. Somewhere, at a distance, a clock clanged into life, striking twelve.

As the sounds of the chimes faded, Byomkesh whispered in my ears, 'Now take the letter in your hand.'

I had almost forgotten that Byomkesh was behind me. Jumping out of my skin, I quickly took out the envelope from my pocket. I walked on for another six or seven minutes. I was only halfway to Kidderpore bridge, when I saw a faint speck of light in the distance and grew alert. There was the voice in my ears again, 'There he is—be ready.'

The speck of light grew brighter. In a few moments one could make out something hurling towards us at some speed, looking even darker than the tar-black road it was travelling on. A few seconds later the figure of a bicycle rider was clearly evident. I stood still and stretched out my hand holding the letter. In front of me the speed of the bicycle too grew more slack.

I waited with bated breath. The bicycle was now within twenty-five feet of me. I noticed that the rider, clad in a black suit, was staring at me fixedly through a pair of goggles.

The cycle proceeded at a moderate speed, targeting me. When the gap between us was about ten feet, suddenly the bicycle bell rang out loudly and simultaneously, I received a jolt in my chest and nearly took a tumble. I could feel the plate tied to my chest shattering into countless pieces.

Then, within a matter of seconds, several things happened. As soon as I staggered to the ground, Byomkesh lunged in front. The bicycle rider was not prepared for someone else behind me. Still, he tried to dodge him, but couldn't escape. Byomkesh shoved him off the vehicle and pounced onto him like a ferocious tiger.

When I rose and went to his aid, I found Byomkesh straddling the opponent and gripping his wrists in a stern vise. The bicycle lay on one side. When he saw me walking up, Byomkesh said, 'Ajit, take the silk cord from my pocket and tie his hands together—hard.'

I took the fine silk cord from his pocket and tightly bound up the hands of the man who lay overthrown. Byomkesh said, 'Good, that's it. Ajit, haven't you recognized this gentleman? This is our friend from this morning, Prafulla Roy. And if you want a better introduction, this is the brain behind the gramophone pin mystery.' He removed the goggles from the man's eyes.

I cannot describe what went through my mind at these words. But Prafulla Roy only gave a viciously toothy laugh and said, 'Byomkeshbabu, you may get off my chest now—I shall not escape.'

Byomkesh said, 'Ajit, please check his pockets carefully for any weapons that he may be carrying.'

One pocket yielded a pair of opera glasses and the other a case of paan—nothing else. I opened the case and found about four paans in it.

Once Byomkesh had released his grip on his victim, Prafulla Roy sat up, subjected him to a long, unblinking stare and spoke slowly, 'Byomkeshbabu, you are brighter than me, because I had underestimated your shrewdness and you hadn't,' he said. 'It never pays to undermine your enemy—this lesson has come to me a little late; there won't be any time to profit from it.' He smiled wanly.

Byomkesh fished out a police whistle from his pocket and

blew on it; then he said to me, 'Ajit, please pick up the bicycle and move it aside. But be careful not to touch the bell—it's a nasty thing.'

Prafulla Roy laughed, 'I see that you know everything—what a genius! You are the only person I feared and that is why I laid this trap today. I had thought you would come alone, we would have a private tryst. But you betrayed me on all counts. I prided myself on my acting prowess, but you are an artiste of a far greater calibre. This morning you stripped me of my mask and laid my mind bare while I only took in your masquerade. Well, my throat feels quite dry—may I have a drink of water?'

Byomkesh said, 'There is no water here, you may have it at the police station.'

Prafulla Roy smiled haggardly and said, 'Really, how silly of me to ask for water here!' He paused a while and then looked yearningly at the box of paan and said, 'Can I have a paan? I know one is not really supposed to indulge a captured criminal with paans, but it would at least quench my thirst.'

Byomkesh gestured to me and I took two paans from the case and put them into his mouth. Chewing on the paan, Prafulla Roy said, 'Thanks. You may have the other two, if you wish.'

Byomkesh was intently looking out for the police and he nodded absent-mindedly. In the distance, we heard the motorcycles approaching. Prafulla Roy said, 'The police is almost here. So you won't let me go?'

Byomkesh said, 'How can I let you go?'

Prafulla Roy laughed wildly and asked again, 'So you're determined to hand me over to the police?'

'Of course I am!'

'Byomkeshbabu, even an intelligent man makes mistakes. You won't be able to deliver me to the police . . .' and he crumpled and fell to the ground.

One motorcycle came up to us noisily and halted. A uniformed officer jumped off it and asked, 'What's up? Dead?'

Prafulla Roy opened his eyes sluggishly and said, 'Well, well, if it isn't the chief himself! Too late, sir, you couldn't get me. Byomkeshbabu, you would have done well to have eaten the paan, we could have journeyed together. I hate to leave a genius like you behind!' Making a vain attempt to smile, Prafulla Roy closed his eyes. His face suddenly went rigid.

In the meantime, a truckload of policemen had arrived. As the Commissioner himself stepped forward with the handcuffs, Byomkesh stood up from his examination of the dead man and said, 'There is no need for handcuffs—the culprit has absconded.'

Byomkesh and I were face to face, sitting in our drawing room. Plenty of air and light were streaming in through the open window. Byomkesh was holding a bicycle bell in his hands, looking it over. An opened envelope lay on the table.

Byomkesh unscrewed the top of the bell, gazed admiringly at the workings inside and said, 'What a brilliant mind. I am sure nobody had even thought that such an instrument can be devised. This coiled spring that you see here is the ammunition—what a deadly power this spring has. How terrible and yet how simple it is. This tiny hole here is the muzzle, from where the projectile shoots out. And this trigger here serves two purposes—the release of the projectile as well as the ringing of the bell. The sound of the bell conceals the noise that the spring makes. Remember, we had talked about this—one sound masks another, but what can cover a smell? That was the day I had received an indication of just how intelligent this man is.'

I asked, 'Tell me something—how did you guess that the thorn-in-the-flesh peddler and the gramophone pin killer were one and the same?'

Byomkesh said, 'I didn't at first. But gradually, almost in my subconscious, those two came together. Look, what is the thorn-in-the-flesh man saying? He is stating very clearly that if there is any obstruction in the way of your happiness and peace, he will rid you of it—of course, in exchange for hard cash. Although there was no mention of the remuneration, it is quite obvious that this wasn't his altruistic philanthropy. And now, look on the other hand, all those who were struck by the gramophone pin, were standing in the way of somebody's happiness. I do not want to raise any accusing fingers at the relatives of the deceased, because something that cannot be proved should not even be implied. But one cannot fail to notice that each of the deceased had no children and their beneficiaries were, in some cases, a nephew or even a son-in law. Can the tale of Ashubabu and his mistress, perhaps, be indicative of the way in which the minds of these would-be beneficiaries were working?

'It was clear, then, that although the two cases of the thorn-in-the-flesh and the gramophone pin appeared to be unconnected, they could be a perfect fit together, like the jagged edges of two broken pieces of a vase can be put together to form a perfect whole. One other thing had struck me in the initial stages—the correspondence between the name of one and the nature of the other. On the one hand you had the thorn-in-the-flesh classified and on the other, people were dropping dead with a thorny object piercing through their heart. Doesn't the resemblance strike you immediately?'

I said, 'Perhaps it does, but I was immune to it.'

Byomkesh shook his head impatiently and said, 'All of this is a matter of simple deduction. It became clear to me almost as soon as Ashubabu's case came into my hands. The actual mystery was the man's identity. This is where Prafulla Roy's true genius is in evidence. Even those who paid the man to commit a murder had no idea of who he was and how he did the deed. His primary defence was his amazing power to conceal his identity. I do not know if I would have ever succeeded in catching him if he hadn't walked into my house the other day, of his own volition.

'Let me explain—the other day, when you stood by the lamp-post, honouring his invitation, your demeanour had aroused Prafulla Roy's suspicions. Still, he foisted the letter onto you and then followed you from a distance. When you eventually came into this house, he was certain that you were my emissary. He was already aware that Ashubabu's case had come into my hands. So he became doubly sure that I already knew a lot. Had it been a different man, he may have given up on the project, cut his losses and run away. But Prafulla Roy, with his extreme impertinence, came to check me out. Meaning, he came to find out exactly how much I knew and what I intended to do on the thorn-in-the-flesh issue. He was not putting his safety on the line by doing this, because it was impossible for me to know that it was he who was at the centre of both the thorn-in-the-flesh and the gramophone pin cases. And even if I had known it, I would not have been able to pin anything on him. But he made one blunder.'

'What was that?'

'He did not imagine that I was waiting just for him that morning. You see, I knew that he would come to check things out.'

'You knew! Then why didn't you have him arrested as soon as he came?'

'Spoken like a true ignoramus, Ajit. All that I'd have gained by arresting him then, would have been a losing battle on a libel suit. Did I have any proof that he was a murderous criminal? There was only one way to catch him—in the act, red-handed, as they say. And that is what I tried to do. Why do you think we went there with plates tied to our chests?

'Anyway, after speaking with me, Prafulla Roy gathered that I knew quite enough—the only thing he didn't realize was that I had seen through him. He decided that it was no longer safe to allow me to live. Hence, he almost issued an invitation to me to take a walk by the racecourse that night. He knew that I had missed him the first time by sending you and so I'd go personally this time. But on one count he still had some doubts—what if I brought the police with me? Which is why he raised the subject of the police. When I reacted so strongly to it, he went away, satisfied. Secretly, he wrote me off as dead.

'The poor chap lost out badly due to that one tiny error. He regretted it amply at the end too and acknowledged that he should not have underestimated my astuteness.'

After a brief pause, Byomkesh said, 'Do you remember, when Ashubabu came here the first time, I had asked him if he heard anything at the time he was hit? He had mentioned a bicycle bell. At the time I hadn't paid any attention to it. That was the piece of the jigsaw puzzle that wasn't quite falling in place. But when I read the thorn-in-the-flesh letter, everything cleared up in an instant. In reply to your question I had said that I have got just one word from the letter—that word was "bicycle"!

'It is amazing that I hadn't thought of the bicycle earlier. As a matter of fact, now when I think about it, I feel it couldn't be anything *but* a bicycle. There can't be any other way to commit a murder so simply and unobtrusively. You are walking on the road and a bicycle comes in front of you. The rider rings the bell for you to move, and then rides away. You fall to the ground, dead. No one can suspect the bicycle-rider because both his hands were holding the handlebars—how would he aim the weapon? So nobody gives him a second glance.

'Just once, the police had shown incredible presence of mind, you may recollect. The last victim of the gramophone pin, Kedar Nandi, died right in front of the police headquarters, at the Lalbazar crossing. The moment he dropped dead, the police halted all traffic and did a thorough search of the person of each and every one present there. But they found nothing. I feel Prafulla Roy was also present in that crowd and he too was searched. He must have had a good laugh to himself then, because it didn't occur to any police constable to check inside his bicycle bell.' Byomkesh began to gaze lovingly at the bell he was holding in his hands.

A gust of breeze lifted the long, official envelope off the table and dropped it to the ground, at my feet. I picked it up and placed it back, saying, 'So what does the Police Commissioner have to say?'

'Oh, many things,' said Byomkesh. 'To start with, he has thanked me on behalf of the police and the government; then, he has expressed his grief at Prafulla Roy's suicide—although this should have made him happy because it has saved the government a great deal of expense and labour. They would have had to prosecute and hang him, you know. Anyway, I shall no doubt receive the award from the government very soon; the Commissioner has informed me that he has arranged for my petition to be cleared as soon as I file it. Prafulla Roy's corpse has not been identified by anyone; the Jewel Insurance Company has looked at it and said that he was not their employee; their staff, Prafulla Roy, is presently in Jessore on business. So, it is obvious that the name, Prafulla Roy, was also an alias. But that doesn't matter, because I shall always remember him as Prafulla Roy. In conclusion, the Commissioner has given me some grim news—this bell has to be returned. Apparently, this is now a property of the government.'

I laughed and said, 'You seem to have grown quite fond of the bell. You just can't let go of it, right?'

Byomkesh joined in my laughter and said, 'That's true. Instead of the two thousand rupees reward, if the government gave me this bell, I would be only too happy to accept it. But—I still have one memento of Prafulla Roy with me.'

'What is that?'

'Don't you remember? That ten-rupee note. I think I shall frame it. It is worth more than a hundred rupees to me now.' Byomkesh went and carefully placed the bell under lock and key in his cupboard.

When he came back, I asked him, 'Well, Byomkesh, tell me truthfully—did you know that the paan was poisoned?'

Byomkesh was silent for a few seconds and then said, 'There is an area of uncertainty between knowing and not knowing, which is the land of the probable.'

A little later he spoke again, 'Do you think it would have been a good thing if Prafulla Roy had gone to an ordinary criminal's death? I do not think so. Instead, this was a fitting end for him, where he showed what a truly great artiste he was, even in an incapacitated state, with his hands and legs in fetters.'

I had no reply to make. It took a lot to comprehend the strange paths through which admiration and sympathy for the criminal led an inquisitor.

'Letter, please!'

The postman delivered a registered letter. Byomkesh tore

open the envelope and extracted a sheet of coloured paper from it, looked it over and then, smiling, handed it to me. It was a cheque for a thousand rupees from Ashutosh Mitra.

The Venom of the Tarantula

It was almost under duress that I got Byomkesh to leave the house.

For the last month he had been concentrating on a complicated forgery case. He would sit with a pile of papers all day and try to conjure up the image of the criminal from it all. As the mystery thickened, so did his conversation trickle gradually to silence. I noticed that this endless ploughing through papers, sitting in the library day after day, wasn't doing his health any good. But every time I brought this up, he would say, 'Oh no, I am quite all right.'

That evening I said, 'I am not going to take no for an answer. We're going for a walk. You need at least a couple of hours' respite in the day.'

'But . . .'

'No buts. Let's go to the lake. Your forger won't give you the slip in two hours.'

'Oh, all right.' He pushed the papers away and set off, but it wasn't difficult to guess that his mind hadn't let go of the problem at hand.

While walking by the lake I suddenly spotted a long-lost friend of mine. We had studied together until the Intermediate class—then he had entered the medical college. I hadn't seen him since. I called out to him, 'Hey, you're Mohan, aren't you? How are you doing?'

He turned around and exclaimed delightedly, 'Ajit! It *is* you! It's been so long. So tell me, how is everything?' After exchanging excited greetings I introduced him to Byomkesh. Mohan said, 'So *you* are Byomkesh Bakshi? Delighted to make your acquaintance. I did suspect at times that the Ajit Bandyopadhyay who writes about your exploits is our old friend, Ajit. But I wasn't quite sure.'

I said, 'So what are you up to nowadays?'

Mohan replied, 'I have my practice here in Calcutta.'

We strolled about and spoke of this and that. An hour passed pleasantly. I noticed that during the conversation Mohan opened his mouth a couple of times as if to say something, but then stopped himself. Byomkesh must have noticed it too because at one point he smiled and said, 'Please go ahead and say what you want to say.'

Mohan said, a little shyly, 'There is something that I want to ask you, but I am hesitant. Actually it is such a trivial problem that it seems unfair to bother you with it. Yet—'

I said, 'That's all right, tell us. If nothing else, it will at least serve the purpose of delivering Byomkesh for a short while from the hands of that forger.'

'Forger?'

I explained.

Mohan said, 'I see! But perhaps Byomkeshbabu will laugh at what I have to say.'

'If it is amusing I shall certainly laugh,' said Byomkesh, 'but from your manner it doesn't seem to be a laughing matter. Instead it appears that a certain problem has kept you pondering—you are desperate to find a solution to it.'

Mohan said excitedly, 'You are absolutely right. Perhaps it is very simple—but for me it has become an irresoluble conundrum. I am not entirely stupid—I think I have my fair share of common sense; yet, you'll be surprised to know how an ailing old man, who is paralysed to boot, is duping me every single day. It isn't just me; he is defeating his entire family's attempts at strict vigilance.'

In the course of the conversation we had sat down on a bench. Mohan said, 'Let me tell you about it as briefly as possible. I am the family-physician in a very affluent household. The family goes back a long way to when the city was just coming up. In addition to other incomes and assets they own a market from which they earn a massive monthly amount as rent. So you can gauge their financial standing.

'The master of this house is Nandadulalbabu. He is actually my only patient in that household. In his heyday he was such a profligate that by the time he reached the age of fifty his health gave up on him. His body plays host to a plethora of diseases. He has long been rendered immobile from arthritis. Now there are signs of paralysis as well. There is a saying among us doctors that there is nothing strange about man's death; it is the fact the he is alive at all that is a source of wonder. This patient of mine is a prime example of that.

'Words fail me in trying to describe the character of Nandadulalbabu to you. Foul-mouthed, mistrustful, crafty, malicious—in brief, I have never seen a meaner nature than his. He has a wife and a family, but he isn't on good terms with anyone. He would like to continue along the same depraved lines as he did in his youth. But his vitality has sapped and his health doesn't permit such excesses any longer. Hence, he bears great bitterness and envy towards everyone—as if they were responsible for his condition. He is always looking for ways and means to pull a fast one on someone to prove his ability.

'His body is weak and he has a heart condition too—hence he cannot leave his room. He sits there in his den, heaping unspeakable indignities upon the entire universe with every sentence he speaks and filling page after page with writing. He has a misplaced notion that he is an unparalleled litterateur; so, now in black, now in red ink, he writes and writes. He is terribly upset with the publishers—he believes that they are in on the conspiracy against him and therefore refuse to publish his work.'

Curious, I asked, 'What does he write?'

'Fiction. Or it may even be autobiographical. Only once did I glance at a page of the stuff; never again have I been able to look at it. After you've read that filth, even a holy oblation won't cleanse you. I am certain that even today's young experimental writers would have a fit if they read it.'

Byomkesh gave a slight smile and said, 'I can see the character before my eyes. But what exactly is the problem?'

Mohan offered a cigarette to each of us, lighted one for himself and said, 'Perhaps you think that such a special character cannot possibly have any more qualities, right? But that is not so. He has another terrific trait—to add to his wonderful health, he has a dangerous addiction.' He took a couple of puffs on his cigarette and continued, 'Byomkeshbabu, you are always dealing with such people; the most inferior class of the society is regular fare to you. I am sure you are familiar with alcohol, marijuana, cocaine and many other such kinds of addictions. But have you heard of anyone being addicted to spider juice?'

I gasped out loud, 'Spider juice? What on earth is that?'

Mohan said, 'There is a certain breed of spiders from whose bodies a venomous juice is extracted—'

Almost as if speaking to himself, Byomkesh muttered, 'Tarantula dance! It used to be practised in Spain—the spider's bite would make people cavort! It's a deadly poison! I have read about it but I haven't come across anyone using it in this country.'

Mohan said, 'You are absolutely right—tarantula. The use of tarantula extract is very prevalent among the hybrid Hispanic tribes of South America. The venom of the tarantula is a deadly poison, but if used in small quantities it can provide a tremendous thrill to the nervous system. As you can guess, this venom is very tempting to someone who cannot live without a constant state of nervous excitement. But continuous use of this stuff can prove to be fatal. The user would be sure to die of a fit of palsy.

'I am almost certain that Nandadulalbabu had picked up this beautiful addiction at some point in his youth. Later, when his body became totally unfit, he couldn't let go of it. It was about a year ago that I came in as his family-physician and at that time, he was a confirmed addict to spider venom. The first thing I did was to prohibit this; I told him that if he wanted to live he would have to give up the drug.

'There was quite a tussle over this—he wouldn't let go of it and I simply wouldn't let him have it. Finally I said, "I shall not let the stuff enter your house. Let me see how you lay your hands on it." He gave a sly smile and said, "Is that so? All right, I *shall* go on having it—let me see how you stop me." And thus, war was declared.

'The rest of the family was, quite obviously, on my side and so it was quite easy to set up a strong barricade system within the house. His wife and children took turns in guarding his room so that there was no means of the drug reaching him. He himself is practically immobile. So he is unable to go out of the house and collect it for himself. After making such rigorous arrangements to prevent him from getting at the drug, I began to feel a sense of immense satisfaction.

'But it was all in vain. In spite of all our precautions he continued to consume the drug. No one could figure out his means of gaining access to it. At first I suspected that someone within the house was secretly supplying the drug to him. So one day, I myself kept guard for the entire day. But amazingly, right under my nose he took the drug at least thrice. I could determine this by checking his pulse, but I could not figure out when and how he did it.

'Since then I have searched every nook and cranny of his room, I have stopped any outsider from coming into contact with him, and yet I have been unsuccessful in stopping him from getting his narcotic fix. This is where things stand.

'Now, my problem is that I need to locate how that man gets hold of the spider venom and how exactly he tricks everyone and consumes it.'

Mohan stopped. I couldn't tell if Byomkesh had become unmindful during the monologue but as soon as Mohan stopped speaking, he stood up and said, 'Ajit, let us go home. I have suddenly thought of something and if my guess is right, then . . .'

I realized that the forger was on his mind again. It was possible that the last part of Mohan's story had entirely slipped by him. A little disconcerted, I said, 'Perhaps you weren't paying attention to Mohan's tale—'

'No, no. Of course I have heard him carefully. It is a most amusing problem and I must say I am also quite intrigued by it; but right now it will be difficult for me to make the time. It *is* a rather difficult case that I am handling now . . .'

Perhaps Mohan felt a little offended, but he concealed the emotion and said, 'Oh of course, in that case just let it go. It certainly isn't right to bother you with such trivial matters. But, you know, if this mystery could be solved, perhaps the man's life could be saved. What can be more frustrating than watching a man—albeit a sinner—die a slow death right before your eyes, simply by consuming poison?'

A trifle abashed, Byomkesh said, 'I didn't say I wouldn't look into it. It will take me at least a couple of hours' cogitation to solve this riddle. It would also help if I could see the man himself. But I may not be able to make it today. It will certainly be a crime to let an unusual man like Nandadulalbabu die. And I shall not let that happen—you may be sure of that. But I need to return to my room right now—I think I may have been able to pin down the forger—I need to take another good look at the papers. Therefore, let Nandadulalbabu continue to consume his poison in peace for just another night—from tomorrow on, I shall put a spanner in his works.'

Mohan laughed and said, 'That is fine with me. Please give me a time that's convenient for you and I shall arrange for the car to pick you up.'

Byomkesh gave it a moment's thought and said, 'I have an idea—it may even help lessen your anxiety for now. Let Ajit accompany you and take a good look around. After hearing his report I should be able to give you the answer to your riddle either tonight or tomorrow morning.'

It was impossible not to notice the shadow of disappointment that crossed Mohan's face at the suggestion that I should go with him instead of Byomkesh. Byomkesh noticed it too and laughed, 'Since Ajit is an old friend of yours, perhaps you do not have much faith in him. But please do not lose heart; in the company of greatness his faculties have now become so unusually sharp that a few examples of his perceptiveness might astonish you. It may even happen that he will solve your problem all by himself and not need my assistance at all.'

But even such high praise couldn't convince Mohan. His face reflected the despondency of an angler who fishes through the day in the hope of hooking a big one and then manages to land only a lowly bluegill. He said, 'All right then, let Ajit come along. But if he isn't able to—'

'Most certainly, in that case you can count on me.'

Byomkesh called me aside and said, 'Take good notice of everything—and don't forget to inquire about incoming mail.'

I had seen Byomkesh solve many a complex mystery and even aided him in some cases. Observing him over the years, I had even picked up some of his modes of investigation. So, I thought to myself, could it be so difficult to solve this simple problem? As a matter of fact, Mohan's mistrust of my capabilities had hurt my pride and I felt a little headstrong urge to solve this mystery all by myself. My mind made up, I followed Mohan away from the lake with resolute steps.

A bus-ride brought us to our destination. It was already dark. The streetlamps had been lit. Mohan walked ahead, showing the way. We walked down a lane off Circular Road; after a few minutes he pointed to a big house with an iron fence around the compound and said, 'This is the place.'

It was an old house, built in the baroque style. In front of the iron gate a watchman sat on a stool. He saluted Mohan and let him through. Then he noticed me and, after casting a suspicious glance my way, said, 'Sir, you are not—'

Mohan smiled and said, 'It's all right watchman, he is with me.'

'Very good, sir.' The watchman stepped aside. We entered the courtyard of the house. As we crossed it and stepped onto the veranda, a young man of about twenty stepped out, 'Is that you, doctor? Do come in.' Then he raised questioning eyes at me, 'This is . . .?'

Mohan took him aside, said something to him and the young man replied, 'Certainly, of course, do let him come and see.'

Mohan then introduced us. The young man's name was Arun; he was Nandadulalbabu's eldest son. We followed him into the house. After passing two doors, Arun knocked on the third. At once a querulous, hoarse voice answered from within, 'Who's there? What is it? Don't bother me now, I am writing.'

Arun said, 'Father, the doctor has come. Abhay, please open the door.'

The door was opened by a youth—probably Arun's younger brother—who looked to be about eighteen. All of us filed into the room. Arun asked Abhay quietly, 'Has he had it again?' Abhay wanly nodded his head.

Upon entering the room my eyes fell first on the bed, which was placed in the centre of the room. Upon it, clutching a pen, slouched the gaunt Nandadulalbabu, leaning against a pillow and glaring at us with eyes burning with hostility. There was a fluorescent light overhead and another table-lamp was placed upon a bedside table; so I could observe the man very clearly. His age was probably on the right side of fifty but all the hair on his head had become grey and his skin had taken on a pallid hue. His structure was bony, with not an ounce of extra flesh on his angular face. The cheekbones seemed to be piercing through his skin and his sharp, slightly crooked nose was jutting out over his lips. The eyes were glittering from an unusual excitement. But within them there lurked the obvious signs that the ebb of the excitement would turn them back into expressionless fish-eyes. His lower lip hung limply. All in all, the entire face had a famished, discontented expression stamped upon every single pore.

As I stared at this ghostly physiognomy for some time, I noticed that his left hand gave a jerk from time to time, as if it had a life that was independent of the rest of the body and had decided to tango all on its own. Those who have seen a dead frog's limbs jump up when they come in contact with electric current may perhaps be able to visualize this nervous twitch.

Nandadulalbabu was staring at me too with vicious eyes, and soon, in that sharp, cackling voice, he ranted, 'Doctor! Who is this with you? What does the man want? Tell him to buzz off—at once—now . . .'

Mohan glanced at me and nodded to indicate that I shouldn't take my host's profanities to heart. He then moved the pile of papers that lay scattered on the bed to make some space, sat down and took his patient's pulse in his hand. Nandadulalbabu sat with a perverted grin stuck on his face and alternated his gaze between me and the doctor. His left hand continued to jerk erratically.

Finally Mohan let go of his wrist and said, 'So you have taken it again?'

'You bet I have—what bloody business is it of yours?'

Mohan bit his lip and then continued, 'You are only doing yourself harm with this. But you wouldn't understand that. You have let the venom addle your brain.'

Nandadulalbabu made a diabolical face and mocked, 'Is that so? I have addled my brain, eh? But you still have a lot of grey matter in there, don't you? So why can't you catch me out? You have placed your guards all around me—so how is it that you can't get to me?' He laughed in a vicious and obscene fashion.

Exasperated, Mohan stood up and said, 'It is impossible to have a conversation with you. I suppose I should just leave you to yourself.'

Nandadulalbabu continued cackling in that irritating manner and said, 'Shame on you, doctor, you call yourself a man? Catch me if you can, or suck on one of these and let me have my fun.' And he waved both his thumbs right under our noses.

Such gross and crude behaviour in front of his sons began to seem unbearable to me. Mohan had probably reached the end of his tether too because he said, 'All right Ajit, look around and take whatever notes you need to take. This is becoming impossible to tolerate.'

All of a sudden the victory-dance of the thumbs came to a stop. Nandadulalbabu raised his reptilian eyes towards me and demanded sourly, 'Who the hell are you and what are you doing in my house?' When he got no answer from me, he continued, 'A smart alec, are you? Well, you better listen—your tricks won't work on me, you get it? Better get out of here as fast as you can or else I'll call the police. Bunch of rogues, scoundrels and thieves, every single one of them!' He included Mohan in his sweeping glance as well. Although he couldn't quite figure out Mohan's reasons for bringing me there, he was obviously deeply suspicious of my presence.

Quite embarrassed, Arun whispered into my ear, 'Please ignore all that he says. Once he consumes the drug, he is completely out of his mind.'

How terrible is the venom that aggravates and brings to the

foreground all that is mean and ugly in a person's nature, I thought. And how would anyone check the moral degeneration of a person who consumes this venom willingly and of his own accord?

Byomkesh had instructed me to take note of everything carefully. So I tried to quickly make a mental inventory going round the room. The room was quite large and sparsely furnished. There was just the bed, a few chairs, an almirah and a bedside table. There was a lamp and some blank sheets of paper and a few other writing accessories on the table. The written sheets were scattered all over the place. I picked up a sheaf. But after reading a few lines I shuddered and had to put them down. Mohan was right. The writing would have made Emile Zola blush. To make matters worse, Mr Litterateur had actually underscored the 'juicier' sections of the material in red ink to draw attention to them. In truth, I could not recall ever having come into contact with a dirtier or a more repugnant mind.

Revolted, I looked up at the man and found that he had gone back to his penmanship. The Parker pen was rapidly filling up the sheet of paper with scrawls. In a little penstand which stood on the bedside table, another crimson Parker fountain pen rested, probably awaiting a lull in the writing when the underscoring would begin.

This is exactly what happened. As soon as he reached the end of the page, Nandadulalbabu laid down the black pen and picked up the red one, only to find that it had run out of ink. He filled it from a bottle of red ink that stood on the table, and went back to underscoring his sparkling gems with a solemn expression.

I turned away and began to inspect the other sections of his room. The almirah contained nothing except for a few half-empty bottles of medicine. Mohan said they had been prescribed by him. The room had two windows and two doors. We had entered through one of these doors and I was told that behind the other lay the bathroom. I inspected that too; there was just the usual bath-linen, soap, oil, toothpaste etc. My queries about the windows revealed that they did not open out into the courtyard; in fact, they remained shut most of the time.

I tried to visualize how Byomkesh would have gone about it had he been there, but I drew a blank. I was just wondering whether to knock on the walls or not—might there be a secret vault or something?—when I suddenly noticed a silver essence-holder in one corner of a shelf in the wall. I examined it eagerly; it held some cotton wool and *attar* in some of the tiny compartments. I asked Arun in a whisper, 'Is he in the habit of using essence?'

Hesitantly he shook his head and said, 'I don't think so; if he had, we would have smelt it on him.'

'How long has this been here?'

'Oh, for as long as I can remember. It was Father who had it brought.'

I turned around and noticed that Nandadulalbabu had stopped writing and was gazing in my direction. Excited, I dipped some cotton wool in the *attar* and dropped it in my pocket.

Then I took one last look around the room before walking out. Nandadulalbabu's eyes followed me; he had that mocking, grotesque smile pinned on his face.

We came out on the veranda and sat down. I said, 'I would like to ask you all a few questions. Please give me honest answers without hiding anything.'

Arun said, 'Certainly, please go ahead.'

I asked, 'Do you keep a constant vigil on him? Who are the ones on guard?'

'Abhay, Mother and I take turns in staying with him. We don't let any of the servants or outsiders go near him.'

'Have you ever seen him consume the stuff?'

'No, we haven't seen him actually putting it in his mouth; but we have found out every time he has ingested it.'

'Has anybody seen what it actually looks like?'

'When he used to take it openly, I did see it—it is a transparent liquid which used to be kept in a bottle for homeopathic medicine. He used to dilute a few drops of it in a glass of fruit juice.'

'Are you certain that no bottles of that kind are still there in the room?'

'Absolutely certain. We have turned the place upside down.'

'Then it obviously comes in from somewhere. Who brings it?'

Arun shook his head, 'We don't know.'

'Is there anybody else other than the three of you who enters that room? Please think carefully.'

'No, there's nobody else. Just the doctor.'

My inquisition ended. What else could I ask? As I sat there trying to come up with something else, Byomkesh's advice came to my mind and I started afresh, 'Does he receive any letters?'

'No.'

'Any parcels or anything else like it?'

Now Arun said, 'Yes, once a week he receives a registered letter.'

I leaned forward eagerly, 'Where does it come from? Who sends it?'

Arun hung his head in embarrassment and spoke softly, 'It comes from within Calcutta. A woman called Rebecca Light sends it.'

I said, 'Oh, I see. Has any one of you seen what it contains?'

'Yes,' Arun said, looking towards Mohan.

I asked impatiently, 'Well, what does it contain?'

'Blank paper.'

'Blank paper?'

'Yes—just a few blank sheets of paper are stuffed into the envelope—there's nothing else.'

Dumbly, I repeated, 'Nothing else?'

'No.'

I was speechless for a few moments and then asked again, 'Are you absolutely sure that the envelopes contain nothing else?'

Arun gave a slight smile and said, 'Yes. Although Father signs and takes the letters from the postman, I open them myself. There is never anything but white sheets inside.'

'Do you open the letter each and every time? Where do you do this?'

'In Father's room. That is where the postman brings the letter.'

'But this is extremely strange. What is the meaning of sending empty sheets of paper by registered post?'

Arun shook his head and said, 'I don't know.'

I sat there a little longer like a dimwit and finally, with a great big sigh, I rose to leave. The first mention of the registered letters had raised my hopes to think that perhaps I had hit upon the solution; but no, that particular door seemed locked and sealed. I understood that although the problem appeared to be quite simple, it was beyond my acumen. Appearances can be very deceptive. It was beyond my capabilities to take on the old geezer with his body riddled with poison and paralysis. What was required here was the razor-edged, crystal-clear intelligence of Byomkesh.

As I was leaving with a crestfallen look, promising to report everything to Byomkesh, something else occurred to me. I asked, 'Does Nandadulalbabu write letters to anyone?'

Arun said, 'No, but he sends a money order every month.'

'To whom?'

With shame writ all over his face, Arun murmured, 'To the same Jewish woman.'

Mohan explained, 'Once she was Nandadulalbabu's . . .'

'I see. How much does he send her?'

'Quite a hefty sum. I don't know why, though.'

The reply drifted to my lips, 'Pension.' But I held my tongue and quietly walked out. Mohan stayed back.

It was almost eight o'clock when I reached home. Byomkesh was in the library. He answered my knock immediately and held the door open, saying, 'How was it? Is the mystery solved?'

'No.' I walked into the room and sat down. Byomkesh had been examining a piece of paper through the thick lens of a magnifying glass. He gave me a piercing look and said, 'Since when have you become this fashionable? Are you using *attar* nowadays?'

'I'm not wearing it, merely carrying it.' I reported everything to him in great detail. He listened attentively. In conclusion I said, 'I couldn't solve it, my friend, so now you have to have a go at it. But I have a feeling that an analysis of this *attar* may reveal something—'

'Reveal what—the spider venom?' Byomkesh took the piece of cotton wool from my hands and held it to his nose, 'Ah, wonderful essence. Pure, unadulterated amburi *attar*. Yes, you were saying something,' he continued as he rubbed some of the *attar* onto his wrist, 'What may be revealed?'

A little hesitantly I said, 'Perhaps under the pretense of using *attar* Nandadulalbabu . . . '

Byomkesh laughed out loud, 'Is it possible to hide the use of something that, by its smell alone, can alert people for miles around? Have you got any indication to believe that Nandadulalbabu actually wears this *attar*?'

'Well, no, I haven't—but . . .'

'No, my dear, you're barking up the wrong tree; try looking elsewhere. Try to think about how the stuff is smuggled into the room and how Nandadulalbabu consumes it in everyone's presence. Why do blank sheets of paper arrive by registered post? What is the reason for sending money to that woman? Have you figured that out?'

Dejected, I said, 'I have thought about all these things, but the solution is beyond me.'

'Think again, harder—nothing will come from nothing, you know. Think deeply, think intensely, think relentlessly,' and so saying, he picked up the lens again.

I asked, 'What about you?'

'I am thinking too. But it is going to be impossible to think intensely. My forger . . .' He leaned over the table.

I left the room and stretched out in the armchair in the living room and started to think again. For God's sake, this couldn't be all that difficult to solve. I was sure I could do it.

To begin with, what was the significance of sending blank sheets by registered post? Was there something written on the sheets with invisible ink? If that were so, how would Nandadulalbabu benefit from it? His quota of venom could not be reaching him that way.

All right, let us assume that the venom somehow managed to get smuggled into the room from outside. But where did Nandadulalbabu hide it? Even a bottle of homeopathic medicine wasn't easy to conceal. He was constantly under surveillance by vigilant eyes. There was even the occasional raid on his room. How then did he do it?

All this intense thinking heated up my brain; five cheroots were burnt to ashes; but I still could not find an answer to even one of these questions. I had almost given up hope when suddenly a marvellous idea occurred to me. I sat up straight in the armchair. Could this be possible? And yet—why ever not? It did sound a bit odd, but what other solution could there be? Byomkesh always said that if there was a logical inference that could be made, even if it appeared improbable, one had to take it to be the only possible solution. In this case too, this had to be, absolutely, the only possible explanation.

I was just going to go to Byomkesh when he himself came in. He took one look at my face and said, 'What is it? Have you figured it out?'

'I just may have.'

'Good. Tell me about it.'

When it came to spelling it out, I felt some pangs of hesitancy, but I brushed them aside and proceeded, 'Look, I just remembered seeing some spiders on the walls of Nandadulalbabu's room. I believe that he—'

'Just grabs them off the wall and gobbles them down?' Byomkesh burst out laughing. 'Ajit, you are an utter—genius. You are matchless. Those house spiders on the wall—if someone ate those there would be some abrasive rashes on the body, but no addictive surges. Understand?'

A little huffily I said, 'All right then, why don't you explain?'

Byomkesh took a chair and put his feet up on the table. Indolently, he lit up a cheroot and asked, 'Have you understood why blank sheets come by post?'

'No.'

'Did you figure out why the Jewish woman is paid every month?'

'No.'

'Haven't you at least worked out why Nandadulalbabu needs to underline his obscene stories?'

'No. Have you?'

'Perhaps,' Byomkesh took a long drag on the cheroot and said, his eyes closed, 'But unless I am absolutely certain about one fact, it will not be fair to make any comments.'

'What is that?'

'I need to know the colour of Nandadulalbabu's tongue.'

It looked like he was pulling my leg. Brusquely I said, 'Are you trying to be funny?'

'Funny!' Byomkesh opened his eyes and saw my expression. 'Are you offended? Honestly, I am not joking. Everything hinges upon the colour of Nandadulalbabu's tongue. If the colour of his tongue is red, then my guess is right, and if it is not—you didn't happen to notice it, did you?'

Irritated, I said, 'No, it didn't occur to me to notice his tongue.'

Byomkesh grinned and said, 'Yet, that should have been the first thing to look at. Anyway, do something—call Nandadulalbabu's son and ask him about it.'

'He may think I am being facetious.'

Byomkesh waved his arms and recited poetically, 'Fear not, oh fear not, there is no need for thee to quail—'

I went into the next room, located the number and dialed it. Mohan was still there and it was he who answered. 'I didn't tell you about it because I hadn't thought that piece of information mattered,' he said. 'Nandadulalbabu's tongue is a deep crimson in colour. It seems a bit unusual because he doesn't take much paan either. But why do you ask?'

I called Byomkesh. He asked, 'It *is* red, right? Well then, it is solved.' He took the phone from me and said, 'Doctor, it's good that I got hold of you. Your riddle has been solved. Yes, it *was* Ajit who solved it—I just helped him a bit. I was so busy with the forger . . . yes, I've got him too . . . You don't have to do too much, just remove the bottle of red ink and the red fountain pen from Nandadulalbabu's room . . . Yes, you got it. Please drop in sometime tomorrow and I shall explain everything. Goodbye. I shall certainly convey your gratitude to Ajit. Didn't I say that his intellect has grown really sharp nowadays?' Laughing to himself, Byomkesh put the receiver down.

After returning to the living room, I said a trifle bashfully, 'I think I am beginning to get it in bits and pieces, but please tell me in greater detail. How did you work it out?'

Byomkesh glanced at the clock and said, 'It is time for dinner. Putiram will be here at any moment to announce it. All right, let me go over it briefly with you. You were on the wrong track from the very beginning. It was important to find out how the stuff entered the room. It doesn't have limbs of its own, hence obviously it was being brought in by someone. Who could that be? Five people have access to the room—the doctor, the two sons, the wife and one other person. The first four people would not deliberately bring the poison to Nandadulalbabu. So this was the work of the fifth person.'

'Who is the fifth person?'

'The fifth one is—the postman. He comes in once a week. It was through him that the poison entered the room.'

'But the envelopes contain nothing but blank sheets of paper.'

'That is the trick. Everyone thinks that the envelope might contain the stuff and so nobody pays attention to the postman. The man is smart; he switches the red inkpot with ease. The point of sending blank sheets of paper by registered post is to give the postman access into Nandadulalbabu's room.'

'And then?'

'You made one more error in your judgement. The money that is sent to the Jewish woman—it's not a pension: that custom doesn't prevail anywhere. It is payment for the drug; the woman supplies it through the postman. So now you see, the venom comes into Nandadulalbabu's hands and nobody even suspects how. But the room is under surveillance at all hours, so how would he consume it? This is where his writing comes in useful. The paper and ink is always at hand and there is no need to get up in order to take in the drug—the task can be accomplished from his seat on the bed. He writes with the black pen, highlights with the red one and at every chance, sucks on the nib of the fountain pen. When the ink runs out he refills the pen. Now do you understand why the colour of his tongue is red?'

'But how did you know it would be the red one? Couldn't it be the black one too?'

'Oh no, can't you see? The black ink is used much more profusely. Would Nandadulalbabu want any superfluous use of that precious stuff? Hence the highlighting—hence the red ink.'

'I get it. So simple—'

'Of course it is simple. But the brain that has come up with such a simple plan is not to be slighted. It is because of its simplicity that all of you were fooled.'

'How did you figure it out?'

'Very easily. In this case two facts seemed to stand out as entirely unnecessary and therefore suspicious. One, the arrival of blank sheets by registered post, and two, Nandadulalbabu's excessive writing and highlighting habit. When I began to mull over the real reasons for these two, I stumbled upon the solution. You see, my forger too—'

The telephone shrilled into action in the next room. Both of us hurried to it. Byomkesh picked it up and said, 'Yes, who is it? . . . Oh, Doctor, yes, tell me . . . Nandadulalbabu is creating a racket? . . . He is ranting and raving? Well, well, that is inevitable . . . What was that? He is cursing Ajit? He is using the "f" and "b" words? . . . That is very wrong . . . very wrong indeed. But if he cannot be shut up, it can't be helped . . . Of course Ajit doesn't take it to heart, he is well aware that good deeds seldom go uncriticized in this world! You have to take the brickbats with the bouquets . . . such is life . . . all right then, goodbye!'

Where There's a Will

It was around ten-thirty in the morning; I was toying with the idea of getting up to take a shower when suddenly the telephone rang in the next room. Byomkesh got up and took the call. I could hear him say, 'Hello, who is that? Bidhubabu? Oh, good morning. How are you? How are things? I beg your pardon? Oh, really? I have to go? Well, all right . . . what is the address? Fine, I'll be there in about half an hour.'

Byomkesh came out of the room fastening the buttons on his kurta and said, 'Come on, let's go visiting. There's been a murder. Bidhubabu has called for us.'

I stood up and asked, 'Which Bidhubabu, the Deputy Commissioner?'

Byomkesh smiled and said, 'Yes, the same. I don't know who I owe this honour to. It was very apparent from his tone that he hasn't called me of his own choice. Orders from above is more like it.'

We had come to know the Deputy Commissioner of Police, Bidhubabu, in the course of our work. He was an ostentatious person who subjected us to bombastic lectures every time we met. He would try, in various ways, to indicate that Byomkesh was his subordinate in both intelligence and expertise. Byomkesh would listen to his declamations in the humblest of manners and laugh quietly in his sleeve. Very often Bidhubabu let slip a lot of secret information from the police files in the course of charting out his own sterling qualities and excellence. So, whenever he needed any information regarding the police, Byomkesh would present himself before Bidhubabu and take in a dose of his bombast.

Bidhubabu had probably not been particulary dull in his younger days. The commitment and enthusiasm he still had was remarkable for a man of his age. But trapped in the monotony of routine police work, his brain had been rendered incapable of anything other than mechanical functioning. In his absence his colleagues referred to him as 'Budhhubabu'—Mr Stupid.

Anyway, we had a quick breakfast and set off. It took us about twenty minutes to reach our destination by bus. The place was in north Calcutta, in the heart of a prosperous residential area. As we were looking for the numbers on the doors, we noticed two constables standing before a house and warily stroking their moustaches. It was evident that this was the scene of the crime.

The constables stood aside when Byomkesh told them who he was. We walked in. From outside the two-storeyed house had appeared small, but inside it was quite spacious and well furnished, indicating that the owner was well-to-do. Large decorative palms stood in clay pots, gracing the hallway. Some goldfish were frolicking in a giant aquarium. The hallway led on three sides to rooms attached with balconies. Facing the entrance, on the fourth side of the hallway, was the staircase leading upstairs.

We gravitated towards a room to the right where a lot of people were milling around. In the centre of the room, the colossal Bidhubabu, complete with his greying moustache, sat at a table frowning away with all his might. The servant had already been interrogated. It was now the turn of the cook. The man, nearly in tears, stood answering Bidhubabu's sharp questions and jumping out of his skin every time he was snapped at. A few subordinate police officers stood around them.

On spotting us, the look of displeasure deepened on Bidhubabu's face. 'So you are here,' he said. 'Have a seat. It's nothing much—a murder, nothing complicated. There are clear indications as to who has done it. The warrant too has been issued. But the chief ordered that you be called in—so . . .' He cleared his throat loudly and continued, 'Ours not to question why—since you're here, you might as well take a look, although there is nothing to look at, really.'

Byomkesh said, 'Sir, since you yourself have taken charge, what can I have to contribute afresh? But since the

Commissioner himself has given the order, I shall stay around and assist you if I may. But what is going on? Who has been murdered?'

Flattery can move mountains. Bidhubabu's countenance softened visibly and he said, 'Karalibabu, who is the master of this house, was murdered in his sleep last night. The mode of killing is a little unusual, so the chief is quite perplexed. But actually it is quite simple—Motilal, one of Karalibabu's nephews, has done the deed and absconded immediately.'

Bent almost double with meekness, Byomkesh said, 'A man of my limited calibre cannot quite grasp the matter unless it is explained to him in great detail. Could you possibly go over the entire story for me, please?'

The cloud of discontent vanished entirely from Bidhubabu's face. He smiled pompously and said, 'Just wait a second while I finish taking this fellow's testimony. Then I shall explain it all to you.'

The cook was still trembling, rooted to his spot; Bidhubabu bellowed at him, 'Be careful and watch what you say. One fib from you and the handcuffs go on—is that clear?'

The cook answered faintly, 'Yes, sir.'

Bidhubabu continued with the unfinished interrogation, 'What time was it when you saw Motilal leave the house last night?'

'I . . . I didn't look at the clock, sir, but it was one or two o'clock.'

'Be specific! Was it one or two?'

'Sir, it was around twelve or one in the night.'

'Make up your mind!' Bidhubabu roared, 'Tell me once and for all—was it midnight or one o'clock or two o'clock?'

The cook gulped and said, 'It was midnight, sir.'

The officer rapidly noted the statement down.

'He tiptoed out like a thief, did he?'

'Well, yes sir . . . you see, he stays out most nights.'

'Keep to the point! Answer what I'm asking you. Did you see Motilal coming down the stairs?'

'No sir. I saw him as he was going out through the main entrance.'

'You didn't see him coming downstairs? Where were you at the time?'

'I . . . sir, I . . .'

'Speak out man, where were you then?'

In a terrified tone the cook stammered, 'Sir, your honour, my friends from back home stay in a chawl in front of this house. So after I finish my work at night I go and sit with them awhile.'

'Oh I see, you were having a lark and lighting up some joints at the time, eh?'

'Your honour . . .'

'So the main entrance was left unlocked, was it?'

The cook shrivelled in fear. Almost inaudibly he muttered, 'Yes sir . . .'

Bidhubabu sat with a slight scowl on his face for some time and said, 'Hmm. So from your parley you could see all those who were going in and out of the house?'

'Yes sir. Nobody else left the house, sir.'

'I see. What was the time when you returned?'

'Sir, about half an hour after Motibabu left I came back and locked up. Sukumarbabu had already returned by then.'

'What! Sukumar—? Where did *he* return from?'

'That I don't know, sir.'

'What time did he return?'

'About twenty or twenty-five minutes after Motibabu left.'

Bidhubabu's scowl grew deeper. He pondered for a while and then said, 'You may go now. Should we need you, you will have to testify again.'

The cook bent low to salute him and made his escape gladly. Bidhubabu then ordered all the other police officials to vacate the room. Byomkesh and I were the only ones left with him. He turned towards us and said, 'Did you see that? One person's statement yielded all the information that I needed to know. If one knows how to cross-examine well—anyway, if I don't tell you about it from the beginning you wouldn't understand. I have collected all these details from the statements of all the members of the household. So listen to me carefully.'

Byomkesh bent his head and gave him a silent hearing. Bidhubabu began, 'The master of this household was called Karalibabu. He was a widower and childless. Quite a prosperous gentleman, he owns four or five houses in Calcutta and has several lakhs in the bank.

'Although he didn't have a family of his own, there was no shortage of wards. Karalibabu was guardian to five people in all—three nephews: Motilal, Makhanlal, Phonibhushan, and his wife's niece and nephew, Satyaboti and Sukumar. All of them live in this very house. They have no one else in the world to call their own.

'Apparently Karalibabu had an irascible nature. He was afflicted with arthritis and other diseases and was getting on in years too; so he didn't go out of his room much. But the entire household feared him like the devil. He had a remarkably whimsical mind—he would change his will at the drop of a hat, and every time, he would will all his property to a different person. His locker has yielded three wills; in the first one he declares Makhan to be his beneficiary, in the second it is Motilal and in the last and final one he leaves everything to Sukumar. This one was drawn up the day before yesterday. Now it is Sukumar who is his beneficiary.

'You see, every time someone fell out of favour with Karalibabu, he struck his name off the will. It was in this context that there was a massive row between Motilal and Karalibabu yesterday afternoon. Motilal is a cantankerous character and, hearing that he had been disenfranchised, he called Karalibabu some ugly names to his face.

'Thereafter, around midnight, Motilal stealthily crept out of the house. The cook and the servant both saw him escape. This morning Karalibabu was discovered dead.

'At first nobody understood how he had died. I came and detected it—he was killed by a needle that pierced his neck just between the medulla and the first vertebra.'

When Bidhubabu paused, Byomkesh raised his head, 'Very strange indeed! Running a needle through the meeting point of the *medulla oblongata* and the first cervical vertebra to kill someone—this is like *The Bride of Lammermoor*!' After a brief pause, he said, 'You've already had a warrant issued in Motilal's name? Does the man work somewhere, is anything known about him at all?'

'Nothing, absolutely nothing,' Bidhubabu said. 'Studied till eighth grade, went to the dogs. Lives off his uncle and leads a degenerate life.'

Byomkesh asked, 'And Makhanlal?'

'That mister too follows suit, but he isn't quite that bad. He does do some cocaine and pot, but hasn't yet joined the band of veteran delinquents.'

'And Phonibhushan?'

'This chap of ours is lame—they say the blind and the lame can be a shade above others; but this guy seems all right. Since he is lame, he cannot go out of the house. Of the three brothers this is the only one who seems close to being a human being.'

'What about Sukumar?'

'Sukumar is a nice boy, a final-year student at the medical college. His sister Satyaboti goes to college too. These two siblings were the only ones who looked after the old man.'

'I presume none of these people are married?'

'That's right, not even the girl.'

Byomkesh stood up and said, 'Sir, come, let's take a look around the house. I suppose the body hasn't yet been removed?'

'No.' A trifle unhappily, Bidhubabu got up and led the way upstairs. The stairs going up started on two ends of the hall, met in a landing in the middle and continued up to the first floor. We could see a door below the staircase. Byomkesh asked, 'Who stays in that room?'

Bidhubabu replied, 'That's Motilal's room. For his own reasons he prefers sleeping on the lower level. The master was a strict disciplinarian and he frowned upon anyone staying out after nine at night. His room is right above that one.'

'Oh—and what about this one?' Byomkesh indicated the room in the corner below the staircase.

'Makhanlal stays in that.'

'They are all in their own rooms I hope, except Motilal of course?'

'Certainly. I have issued strict orders that without my permission no one is to leave the house; constables are standing guard over the house.'

Byomkesh mumbled something approvingly under his breath. On the first floor, Bidhubabu pointed to a closed door facing the staircase and said, 'This was Karalibabu's bedroom.'

At the threshold of the room Byomkesh suddenly went down on his knees and said, 'What are these marks?'

Bidhubabu also bent forward to check and then straightened up and said derisively, 'That's tea. Every morning the girl—Satyaboti—used to bring him a cup of tea and wake him up. This morning when she got no answer she stepped into the room and found him dead. Probably at that moment some tea had spilled to the ground.'

'Oh—so she was the first one to know about his death?'

'Yes.'

The door was locked. Bidhubabu unlocked it and we entered the room.

It was a medium-sized room, sparsely but neatly furnished. A Mirzapuri carpet covered the floor. In the centre of the room was a teapoy covered with an embroidered tablecloth; in one corner there was a clothes-horse—a folded dhoti and kurta hung on it and polished shoes were arranged in a row below it. To the left was the bed, atop which lay something wrapped in a sheet—it looked like someone lying on his side and sleeping with the sheet pulled up to his ears. On a small stand beside the bed some bottles of medicine and measuring-cups stood neatly arranged in a row. At the head of the bed there was an earthen jug containing water, its top covered by an upturned glass. In general, it was possible to guess from the condition of the room that its occupant liked to keep his belongings tidy. It was difficult to imagine that the man who lay all wrapped up on that bed had actually been murdered in that very room the night before.

On the teapoy stood a cup of tea. Byomkesh studied this cup for a long time. Eventually, very softly, he murmured, as if to himself, 'Half the tea in the cup has spilled onto the saucer, the cup is half empty, the saucer is full—how did that happen?'

Bidhubabu emitted an impatient sound and said, 'That is what I was telling you, the girl—'

'I've heard that,' Byomkesh said. 'But why?'

Bidhubabu did not think it necessary to answer this apparently meaningless question. He made a face and went and looked out of the window.

Very cautiously Byomkesh picked up the teacup. A whitish layer had formed on the tea; he gently stirred it with a spoon and took a small sip. Then he put the cup down, wiped his mouth and went to stand beside the bed.

After fixedly staring at the bed for some time, Byomkesh asked, 'The body hasn't been moved, right? It is exactly as it was found?'

Bidhubabu, who was still staring out of the window, replied, 'Yes. Only the sheet has been pulled over his face—and I have extracted the needle.'

Slowly Byomkesh pulled the sheet back. A thin, wiry old man lay on his side on the bed. He looked like he was fast asleep. He had greying hair and the skin on his forehead had crinkled to form a few ridges. There was no sign of pain on his face. Byomkesh examined the body without moving it in any way. He swept aside the hair from the back of the neck and checked; he also examined something near the nose carefully. Then he called Bidhubabu over and said, 'Sir, I am sure you have examined the body very thoroughly, but I would like to draw your attention to two things. There are marks of three attempts at piercing his neck with a needle.'

Bidhubabu hadn't noticed this earlier. Now he looked and said, 'Yes, but that's nothing much. It obviously took him three attempts to find the meeting point of the medulla and the vertebra. What's the second thing?'

'Have you noticed the nose?'

'The nose?'

'Yes, the nose.'

Bidhubabu bent over the nose. I did likewise and saw that around the nostrils there were some tiny black spots like the ones you get when your skin stretches in winter.

Bidhubabu said, 'Perhaps he had a cold. You get such marks

when you wipe your nose too frequently. But what, pray, have you deduced from that?' Bidhubabu's tone was thick with sarcasm.

'Nothing . . . nothing. Come, let us go into the room next door. That was perhaps Karalibabu's living room?'

The next room contained a table, chairs, a typewriter and bookshelves. Evidently, this was the room where Karalibabu used to spend most of his time. Bidhubabu indicated the locker attached to the desk and said, 'His wills were found there.'

Byomkesh examined this room too in great detail, but nothing new was found. The locker didn't contain any more papers. On the other side of the room there was a small toilet. Byomkesh took a peep into that and came back saying, 'There is nothing more to see over here. Let us go to Sukumarbabu's room—isn't he the beneficiary? Oh, by the way, can I have a look at the needle?'

Bidhubabu took an envelope out of his pocket. Byomkesh took the needle out of it and held it up between two fingers. It was a little thicker than an ordinary darning needle, more like the ones used for crocheting. From the eye dangled a piece of thread.

Byomkesh stared at it with wide eyes for a while and muttered softly, 'Strange! Very strange.'

'What's strange?'

'The thread. Don't you see, the needle is threaded—black silk thread!'

'I can certainly see that. But what, pray, is so strange about a needle being threaded?'

Byomkesh glanced quickly at Bidhubabu's face. Then, as if abashed, he said, 'Well, really now, what is so strange about it indeed? Needles are usually threaded—that's precisely why they were created!' He replaced the needle in the envelope, handed it back to Bidhubabu and said, 'Let us go look up Sukumarbabu now.'

On turning left on the corridor, the room at the corner belonged to Sukumarbabu. The door was closed; Bidhubabu pushed it open without knocking. Sukumar was sitting with his elbows on his desk, holding his head in his hands. He stood up as we entered. The bed was on one side of the room and on the other side were the desk, a chair and a bookshelf. Some chests were piled up along one wall.

I would guess Sukumar's age at twenty-four or twenty-five; he was a handsome chap with a well-built muscular body. But this terrible mishap in the house had taken its toll on him; he looked shrunken and pale and there were dark circles under his eyes. On seeing the three of us barge in, a shadow of fear flitted across his eyes.

Bidhubabu said, 'Sukumarbabu, this is Byomkesh Bakshi. He would like to speak to you.'

Sukumar cleared his throat and said, 'Sit down, won't you?'

Byomkesh sat down in front of the desk. He picked up a book that lay on the desk and glanced at it—*Gray's Anatomy*. As he turned the pages he asked, 'Last night, from where did you return at midnight, Sukumarbabu?'

Sukumar was startled. He replied faintly, 'I had gone to see a film.'

Without raising his head Byomkesh asked, 'Which cinema hall?'

'Chitra.'

Bidhubabu said in a disapproving tone, 'You should have told me about this earlier; why didn't you?'

Sukumar stuttered, 'Well, sir, I didn't think it was important, that is why . . .'

With a grave countenance Bidhubabu said, 'We are to determine whether it is important or not. Is there any proof that you had gone to Chitra?'

Sukumar thought for a while with his head bent, then brought out a piece of coloured paper from the pocket of his kurta which hung on the rack. The chit of paper was the counterfoil of the cinema ticket; Bidhubabu examined it thoroughly and carefully placed it inside a notebook.

Turning some more pages of the book, Byomkesh asked, 'Is there a reason for your going to the show at nine-thirty rather than the one in the evening?'

Sukumar's face blanched as he replied softly, 'No reason as such . . . there wasn't . . .'

Byomkesh said, 'Surely you were aware that Karalibabu disliked anyone staying out until late at night.'

Sukumar was unable to reply. He just stood there with a haggard expression.

Suddenly Byomkesh looked Sukumar full in the face and asked, 'When was the last time you saw Karalibabu alive?'

Sukumar gulped and said, 'At about five in the evening.'

'Did you go to his room?'

'Yes.'

'Why?'

Sukumar made a visible effort to bring his voice under control and spoke slowly, 'I had gone to say a few words to Uncle about the will. He had deprived Motida and made the will in my favour; on this matter he had a row with Motida in the afternoon. I had gone to tell Uncle that I didn't want his legacy all to myself and that he should divide it equally amongst us.'

'Then?'

'When he heard what I had to say he ordered me out of the room.'

'And you left?'

'Yes. From there I went to Phoni's room. As I sat talking to him it grew late. I was feeling dispirited and so I thought I would go and see a film; Phoni also advised me to go. So I slipped away quietly thinking Uncle won't come to know of it.'

It was apparent that Bidhubabu was completely satisfied with Sukumar's defence. But Byomkesh's face remained deadpan. In a somewhat severe tone Bidhubabu said, 'Byomkeshbabu, why don't you state what's on your mind? Are you suspecting Sukumarbabu to be the murderer?'

Byomkesh stood up and said, 'Oh no, no, certainly not—come on, let's go to Sukumarbabu's sister's room now.'

Bidhubabu said rather rudely, 'Fine. Come. But she doesn't know a thing and it really isn't necessary to bother the poor girl needlessly. I have already taken her statement.'

Diffidently, Byomkesh said, 'Well, certainly, certainly, but yet if I could just . . .'

The girl's room was at the other turn of the corridor.

Bidhubabu knocked on the door. About half a minute later a seventeen or eighteen-year-old girl opened the door and on seeing us, moved aside. With hesitant steps we walked in. Sukumar, who had followed us, went and collapsed on the bed wearily. I had taken a look at the girl when we entered. She was slender, dark and tall. Incessant weeping had turned her eyes red and her face slightly puffy. Hence it was impossible to tell whether she was pretty or not. Her hair was tangled and unkempt. While I felt annoyed with Byomkesh for being cruel enough to cross-examine this grief-stricken girl, it was clear that there was a deliberate design lurking behind the somewhat hesitant manner he had decided to put on.

Byomkesh brought his palms together in greeting and said courteously, 'I am afraid I shall put you to some trouble. I hope it won't upset you. When such a grave tragedy takes place in the house, along with all the other hassles one also has to bear with the minor disturbances that the police create . . .'

Bidhubabu retorted angrily, 'Don't discredit the police, you are not part of the force.'

Byomkesh went on as if he hadn't spoken, 'Not too much, just a few standard questions. Please sit,' and he indicated one of the chairs in the room.

The girl gave Byomkesh a scornful look and said in a muffled voice cracked with grief, 'Please ask whatever you want to. I can answer without sitting down.'

'You don't wish to sit? All right then, let me have a seat at least.' Byomkesh sat down and looked around the room once. Just like Sukumar's room this one too was done up very simply. There was nothing ornate about the furnishings: a bed, a desk, a chair and a bookshelf. The only additional item was a dressing table with drawers.

A little abstractedly, Byomkesh raised his eyes to the beams on the ceiling and asked, 'You are the one who used to wake Karalibabu everyday with his morning cup of tea?'

The girl silently nodded her head to indicate assent.

Byomkesh said, 'So this morning it was when you went to give him his tea that you first came to know of his death?'

The girl nodded again.

'You didn't know about it beforehand?'

Bidhubabu muttered irritatedly, 'Needless question, needless. Absolutely idiotic.'

Byomkesh continued as if he hadn't heard, 'Did Karalibabu keep the door of his room open at night?'

'Yes. Nobody in this house was allowed to shut the doors of their rooms. Uncle too used to leave his door ajar while sleeping.'

'Is that so. Then . . .'

As if his patience had just snapped, Bidhubabu exclaimed, 'Enough of this. Now come along, will you? It is absolutely unnecessary to bother the poor thing with all kinds of superfluous questions. You wouldn't know how to cross-examine if—'

At this point the mask of politeness slipped from Byomkesh's face. Like a wounded tiger he whirled on Bidhubabu and in a murderous but low tone, said, 'If you continue to hinder me I shall be compelled to inform the Commissioner that you are interfering with my investigation. Are you aware that such cases do not fall under the domain of the general police—it comes under the CID?'

Bidhubabu couldn't have been more surprised if he had received a slap on the face. He subjected Byomkesh to a few moments of glowering. Then he made as if to utter something but swallowed it back and stomped out of the room instead.

Byomkesh turned back to the girl and said, 'You did not know about Karalibabu's death beforehand? Please think carefully before you answer.'

'I have thought it over. I did not know.' There was a trace of obduracy in the girl's voice.

Byomkesh sat silently for some time with his brow furrowed. Then he said, 'Anyway. Now tell me something else; how much sugar did Karalibabu take in his tea?'

The girl stared wide-eyed now and finally said, 'Sugar? Uncle liked his tea a trifle sweet, about three or four teaspoons . . .'

The next question came like a bullet fired from a gun, 'Then why didn't you put any sugar in his tea this morning?'

The girl's face went ashen and she looked around her, eyes dilated with fear. Then she bit her lip and brought herself under control with great difficulty and said, 'Perhaps I forgot. I haven't been keeping very well since yesterday . . .'

'Did you go to college yesterday?'

'Yes,' came the muffled yet defiant reply.

Raising himself from the chair, Byomkesh said very slowly, 'If only you would tell us everything it would help us immensely; you may benefit from it too.'

The girl stood there with her lips pressed together; she did not speak.

Byomkesh repeated, 'Will you tell us everything, please?'

The girl said slowly, drawing each word out, 'I don't know anything further.'

Byomkesh sighed. All this while, as he was talking, he had been looking at a sewing basket placed on the desk. Now he went and stood close to the desk. Pointing at the basket he said, 'I presume this belongs to you?'

'Yes.'

Byomkesh opened the basket. Inside it lay an incomplete tablecloth and multicoloured strands of silk threads in a tangle. Byomkesh picked up the tangled threads and started muttering to himself, 'Red, purple, blue, black, . . . hmm . . . black . . .' He put the ball of thread back in the box and looked for something else inside it, opening up the folded tablecloth too. Then he turned to the girl and asked, 'Where's the needle?'

The girl had been turned to stone; all she could come out with was, 'Needle?'

Byomkesh said, 'Yes, the needle. I presume you stitch with a needle. Where is it?'

The girl was about to say something, but could not. Turning suddenly, she blurted out, 'Dada!' and, running to where Sukumar was sitting, she laid her head on his lap and broke into tears. The sobs racked her body.

A dazed Sukumar tried to lift her face up and kept repeating, 'Satya . . . Satya . . .?'

Satyaboti did not raise her head. She just continued to weep. Byomkesh went very close to them and said softly, 'You didn't do the right thing, you know. You should have told me all. I am not part of the police. Had you confessed to me, you may have profited from it. Come on Ajit, let's go.'

After leaving the room, Byomkesh carefully shut the door behind him. He stood with a frown on his face for some time; then suddenly he looked up and said, 'Now? Oh yes, Phonibabu. Come, I think that's his room over there.'

After passing Karalibabu's room along the corridor and turning the corner, we came to a room on the left. Byomkesh knocked on the door. A young man of twenty-one or twenty-two opened the door. Byomkesh asked, 'Are you Phonibabu?'

He nodded and said, 'Yes. Please come in.'

His very posture made one feel there was a deformity somewhere in his body, but its exact nature could not be spotted immediately. He was quite well-built but his face was a trifle haggard, as if a protracted but suppressed suffering had lent his face some extra wrinkles. As we entered the room he hobbled ahead and indicated a chair, saying, 'Please sit down.' His gait revealed exactly where the deformity lay. His left leg was abnormally thin, almost like a dead limb. Hence he limped quite a bit when he walked.

I sat on one end of the bed and Phoni sat down beside me. Byomkesh seemed to be lost for words at first, then said, rather uncertainly, 'I suppose you are aware that the police is suspecting your brother Motilal on this matter?'

'I know,' said Phoni. 'But from my side I can vouch for it that Motida is innocent. He is very belligerent and combative—but I cannot believe that he is capable of murdering Uncle.'

'Not even his hostility at being deprived of the legacy can make him do the deed?'

'That motivation applies not to Motida alone but to all of us—all three brothers. Then why should only Motida be suspected?'

Byomkesh avoided the question and said, 'I presume you have already told the police all that you know; still, I would like to ask a few—'

Phoni was slightly taken aback, 'You are not a policeman then. I thought perhaps you were from the CID.'

Byomkesh laughed and shook his head, 'No, I am just an Inquisitor, a Seeker of Truth.'

In wide-eyed wonder Phoni said, 'Seeker of Truth? Byomkeshbabu? You are Byomkesh Bakshi, the Inquisitor?'

Byomkesh nodded and said, 'Now please tell me, how were Karalibabu's relations with the other members of the household? In other words, who he liked, who he disliked—all these details.'

Phoni sat with his face held between his palms for a while, then he smiled wanly and said, 'You see, I am lame—God's curse is on me—so I have never been able to mix very well with other people. This room and these books have been my sole companions all my life. It will be quite impossible for me to say accurately whom Uncle loved the most amongst all of us. He was of a very testy disposition and he certainly didn't wear his heart on his sleeve. But from what I could gather through tacit gestures I would say he cared for Satyaboti the most.'

'And you?'

'Me . . . perhaps because I am lame he pitied me somewhere deep down—but more than that . . . I do not wish to disrespect the deceased, especially when he has been our benefactor—if he hadn't taken us in we would have starved to death—but Uncle did not know what love really is.'

Byomkesh said, 'I presume you are aware that he has bequeathed all his wealth to Sukumarbabu.'

Phoni smiled a little, 'I've heard about it. Well, there's no doubt that Sukumarda is the best person to inherit the property, but that doesn't really tell you anything about Uncle's real wishes. He was an astonishingly whimsical person; the moment he was displeased with someone, he would go tap-tap on the typewriter and change his will. There is perhaps no one left in this house whom Uncle hasn't made his will out to at some time or the other.'

Byomkesh said, 'Since the final will is in Sukumar's name it is he who will inherit all.'

Phoni asked, 'Is that what the law says? I am not very

knowledgeable about these things.'

'That is how the law goes.' Byomkesh seemed to hesitate a bit, then asked, 'Under the circumstances what are you going to do? Have you decided anything yet?'

Phoni ran his fingers through his hair and stared out of the window, 'I don't know what I shall do or where I shall go. I have no qualifications, so I am incapable of earning my own bread. If Sukumarda gives me shelter I shall stay under his roof—or else I'll end up on the streets.' His eyes filled with tears. I quickly turned my face the other way.

Byomkesh said, somewhat absently, 'Sukumarbabu returned home at midnight last night.'

Phoni was a little startled, 'Midnight! Oh yes, he had gone to see a film last night.'

Byomkesh asked, 'Can you take a guess as to exactly when Karalibabu was murdered? Did you hear any sound, of any sort?'

'Nothing. Perhaps early in the morning . . .'

'No. He was murdered at midnight.'

Byomkesh got up, glanced at his watch and exclaimed, 'Oh, it's two-thirty—that's enough, come on Ajit. I am quite hungry, we have hardly eaten anything . . . goodbye.'

At this point there was a commotion downstairs; the next moment an excited young man shoved the door of our room open and burst in saying, 'Phoni, they've arrested Motida and brought him—' He stopped short when he saw us.

Byomkesh said, 'Are you Makhanbabu?'

Makhan went pale with fear and blurted out, 'I . . . I don't know anything.' He scrambled out of the room.

We came down the stairs and found utter pandemonium in the sitting room. Bidhubabu wasn't there; the inspector from the local police station had taken his place. Two constables were holding on to a man who looked half-crazed and was bawling away, 'Uncle has been murdered? Please sirs, I don't know anything . . . I can swear by anything . . . I'm just a foolish old drunkard . . . I've spent the night with Dalim, she is my witness . . .'

The inspector knew his job well. He had been sitting quite

still through all this. When he saw us coming he said, 'Byomkeshbabu, here is Motilal—Bidhubabu's suspect. If you have any questions, you may ask him.'

Byomkesh asked, 'Where was he taken under arrest?'

The sub-inspector who had arrested him said, 'In the room of a disreputable woman in the notorious red-light area—'

Again Motilal started howling, 'I was fast asleep in Dalim's house—which lying rascal is saying—'

Byomkesh held up his hand and stopped him, 'Don't you usually return home at the crack of dawn? What happened today?'

Like a demented man Motilal looked around him with bloodshot eyes and said, 'Why? . . . . What? I—I was drunk—I had finished off two bottles of whisky . . . I couldn't wake up . . .'

Byomkesh looked at the inspector and inclined his head slightly. The inspector said, 'Take him away and keep him under custody.'

Motilal screamed and yelled as he was dragged away. Byomkesh asked, 'Where is Bidhubabu?'

'He went home about a quarter of an hour ago—he said he'll be back at about four in the afternoon.'

'All right, then we shall get going too; we'll come back tomorrow morning. By the way, have all the rooms in the house been searched?'

'Karalibabu's and Motilal's rooms have been searched. Bidhubabu did not think it necessary to search any of the other rooms.'

'Did anything come out of Motilal's room?'

'Nothing at all.'

'I didn't get to see the wills. I presume Bidhubabu has sealed them. That's fine, they can wait until tomorrow. All right, see you later. Please keep me informed if anything new develops here.'

We came back home. That night Byomkesh drew up a blueprint of Karalibabu's house and showed it to me, saying, 'Just below Karalibabu's room is Motilal's room. Makhan stays next door to him. Below Phoni's room is the drawing room where the police have set up shop for now. Satyaboti's room is right above the kitchen. And the cook sleeps right below Sukumar's room.'

I asked, 'What is the use of this plan?'

'Nothing.' Byomkesh began to study the blueprint intently.

I asked, 'What do you feel? Motilal hasn't committed the crime? Is that it?'

'No, he hasn't. You can rest assured about that.'

'Who did it then?'

'That is difficult to say. If Motilal is excluded, four of them remain—Phoni, Makhan, Sukumar and Satyaboti. Any one of them could have done it. The motive is the same in all their cases.'

I was astounded. 'Satyaboti too?'

'Why not?'

'But she's a woman . . .'

'When a woman loves somebody, there is nothing she would stop at for him.'

'But what would be her self-interest in it? As per Karalibabu's will it is her brother who gets everything anyway.'

'Don't you get it? When a person who changes his will at the drop of a hat is finished off, the question of his changing it again doesn't arise.'

I was dumbfounded. I had not thought of it this way at all. I said, 'So then do you think it was Satyaboti who . . .'

'I did not say that. It could be Sukumar. It may even be a complete outsider. But Satyaboti is certainly no ordinary person.'

I ruminated awhile. In the last few hours so much varied and self-contradictory material had come our way that it was becoming impossible to create a coherent picture out of it all. The whole thing was such a tangled mess that thinking about it only made it worse. Eventually I asked, 'What did you make of the body?'

'I deduced that just before murdering Karalibabu, the killer had used chloroform on him.'

'How did you come upon that piece of information?'

'The murderer had pierced his neck three times. If he hadn't been chloroformed, Karalibabu would have woken up. Do you remember those spots on his nose? Those are the marks of chloroform.'

'What is the significance of piercing him thrice with the needle?'

'It means that the first two times the murderer was unable to find the right spot. But that is not very relevant. What *is* relevant is, why did the murderer leave the needle stuck to the dead body? If you remove it after the deed is done, you do away with the evidence. Then why leave it lying around?'

'Maybe it slipped his mind in the rush. But one more thing—how do you know the murder was committed at midnight?'

'That is just a guess. But if ever Satyaboti reveals the truth, you'll see I am right. The doctor's report will also confirm that.'

Byomkesh sat and stared at the ceiling for some time and then said, 'On Sukumar's desk there was a book—*Gray's Anatomy*. In the entire text only a few lines on a certain page were underscored with a red pencil.'

'Really? What did those few lines say?'

'They said—"if a needle is stabbed into the meeting point of the medulla and the first vertebra, death would be instantaneous".'

I jumped up, 'What! Then . . .?!'

'The strange thing is, I couldn't find the red pencil anywhere on Sukumar's desk.' Suddenly Byomkesh began pacing the floor with deep worry-lines creasing his brow. My head was bursting with questions but I didn't dare interrupt his train of thought. I knew that questions asked at this time would receive a snarl in response.

After getting into bed at night, he asked one question, 'You are a writer. Tell me, where did the word thimble originate?'

Surprised, I said, 'Thimble? You mean that thing which tailors have on their fingers when they are darning?'

'That's right.'

I began thinking, but nothing came to mind. So I said, 'It probably had something to do with "thumb". It's a protection for the thumb after all, isn't it? Maybe it's a combination of "thumb" and "humble" . . .'

'Stop being fanciful,' Byomkesh said, 'I want a straight answer.'

I had to admit that I had no idea. I countered, 'Do you know?'

'No. If I'd known, why would I have asked you?'

Byomkesh didn't speak anymore. I too dozed off thinking of the strange quirks of language.

The next morning when I woke up I found that Byomkesh had already left. I was a little miffed. But I guessed there was a reason for leaving me behind—perhaps I would have come in the way of his investigation. When he returned, it was eleven o'clock. He took off his shirt, switched on the fan and lit a cigarette. I asked, 'How did it go?'

He drew in a mouthful of smoke, began to let it go slowly and spoke, 'I got to see the wills. They were witnessed by the cook and the servant—their thumb impressions are on the wills.'

'And . . .?'

'I have told them to search all the other rooms of the house well. But Bidhubabu has decided to do the exact opposite of whatever I say. Eventually I coerced him by saying that if he doesn't conduct the search, I would complain to the Commissioner.'

'What else?'

'What else. He is still after Motilal.' After a few minutes' silence he said, 'The girl is very strong; the way she has sealed her lips . . . she just won't budge. Yet she holds the key to this whole mystery. Anyway, let us see, if Bidhubabu changes his mind about the thorough search of all the rooms, something may come up from somewhere.'

'What exactly are you expecting will turn up?'

'Who can tell? Something insignificant, perhaps a receipt from a chemist's, or a pencil, or—but there's no point in speculating. Let's get going, it's time to start the day.'

Byomkesh spent the afternoon lazing in his armchair with

his eyes shut. It seemed as if he was waiting for something. As the clock struck three, Putiram came and made tea for us. Byomkesh drank it up in silence and went back to his old pose.

At about four-thirty the telephone rang in the next room. Byomkesh sprang up and picked it up, 'Yes, who is it? Oh, Inspector, anything new? . . . Sukumarbabu's room has been searched? Good, good, so Bidhubabu finally . . . What was found in his room? . . . What? Sukumarbabu has been arrested! . . . And then—did you find anything else? A bottle of chloroform . . . it was in the bookshelf, behind the books? . . . And? . . . Will? . . . Phonibabu! . . . Yes, you are right, by the law of permutations, it was now his turn . . . Has Sukumarbabu's sister been arrested as well? . . . No! Fine . . . Was there anything else in the room, like a red pencil for example? No? Strange. Any needlework material? . . . Well, really . . . Is Bidhubabu there? He has gone to release Motilal? Hmm, at last good sense has prevailed. Which rooms other than Sukumarbabu's have been searched? None! . . . What was that . . . Bidhubabu did not consider it necessary! What *does* Bidhubabu consider necessary?! Am I needed there today? I could take a look at the new will . . . Oh, he has taken it with him . . . All right, tomorrow morning will be fine. As long as the red pencil and the needlework material don't show up . . . beg your pardon, what were you saying? Incriminating evidence has been found against Sukumar? Yes, you could say that again. Has the doctor's report come in? What does he say about the time of death? About three hours after dinner . . . approximately midnight . . . I see. All right, I'll certainly come over tomorrow morning.'

Byomkesh put back the receiver and returned to his seat. The worried frown on his brow indicated that he wasn't entirely satisfied. I asked, 'So it really was Sukumar? You suspected him right from the start, didn't you?'

After a few minutes' silence, Byomkesh said, 'All the evidence in this case seems to point towards Sukumar being the murderer. Look, even the very nature of Karalibabu's death seems to be crying out that it is the work of a medical man. Those who know nothing of anatomy cannot kill like that. The needle which was used for the murder was also filched from his sister's sewing basket; so much so, that even the thread was the same. Sukumar returned home at midnight and that is exactly when Karalibabu died. On searching Sukumar's room a bottle of chloroform and a typed will were discovered—it is Karalibabu's last and final testament where he deprives Sukumar and leaves everything to Phoni. Sukumar himself has admitted that he had a row with Karalibabu that evening—so he must have known that Karalibabu was going to change his will again. The motive for the murder is also very clear.'

'It's all sorted out, then—it was Sukumar who did it . . .'

'Where is there room for doubt?' A few minutes' pause and Byomkesh asked, 'Tell me, what did you make of Sukumar? Did you find him to be stupid?'

I said, 'No. On the contrary—he seemed pretty intelligent.'

Byomkesh said pensively, 'That is where I am stumped. Why would an intelligent man behave so stupidly?' Suddenly Byomkesh sat up straight. I too had heard the soft footsteps outside the door. Byomkesh called out, 'Who is that? Please come in.'

There was no answer at first. Then the door opened very slowly, and in great stupefaction I saw before me—Satyaboti!

Satyaboti entered the room and shut the door behind her. For a little while she stood there stiffly. Then she suddenly burst into tears and said in a choking voice, 'Byomkeshbabu, please—please save my brother.'

I was totally befuddled by her sudden appearance. But Byomkesh sprang to her side; perhaps her head had started spinning because she stretched out her hand blindly—Byomkesh took her by the hand and led her to a seat. At a signal from him I switched on the fan.

For the first few minutes Satyaboti covered her eyes with the end of her sari and shed unbridled tears; wordlessly we turned the other way to give her some privacy. Even in our eventful lives such a staggering event was a first. I had seen Satyaboti only once; she had not seemed different in any way from the average educated Bengali girl. Hence, it was remarkable, even unthinkable, that in a time of crisis she would shake off all inhibitions and come to us so directly. When calamity strikes, the greater percentage of Bengali girls turn into wooden dolls. This lanky, dusky girl suddenly acquired a wondrous halo in my eyes. From the tip of her old, dusty, gold-threaded slippers to the ends of her tangled, carelessly-wound plait, everything about her seemed to glow with an unearthly light.

She wiped her eyes, looked up and repeated, 'Byomkeshbabu, please save my brother.' I noticed that although she now had a grip on herself, her voice was still shaking.

Byomkesh spoke slowly, 'I heard that your brother has been arrested, but—'

Fervently Satyaboti exclaimed, 'He is innocent, he doesn't know anything . . . he has committed no crime—' and she burst into tears again.

I could see that Byomkesh was affected deep down, but outwardly he remained calm as he said, 'But all the proof that has accumulated against him . . .'

Satyaboti said, 'They are all false. Dada is incapable of murdering someone for money. You don't know the kind of person he is. Byomkeshbabu, we do not want Uncle's money. Please save us from this danger and we shall stay indebted to you for life.' Tears streamed down her cheeks, but this time she made no attempt to wipe them away; perhaps she wasn't even aware of them.

When Byomkesh spoke this time, I noticed an emotion in his voice which hadn't been there before. He said, 'If your brother is really innocent, I shall do my best to save him, but . . .'

'He *is* innocent. You don't believe me? I can swear on my honour, Dada could not have done this—he cannot harm a fly.' Suddenly she went down on her knees and grabbed Byomkesh's feet.

Byomkesh sprang up and moved aside, 'What are you doing . . . please . . .'

'Promise—please promise me first that you'll release Dada?'

Byomkesh firmly took her by the hands and forced her to return to her seat. Then he sat before her and said in a resolute voice, 'You are wrong about one thing—I am not the person who can release Sukumarbabu. Only the police can do that. I can only try to prove that he is innocent. But in order to do that I need to know all the facts. Can't you understand, as long as you keep things from me I shall not be able to give you any assistance at all.'

Satyaboti lowered her eyes and said, 'I have not kept anything from you.'

'Yes you have. That very night you had gone to Karalibabu's room and come to know of his death, but you didn't tell me that.'

Satyaboti stared at Byomkesh in wide-eyed panic; then she lowered her head and sat mute.

Byomkesh asked mildly, 'Now will you tell me everything?'

Satyaboti raised her eyes and said, 'How can I? It will only go towards incriminating Dada further.'

In an imploring tone Byomkesh said, 'Look here, if your brother is innocent, the truth cannot harm him in any way. You can tell me everything without any fear; don't hide anything.'

Satyaboti sat with her head bowed and thought for a while; then in a broken voice she said, 'All right. I have no other choice . . .' She wiped her eyes which were brimming with tears, calmed herself and began to speak:

'That evening Dada had a small row with Uncle. Uncle had left Dada everything in his will and he and Motida had fought at length over this in the afternoon. When he returned from the college and heard about this, Dada went to tell Uncle that the property should be left equally to all of us and not to him alone. Uncle hated arguments; he lost his temper and said, "You know better than me, do you? Get out of here—you will not get a single paisa from me!"

'Dada had not known that Uncle would flare up like this. He left the room and went to Phonida. Phonida is lame, he cannot leave his room—so Dada used to spend some time with him every evening. Perhaps you have met Phonida? He has never been to school, but he is quite well-read. From the books on his shelf you can tell that he has a hold over several subjects. I used to go to him for help with my studies sometimes. Anyway, after the argument with Uncle, Dada felt very despondent and at around eight in the evening he told me, "Satya, I am going to see a film. It'll be close to midnight before I get back. Leave the main door open for me." He finished his dinner and quietly slipped off.

'Our cook goes and chats with the folks from his village after we are done with our dinner. He is out till quite late. I knew that and so I didn't stay up to open the door for Dada. At about ten o'clock, after I had cleared away the dinner things and put everything away, I went upstairs and got into bed.

'I had fallen asleep when suddenly something woke me up. I thought I heard some noises in Dada's room. It was like the noise you hear when someone drags something heavy, like a desk or a large box across the floor. I thought Dada had returned from the cinema. I tried to go back to sleep. For some reason, sleep just wouldn't come. I stayed awake for a while. There were no more noises from Dada's room. I thought he must have turned in for the night. After about a quarter of an hour I heard a faint sound in the corridor, as if someone was tiptoeing along it. I found that very strange. Dada must have been asleep for a while. So who could that be? I got up softly and pushed the door open just a crack—and I saw Dada silently enter his room and shut the door behind him. The corridor was flooded with moonlight and I could see Dada very clearly.'

Byomkesh interposed, 'Just one clarification—did Sukumarbabu have his shoes on?'

'Yes.'

'Was he carrying anything?'

'No.'

'Nothing? A piece of paper or a bottle?'

'Nothing.'

'What time was it—did you check?'

Satyaboti said, 'That wasn't necessary. It was striking midnight on every clock in town.'

'I see.'

She continued, 'At first I did not understand what was

going on. Dada had come back fifteen minutes ago—I knew that from the noises in his room—then where could he have gone again? Suddenly it struck me that perhaps Uncle had been taken ill and Dada had gone to his room. Uncle suffered from arthritic pain sometimes at night—he wouldn't be able to get any sleep. At such times he needed medication to sleep. I slipped out quietly and went towards Uncle's room. He always kept his door unlocked . . . I entered the room. It was dark, but a smell hit my nose. I cannot explain to you exactly what kind of a smell it was—it wasn't strong or sharp, but . . .'

'Was it a sweet smell?'

'Yes, exactly—it was a syrupy smell.'

'Hmm . . . chloroform. Continue.'

'The light switch was next to the door. I switched it on and saw that Uncle was lying on the bed. It looked like he was sleeping. His posture did not indicate in any way that he . . . But still, for some strange reason my heart began to beat fast. That smell seemed to cut off my breath like a wet rag pressed to my nose. For some time I just stood by the door. I tried telling myself that it was the smell of medication and Uncle had just taken pills and gone to sleep. My legs were shaking, but I approached the bed cautiously. I bent forward and noticed that he wasn't breathing. I cannot describe what was going on inside me then—I felt as if I would swoon at any time. Perhaps my head did actually spin. In order to steady myself I reached out and touched Uncle's pillow. My hand fell on his neck—I felt something sharp pricking it. I looked and saw that a needle has been pierced right through his neck; the thread was still threaded through it.

'I could stay there no longer. But I do not know how I had the strength to switch off the light and walk back to my room. By the time my senses returned I was sitting on my bed, shivering hard and weeping.

'The rest you already know. I did not suspect Dada, because I know he could not have done this; still, it didn't take me long to figure out that I couldn't talk about this to anyone, or I would only make things worse for him. The following morning I somehow managed to make a cup of tea and take it to Uncle's room . . .'

Satyaboti's voice grew faint and she trailed off. From the unnatural paleness of her face and the terror in her eyes it was easy to see the immense quandary and agony that she had faced the other night. I looked at Byomkesh and saw that his eyes were glittering. He exclaimed, 'I have never met a girl as extraordinary as you. Anyone else would have screamed the place down, swooning . . . raising hell . . . hysterical—you are . . .'

Satyaboti whispered, 'Only for Dada's sake . . .'

Byomkesh stood up and said, 'Please go home now. I shall be over there tomorrow morning.'

Satyaboti also stood up; nervously she said, 'But you did not say anything.'

Byomkesh said, 'There is nothing to say. I do not want to raise your hopes and then disappoint you. There is a veritable whatsitsname called Bidhubabu involved, you see. Anyway, I can say this for certain, had you told me all this on the very first day, perhaps everything would have gone much more smoothly.'

Tearfully Satyaboti said, 'Will any of what I have just said cause harm to Dada? Are you certain? Byomkeshbabu, I have no one else . . .' She choked on her tears.

Byomkesh quickly went and held the main door open for her, tried to smile and said, 'You hurry along now—it's getting late. Ours here is a bachelor-pad too . . .'

Satyaboti hurried out, a trifle contrite; just as she crossed the threshold Byomkesh said something to her in a soft undertone, which I was unable to hear. Satyaboti looked back, startled. For a moment her grateful, pleading eyes were before me. Then she quickly raised her hands in a brief gesture of greeting and went rapidly down the stairs.

After shutting the door Byomkesh came and sat down, looked at his watch and said, 'It's seven o'clock already.' Then he seemed to be doing some mental calculations after which he said, 'There's still a lot of time.'

Eagerly I pounced on him, 'Byomkesh, what do you make

of it all? I didn't get anything—but from your manner I feel as if you have already come to know all the facts.'

Byomkesh shook his head, 'Not everything, not yet.'

I said, 'Whatever you might say, my firm belief is that Sukumar did not do the deed—whatever evidence there might be against him.'

Byomkesh laughed, 'So who did it then?'

'I don't know about that, but it certainly wasn't Sukumar.'

Byomkesh remained silent; he lit a cigarette and began to smoke in silence. I figured he wouldn't say anything more now. I too began to ponder in silence over the amazing complexities of this case.

Much later, Byomkesh suddenly asked, 'I suppose you couldn't call Satyaboti beautiful, could you?'

Intrigued, I looked up and said, 'Why do you ask?'

'Just asking. I think generally people would say she is too dark.'

I failed to understand the link between the problem in hand and Satyaboti's looks. But it was impossible sometimes to follow the intricate route that Byomkesh's mind took. I considered the matter gravely and said, 'Yes, people would call her dark—but not exactly unattractive, I think.'

Byomkesh laughed and jumped up saying, 'You mean, as the poet said,

Dark you say she is, dark as the darkest night
But I have seen her deep dark doe-like eyes . . .

Right? Oh, by the way, Ajit, what is your age, precisely?'

Astounded, I said, 'My age . . . ?'

'Yes—tell me exactly, to the year, month and day.'

Perhaps he was going to find the solution to the mystery of Karalibabu's death in my precise age. With Byomkesh, you never knew. I did some mental arithmetic and said, 'My age is twenty-nine years, five months and eleven days. Why?'

Byomkesh heaved a great sigh of relief and said, 'Good, you are elder to me by a full three months. I am so relieved. But do keep this in mind, won't you?'

'What are you talking about?'

'Oh, nothing. Anyway. My head is going round in circles from concentrating too hard on this case. Come on, let us go and see a film tonight.'

Byomkesh never went to the cinema. He just did not like either plays or films. So I was amazed, to say the least. I said, 'What has got into you today? Have you gone absolutely crazy?'

Byomkesh laughed and said, 'Not impossible. I was born under the lunar ascendant, you see. Mr Bhattacharya had cast my horoscope and immediately pronounced, "This boy will turn out utterly deranged." But it's getting late. Come, let us eat and get going. There is a good movie showing at Chitra, I hear.'

So, after dinner we landed up at Chitra. The film started at nine-thirty. It was a trifle longer than usual and so it was close to midnight when the film ended. Our house was some distance away. Some stray buses were still plying. As I headed towards the bus stop, Byomkesh said, 'No, come on, let's walk for a while.' He set off at a brisk pace. When he turned into a narrow lane after Cornwallis Street, I realized he was going in the direction of Karalibabu's house. I couldn't comprehend what he wanted to do there at this time of the night. But anyway, I followed him without uttering a word.

We are walking slightly faster than usual. Yet it took us a while to reach Karalibabu's house. There was a street lamp at the corner across from the house. Byomkesh stood below it, rolled up his shirt-sleeves and looked at his watch. But there was no need for it because just at that moment an array of clocks struck, announcing midnight.

Byomkesh cheerfully treated me to a slap on the back and said, 'It works. Come, now let's try to get a taxi.'

The following morning at about eight-thirty we landed up at Karalibabu's house. Some police officials were there, along with Bidhubabu. The latter was a little embarrassed on seeing Byomkesh, but he hid it well and solemnly said, 'Byomkeshbabu, perhaps you know that I have put Sukumar under arrest. It is he who is actually the killer. I knew that all along—I was just playing it by ear.'

'Indeed!' Byomkesh said, and looked attentively at Bidhubabu's large ears, as if he expected these to perform some new trick at any moment. In their attempts to choke back their laughter, the inspector and the sub-inspector ended up with ridiculously grave expressions and turned the other way.

Bidhubabu asked, a trifle suspiciously, 'What brings you here today?'

Byomkesh replied, 'Nothing really. I heard another new will has been dug out. So I thought I would take a look at it.'

After cogitating for some time on whether to show Byomkesh the will or not, Bidhubabu reluctantly opened a file and extracted a document. He said, 'Watch out, don't tear it or anything; this will is the most important proof against Sukumar. After killing Karalibabu, Sukumar stole this and hid it in his room. Do you know where he hid it? Those three chests that are piled up one on top of the other in his room—it was tucked right under the bottom one.'

Byomkesh gave a laugh and said, 'Great, everything is falling into place. But tell me one thing, why didn't Sukumar tear up the will into little bits?'

Bidhubabu made a derisive noise through his nose and said, 'Ha, he didn't have that sense. He thought we would not search his room.'

'Did Sukumar say anything when you arrested him?'

'What can he say except what they all say, "I don't know anything"—pretending to be stunned.'

Byomkesh surveyed the will from all possible angles, then carefully opened it up and began to read it. I too craned my neck and saw that on a sheet of white foolscap paper the following words were typed:

On this Twenty-second day of September, Nineteen Thirty-three (by the Christian calendar), I am making this will in complete possession of my senses. After my demise all my movable and immovable property as well as all monetary assets will be inherited by my youngest

nephew Phonibhushan Kar. All other wills that were
made previously are hereby rendered null and void.
Signed: *Karalicharan Basu*.

On reading the will Byomkesh leaped up, his face suffused
with excitement, and said, 'Bidhubabu, this is fantastic, the will
isn't—' he stopped and held out the piece of paper in front of
Bidhubabu. Bidhubabu scanned the whole thing again from
the beginning to the end with increasing bewilderment and
enquired, 'What is it? I cannot see . . .'

'Don't you see?' Byomkesh pointed to the space below the
signature.

At that Bidhubabu's eyes grew large and he said, 'O—h,
witnesses . . .'

'Quiet!' Byomkesh indicated silence and glanced at the
closed door. He waited for a few moments and then walked up
to the door on tiptoes and suddenly flung it open. Makhanlal
had his ear to the door; he tried to make a speedy escape.
Byomkesh caught hold of his sleeve and dragged him inside
the room. He pushed him roughly onto a chair and said,
'Inspector, please keep an eye on him—don't let him go; and
also don't allow him to talk.'

Makhan had shrunk to half his size in terror. He started to
say, 'I . . .'

'Silence! Bidhubabu, please send for another warrant from
the magistrate. There is no need to give the suspect's name—we
can fill that in later.' He went very close to Bidhubabu, lowered
his voice and said, 'Until then, you can play this fellow by ear.'

Stupefied, Bidhubabu said, 'But I don't understand—'

'Later. Meanwhile, please get the warrant ready. Come on,
Ajit.'

Byomkesh took the stairs rapidly and knocked on
Phonibhushan's door. It opened. A little taken aback at seeing
us, Phoni said, 'Byomkeshbabu!'

We entered the room. Suddenly, Byomkesh no longer
seemed rushed for time. He gave a little laugh and said, 'You
will be happy to hear that we now know who Karalibabu's
murderer really is.'

Phoni smiled wanly and said, 'Yes, I have heard that Sukumarda has been arrested. But I still cannot come to terms with it.'

'It really is hard to accept. There is also a new will that was found in his room—according to that you are the beneficiary.'

Phoni said, 'I have heard that too. Ever since I came to know, there's a bitter taste in my mouth. Just for a few thousand rupees Uncle had to lose his life.' He heaved a sigh and continued, 'Wealth, the root of all evil! He has left me all his wealth, but I cannot rejoice, Byomkeshbabu. I would rather he didn't give me the money and stayed alive instead.'

Byomkesh was standing in front of the bookshelf, glancing at the books. A trifle self-absorbed, he said, 'True, true. A wealthy man is never happy, as the cliché goes. What is this book? Physiology! I see, it is Sukumar's book.' Byomkesh took it off the shelf and glanced at the fly-leaf.

Phoni gave a short laugh and said, 'Yes, Sukumarda often lent me his books from medical school. How strange life is—in this household Sukumarda was the only person whom I considered to be my friend . . . in fact even more than my brothers—and he was the one who . . .'

Byomkesh took down some more books and said in a surprised voice, 'You are quite a bookworm, aren't you? And do you always mark your books as you read them?'

Phoni said, 'Yes. I have no hobbies other than reading. Books are my only companions. Only Sukumarda used to spend some time with me every evening. Byomkeshbabu, please tell me, has Sukumarda really done this—is there no scope for doubt?'

Byomkesh sat down on the chair. He said, 'The evidence that has been culled against the culprit does not leave any room for doubt any more. Please sit—I shall tell you everything.'

Phoni sat on the edge of the bed. I sat down beside him. Byomkesh said, 'Look, there are two kinds of murder—one is committed in the heat of the moment, what we call a "crime of passion"; the other is premeditated. A murderer who kills in the heat of the moment is easy to catch—in most cases he himself confesses his crime. But when a man commits a premeditated crime, calculated to deflect all suspicions away from himself, it becomes difficult to catch him out. In such cases, we do not know who the offender is, but begin to suspect a host of other people. What is to be done in a situation such as this? The only way, at this point, is to judge from the mode of killing, who the real murderer might be.

'In the present case we noticed something strange— apparently the murderer is simultaneously clever and stupid. He has committed the murder very intelligently, but has gone and hidden all the instruments of killing in his own room. You tell me, was there any need to do the deed with Satyaboti's needle? Were there no other needles in this town? Also, did he have to hide the will so carefully? If he had ripped it up, no one would have been the wiser. What does all this indicate?'

Phoni was listening with his chin resting on his palm. He asked, 'What?'

Byomkesh said, 'A person who is naturally moronic can never act intelligently. But one who is quick-witted can pretend to be dull. So it is very evident that the culprit, whoever he is, is smart. But clever people also make mistakes and an attempt to appear dim-witted does not always succeed. In this case too, the culprit made some minor errors and that is what has helped me to catch him.'

Phoni asked softly, 'What mistakes did he make?'

'Wait.' Byomkesh rummaged in his pocket and brought out a sheet of blank paper. 'I need to draw out a plan of this house first. Do you have a pencil—anything that writes will do.'

There was a book beside the pillow on Phoni's bed. He opened it and took out a red pencil and handed it to Byomkesh. Byomkesh took the pencil and looked at it carefully. Then with a slight smile he said, 'Actually, it isn't necessary to draw the sketch after all. I can just explain in words. The culprit committed three blunders. First: he marked out a few lines in a copy of Gray's Anatomy. Second: he made a noise while heaving the chests around. Third, and most important: he was not conversant with legalities.'

Phoni's face had gone all white. He managed to utter, 'Not conversant with legalities?'

Byomkesh said, 'No, and that is precisely why his crime, planned so carefully, was completely futile.'

Phoni licked his parched lips and stammered, 'I . . . I'm really unable to follow you.'

Byomkesh drew his words out, 'The will which has been unearthed from Sukumar's room is absolutely null and void as a legal document. It doesn't have the witnesses' signatures.'

It seemed as if Phoni would pass out. There was a long silence; Phoni stared at the floor with stony, unseeing eyes. Then he grasped his hair in his clenched fists and muttered almost to himself, 'All in vain, an utter waste—!' He looked up and said, 'Byomkeshbabu, would you please allow me to be alone for a bit? I am feeling very unwell.'

Byomkesh stood up and nodded, 'I will give you half an hour. Please prepare yourself.' At the door he turned back and said, 'You threw the thimble away, didn't you? You must have taken it—I didn't find it in Satyaboti's basket. I don't know why you didn't leave it in Sukumar's room along with the chloroform. In the scramble you probably forgot to take it off, right? That must be it. But tell me, who got the chloroform for you—Makhanlal?'

Phoni lay back on his pillow and said wearily, 'Please come back in half an hour—'

We shut the door as we left, came downstairs and sat down. Makhanlal was still being held prisoner by the inspector and the sub-inspector. Byomkesh frowned at him and asked, 'When did you bring Phoni chloroform?'

Startled, Makhan said, 'I don't know anything . . .'

'Tell me the truth or I shall put your name down in the warrant.'

Makhan burst into tears and said, 'Very honestly, sir, I am not involved in all this at all. Phoni said he has trouble going to sleep and a drop of chloroform would help. So . . .'

'I get it. Bidhubabu, you may release this man now.'

As soon as they let him go, Makhanlal vanished. Byomkesh asked, 'Has the warrant come through yet?'

'No, but it'll be here at any moment. But who is it for?'

'For the man who killed Karalibabu.'

Extremely displeased, Bidhubabu shook his head and said, 'Byomkeshbabu, this is not the time to fool around. Just because the Commissioner has a lot of regard for you, you have been bossing me around; that too I have tolerated. But I shall not stand for asinine jokes.'

'I'm not joking at all. It's the absolute, distilled truth . . . listen to me carefully.' Byomkesh explained everything to him briefly.

Bidhubabu remained dumbstruck for a while and then exclaimed, 'If that is the case, then why have you left him alone? What if he runs away?'

'He won't run away. He will plead guilty. And that is our only hope because his crime will be very difficult to prove in court. You know what juries are like—they are only too eager to give a verdict of "not guilty".'

'That I am well aware of . . . but . . .' Bidhubabu sat down again.

Exactly after half an hour we returned to Phonibhushan's room. Bidhubabu opened the door and stomped inside, ahead of the rest of us, and came to a sudden halt. Phoni lay on the bed, his right arm hanging out; just below, the floor was caked with blood. His slashed wrist was still dripping with dark red globules.

Byomkesh gazed at him for a while and said, 'I didn't think he would go this far. But what other options were left for him anyway?'

There was a note resting on Phoni's chest. Picking it up, Byomkesh read it out loud. This is what it said:

Byomkeshbabu,
Goodbye. I am lame and worthless—there is no room for me here; let me see if I can be accommodated up there.
I know that you would not have been able to prove my guilt in court. But there is no point in my staying alive. When the money is gone, what will I live in hope of?
I am not sorry that I murdered Uncle. He had no love for me; he often mocked and ridiculed my deformity.

But I do wish to beg forgiveness of Sukumarda. Yet, there was no one else that I could frame. Moreover, if he had gone to prison, I would have profited in yet another way. But the secret which I have always felt ashamed to express to anybody on account of my handicap, shall remain that way.

I shall not disclose how I got hold of the chloroform; the person who got it for me did not know my intentions. But perhaps he suspected something later.

You are an amazing person—you didn't even leave the thimble out. You were right, I had forgotten to take it off. I noticed it after I came back into my room. It must be lying around here somewhere. That night when I had stolen the thimble and the needle from Satyaboti's sewing basket, she was cooking in the kitchen.

If it had been anybody other than you, he would not have caught me out. But yet I cannot bring myself to feel hatred for you. Farewell. I am bound for a distant abode.

Yours,

Phonibushan Kar.

Byomkesh handed Bidhubabu the note and said, 'I think there is no reason now to hold Sukumar prisoner any longer. His sister must be informed too. I think she is still in her room. Come on, Ajit.'

About a week or so later the two of us were sitting in our living room, sipping our evening tea in companionable silence.

Over the last few days Byomkesh had been going out every afternoon without fail. He didn't tell me where he went and I didn't ask either. Sometimes he got cases that were to be kept a secret, even from me.

I asked, 'Are you going out today?'

Byomkesh glanced at his watch and said, 'Yes.'

A little diffidently, I asked, 'Is this a new case you have taken on?'

'Case? Yes—but it's top secret.'

I dropped the matter. Instead, I asked, 'Is everything cleared up for Sukumar?'

'Yes—he has applied for probate.'

I said, 'Byomkesh, tell me, exactly how did Phoni commit the murder—give me the details. I am still unable to untangle the whole mess.'

Byomkesh put his empty teacup down and said, 'All right, let me narrate the incidents in their proper sequence. That afternoon Motilal had a row with Karalibabu. In the evening Sukumar heard about it and went to reason with Karalibabu. He got thrown out of there and stayed in Phoni's room until about seven-thirty in the evening; he then had his dinner and went off to the movies. Till here there is no confusion, right?'

'No.'

'Between eight and nine at night—when Satyaboti was in the kitchen, Phoni pilfered the thimble and the needle from her room. He had anticipated that Karalibabu would change his will again and this time he would be the beneficiary. He decided he wouldn't give the old man another chance to change his mind. Phoni could not stand Karalibabu; handicapped people are often very sensitive about their deformity. They can be very vindictive towards people who taunt them about it. Phoni had probably been contemplating the murder for quite some time.

'From the statement given by the cook, we know that Motilal left the house sometime around eleven-thirty. Under the influence of opium, people often have no sense of time. That's why the cook was so uncertain. According to my calculation, Motilal left the house at exactly twenty-five past eleven. He always had that weakness—he hardly ever stayed home at nights.

'After Motilal left, Phoni came out of his room. Motilal's room was right below Karalibabu's. Phoni did not want the noises to alert Motilal—hence the wait. It took him about five minutes to get Karalibabu under chloroform. Then Phoni pierced his neck with the needle, ineptly. It took him three tries to get it right. If it had been a medical student like Sukumar, it could never have taken him that long.

'After that, Phoni went into the next room and took

Karalibabu's last will out of the safe. His guess was right; the will was made out in his name.

'All this took him a total of ten to twelve minutes.

'Now, the question was, what should he do with the will? He could have left it where he found it. But that would not have served to tighten the noose around Sukumar's neck. And in order to save his own skin, he had to inculpate someone else.

'So he hid the will and the bottle of chloroform in Sukumar's room. He knew that after such a crime, all the rooms would be searched and then the will would come out. It was like killing two birds with a single stone—Sukumar would hang, and Phoni would get the property.

'When he moved the chests to hide the will, there was some noise. That is what woke Satyaboti. It was then a quarter to twelve. She thought Sukumar had returned from the cinema. But in reality, Sukumar could not have returned then. He returned when—yes, when all the clocks were striking the midnight hour. Anything else that you need explained?'

'What is the reason behind there being no witnesses' signatures on the will?'

Byomkesh thought for a while and said, 'Possibly Karalibabu drew it up after dinner, so nothing else could be done about it that night. Perhaps he wanted the cook and the servant to sign on it the following morning.'

A few minutes passed as we smoked silently. Then I asked, 'Did you meet Satyaboti again? What did she say? Thanked you profusely, did she?'

With a disappointed countenance, Byomkesh replied, 'No—she just covered her head with the end of her sari and touched my feet.'

'Quite a girl though, isn't she?'

Byomkesh stood up and shook his finger at me, 'You are older than me, remember?'

'Yes—but why?'

Without answering, Byomkesh went into the next room. After a few minutes he came out, dressed to the hilt. I said, 'Your secret client seems to be very particular. Likes the detective decked up in silk kurtas, eh?'

Byomkesh wiped his face on a perfumed handkerchief and said, 'Hmm, seeking truth is no laughing matter. One must be adequately prepared.'

I said, 'But you have been a truth-seeker for a while now. I have never seen you so dressed up before.'

Byomkesh pulled a grave face and said, 'As a matter of fact, it is only very recently that I have begun to seek Truth in true earnest.'

'Whatever do you mean?'

'The meaning runs deep. Think vernacular.' With a mischievous smile, Byomkesh moved towards the door.

'Truth—? Satya! Oh!' Light dawned. I leaped up and grabbed him by the shoulder. 'Satyaboti! So that's the great Truth you've been after these last few days! Eh—Byomkesh? Et tu, then? So the bard was right when he wrote, all the world's a snare—of love!'

Byomkesh said, 'Watch it! You are older than me and that makes you her revered brother-in-law. No bachelorly banter will be permitted! From now on, I too shall call you brother, to make things easier.'

I asked, 'Why am I such a bugaboo?'

He said, 'I am infinitely suspicious of the entire breed of authors.'

I heaved a sigh and said, 'Fine, so I'll play the brother from now on.' I placed my hand on Byomkesh's head in mock-benediction and said, 'Go on then, mate, it's almost four. You had better make a move. My blessings are with you. May you always be devoted to Truth, in whatever form, womanly or otherwise.'

Byomkesh went out.

Calamity Strikes

With a dejected sway of the hand Byomkesh deposited the newspaper on my lap and said, 'Nothing anywhere, absolutely nothing. The press people could try bringing out blank sheets instead. At least it would save them the printing costs.'

I couldn't resist a dig, 'Isn't there anything in the advertisements? Don't you always say that all the news in the world is crammed into the classified columns?'

With a downcast expression Byomkesh lit a cheroot and said, 'No, there isn't much even in the personal notices. Someone has placed an advertisement seeking to marry a widow. Why the insistence on a widow when there is no dearth of unmarried females? I am sure he is up to no good.'

'Oh, of course. Anything else?'

'An insurance company has placed a huge notice saying that they will jointly insure the husband and the wife and if, for some reason, one of the pair were to die, the other would get all the money. These insurance companies can make life so difficult—they won't even let people die in peace.'

'Why is that so? Do you see an ulterior motive here as well?'

'The insurance company may not stand to gain anything, but it isn't good to breed criminal intentions in people's minds either.'

'Sorry? What was that again?'

Byomkesh did not reply. He released a deep, mournful sigh, put his feet up on the table, raised complaining eyes to the beams overhead and continued to smoke in silence.

It was winter. The Christmas vacations were under way. Calcuttans were celebrating by going on excursions away from the city, while those who lived elsewhere were celebrating by visiting Calcutta. This was a few years ago, when Byomkesh was still unmarried.

As was our daily practice, the two of us were having our morning tea together and dissecting the newspaper. After three long months of sitting idle, even Byomkesh's iron-strong patience had begun to wear thin. Time seemed to hang loosely on our hands. Each day passed in looking the newspapers up for possible leads; but the humdrum and colourless information that filled the dailies had proved entirely useless thus far. Boredom sat heavy on my heart. I could only guess what Byomkesh's state of mind was like, deprived of all food for thought. I had not helped his misery much by chaffing continuously at him, as if to imply that it was he who was responsible for our dreary state of inaction.

This morning, the resigned look on his face made me feel sorry. It was bad enough for him to have to deal with the cul de sac that his mind was caught in; he could do without my pushing and prodding which only made matters worse. I decided not to plague him with any more questions and quietly withdrew to the pages of my newspaper.

At this time of the year there was always a surfeit of conferences and conventions. This year was no exception. The newsmongers made up for the lack of juicier news by filling the pages with tedious descriptions of these events. I noticed that in Calcutta itself some five conventions were currently under way. In addition, the All India Science Congress was going on in Delhi. Many stalwart scientists had come together from diverse corners of the country and were presumably engaged in contributing to Delhi's pollution with the fumes of their noxious rhetoric. Even the second-hand smoke that I had to ingest courtesy the newspaper report was enough to line my cranium with soot.

I often wondered why our scientists talked more than they worked. The greater the scientist, the bigger was his prattle. Even if they were to discover something like the steam engine or the aeroplane, I would be willing to listen to their drivel patiently. But far from that, they could not even invent an insect repellent that worked! Nonsense of the first order!

During my disinterested scrutiny of the description of the science congress, one name suddenly caught my attention. It was of a renowned professor and researcher from Calcutta, Debkumar Sarkar. He had delivered a long speech at the convention. It wasn't as if other Bengali scientists had been particularly reticent; many had regaled the audience at length with their learned opinions. But the reason why Debkumarbabu's name interested me was that he was our neighbour; he lived two houses down from ours, at the end of the row. Although we had never been introduced, we knew of Professor Sarkar through our connection with Habul, his son.

Habul was a great admirer of Byomkesh's. The youngster was about eighteen or nineteen years of age, studying in college. A simple young soul, he wouldn't talk much before us, but just gape at Byomkesh, quite overcome with awe. With a mild smile Byomkesh would accept his homage. Sometimes we invited Habul to tea, thrilling him to bits.

Naturally, I was a trifle curious to know what our young friend's father had to say. Glancing through the report, I felt what he had said about the difficulties and deprivations of Indian scientists wasn't entirely untrue. I thought that if I read it out loud it might serve to distract Byomkesh and perhaps cheer him up somewhat. So I said, 'Hey, listen to what our Habul's father has had to say in Delhi.'

Byomkesh didn't lower his eyes from the ceiling, nor did he express much enthusiasm. Undeterred, I began to read:

'There is no denying the fact that without the aid of scientific knowledge no nation can achieve greatness. There is a prevalent belief that Indian scientists lack the powers of invention and are incapable of productive research—this is often cited as the reason why India is still not self-sufficient. But this belief is completely baseless, and our glorious past is proof of that. It is needless to mention in such erudite company that it was in India that the first seeds of modern science had germinated and then gradually spread, like pollen dust on gusts of wind, to locales far and wide. Mathematics, astronomy, medicine and architecture are the four pillars of modern scientific thought, and India was the founding ground of all four.

'However, it would be futile to dispute that at present this exceptional inventiveness of ours is on the wane. Why is this so? Has our mental prowess diminished? No, certainly not. There are other reasons for the barren harvests of our talent.

'In ancient times the sages and learned men lived under royal patronage. They did not have to worry about resources; if they needed money, the king provided it amply. The boundless wealth of the royal treasury could fulfil any demand in the cause of their quest. Relieved of economic cares, the scholars devoted themselves to their research which, eventually, always came to fruition.

'But what is the condition of our scientists today? The state does not patronize scientific research; nor are the wealthier sections of society very eager to spend money on research projects. We have to work within the constrained resources that a handful of universities and some meagre grants from here and there are able to afford us. Our success, too, is commensurate with our circumstances. Just as the mouse, in spite of all its efforts, is unable to carry the burden of an elephant on its back, we too are ill-equipped to make pathbreaking discoveries when the purse-strings are so tightly drawn. A famished mind cannot conceive the colossal.

'Still, I can confidently claim that if we could pursue our research with a mind unfettered by financial concerns, we would not have been lesser to any nation on earth. But alas! Money is not to be had—and our pursuit of the obtuse coffers of wealth obscures our attainment of finer intents. But, in spite of all this, what we have accomplished under such penurious conditions is a matter of pride and not of shame. Does anyone keep a count of the innumerable inventions that are achieved, often surprising even the inventor himself, in our little laboratories? The innovator carefully conceals his discovery deep within his heart and continues to wander in search of greater knowledge. But he is alone; there is nobody who will come to his aid; instead, he fears that the moment someone else gets a hint of his discovery, the credit will be snatched away from him. There are plenty of grasping thieves waiting to defraud the inventor and appropriate the discovery.

'Hence, I appeal to you—we need more funds, we require

more support, we must have unlimited resources for research
and the guarantee of proper credit for our inventions. We
want . . .'

'Stop!'

The professor's style was rather grandiloquent and I had
got carried away. Suddenly Byomkesh snapped, 'Enough!'

'What's the matter?'

'We want this, we want that, we must have the other. I'm
sick and tired of all this blustering. Really, the grass is always
greener . . .'

I said, 'That is the fun, my friend. There is always an excuse
for one's failures. Debkumarbabu's speech is evidence of the
fact that even the pedagogues of our country are not immune
to this tendency.'

A brief smile peeped out from behind the exasperated
expression on Byomkesh's face. 'Habul may look to be a
simple-minded boy,' he said, 'but he is quite intelligent. Being
his father, how can Debkumarbabu go around dumping such
gibberish on all and sundry like a veritable whatsitsname?'

'It isn't necessary for an intelligent boy's father to be smart.
Have you ever seen Professor Sarkar?' I asked.

'I am not sure. I have not felt an irresistible urge to lay eyes
on him. But I have heard that he has married a second time.
What greater proof of a man's stupidity can there be?' And
Byomkesh wearily closed his eyes. The clock struck
eight-thirty. I couldn't think of anything to do and finally I was
about to ask Putiram for a second cup of tea when suddenly
Byomkesh sat up straight.

'I can hear footsteps on the staircase.' He pricked up his ears
for a few seconds and then sat back dejectedly. 'Habul. I
wonder what he wants. He seems to be in a hurry.'

Moments later the door was flung open and Habul rushed
in. His hair was in disarray, his eyes were popping out as if he
had been frightened out of his wits. Habul had never been
handsome; he was rather plump and had a round face on which
a shadowy beard was beginning to sprout. Now he was really
a sight. I got up hurriedly and said, 'Hello, Habul. Whatever is
the matter?'

But Habul's demented eyes were fixed upon Byomkesh. My question probably never reached his ears. He stumbled over to where Byomkesh sat and blurted out, 'Byomkeshda, it's terrible! My sister Rekha has suddenly died.'

And he began to howl.

Byomkesh took Habul by the hand and sat him down on a chair. For a while there was no consoling him, he just wept helplessly. Such an unexpected catastrophe had really shocked him out of his senses.

We did not know that Habul had a sister. We had never been very curious about his family. I had only heard that after Habul's mother died, Debkumarbabu had remarried. I had also gathered that there wasn't much love lost between the stepson and the stepmother.

After a few minutes, Habul calmed down a bit and began to tell us what had happened. Debkumarbabu was away in Delhi; Habul, his stepmother and his younger sister, Rekha, were at home. This morning, as always, Habul had retired to his room on the second floor to study. After the clock struck eight, he suddenly heard his stepmother shriek and ran downstairs. He found her standing in front of the kitchen and wailing. He couldn't make sense of what she was saying. So he walked into the kitchen and saw that his sister, Rekha, was kneeling before the stove.

He asked her what the matter was, but she did not answer. He then went close to her and shook her. It was then that he realized that she was dead. Her body was stone cold and her limbs had become rigid.

At this point in the narration, Habul began sobbing again. 'What shall I do, Byomkeshda? Father isn't here . . . so I came to you. Rekha is dead—oh God! How could this happen, Byomkeshda?'

Habul's state of anguish brought tears to my eyes too.

Byomkesh placed a hand on his shoulder and said, 'Habul, be a man. You need to keep your wits about you in a crisis. Tell me, was something wrong with Rekha? Did she have a heart ailment?'

'I don't know . . . I don't think so.'

'How old was she?'

'Sixteen. She is two years younger to me.'

'Did she have any illness recently? Beriberi or something like that?'

'No.'

Byomkesh reflected for a few seconds and then said, 'Come, let us go to your house. I cannot say anything unless I see what has happened for myself. You need to wire your father and ask him to come immediately. But that can wait for a couple of hours. Right now we need a doctor. Doesn't Dr Rudra stay near your place? All right—come, Ajit.'

Soon we reached Debkumarbabu's house. The front of the house was narrow, as if due to pressures from the houses on either side it had been squeezed into growing vertically. On the ground floor there was only a living room, with the kitchen, pantry and bathroom beyond it. As we stood at the door, a shrill female voice fell on our ears. Someone was shrieking without pause. The tone carried every sign of distress and agitation, but none of sorrow. It was obviously the stepmother lamenting the death of the young girl.

An aged servant stood in front of the house, looking quite lost. Byomkesh said to him, 'You work here, don't you? Go and call the doctor from the house across the street.'

The man seemed glad to have something to do. He said, 'Yes sir,' and promptly disappeared. We followed Habul inside.

The woman whose voice we had heard from outside was standing at the bottom of the stairs and having an endless conversation with herself. The sound of our footsteps startled her. She cast an apprehensive glance at us. On seeing two strangers coming in with Habul, she quickly drew the end of her sari over her head and hurried up the stairs. I was able to see her face for an instant. I felt as if a shadow of annoyance mixed with fear crossed her face before the sari veiled it.

Habul murmured faintly, 'My mother . . .'

'I see,' said Byomkesh. 'Which way is the kitchen?'

Habul pointed to it. Around a medium-sized, quadrangular

courtyard, there were several rooms; of these, the largest one was the kitchen. On one side of it was a tap from which a steady trickle of water had made the doorway slippery. We took our shoes off and went in. The room was very dark, with no windows for light to enter.

Habul reached beside the door and switched on a fumy light-bulb. Now we could see the inside of the room more clearly.

Against the wall opposite the door, there were two adjacent coal stoves piled high with broken bits of fuel; but neither was lit. In front of one unlit stove was a girl bent on her knees, like a woman kneeling in prayer at an altar. Her body was tilting forward; her head too had fallen on to her chest. One hand hung limp at her side. But there were no obvious signs of death. Delicately, Byomkesh bent down and took her pulse. I could tell from his face that there wasn't one.

Byomkesh let go of her hand and slowly held her chin and lifted her face up. The lifeless body had already begun to stiffen, so the face only lifted by a few inches.

The girl was quite attractive. She was fair with an angular face and naturally pouting lips. For her sixteen-odd years, her body was quite filled out. Her long tresses, which she had probably undone before going to take her bath, still lay loose over her back. She was wearing a plain cotton striped sari, three gold bangles on each arm, a pair of light earrings and a slim gold chain on her neck.

Byomkesh took a good look at her from up close. Then he stood up and moved a few paces away to look at her from a distance. After watching her carefully for a while, he approached her once again. He raised her right hand and examined the palm. It was smeared with coal dust; obviously she herself had filled the stove with the fuel. The fingers were slightly bent and the tips of the thumb and the index finger were joined together. When Byomkesh separated the two gingerly, a tiny object dropped to the ground. Byomkesh picked it up, placed it on his palm and held it up to the light. I too leaned forward to see what it was. It was the burnt end of a matchstick, the little bit that remains after the match has completely burnt out.

Byomkesh studied it intently for a while and then threw it away. Then he picked up the girl's left hand. The fist was clenched; when he unclasped the fingers, we could see that there was a matchbox in it. Byomkesh opened the box; there were a few matchsticks left in it. Reflectively, he said, 'Hmm, that is what I thought. Death came just as she had lit the matchstick and was about to light the stove.'

Byomkesh moved away from the body and began to look around the room. He took a close look at the wet footprints marked upon the floor. Finally he shook his head and declared, 'No, there was no one else in the room at the time of her death. Later a woman entered, and then Habul came in.'

At this point there were noises outside. Byomkesh said, 'That is probably Dr Rudra. Habul, please bring him in.'

Habul went out. I took this opportunity to ask Byomkesh, 'Have you found anything?'

Byomkesh frowned slightly and shook his head, 'Nothing. Only this much is apparent—that until the moment of her death, the girl did not know that she was about to die.'

Habul returned with Dr Rudra. He was middle-aged and one of Calcutta's most renowned physicians. But he was notorious for his rudeness and bad temper. He would always be in the worst of moods; so much so, that his behaviour in the presence of even a dying patient was such that it would have put anyone but him out of business. He owed his roaring practice solely to his gift for medicine. Other than that, there was not a single human quality to be found in him.

Dr Rudra's appearance said a lot about his personality. He was dark as dark can be; his bloodshot eyes set within his ugly, horse-like visage, seemed to scorn all those they fell upon. The shape of his lips too carried that disdain. When he entered the room, it felt as if hauteur personified had come in, dressed in trousers, coat and shoes.

Silently, Habul pointed to the body of his sister. In his habitual rough tone, Dr Rudra asked, 'What is it? Is she dead?'

Byomkesh said, 'Please take a look and tell us.'

Dr Rudra raised his arrogant eyes at Byomkesh and said,

'Who are you?'

'I am a friend of the family.'

'Oh!' He ignored Byomkesh completely and asked Habul, 'Who is this? Debkumarbabu's daughter?'

Habul nodded.

A shade of curiosity passed across Dr Rudra's raised eyebrows. He looked at the corpse and said, 'Her name is Rekha?'

Habul nodded again.

'What happened?'

'Nothing. Just—suddenly . . .'

Dr Rudra knelt down beside the body. For an instant he felt the pulse and pulled an eyelid up briefly to check the pupil. Then he stood up and said, 'She has expired. It occurred almost two hours ago. Rigor mortis has set in.' He said this with great relish, as if it was a wonderful piece of news that was bound to delight his listeners.

Byomkesh queried, 'Is it possible to identify the cause of death?'

'That can only be known after an autopsy. I am going—send my fees of thirty-two rupees to my house. And yes, do inform the police, it is an unnatural death.' Having made his pronouncement, Dr Rudra strode out.

As we walked out of the kitchen, Byomkesh said, 'Of course it is necessary to inform the police, or there may be problems later on. I happen to know Birenbabu, the inspector of the local police station. I shall let him know.'

He jotted down a few lines on a piece of paper and handed it to the servant, asking him to deliver the note to the inspector. Then he said, 'There is no need to disturb the body further; the police will handle it once they get here.' He secured the chain on the door and said, 'Habul, it would be useful if we could take a look at Rekha's room.'

In a sombre voice Habul said, 'Come,' and led us upstairs. After the initial burst of weeping, he seemed to have gone into a trance, responding mechanically to whatever anyone said to him.

On the first floor there were three rooms, of which the last belonged to Rekha. The other two were probably Debkumarbabu's and his wife's bedrooms. When we entered Rekha's room, we saw that, although small, it was well maintained. The furniture, what little there was of it, was clean and polished. On one side there was a single bed; on the other side, by the window, there was a desk. Beside it, on a tiny shelf, two rows of Bangla books stood neatly arranged. On a bracket hung a mirror and at its foot there were brushes, ribbons, hair clips etc. Every part of the room had the touch of a skilful and educated girl stamped upon it.

Byomkesh began to pick up this and that, going round the room. He examined the hair clips and ribbons. Then he went and stood by the window. It overlooked the street. A short step away, on the other side of the street, was Dr Rudra's huge mansion and his chamber. The terrace of that house was clearly visible from this window. Byomkesh stood there, gazing outside. Then he turned back and pulled out the drawer attached to the desk. It wasn't locked and so it opened easily. There wasn't much in it: a couple of notebooks, a letter-pad, a bottle of perfume, needle and thread. Byomkesh picked up a bottle and looked at it; there were some white tablets in it. He said, 'Aspirin. Did Rekha take Aspirin?'

'Yes, sometimes, when she had a headache,' replied Habul.

Byomkesh put the bottle back in its place and began to pace the floor fretfully. He finally came to a standstill before the bed. The bed showed clear signs of having been slept in. The quilt lay all in a heap near the foot and the pillow carried the indent of the head. For a few moments my mind was gripped by a deep depression. So this was life—while the very marks of one's last repose were still fresh, the person had already set off on an unknown, infinite journey.

Engrossed in thought, Byomkesh lifted the pillow. A piece of paper, light green in colour, lay beneath it. Startled, Byomkesh picked it up and looked at it closely. It was a folded sheet from a letter-pad. He hesitated only slightly and then unfolded the letter and began to read it. I too craned my neck to read over his shoulder. In a feminine hand, the letter said:

Nontuda,

Our wedding has been called off. Your father asked for ten thousand rupees. It is impossible for my father to come up with that kind of money.

Perhaps you know that I shall not be able to marry anyone except you. But living in this house too is becoming unbearable. Can you bring me some poison? I know your pharmacy has a variety of them. Please give me some; if you don't, I shall choose some other means to die. As you already know, I keep my promises.

Always,
Your Rekha.

Byomkesh read the letter in silence and then handed it to Habul. He read it and broke down again, weeping. Tearfully, he said, 'I knew this would happen, Rekha would kill herself . . .'

'Who is Nontu?'

'Nontuda is Dr Rudra's son. Marriage negotiations between Rekha and him were under way. Nontuda is a good man. But that brute angered Father by demanding ten thousand rupees . . .'

Byomkesh ran his hand over his face once and said, 'But—no, let it go.' He took Habul by the hand, sat him down on the bed and began to console him in the gentlest of tones.

In a choked voice Habul said, 'Byomkeshda, I had just that one sister to call my own. Mother is gone and Father doesn't have much time for us . . .' He buried his face in his hands and began to sob helplessly.

After a while, under Byomkesh's care, Habul seemed to recover a little. Byomkesh stood up and said, 'Come, the police will soon be here. I need to ask your mother a few questions before they come.'

Habul's stepmother was in her own room. Habul went and conveyed Byomkesh's request to her. She came over to the door, her face partially hidden by the sari drawn over her head. Earlier I had caught a glimpse of her. This time I took a good look.

She was about twenty-seven or twenty-eight years of age; slim and tall, fair-complexioned, with a comely facial structure. Yet, far from being beautiful, she wouldn't even pass as reasonably attractive. An abiding harshness in the eyes was responsible for the lines between her brows. The thin, shapely lips curled nastily, as if perpetually derisive of the flaws in others. Her displeased expression made me feel that she had never known a day's happiness after her marriage. She didn't have children of her own and because of her nature, had even failed to love her husband's children from his first marriage. Hence, her unsympathetic heart had remained barren and arid as a desert.

I noticed something else too. She was probably finicky about her personal hygiene and her room. The manner in which she came and stood at the door made me feel as if she was trying to guard herself and her room against all kinds of defilation. Just in case we entered and contaminated the chaste premises of her room, she was standing guard before it.

Naturally, we made no attempt to enter the room and stood outside instead. Byomkesh asked, 'Did you see Rekha this morning?'

In response to this innocuous question, the lady let loose a barrage of sentences. I realized that along with all the other stereotypically feminine virtues, she wasn't lacking in loquacity either—if she got a chance to speak, there was no stopping her. As if Byomkesh's question had given her the cue, she embarked on a long monologue that touched on almost everything that was on her mind. This morning, when she realized that the maid wasn't going to turn up, she had asked Rekha to clean the kitchen and to light the stove. Of course, that was not to say that she ever let her stepchildren do a single household chore. As long as she had the ability, she did it all herself. But it was impossible to do every little chore single-handedly. Hence she had asked Rekha to light the stove while she herself cleaned her own bedroom and took a bath. After her bath she went on upstairs, knowing nothing of what was going on in the kitchen. Later, when she had changed, towelled her hair dry, taken the gods' names ten times and came downstairs, she found . . . the calamity! She never meddled with her stepchildren. But such was her misfortune that she had to deal with all the problems every time. After what had happened, all the blame would probably fall on her, especially once the master of the house came back—the commotion that he would cause was beyond belief. She was already in disfavour with him; he'd be only too happy to see her dead.

As the stream of words showed signs of slowing down, Byomkesh asked very deliberately, 'Did you happen to say any harsh words to Rekha this morning?'

At this the lady was inflamed. 'Harsh words do not cross my lips; that is not how I was brought up. Ever since I have set foot in this house, I have been living with my stepchildren. Can anybody claim that I have ever said a rude word? But, yes, this morning when I sent Rekha to light the fire, she returned from the kitchen and said, "I can't find the matches," and she walked in and took the matchbox from my shelf. I was wiping the floor at the time and I said, "You came in just like that—before you have had a bath? At your age, don't you have this sense? If you needed matches, you could have always had them brought from the shop." This is all I said, not a single word more. If that is a crime, then I am guilty.'

In a calm tone Byomkesh said, 'It is not a question of being guilty; but why did Rekha come into your room for the matches? Are they usually kept in your room?'

The lady replied, 'Yes. I cannot sleep in the dark, so I have an oil lamp in my room. The lamp and a box of matches are kept on a shelf. Everyone knows it, Rekha knew it too.'

I peeped into the room and saw that at the head of the bed, against the wall, there was indeed a tiny shelf on which a small lamp stood. This was a chance also to take a look at the rest of the room. An excessive immaculateness seemed to have petrified the furniture. So much so, that even the goddess Kali, from her picture on the wall, seemed to stick her tongue out warily, for fear of violating the purity of the room.

Furrowing his brows, Byomkesh asked, 'Oh—so that was

the last time you saw Rekha? After that you didn't see her alive?'

'No, and—' The lady was about to embark upon another discourse when the servant called out to us from below that the inspector had arrived.

We trooped downstairs.

Byomkesh was well acquainted with Birenbabu; each understood the other's worth. Birenbabu was a middle-aged man with a healthy, well-built body. He was known to be a bright and judicious operator. Byomkesh held him in high esteem especially because he did not have a bloated sense of self-importance that was so typical of the police, or the desire to show his opponent down in any way. I had even been witness to a few cases where Byomkesh had actually sought Birenbabu's help. He had an immense amount of knowledge about the lower classes of criminals and pickpockets.

When we greeted him, he looked at Byomkesh and said, 'What's the matter, Byomkeshbabu? Is it something serious?'

Byomkesh replied, 'I shall let you be the judge of that,' and led him inside.

It was two o'clock by the time we had sent the body away for the post-mortem, dispatched a telegram to Debkumarbabu and wrapped the matter up to the best of our ability. By the time we returned home and finished our lunch, the short winter day was drawing to a close.

Byomkesh remained morose and silent. I, too, was feeling rather uncomfortable. While we had been rather anxious for something interesting to turn up, who would have thought it would present itself in this cruel fashion? I was constantly reminded of Habul's face and felt very melancholic.

Gradually dusk rolled in; Byomkesh continued to sit by the window in silence, staring out unseeingly. Finally I asked, 'It *is* suicide, isn't it? What do you feel?'

Byomkesh was startled, 'Eh? Oh, you mean Rekha? What is *your* opinion?'

Although I wasn't entirely sure, I said, 'What else can it possibly be? Her intent is pretty obvious from that letter.'

'That it is. But what would you say was the method by which she committed suicide?'

'Poison. That too she states categorically in the letter . . .'

'She does. But I don't quite understand how she could consume the poison even before she had laid her hands on it. She did ask for it in the letter; but seeing that the letter didn't even reach its destination and was found lying under her pillow instead, where did the poison come from?'

I said, 'The letter said that if she didn't get poison, she would try any other means . . .'

'But do you think it is possible that she would try other means even before sending the letter?'

I remained silent.

A few moments later Byomkesh said, 'Moreover, nobody commits suicide while kneeling down to light a stove. Rekha's death came without warning—like a bolt from the blue. So furious, so infallible was this fiery bolt, that she didn't have a second to move. Even the matchstick she had lit burnt out in her hand.'

'How is such a death possible?'

'That is what I cannot figure out. I know that from among the known poisons, none except hydrocyanic acid has such fatal effects. But . . .'

Byomkesh left the sentence hanging.

A little diffidently, I said, 'I do not know much about these things, but isn't it possible that the death came from a sudden heart failure?'

Byomkesh continued to ruminate and said, 'That is the possibility which is beginning to look more and more probable. Rekha used to take aspirin for her headaches. Perhaps she had a weak heart too . . . but no, something doesn't seem quite right. I cannot accept the possibility of a heart failure so easily, although all the evidence and logic seems to point towards it.'

He gave a perplexed laugh. 'My brain and my instincts are not seeing eye to eye. I cannot get rid of the feeling that the death is an unnatural one, an uncommon one, and something about it is gravely wrong. But let that be; it is pointless to fret over it now—the doctor's report tomorrow will clarify all.'

The room was in darkness; Byomkesh switched on the lights.

At this point there were a few soft knocks on the door. There had been no footsteps on the stairs. Byomkesh raised his eyebrows and called out, 'Who is that? Come on in!'

An unknown youth entered quietly. He was well-built and quite handsome, but a shadow of grief marked his wan face. He was wearing rubber-soled shoes on his feet; this was why we hadn't heard his footsteps. He took a few steps into the room hesitantly and said, 'My name is Manmathanath Rudra . . .'

Byomkesh looked him over swiftly and said, 'So you are Nontu? Do come in.' He indicated a chair.

Manmatha sat down and asked haltingly, 'Do you know me?'

Byomkesh sat opposite him and said, 'Recently I have had the occasion to know your name. You wish to know about Rekha's death?'

The young man's voice shook slightly as he said, 'Yes, how did she die, Byomkeshbabu?'

'That is not known yet.'

Manmatha held Byomkesh with his unusually bright eyes and asked, 'Do you suspect that she committed suicide?'

'Not possible.'

'Then, has somebody—'

'I cannot say anything for certain as yet.'

Manmatha covered his face with both his hands and sat for a while. Then, raising his head, he said indistinctly, 'Perhaps you have heard, Rekha and I were—'

'Yes, I know.'

Until now Manmatha was holding onto the last vestiges of his restraint; but now he broke down and began to speak in a choked voice, 'I have always been in love with her, ever since I used to go to their house to play, when Rekha was hardly six. Later when the marriage proposal came up, Father made things so difficult for them that the negotiations broke down. But I had decided that I would go ahead, against my father's wishes. Father and I had a huge row over this. He said he'd throw me out of the house. Yet I . . .'

Byomkesh asked, 'When did you have the row with your father?'

'Yesterday afternoon. I said to him that I wouldn't marry anyone other than Rekha. Who was to know that she . . . But why did this happen, Byomkeshbabu? Who had anything to gain by taking her life?'

Byomkesh was doodling with a pencil on the table; without looking up, he said, 'Your father stands to gain.'

Startled, Manmatha stood up, 'Father! No, oh no—what are you saying? Father . . .' Eyes wide with terror, he looked around blankly and then stumbled out of the room without uttering another word.

I turned towards Byomkesh and saw that he was deeply engrossed in his scribbles and doodles.

We eagerly awaited the doctor's report all through the next morning. But it did not come. Byomkesh called the police station, but they had no information either.

Around four-thirty in the evening Debkumarbabu arrived. He had left Delhi as soon as he received Habul's telegram, and had arrived here in the afternoon.

He was around forty, but his grim expression made him look much older. He was burly, balding and wore thick glasses. He appeared to be the absent-minded sort—in other words, he lived more in the cerebral than in the corporeal world. His buttoned-up coat and the owlish face with round spectacles were not unfamiliar to anyone in the student circles of Calcutta; as a neighbour, I too had run across him a few times. But now I saw that his face was quite drawn and pallid. There were dark circles under his eyes, his cheeks were sunken and he no longer had an air of vigour about him.

He looked at me through his thick glasses and asked, 'Are you Byomkeshbabu?'

I pointed to Byomkesh. Debkumarbabu turned towards him and said, 'Oh.' He placed his sturdy walking-stick on the table.

Byomkesh muttered a few commonplaces conveying

sympathy. Perhaps they didn't even fall on Debkumarbabu's ears. His keen eyes went around the room once. In a fatigued voice, he said, 'I left Delhi at ten in the morning yesterday and reached here at two-thirty this afternoon. Nearly thirty hours in the train . . .'

We remained silent; the signs of physical stress were evident in every line of his body.

Debkumarbabu turned towards Byomkesh and said, 'I have heard about you from Habul—I am eternally grateful to you for your help and support in our time of trouble.'

Byomkesh said, 'Please don't mention it. If I have been able to assist at all, it was my duty as a neighbour.'

'If you say so. But you are a busy man—' Abruptly, he asked, 'What was the matter with her? Do you have any idea? No one at home could tell me much.'

Byomkesh narrated all that he had seen. While listening, Debkumarbabu inattentively pulled a cigar out of his pocket, held it to his lips and then kept it down unlit upon the table. My eyes were on his face and I realized that he was listening to Byomkesh with such rapt attention that he had no idea what his hands were doing in nervous excitement. Once he took off his glasses and stared straight at me, with his huge eyes, for nearly two minutes. Then he put the glasses back on and shut his eyes.

When Byomkesh finished his narration, Debkumarbabu remained silent for a while and then suddenly said, 'Ohh, that Dr Rudra entered my house, did he! The monster—the scoundrel! There is nothing that he cannot do for money. He is a fiend!' In his excitement he gripped the walking-stick and stood upright; his face suddenly took on a vicious hue.

But within a few seconds he regained his composure. Perhaps he felt a little discomfited when he noticed the surprised looks on our faces. He cleared his throat and said, 'I should leave now. Byomkeshbabu, I'd just like to thank you once more.' He moved towards the door.

At the door he stopped short and crinkled his brow, as if suddenly struck by a thought. Then he turned around and said, 'If I had the money, I would have hired you to conduct the investigations on this case. But I am not well-off—I cannot afford it.'

Byomkesh was about to say something, but he waved his stick and stopped him, 'I cannot possibly accept somebody's services without paying for them. The police are investigating already; let them do what they can. Besides, what is there to investigate anymore? No amount of investigation can bring my daughter back.' Without any words of farewell, he turned around and left.

After this remarkable visit, for several minutes we sat there, dumbstruck. Eventually Byomkesh gave a huge sigh and remarked, 'One misapprehension has been corrected. I had come to believe that Debkumarbabu didn't care for his children from his first marriage—that isn't true. At least as far as his daughter was concerned, he loved her very dearly.'

Debkumarbabu had forgotten the cigar; Byomkesh glanced at it and said, 'Strange, absent-minded man,' and began to pace the floor slowly.

'I noticed he is furious with Dr Rudra,' I said.

Byomkesh didn't deign to reply.

In the evening Birenbabu, the inspector, arrived with the post-mortem report. He said, 'The report reveals nothing. After repeated tests, the cause of death still could not be determined.'

I read the report. The doctor said that the body bore no marks or wounds. There was no poisonous substance in the bloodstream. The heart was strong and normal and so death was not caused by its sudden failure. It would appear that a sudden paralysis of the nervous system had caused the death. But the doctor was unable to say how this nervous paralysis occurred. He had never seen such a strange case, where there was hardly any visible signs of death.

Byomkesh held the piece of paper in his hand and sat there thinking. Furrows appeared on his brow.

Birenbabu said, 'This case will certainly go to the coroner's court; there the verdict will be "death due to unknown causes". Thereafter we—meaning the police—are free to either continue or discontinue our investigations. Byomkeshbabu, what do you think? After such a post-mortem report, will an investigation yield any results?'

Byomkesh said, 'I do not know if there will be any results, but investigations should continue.'

Birenbabu asked eagerly, 'Why do you say that? Do you suspect anyone in particular?'

'Not exactly any one individual in particular. But I am quite convinced that there has been foul play.'

Birenbabu nodded in agreement and said, 'I think so too. What did you think of Debkumarbabu's wife?'

Byomkesh remained silent for a while. Then he spoke slowly, 'Look, I feel there is no point in barking up this or that tree. In order to solve the mystery the first thing that we need to know is the cause of death. As long as we do not know this, merely suspecting one individual or another is quite pointless. Of course, it is to be kept in mind that at the time of Rekha's death, only her stepmother and her brother were present in the house. But that shouldn't allow us to lose sight of the main problem at hand.'

'But when the doctor cannot figure out . . .'

'The doctor has seen only the corpse, we have seen much more. Therefore, it isn't impossible that we shall work out what the doctor hasn't been able to.'

In a doubtful tone Birenbabu said, 'That's true—but . . . anyway, you have been there on Debkumarbabu's behalf from the very beginning and will be there till the end; so we can work our way through, consulting each other as and when necessary.'

With a short laugh Byomkesh said, 'Oh no. Just a short while ago Debkumarbabu was here—he has relieved me of my duties.'

Surprised, Birenbabu remarked, 'Is that so!'

'Yes. He does not want to accept my services without the due remuneration—and he lacks the funds to employ me rightfully.'

'Well, well. And why does he lack the funds? He is employed in a fairly good position; I have heard that he draws quite a respectable salary.'

'That may be so.'

A frown cast its shadow over Birenbabu's brow, 'Hmm, I shall need to look into Debkumarbabu's financial situation. But what could be his reasons for refusing your help? Could it be possible that he is trying to shield somebody?'

I burst out laughing. The very notion of Debkumarbabu employing strategic moves to shield someone by refusing Byomkesh's services was completely ridiculous.

Birenbabu asked a trifle sharply, 'Why did you laugh?'

Rather embarrassed, I replied, 'Have you seen Debkumarbabu?'

'No.'

'If you see him, you'll know why I laughed.'

Birenbabu rose to leave. 'I shall investigate this case,' he told Byomkesh, 'till I reach the bottom of it—let me see if I can solve it. But you are not free yet. Debkumarbabu may have let you off, but do remember that when the need comes, I shall come to you for help.'

'That will be very nice indeed,' said Byomkesh. 'I shall be happy to assist you to the best of my ability. I also have a personal stake in this case—due to its relation with Habul.'

'Of course. But can you give me some pointers as to which path I should follow just now? There have got to be some clues which will give me a lead.'

Byomkesh thought for a moment and said, 'Why not start with Dr Rudra? Perhaps he holds the key to the way out of this maze.'

Birenbabu looked startled, 'Oh? All right—if you say so . . .'

Head bent, deep in thought, he took his leave.

About five or six days passed without any further incident. Byomkesh seemed to have gone back into his inertia. He did nothing else except read the newspaper in the morning and stare out of the window with unseeing eyes in the evening, feet planted on the table.

Birenbabu had not showed up during this time and so we had no idea how far his investigations had progressed. The only visitor we had was Habul, who came in every once in a while. When he came, Byomkesh tried to shake off his ennui and cheer the young fellow up with various kinds of stories. But it was as if a melancholic listlessness had taken permanent hold of Habul's mind. He would sit silently with eyes that were like pools of pain; then he would slowly get up and walk away. When asked what was going on at home, he couldn't even give proper answers. But we gathered that his stepmother's tongue had become sharper, if anything.

Finally, one day he heaved a great sigh and said, 'Father is going to Patna tonight; he has to deliver a lecture at the university there.' I guessed that, unable to tolerate the incessant harangue from his wife on top of his grief, Debkumarbabu was making his escape. The domestic strife in this absent-minded scientist's life was truly pitiful.

That day, after Habul left, Birenbabu paid us a visit. It was obvious from his countenance that he hadn't been able to get very far. Byomkesh greeted him graciously and offered him a seat. It was time for our evening tea and it arrived soon.

Byomkesh looked at Birenbabu and asked, 'So—how is it going?'

Taking a sip from his cup, Birenbabu answered gloomily, 'No progress in any direction. Whichever way I turn, there is nothing tangible, nothing concrete. Far from getting any proofs, even suspicions are few and hard to come by. Yet, I have come to believe even more strongly that this mystery runs deep; the more I fail at every step, the stronger this conviction grows.'

Byomkesh asked, 'Have you discovered anything new about the cause of death?'

Birenbabu shook his head, 'I went to see the doctor. Of course, he isn't willing to commit himself to anything outside of what the report says. But I think he has a theory. He feels that the vapour from some unknown poison was inhaled and caused a heart failure. He only hinted at this vaguely, but it was clear that this is what he believes.'

Byomkesh thought for a while and said, 'Did you tell him that the victim died while lighting the stove?'

'Yes.'

After a few more minutes of silence Byomkesh said, 'All

right. And on the other side? Did you inquire about Dr Rudra?'

'Yes. As far as I could gather, the man is a complete rogue and a money-sucking leech. There are rumours that he has finished off a few victims of tetanus by experimenting on them with an injection of his own invention. But sadly, in this case, there is no evidence to link him to the murder. It is true that there were some talks of marriage between Debkumarbabu's daughter and Rudra's son. He had demanded a dowry of ten thousand rupees. Debkumarbabu doesn't have so much money and so he had to call off the negotiations. But Rudra's son is a gentleman. He had some major rows with his father on this issue. Meanwhile this tragedy occurred—the girl died quite suddenly. Since then, I have come to know that the boy has left the house; he believes that his father is indirectly responsible for the girl's death.'

The news of Manmatha leaving his house was new, but all the other information was old hat to us. Perhaps the repetition of these facts had made Byomkesh a little unmindful. When Birenbabu stopped, he queried, 'You had said you will look into Debkumarbabu's financial situation; did you do that?'

'I did. He is not very well-off. There are no debts, but it would be impossible for him to cough up ten to twelve thousand rupees for his daughter's wedding. The man is perhaps a little careless about money or lacks his fair share of pragmatism. He does draw a decent salary from the college, some eight hundred rupees, but you'll be surprised to know that the lion's share of that money goes into the coffers of his insurance company. He has a life insurance policy made out for fifty thousand rupees; not only that, he has insured himself so late in life that the amount of the premium is really large. After that, there isn't much left over.'

Astounded, Byomkesh exclaimed, 'Fifty thousand rupees! That's—! Is it in his own name?'

'Not just his—it is a joint policy held by himself and his wife. It has been only a year since he got it done. This is his second marriage—if something happens to him suddenly his poor widow should not suffer—I suppose that is why he has gone in for a joint policy. The children have no rights over this money.'

'Hmm. Anything else?'

'What else? I even had someone keeping an eye on Debkumarbabu's son, Habul, in case something comes of it. The boy seems to have gone a bit crazy; he doesn't go to college much, just roams the streets, and sometimes sits quietly in the park. Apparently, he visits you as well, about once a day.'

I suddenly noticed that Byomkesh was no longer languid; it was as if his mind had suddenly come alive. After a long time, his eyes were glittering with hidden excitement. Without knowing why, my heartbeat quickened too.

But Byomkesh didn't express any signs of this urgency. In the same listless tone as before, he remarked, 'You can rule out Habul. Are you leaving? You will be at the police station, right? All right, if I need anything, I shall give you a call.'

Taken aback a trifle, Birenbabu went on his way. After his departure, Byomkesh paced the floor for a while; I saw that his eyes were gleaming with the old light. I was about to inquire why he had forced Birenbabu to leave, when he suddenly picked up his shawl from the back of a chair, draped it around himself, and said, 'Come on, let's go for a walk. This closed room is stifling me.'

The two of us set off. Byomkesh had a characteristic reluctance to leave the house without reason. If there wasn't any work to be done, he liked to sit in a corner quietly. In his company I too had become rather inactive physically, and my habit of venturing out by myself had deserted me entirely. Therefore, on this day, I was happy to see that Byomkesh's overheated brain had actually led him to seek some fresh air in an open space.

But as we continued to walk, my happiness gradually dissolved. Byomkesh was walking so haphazardly in the crowded streets that I felt he would meet with an accident at any moment. I tried to guide him along, but he was proceeding at an irrevocable speed, pushing and shoving everyone in his way—stepping on an old man's foot, jostling a young girl with books in her hand, oblivious to everything around him, like the wheels of the juggernaut. In fact, I had never seen him quite so abstracted. I, of course, was aware that his mind, having got the scent of its quarry, was running way ahead of his physical senses. But how were the pedestrians, who hadn't a clue about his emotional state, to know that?

In this manner, leaving a trail of abuse and frowns in our wake, we managed to reach College Square. The whole place was swirling like a whirlpool, with the milling crowds of students talking and laughing among themselves. Without further thought, I gripped Byomkesh's arm and dragged him inside. At least here we wouldn't have a chance of annoying old men or young women. If a discourtesy was caused, it could be shrugged away. The students in our country are rarely prone to squabbling.

With the pool in the centre, two streams of people were moving in opposite directions; we merged with one of these streams and so the possibilities of a collision grew even less. Byomkesh, with his brows knit in profound thought, was still unaware of his whereabouts. His shawl was slipping off his shoulder from time to time, but he was totally unconcerned.

I began to wonder, what was it about Birenbabu's conversation that had caused Byomkesh's torpid brain to shift gears and suddenly begin to move at the speed of the Punjab Mail? Was the mystery of Rekha's death about to be solved?

After walking about for half an hour or so, Byomkesh gradually began to regain his senses; he cast a casual glance at me and said, 'Debkumarbabu is leaving for Patna today, isn't he?'

I nodded.

'He cannot be allowed to leave. He . . .'

Byomkesh looked ahead and quickened his pace, leaving the sentence incomplete. I noticed that a crowd of people had gathered around a bench in one corner. They were exclaiming excitedly. Those who were on the periphery of the crowd were craning their necks to see what had happened. From their disposition it was obvious that something unusual had taken place.

On reaching the spot Byomkesh asked a young man, 'What is the matter?'

The youth said, 'I am not sure. I think someone, who was sitting on this bench, has died quite suddenly.'

Byomkesh made his way forward through the crowd. I followed suit. When we reached the bench, we saw that a youth was sitting on it, leaning forward as if he had fallen asleep. His head had drooped to his chest and his legs were stretched out in front. A cigarette dangled from his lips—but it hadn't been lit. In his left fist was a matchbox.

A student of medicine was feeling for the pulse. He said, 'There isn't one—he is dead.'

It was almost dusk and amidst the crowd, it was difficult to see. Byomkesh held the dead youth by the chin and raised his face to take a look, then let go of it as if struck by lightning. My heart too leapt to my throat. It was—our Habul.

The police arrived on the scene soon enough. We gave them Debkumarbabu's address and left the scene. The streetlights had already come on. Walking back home with brisk steps, Byomkesh said in a horrified, controlled whisper, 'Oh! What a cruel revenge of fate! What a devious joke!'

My brain had gone absolutely dull; but amidst the grief, I could only think of one thing: if there was a world beyond death, then the beloved sister whose death Habul had bemoaned so broken-heartedly, would have been reunited with him by now.

When we reached home, Byomkesh went into his library and shut the door. I could hear him speaking on the telephone.

He came out nearly an hour later and, in a weary tone, asked Putiram for some tea. He then sat down with his chin tucked into his chest. I didn't want to disturb him any further by asking questions.

At eight-thirty Birenbabu arrived. Byomkesh asked, 'Have you brought the warrant?' Birenbabu nodded. We started out again.

In a couple of minutes we stood before Debkumarbabu's house. The house was deathly silent; there were no lights at the windows upstairs; only the living room had lights on. Birenbabu knocked on the door, but no one answered from within. He pushed at the door and it swung open. We trooped inside.

There was a couch in the tiny living room, on which Debkumarbabu sat in absolute stillness. Upon our entry he raised his bloodshot eyes in our direction. After gazing at us for a few seconds, a bitter smile manifested itself on his face. He shook his head and murmured, 'The fruits of my labours—all came to nothing. I churned the oceans—all for a pot of poison.'

Birenbabu took a step towards him and said, 'Debkumarbabu, we have an arrest warrant in your name.'

As if coming out of a trance, he looked at the inspector's uniform and said, 'You have come—that is good. I was about to go to the police station myself.' He stretched out his hands and said, 'Handcuff me.'

Birenbabu said, 'That won't be necessary. Please hear out the charges brought against you,' and he made as if to read them out.

But Debkumarbabu had again become inattentive; he put his hand in his pocket and groped around for something as he muttered to himself, 'Fate! Or why would Habul too use that same matchbox? To think of what I had planned and where it has led me! I had wanted to give Rekha a grand wedding, have a big laboratory of my own, send Habul abroad for further studies . . . ' He fished out a cigar from his pocket and put it to his lips.

Byomkesh pulled out his own matchbox and lit the cigar for him. He said, 'Debkumarbabu, you will have to surrender your matchbox to us.'

Debkumarbabu looked up quickly and said, 'Byomkeshbabu, you are here too? Don't worry, I shall not kill myself. I have murdered my son and my daughter, I wish to die a criminal's death on the gallows.'

Byomkesh said, 'Please give me the matchbox then.'

Debkumarbabu brought it out of his pocket and placed it before us and said, 'Here you are. But do be careful, it is a terrible thing. Each and every matchstick has a poisoned flame. Once you light it, there is no escape . . .'

Byomkesh handed it to Birenbabu. He placed it in his pocket with great caution. Debkumarbabu continued, 'What an invention it was! Death in a flash, but no traces left behind. It would have changed the face of modern warfare! Not a mere poison, this is a scourge! But . . . it has all come to nought.' He let go a deep sigh from the depths of his heart.

Gently, Birenbabu said, 'Debkumarbabu, it is time to go.'

'Come.' He stood up promptly.

Rather hesitantly, Byomkesh asked, 'Is your wife here, at home?'

'Wife!' Debkumarbabu's eyes became glazed with a demented look. He roared out in wild laughter and said, 'Wife! After my execution, she is the one who will get all the money from the insurance company. Isn't it an irony of fate? Come, let's go.'

A taxi was called. Byomkesh led Debkumarbabu by the hand and reached him to it. Birenbabu got in beside him. Two constables had materialized out of nowhere; they too got into the car.

Debkumarbabu called out from inside, 'Byomkeshbabu, you had wanted to solve the mystery of my Rekha's death—I am grateful to you—'

We remained standing on the pavement as the taxi went on its way.

For a couple of days afterwards Byomkesh didn't bring this case up at all. I could guess at his state of mind, so I didn't urge him either. On the evening of the third day he started speaking of his own volition. Haphazardly, talking almost to himself, he began, 'There is a phrase in English—vengeance coming home to roost—that is what happened to Debkumarbabu! He had wanted to kill his wife, but such was the will of fate that both times he aimed his lethal arrows, they struck his son and daughter, who were dearer than life to him.

'Quite unexpectedly, Debkumarbabu had come upon an extraordinary invention. But due to a lack of funds, he was unable to make proper use of it. With an invention such as this, you cannot apply for a patent, because it has no value in the commercial market. But if war-prone, expansionist nations like Germany, Japan or France ever got wind of the formula, they would immediately start producing this lethal poison in their laboratories. The inventor wouldn't be able to do a thing and he wouldn't stand to gain anything out of his invention.

'So Debkumarbabu kept it all under wraps. He needed funds badly because much experimentation was needed to find out all the uses of the poison. But where was the money? In order to conduct such a huge experiment in complete secrecy, he would need his own laboratory, and that requires massive resources. Where would so much money come from?

'Meanwhile, at home, Debkumarbabu's wife was making his life quite miserable. Those who are involved in rigorous cerebral activities require some peace on the domestic front—but this was completely lacking in his life. The company of his finicky, unsympathetic and prattling wife was driving him around the bend. Debkumarbabu is not a violent person by nature. If he was given a peaceful atmosphere in which he could pursue his scientific activities, he would want nothing else. From the love he bore for his children, one can imagine that he has a very caring nature. His second wife, had she tried, could have also received her share of his affection. But she was made in a different mould. In fact, Debkumarbabu had begun to hate the very sight of her.

'A man does not usually have a desire to kill his wife; when he is driven to this extreme, it is because he has reached the end of his tether. Debkumarbabu too had come to a breaking point. Then the deadly poison came into his possession. Here was a way of disposing of his wife. Deep in the recesses of his mind, he began to hatch a plot.

'Then he saw the advertisement put out by the insurance company for joint life-insurance policies—the husband and wife could take out the policy together and when one of them died, the other one would get the money. Now all his doubts were resolved. Where would he get such an opportunity again? If he could take out that policy and then kill his wife with the poison he had invented—it would be like killing two birds with one stone; he would get the money he wanted and his wife too would die in a manner which would be impossible to detect.

'Debkumarbabu took out a policy for fifty thousand rupees at one shot, and then began to bide his time. It wouldn't do to rush things—the insurance company would get suspicious. A year went by. Finally, he made up his mind to shoot his deadly arrow during the Christmas vacations.

'The poison he had invented had explosive properties; in its normal state it was quite harmless, but once it came in contact with fire, its lethal powers evolved in the form of a chemical vapour. If a whiff of that vapour entered someone's nose, death was certain and instantaneous.

'Debkumarbabu figured out an ingenious plan for targeting his wife with this poison. Such ingenuity is only possible from a scientific mind. He coated some matchsticks with the poison. I do not know the process by which he did this, but the result was that whoever struck one of these matchsticks would inhale the vapour and die immediately. Having got these matchsticks ready, Debkumarbabu began to prepare for the science congress in Delhi. Gradually, the day of his departure drew close. At some point, he placed one of these matchsticks in the matchbox that was kept in his wife's room, and left for Delhi. He knew that every night his wife lit the lamp by striking a match from that matchbox—this wasn't for use elsewhere. Today or tomorrow, at some point the lady would strike the fatal match. Debkumarbabu would be far away in Delhi— nobody would suspect that this could be his handiwork.

'Everything was perfect, but destiny begged to differ. Rekha went to light the stove, couldn't find the matches, borrowed her stepmother's matchbox and struck the fatal matchstick.

'Debkumarbabu returned from Delhi. After this calamity, his heart hardened against his wife more than ever before. He became stubborn—since his daughter had been killed, she too would have to die. A few days passed. Again he kept one poisoned matchstick in the matchbox and prepared to leave for Patna.

'But calamity struck again—this time even before Debkumarbabu had a chance to leave. Habul was in the habit of smoking; perhaps he was out of matches and so he took some matchsticks out of his stepmother's matchbox and went for a stroll. Then . . .

'Debkumarbabu had churned the high seas of science and had come up with what he thought was the most wonderful of inventions. Little did he know that he had only succeeded in dredging up the most poisonous, the most satanic of vipers. His little flames of poison ruined everything that he held dear.'

Byomkesh heaved a deep sigh and stopped.

After a pause, I asked him, 'Tell me, when did you first suspect that Debkumarbabu was the culprit?'

'The moment I heard that he had taken out a life insurance policy for fifty thousand rupees,' Byomkesh replied. 'Until then, there wasn't even a satisfactory motive for murdering Rekha. It wasn't clear who would gain from her death, or whose way she was in. We did not realize then that Rekha wasn't the murderer's target.

'But one other tiny clue had fallen into my hands from another source. When Rekha's autopsy yielded no results, there was only one possibility left open—that the poison that had caused her death was not yet known to scientists. In other words, it was a new discovery. Do you remember Debkumarbabu's speech in Delhi? At that time we had brushed it aside as the blustering of the unsuccessful; how were we to know that he had truly made a momentous discovery and that his speech contained oblique references to it?

'Be that as it may, the question was, where did this new discovery come from? There were two scientists on the scene—one, Dr Rudra and two, Debkumarbabu. One of these two would have to be the inventor of this poison. But Dr Rudra was more of a suspect because being a doctor, he had easier access to poisonous substances. Moreover, if Debkumarbabu was the inventor, why would he poison his own daughter?

'Hence it was Dr Rudra who was the obvious suspect. And yet, my mind wasn't completely at ease. Dr Rudra is obviously a scoundrel, but would he go so far as to kill a young girl just because his son had fallen out with him over her? And even if he wanted to, how would he get access to her? How would he plant the poison in someone else's house? Rekha and Manmatha used to meet and throw letters across the terraces to each other, but Dr Rudra was not privy to such practices!

'In some corner of my mind, there was always an amorphous idea that the death was caused by some poisonous vapour. Think about it. Rekha held a burnt-out matchstick in one hand and a matchbox in the other—meaning her death had occurred immediately after she struck the match. That could be a coincidence, or there could be a cause-and-effect relationship between the two. Debkumarbabu, however, had been very clever. He had put only one poisoned matchstick in the box, so that an examination of the other matches would yield no results. I had brought back the matchbox and examined it too—but in vain. In the case of Habul too, there was just that one poisoned matchstick in the box. But such was the cruelty of fate that the first match he happened to strike was the poisoned one.

'Ajit, you are a writer. Don't you think there is a lesson to be learnt in all this? The day that man discovered the tools to kill another human being, he also brought into being a weapon that could boomerang upon him at any time. The sophisticated weaponry that is, in great secrecy, being produced all over the world today, might one day serve to destroy the entire human race. Like the demon who sprung into being from Brahma's imagination, like Frankenstein's monster, it won't even spare its creators. Don't you think so?'

The room was in darkness and I could hardly see Byomkesh. I felt as if his final words were not mere musings, but a prophecy of sorts.

An Encore for Byomkesh

Debkumarbabu's trial had come to an end at the High Court. It was early February. The severity of winter was subsiding gradually. At times a light breeze brought the reminder that spring was not far away, but the warm rays of the morning sun still seemed inviting enough.

That morning, I was sitting by the window and soaking up the sun while turning the pages of the newspaper. Byomkesh had left on some errand soon after breakfast. He had said he would be back by ten o'clock.

The newspaper contained a report of the final phase of Debkumarbabu's trial. I had no need to read about it because Byomkesh and I had been present in court through the entire proceedings. So I was turning the pages lazily and thinking about Debkumarbabu and his impossible obduracy. If he had been a little flexible, perhaps his conviction for murder could have been averted, since high politics did not always go by the penal code. But Debkumarbabu had decided not to reveal the formula of his invention, and there was no way to make him change his mind. An extensive investigation of the matchsticks, too, had failed to reveal the exact composition of the poisonous substance. So, the legal juggernaut had run its full course and brought the tragic matter to its conclusion.

I was still reflecting on the newspaper report when the telephone rang. I went and picked up the receiver. It was Inspector Birenbabu from the police station. His voice had an agitated edge to it. 'Is Byomkeshbabu at home?' he asked.

'He has just stepped out. Is it anything urgent?'

'Yes—when will he return?'

'At about ten o'clock.'

'All right then, I shall be there around ten. I have some bad news.'

Before I could ask him what the bad news was, he had hung

up. I went back to my seat. My watch said it was nine o'clock. Although I felt restless, I picked up the newspaper and tried to go through it again, waiting for the clock to strike ten.

But I did not have to wait that long. Byomkesh returned within the next half hour. When I told him about Birenbabu's call, he looked surprised and said, 'Really? I wonder what it is now.'

I shook my head in silence. Byomkesh summoned Putiram and directed him to make some tea. This was a prerequisite to greeting Birenbabu. He had such a fondness for the beverage that it brooked no consideration for time and place.

After ordering the tea, Byomkesh stretched out on a chair and took out his packet of cigarettes; he held one between his lips and, taking a matchbox out of his pocket, remarked, 'If Birenbabu says it is bad news, it must be something serious. Maybe—'

He stopped short. I looked up and found him gazing in astonishment at the matchbox he was holding. Putting down the unlit cigarette, he spoke slowly, 'This is very strange! How did this matchbox come to be in my pocket?'

'Which matchbox?'

Byomkesh held the box up for me. It looked no different from an ordinary matchbox. Seeing the mystified look on my face, Byomkesh said, 'Perhaps you can see that the label on the box shows a woodcutter with an axe on his shoulder, about to chop up a palm tree. But in our house . . .'

I butted in, 'I get it—we always buy the Horse brand.'

'Exactly. So, when I went out, I had a Horse brand matchbox in my pocket, naturally. But when I come back, the horse has turned into a woodcutter. The thing is, even in this age of scientific advancement and evolution, isn't this a bit much?' He raised his voice and called out, 'Putiram!'

Putiram came and stood before us.

'Which brand of matches did you buy this time?'

'The Horse brand, sir.'

'How many did you bring?'

'One dozen, sir.'

'Did you pick up the Woodcutter brand, by any chance?'

'No, sir.'

'All right, you may go.'

Putiram went back inside.

Byomkesh's brows drew close in a frown as he continued to ponder over the matchbox. After a while, he said, 'Now I remember—when I lit a cigarette in the tram, the man sitting next to me asked for the matches. He returned the box after lighting his own cigarette and I dropped it into my pocket without looking at it .... Ajit!'

'Yes?'

Byomkesh stood up and exclaimed, 'Ajit, that is the man who switched the matchboxes.' I noticed that his face had suddenly gone deathly pale.

I asked, 'Who was he? Do you remember what he looked like?'

Byomkesh shook his head and said, 'No, I didn't get a good look. As far as I remember, he wore a monkey-cap covering most of his face, and had dark glasses on.' Byomkesh paused for a few moments; then he looked at the clock and asked, 'What time did Birenbabu say he would be here?'

'At ten.'

'Then it is almost time. Ajit, do you know why Birenbabu is coming today?'

'No—do you?'

'I have a feeling—I suspect—'

At this moment we heard Birenbabu's heavy footsteps on the stairs and Byomkesh's sentence remained incomplete.

Birenbabu entered the room and gravely took a seat. Byomkesh handed him a cigarette and said, 'Please use your own matchbox to light it. When was Debkumarbabu's matchbox stolen?'

'Day before yesterday,' said Birenbabu without thinking. Then he looked up in amazement, saying, 'But how did you come to know? This is top secret—no one knows as yet.'

'The thief himself has chosen to notify me,' said Byomkesh. He told Birenbabu about the incident in the tram.

Birenbabu took it all in with great attentiveness. Then he looked at the matchbox and kept it aside warily, saying, 'This box holds one lethal matchstick. My God! Do you have any idea about who might be behind this?'

'No. But whoever it is, there is no doubt about one fact: he wants me dead.'

'But why? Why you in particular?'

I said, 'Perhaps he thinks that if Byomkesh is dead, it would be nearly impossible for anyone else to catch him; so he is trying to remove the obstacle from his path in advance.'

Byomkesh shook his head, 'I don't think so. There are many officers of the police force who are no less than me in intelligence and competence. Take Birenbabu for example. If the thief was trying to do away with his main adversary, he would have tried to kill Birenbabu and not me.'

Although the flattery was a bit extreme in nature, I noticed that Birenbabu was quite gratified. He said, 'No, oh no—but—what other reason could there be?'

Byomkesh looked thoughtful. He said, 'That is what I cannot figure out. If memory serves me right, I do not have any personal enemies.'

Birenbabu exclaimed, 'Now that's strange! You have been going after thieves, swindlers and miscreants for years, and you say you have no enemies? I thought it was our business to make enemies.'

Putiram brought the tea. Byomkesh handed a cup to Birenbabu and said with a laugh, 'That is true. But most of my enemies are no longer alive. Anyway, why don't you tell us how the matchbox came to be stolen?'

Birenbabu took a sip from his cup and said, 'It is difficult to tell exactly how it was stolen. As you are aware, the matchbox was an exhibit at Debkumarbabu's trial; so it had passed from police custody into the court's possession. The trial came to a close day before yesterday. Since then it is nowhere to be found.'

'And?'

'What else! A few peons and subordinate employees have been detained on suspicion. But that is as far as it goes. It has created quite a stir in important circles and the government is deeply concerned as well. Now you are our only hope.'

'What do I have to do?'

'There are orders from the government that the matchbox has to be retrieved at any cost, even if the thief cannot be caught. Apparently, international accord is at stake.'

'All right. But do you have permission from the authorities to invite me to take on the investigation?'

'I do. Let me tell you about this in detail—the moment the box disappeared, the case went into the hands of the CID. But these three days of their labour have yielded no fruits. Meanwhile, the government is sending out urgent messages three or four times a day. So, eventually, the chief decided to seek your help. He believes that if anyone can solve this mystery, it is you.'

Byomkesh stood up and walked around the room once. Then he said, 'Then there is no argument, of course. But I would like to speak to the Commissioner once.'

'You will be able to see him whenever you want to.'

'All right.' Byomkesh reflected for a few moments and then said, 'Not today, I shall go in to see him tomorrow. I need to do some thinking today.'

Birenbabu said, 'But—the sooner . . .'

'I understand that—but it wouldn't do to rush into this. We have to find an unknown man and we do not have any clue that can lead us to his identity. Wouldn't it be better to work out a strategy first?'

'Yes, I suppose you're right.'

'In the meantime, keep trying to get a confession out of the men you have already arrested. In case—'

Birenbabu gave a grave laugh, 'We have been trying to do just that for the past three days, to no avail. If you wish to take a shot at it, you are most welcome.'

Byomkesh replied gloomily, 'If the police haven't succeeded, I don't think I shall be of any use. Perhaps they are innocent. Well then, we shall stick to the plan and I shall meet the Commissioner tomorrow. We can take it from there. I have a vested interest here since the our dear Mr Thief has chosen me as his first target.'

Birenbabu took his leave. After he left, Byomkesh picked up

the matchbox and took it into the library. Then he knitted his brows and began to pace the floor with his hands clasped behind him.

When the clock struck eleven, Putiram came and reminded him to take his bath and have his lunch. But Byomkesh barely heard him. He muttered an absent-minded 'Hmm' and continued with his pacing around the room.

There was a knock at the door. It was the postman. He handed Byomkesh an envelope and said, 'Is this yours?'

Byomkesh looked at the address and said, 'Yes, it is. Why do you ask?'

The postman replied, 'Because another gentleman from the mess downstairs claims that it is for him.'

'Really! You mean to say that there is another Byomkesh Bakshi?'

'He said his name is Byomkesh Bose.'

Byomkesh took a good look at the envelope and said, 'Oh, well, he might be right. I can't quite make out the word that's scrawled after "Byomkesh". The stamp says it is from Bagbazar, which means it is a local letter. Who would address an envelope to me from within Calcutta? Anyway, the contents should reveal something. If it isn't mine—but I had no idea that there was another Byomkesh in the mess downstairs.'

The postman left. Byomkesh slit the envelope open with his letter-opener, glanced at the contents and passed it to me, saying, 'It's not for me. It's from one Kokanad Gupta—strange name—I don't remember ever coming across it before.'

The letter said:

Dear Byomkeshbabu,

My respectful greetings to you. It has been some time since I last met you, and yet I can never forget you. I am eager to meet you again. Would you recognize me? Who knows, after such a long time, you may not even be able place this humble admirer of yours.

I am eternally in your debt. What I am today is entirely due to you. Since I have had to stay away for a long time, I have not been able to repay even a fragment of your debt. But now that I have returned, I intend to do my best.

Please know that you are always in my thoughts.

Yours truly,

Kokanad Gupta.

After reading the entire letter I said, 'We should not have read this note. Although it does not contain anything of a personal nature, yet there is a lot of genuine fondness expressed here that outsiders should not be privy to.'

Byomkesh said, 'I fully agree with you. Reading this letter makes one feel embarrassed, as if one has read a lover's note by stealth. But I didn't have a choice! I had to make sure that the letter wasn't for me. And it certainly isn't. I do not know anyone named Kokanad Gupta, and even if I did, I cannot recall having done him a huge favour.'

'In that case we should return the letter to its rightful owner.'

'Yes. Let me call Putiram.'

But before Putiram could appear, the rightful begetter of the letter arrived in person. We had a nodding acquaintance with nearly all the inmates of the boarding-house below us, but we had never encountered this gentleman before. The man was short and slender, perhaps in his mid-forties—though his face did not give away his age. From his forehead to his neck, his face had burnt and the skin stretched in such a way that it was impossible to guess what he had looked like initially. At first glance it seemed almost as if he had donned a hideous mask. He had no facial hair; even his eyelashes were gone. The still, unblinking stare in his eyes was somewhat unnerving.

The man's appearance had us both transfixed. His voice, which was quite normal, brought us back to reality. He stood at the door and said, with some hesitation, 'My name is Byomkesh Bose. A letter . . .'

Byomkesh hastened to say, 'Do come in. I was about to send the letter down to you. It was nice of you to come by. Please take a seat. I hope you won't take offence, but I opened it, thinking it was mine. Here it is.'

The gentleman took the letter and perused it slowly. Then he said, 'Kokanad Gupta! But I don't think . . .' He looked at Byomkesh and asked, 'It is not yours? I presume you have read the letter?'

A little embarrassed, Byomkesh said, 'I have—thinking it was for me. But from the contents I don't think it's mine. I mistook the word "Bose" on the envelope for "Bakshi". I suppose you know that my name is Byomkesh Bakshi?'

'Of course I do. You are the pride and joy of our mess. I heard about you as soon as I came here. But I cannot say whether the letter is for me or not. The name Kokanad Gupta sounds familiar, but . . . anyway, if you say it isn't yours, then it must be mine.'

Byomkesh laughed and said, 'It befits a truly benevolent soul to forget a good deed after he has done it.'

'No, no, it's not that—it has been a long time and I don't quite seem to recall what it's all about. Perhaps it will come back to me later. All right then, goodbye.' He rose to leave.

Byomkesh asked, 'How long is it since you have come to stay here?'

'Not very long. About a week or so.'

'Oh.' Byomkesh laughed, 'Well, at least I have found a namesake at last. All right then, see you later. But do drop in for a chat sometimes.'

The gentleman nodded agreeably and left. Byomkesh took one glance at his watch and began to unbutton his shirt, saying, 'It is rather late now. Let us bathe and have lunch. Then we can concentrate on the matchbox mystery in peace. There is a lot to think about. We have to conjure up a criminal out of thin air. Tell me, do you feel we have met this second Byomkeshbabu somewhere before?'

I replied confidently, 'No. I have never seen that face before. Have you?'

Byomkesh pondered for a moment and said, 'Well, perhaps not. But that gait seemed familiar; I seem to remember it from somewhere. Not recently, but long ago. Anyway, no more nonsense now.' He began to massage oil into his hair as he proceeded towards the bathroom.

I had always observed that when Byomkesh got some food for thought, he went into an inert trance. At such times it became impossible to have a conversation with him. Either my words would fall on deaf ears or he would lose his temper and snap at me irritably. But this particular afternoon when he sat in the living room after lunch and burnt several cigarettes to ashes, I could make out that something was getting in the way of his single-minded deliberation. For some reason he was unable to focus his energies on the case at hand. Finally, when he got up and started pacing from room to room restlessly, I asked him, 'What is the matter with you today? Why are you fidgeting?'

Abashed, Byomkesh dropped into a chair and said, 'I don't know why, but I simply cannot concentrate today; all I can think of is a lot of nonsensical . . .'

I said, 'When there is a serious matter at hand, you shouldn't let any nonsense get in the way.'

A little irritably, he retorted, 'Do you think I am doing this on purpose? That letter this morning . . .'

'Which letter?'

'Oh you know, the Kokanad Gupta one. That is all that I can think of.'

Astonished, I said, 'But what is there in that letter for you to—'

'Nothing. And yet I feel, what if that letter was really meant for me—if—'

'I don't understand. You don't know the author of the letter. Another gentleman has already claimed the letter as his. Then how could it be meant for you?'

'That is true. But can you recollect the contents of the letter?'

'It had nothing but a bunch of sentences dripping with gratitude. Why are you letting it distract you from the case?'

'You are right,' Byomkesh got to his feet. 'Indulging the brain in these meaningless reflections can become habit-forming. No—from now on, I shall think only of the matchbox and nothing else. I am in the library—when the tea is ready, just call me.' He went into the room and shut the door firmly, as if determined to keep the pointless thoughts out.

The evening passed into night, but Byomkesh was far from being at peace with his restless mind. It was clear that he had still not been able to decide on a course of action.

It was well past midnight. I was deep in slumber, tucked inside a warm blanket, when Byomkesh's insistent poking woke me. I asked, 'What is it?'

He said, 'Listen, I have a plan.'

I pulled the blanket over my head and said, 'A plan! At this time of night!'

Byomkesh said, 'Yes, listen. The man who has stolen the matchbox is the same as the one who is trying to kill me, right? Now just think, if I were to really . . .'

I dozed off.

In the morning, at the breakfast table, I asked, 'What is it you were saying last night—I didn't get to hear all of it.'

Byomkesh kept his eyes on the newspaper and said, with a sour expression, 'Of course you didn't. How would you? I tell you I am about to die and you snore away to glory. That's what real friends are for!'

I flinched, 'You're about to what! What are you saying?'

'I am saying that I shall die very soon. But before that I need to meet the Commissioner once.' He looked at his watch and said, 'It is a quarter past eight now. Nine o'clock should be fine.'

'I cannot figure out a word of what you are saying.'

Byomkesh gave me an amiable smile and went back to the newspaper. I realized that what he had blabbered out the night before was not going to come out of him easily again. I was sure he had cooked up an extraordinary strategy and I couldn't wait to hear what it was. I cursed myself for falling asleep in the middle of his revelation.

Some five minutes passed in absolute silence. I was beginning to wonder whether I could get Byomkesh to spell his plan out by making some stupid comment, when suddenly he looked up from the newspaper and asked me, 'Would you be interested in buying a box of matches for one lakh rupees?'

'What kind of a question is that?'

'A gentleman has made the offer. Here—have a look.'

Byomkesh passed me the newspaper. I saw the advertisement at the centre of the second page, bracketed for prominence:

For sale, a box of matches. Price one lakh rupees. Contains twenty matchsticks. Price for each five thousand rupees. Will also sell separately. Interested buyers should advertise in the newspapers. This priceless commodity will stay in the market for only a week, after which it will be exported. So hurry!

All the while that I was reading this strange insert, Byomkesh was getting dressed to go out. When I looked up at him with a bemused expression, he said, 'Very clever. First he steals the matchbox and then he wants to sell it right back to the government. If the government refuses, he has threatened to find buyers in Japan or Italy. Come on.'

'Where?'

'Let us take a shot at the newspaper office, in case something turns up—though the chances are slim.'

I got dressed hastily and went out with him.

It wasn't long before we got to meet the editor-in-chief at the office of the Daily Kalketu. When he heard Byomkesh's request he said, 'The classifieds are not really in my department, but I happen to know about this one. The envelope came by registered post, and I received it. I remember it because it was the strangest advertisement I have ever come across.'

Byomkesh asked, 'So you didn't happen to see the advertiser?'

'No. As I told you, it came by post. The envelope contained twenty rupees in cash and the draft for the classified. There was no name of the sender. I was really amazed, but it was the middle of a busy day, so I handed it to the manager of the classifieds section and then forgot all about it. But what is the matter? Seems to me as if—matchbox and all—is it something serious?'

Byomkesh laughed out loud and replied, 'Not serious enough to hit the headlines as yet. Tell me, do you have no information at all about the sender? An address?'

The editor shook his head, 'The envelope had nothing but

the money and the draft.'

'You said it was a registered letter. So the sender's name and address must have been mentioned on the envelope?'

Surprised, the editor replied, 'I suppose so, but I don't think I noticed. But it should have been on it. As far as I know, the post office doesn't accept registered letters without the sender's name and address.'

There was a huge waste-paper basket next to the desk and the editor dug into it and began to rummage through a heap of crumpled papers. Then he straightened up with a victorious smile and said, 'I've got it—here you are!'

It was an ordinary registered letter with the sender's name and address on one corner. It read:

B.K. Sinha
18/1, Sitaram Ghose Street
Calcutta.

Byomkesh jotted the address down and said, 'I see it is in our neighbourhood. We shall take our leave now—there is no sense in wasting your precious time unnecessarily. Thank you very much.'

The editor said, 'There is no need to thank me. Just see to it that we get a tip-off if there is some sensational news. I suppose you know that we were the first ones to print the news of Debkumarbabu's case.'

'Oh yes, certainly.' We left the office and headed straight for Sitaram Ghose Street. The house numbered 18/1 was a small two-storeyed affair. Some quilts and sheets were drying out on the railings; the murmur of young children memorizing their lessons could be heard from inside.

Byomkesh said, 'Wrong address. Anyway, since we have come, let us check it out.'

After some knocking and shouting a domestic came out of the house, 'Who would you be looking for, sir?'

'Is the master at home?'

'No.'

'Who lives here?'

'The Inspector of Police.'

'Inspector? What is his name?'

'Birenbabu.'

Byomkesh stared at him, open-mouthed, for a while. Then he guffawed and said, 'Oh, I get it. When your master returns, tell him Byomkeshbabu was here to pay his respects.' He continued to chuckle as we walked away.

I said, 'You seem to be quite delighted.'

'What else can I be!' said Byomkesh. 'This man has such a tremendous sense of humour that he cracks jokes even at the government's expense. If such a man wishes to play a prank on me, it would be rude not to play along. You go on home, I have some work to do. I shall discuss everything with you when I return.'

We had arrived at Harrison Road. Byomkesh jumped onto a passing tram.

That afternoon Byomkesh deigned to reveal his strategy to me. The plan did not inspire any hopes in me. It was like dropping a line into an unknown lake, in the hope that some fish may take the bait. When I said as much, Byomkesh said, 'Well, of course, it is surely a shot in the dark and there is no guarantee of success. If it doesn't work, we shall have to think of something else.'

I asked, 'Has the Commissioner agreed to this?'

'Oh yes.'

'Is there anything I can do?'

'Just keep this to yourself, that's all. I'm going to leave right now. If I am to die, I should hurry up and have it done with. After all, how long can one matchbox last? If you wish, you may go to Srirampore tomorrow to take a look at the unidentified corpse.'

'In the meantime if someone comes looking for you, what should I say?'

'Tell them that I have left the city on a secret mission and you do not know when I shall return.'

'Birenbabu may drop by in the evening. Should he be given the same story?'

Byomkesh knitted his brows and remained in thought for a few moments and then said, 'Yes, tell him the same thing. You mustn't reveal the plan to anyone at all.'

'Fine.' I was a little surprised. Birenbabu was part of the police and also the officer in charge of this case. Why should he be kept in the dark?

As if he sensed my unspoken doubt, Byomkesh said, 'There is no particular reason for not telling Birenbabu, except an ordinary precaution. At present nobody knows about this plan except you, the Commissioner and me. Of course, tomorrow some more people will come to know of it. But for as long as possible, it should be kept completely under wraps. The learned Chanakya says that the key to successful politics lies in the secrecy of the scheme. So you are to keep your lips firmly sealed.'

About half an hour after Byomkesh left, Birenbabu called.

'Where is Byomkeshbabu?'

'He has gone out of Calcutta.'

'Where has he gone?'

'I don't know.'

'When will he return?'

'There is no certainty; it may be a while, maybe a few days.'

'A few days! Why were you people at my house this morning?'

I played dumb and said, 'I don't know.'

At the other end of the line, Birenbabu made some disapproving noises, 'Looks like you know nothing. Do you at least know which assignment has taken Byomkeshbabu out of Calcutta?'

'No.'

Birenbabu slammed the phone down.

It was four o'clock. I ordered Putiram to make some tea and was just wondering what I could do next, when there was a soft knock on the door. I got up, opened the door and found our scalded friend of the previous day. He was carrying a newspaper.

He said, 'Byomkeshbabu isn't in?'

'No. But do come in.'

There was no purpose to the visit. He had just dropped by to honour the invitation extended the other day. I too was at a loss as to how I would spend the evening. So I was delighted to have Mr Bose's company. He took a seat and said, 'There was a very strange classified in today's paper, I thought it might interest you. Perhaps it hasn't caught your attention.' He opened the newspaper and handed it to me, saying, 'Have you seen it?'

It was the same advertisement! I was in a quandary. I was a very bad liar and invariably got caught out. Yet Byomkesh had quoted Chanakya to me and ordained me to keep my lips sealed. I was struggling to find a solution to my dilemma when Mr Bose smiled and said, 'You *have* read it, but Byomkeshbabu has forbidden you to reveal anything, is that it?'

I remained silent.

Byomkesh Bose went on, 'Lately matchsticks have been much in the news. Just the other day Debkumarbabu's trial came to an end, that too was about matchsticks; and again there is this classified selling matchsticks—the price is one lakh rupees for a box! Naturally one begins to wonder if there is a connection between the two.' He looked at me inquiringly. I still held my tongue.

He said, 'Anyway, let that be. You are going to suspect me of trying to get your secrets out in the open.' He changed the subject and I heaved a sigh of relief.

Putiram brought in the tea. The discussion shifted to cricket, politics, literature and various other topics. I found Mr Bose to be quite genial and sociable. He was also very knowledgeable.

At one point I asked, 'So what is it that you do exactly? I hope you do not mind my asking.'

He remained quiet for a few moments and then said, 'I work for the government.'

'A government job?'

'Yes, but the job doesn't really involve regular working hours; it is a peculiar kind of job.'

'Oh—so what do you have to do?' I knew I was crossing the bounds of decency, but my curiosity urged me on.

Very slowly he replied, 'In order to maintain law and order

in the country, the government needs to conduct some of its activities in private, to gather a lot of information and keep an eye on some of its subjects. My job involves that sort of activity.'

In hushed wonderment I asked, 'You're a CID officer?'

He smiled, 'There can be policing over the police as well. This home of yours is very peaceful; it is a boarding-house without the hassles of one. How long is it since you have been here?'

Since he had deftly changed the subject, I couldn't proceed any further. I replied, 'I have been here for the last eight years. Byomkesh has been here longer than that.'

We spoke of this and that for some more time. When I inquired about how his face came to be disfigured, he replied that an acid bottle had slipped from his hands and spilled its contents on his face while he was working in a laboratory some years ago.

Eventually, he rose to leave. On his way out, he suddenly turned around and asked, 'I believe you are acquainted with Inspector Biren Sinha. Can you tell me what sort of a person he is?'

'What kind of person? We know him through our work. I have no idea about him personally.'

'Would you say he is a greedy person?'

'Please forgive me Byomkeshbabu, but I really don't have much to say about him.'

'Oh, I see. All right then, see you later.'

He left. But his words continued to play on my mind. Why was this man interested in Birenbabu's character? Was Birenbabu greedy? In general, police officers were supposed to be susceptible to the lure of Mammon. But I had never heard even a whisper about Birenbabu's integrity. What was the significance of this question then? And why did this secret agent of the government ask me about him? Suddenly I remembered that Byomkesh had forbidden me to reveal the plan about his disappearance to Birenbabu too.

The next morning I scanned the newspaper as soon as I woke up. The news that I was looking for was prominently displayed at the very beginning of the classifieds section:

> Last evening at about five-thirty, an unidentified corpse was discovered in the waiting room of the Srirampore railway station. There were no wounds on the body. The cause of death is still unknown. The deceased is about thirty years old, good looking and clean-shaven. He was wearing a brown kurta and a white shawl. The young man had arrived from Calcutta by the 4:53 local train; the ticket was found in his pocket. If anyone can identify the body, please contact the Srirampore hospital authorities.

Hastily I washed up, had a quick breakfast and headed out. On the first floor landing, I heard someone call me from behind, 'Ajitbabu, where are you off to so early in the morning?'

I turned and saw that Byomkesh Bose was standing at the entrance to his room. Today the lies rolled off my tongue quite smoothly. 'I am going to Diamond Harbour, to a friend's place. There is no telling when Byomkesh will be back—so I thought I'll make a short trip.'

'That's nice. Have you read the newspaper this morning?'

I had the *Daily Kalketu* in my hands. I said, 'No, not yet. I shall read it in the train,' and was on my way.

I walked the short distance to Sealdah station, which was the departure point for the Diamond Harbour train. I then took a tram to Howrah station, from where the train bound for Srirampore would leave. When one is a novice at lying, the tension of getting caught is always alive in one's mind. But the more one practises the art of lying, the more adept one gets at it. Anyway, I boarded the train from Howrah and reached Srirampore at about nine-thirty.

A gentleman was standing guard in front of the hospital. When I asked him about the unidentified body, he gave me the once-over and then indicated a tiny hut at the far end. The room was outside the main hospital building and was guarded by a policeman.

I approached the small enclosure of wire and glass and expressed my intentions; it wasn't too difficult to gain entry. I found Byomkesh lying upon a concrete platform. His body was covered with a sheet from neck downwards. His face was still in a deathly repose.

I stood beside him and murmured softly, 'Awake, Sleeping Beauty.'

He opened his eyes.

'How long have you been holding this pose?'

'Nearly two hours now. I would really appreciate a cigarette.'

'Impossible. A funeral I could get you, but cigarettes are an absolute no-no for the dead.'

'Are you sure? Aren't there any sanctions in the ancient laws?'

'No. So how many people have come to see you so far?'

'Just three. Locals, all of them—the "nothing better to do" types.'

'So what now?'

'There is no reason to give up yet. We have the whole of today and part of the morning tomorrow as well.'

'For two whole days you'll lie here like this? Suppose "he" doesn't even notice the advertisement?'

'He is bound to notice it. He is scanning the newspapers carefully nowadays.'

'That is true! Anyway, tell me what I am to do now.'

'You are to stay hidden somewhere close to this room and observe those who are coming to look at me. The police is also on duty. Whoever is coming to take a look at this unfortunate soul, is walking out with a spy tailing him. But the more the merrier. If you can spot any known faces, come and alert me at once. My problem is that I am not allowed to open my eyes and so I do not have the honour of catching sight of the people who are coming here. If the corpse were to take little peeks, it would cause a furore indeed.'

'All right, I shall stay close at hand. But the police wouldn't cause any trouble, would they?'

'Just inform the guard at the door about your identity and there'll be no trouble. The guard is not what he seems; he's dressed like a police constable, but actually he is a CID officer.'

I stepped outside and disclosed my identity to the constable in disguise. He pointed to a shrub at a distance. This shrub was situated in such a way that if I hid behind it, I would be able to see the doorway to the enclosure quite clearly and yet no one would know that I was there.

I went and took up my position behind the bush. Although I was enclosed from all sides, there was nothing overhead. Relaxed, I began sunning myself and lit a cigarette. Gradually, as the day wore on, the number of interested visitors began to grow. I inspected them enthusiastically. All of them were strangers; from their demeanour it was quite clear that they were treating this as a novel diversion. It was almost eleven. The sun overhead had grown a little hotter. I pulled the shawl over my head as I sat there.

Gradually a feeling of despondency was creeping in on me. Why would a man who had stolen the matchbox come to identify an unclaimed body in Srirampore? And even if he did, how would we spot him from amongst so many strangers? It was true that the police would pursue each and every visitor, but what good would that do? I felt Byomkesh had set a wild-goose chase in motion.

I was lost in these thoughts though my eyes were on Byomkesh's hut. Suddenly I was brought back to reality with a jolt. A man had entered the room with hurried footsteps; he rushed out again in a matter of seconds, nodded once at a question from the guard, and hurried away.

The man was Byomkesh Bose from our downstairs mess. I was so stunned on seeing him that for a few seconds after he left, I remained rooted to the spot. Then I charged into the hut in excitement.

Perhaps on hearing my approaching footsteps, Byomkesh had gone back to his deathlike stance. I went close to him and blurted out excitedly, 'Hey, guess who was here just now? Your namesake—the new Byomkeshbabu from the mess.'

Byomkesh catapulted into a sitting position and looked at me in wide-eyed amazement, 'Are you sure? Absolutely beyond a doubt?'

'Absolutely.'

'Come on then—he can't have got far.'

Byomkesh had his clothes on, but he was barefoot. He ran out as he was.

The man who I had seen in front on the hospital was still there.

Byomkesh asked him, 'Where is he, the man who was just here?'

The gentleman looked extremely distraught as he said, 'Was that the man?'

'Yes—he is the one who has to be arrested.'

The gentleman was aghast, 'He has escaped.'

'Escaped!'

'He came in a taxi from Calcutta and went back in it. We did not arrange for motorcycles and so—'

Byomkesh gnashed his teeth and said, 'You will have to answer for this. Come on Ajit, if we can get hold of a taxi—perhaps even now . . .'

But there were no taxis around. So we had to take a bus bound for Calcutta. On the way I asked, 'So that was the man?'

Byomkesh nodded, 'Hmm.'

'But how did you work it out?'

'That's a long story. I shall tell you later.'

'Tell me, why did he run away in such a hurry? If you are already dead . . .'

'He is a predatory hound. He sensed the trap as soon as he stepped into the room. So he rushed out immediately.'

When we reached the mess at half past noon, we found the manager standing at the foot of the stairs. Byomkesh asked him, 'Did Byomkeshbabu come here?'

The manager stared at Byomkesh's bare feet incredulously and said, 'The second Byomkeshbabu? He left a while ago. There was an urgent message from his home and so he had to leave in a hurry. He too was looking for you. He asked me to convey his greetings to you and to tell you that you need not feel disappointed, for you will meet him again soon.'

Byomkesh managed to withstand this mammoth jolt of civility and asked, 'Which is his room?'

'Room number five.'

The door was locked; Byomkesh asked, 'Where is the key?'

The manager said, 'I have the duplicate with me, but—'

'Open it.'

As he fished out a bunch of keys from his pocket, the manager asked anxiously, 'What . . . what is the matter, Byomkeshbabu?'

'Nothing much—the man who was in this room happens to be a branded criminal.'

The manager opened the door quickly and stood aside.

Upon entering the room, Byomkesh threw a quick glance all around and said, 'It looks as if he hasn't taken anything with him; his boxes and belongings are still in place.'

The manager said, 'He has just taken a small bag and a flask. Everything else is still here. He said he would be back in a couple of days and so I thought . . .'

Byomkesh said, 'Right. Now, could you please send word to the police inspector, Birenbabu—tell him that the thief has been found and he should come immediately. In the meantime we shall take a look around this room.'

After the manager left, Byomkesh began to inspect the furniture in the room. Nearly all the rooms in this boarding-house were quite large—two or three people shared each one. But this was a smaller room, designed for a single occupant. The rent was also higher than the norm. As a result, the room stayed empty most of the time. It was ideal for someone who wished to live in a mess and yet maintain his privacy.

There was nothing in the room except for a couple of trunks and bedding. Byomkesh scrutinized the bed and remarked, 'It is winter and yet he hasn't taken either the blanket or the pillow with him. Do you know what that means?'

'No. What does it mean?'

'He must have another set waiting elsewhere.'

Byomkesh turned the bed upside down, but it yielded nothing.

I asked, 'Are you expecting to find the matchbox here? You think he would leave it behind in his room?'

'No—he wouldn't have come back then. I am looking for

his present address—something that will indicate his real name and address. I suppose even you have figured out by now that his real name isn't Byomkesh Bose?'

'Er ... I mean ... yes, of course I have. But what is the reason for adopting that particular alias?'

Byomkesh flopped down upon the bed and began to look around him as he said, 'The reason is revenge. Ajit, the psychology of revenge is very strange. Since you are a writer, you know a lot about human psychology. So you probably know that revenge accomplished from behind the scenes brings no joy to the avenger; with each and every blow he wants to announce that he is having his revenge. If the enemy fails to discern the source of the blow, half the fun of revenge is gone. That is why this gentleman had to announce his presence to me. If this had been the stone age instead of the civilized twentieth century, such dissimilation would not have been necessary—he could have simply come and bludgeoned me with a rock. But in this day and age that doesn't work—it can earn him the death penalty. But, though the mode of revenge may have changed, the mindset remains the same. It was this emotion that had made him rush to Srirampore for a glimpse of my dead visage.' Byomkesh gave a whimsical laugh, 'Do you remember the letter? It *was* meant for me—he had written it himself. Behind the words dripping with gratitude was a simple message. He made it as clear as possible that he had not forgotten anything and was eager to repay my debt. We, of course, misread the letter—but I had a doubt. Perhaps you remember.'

I saw the words in the letter in a new light. I said, 'I do remember. But who knew then that ... tell me, the man is an old enemy of yours, right?'

'There is no doubt about that.'

'But you cannot figure out who he is?'

'Perhaps I can. But let that be for now—let's take a look at his boxes.'

One of the trunks was unlocked. Byomkesh fiddled around with the lock of the other one and it came apart. There were some warm jackets and kurtas in there. When we took them out, we found some spirit gum and some plaited faux hair at the bottom of the trunk. Byomkesh held them up and said, 'Hmm. Someone whose face has been disfigured by acid, will naturally need to don some disguises at times. Perhaps he had changed his appearance when he switched my matchbox in the tram.'

He kept these aside and dug into the box again, saying, 'But what's this?'

It was a bundle wrapped in a fabric which felt like oil-cloth.

Carefully, Byomkesh put it down on the floor and unwrapped it. An empty bottle of about half an ounce, some broken pieces of red sealing wax and a half-burnt candle were revealed.

Byomkesh opened the bottle and took a sniff, inspected the sealing wax and the candle and, finally, picked up the oil-cloth and began to scrutinize it. I noticed that it wasn't an ordinary oil-cloth. It was a waterproof material of very high quality—a little bluish and translucent—about the size of a handkerchief. At present a quarter of the sheet was missing from one corner—it appeared as if it had been torn off.

Byomkesh said with great deliberation, 'Bottle, sealing wax, candle and waterproof: all in one place. Have you deduced the implication of all this?'

'No. What is it?'

'Didn't you get a clue from the waterproof?'

In sheer despair I replied, 'Nothing. What have you deduced from it?'

'Everything, except the man's present address. Come on, we are done here.'

At this moment the manager returned and said, 'I have notified the inspector, he will be here any moment.'

'Fine. Well, sir, when this namesake of mine left, I am sure you had gone upto the entrance with him?'

'Yes, yes, I did.'

'Did you happen to notice the number of the taxi?'

The manager shook his head and said, 'No. All I noticed was that it was a blue taxi, quite old, and that the driver was a Sikh.'

Byomkesh was silent for a few moments and then he asked, 'Was anyone else at the door at the time?'

The manager thought for a while and then said, 'I don't remember any of the gentlemen being there. But Putiram, your domestic, was sitting in the yard. Since you weren't at home, perhaps he was taking a short—'

Byomkesh sighed and said, 'Putiram's presence or absence doesn't make a difference. He doesn't know English and so even if he did notice the number-plate of the taxi, he wouldn't have been able to read it. Come on then Ajit, it is nearly half past one and my stomach is making strange sounds. Sir, would you be able to fix us up with a meal today—if it's not very inconvenient for you.'

The manager said, 'Certainly—it is no trouble at all. Byomkeshbabu's—I mean the second one's—share of the lunch is still there. You two go and have a shower and I shall send the food upstairs.'

Byomkesh gave a laugh and said, 'Beautiful—the second Byomkeshbabu's lunch will now be eaten by the first Byomkeshbabu. That's the way of the world, isn't it, Ajit? I only wish I knew where the second Byomkesh is now and whose lunch he is having.'

We were still eating when Birenbabu arrived. We gulped down the last few mouthfuls and entered the living room. Birenbabu stood up and raised questioning eyes at Byomkesh.

Byomkesh said, 'I see that you haven't had lunch yet.'

'No. I was on my way home for lunch when I got your message. What's the matter Byomkeshbabu—have you nabbed him?'

'Later. First let me get you something to eat.'

'I don't want anything to eat. But a cup of tea—'

Byomkesh laughed and said, 'Of course; but also a couple of eggs, I think. Putiram!'

After Putiram took the order and left, Byomkesh reported everything to Birenbabu in detail. He was a little hurt that so much had been done without his knowledge. Byomkesh did his best to comfort him in the gentlest of terms; still he remarked a trifle petulantly, 'If I had known about all this, he would not have slipped through our hands so easily. Now it will be difficult to catch him. Perhaps he has already got away from Calcutta.'

Byomkesh stared at the floor as he said, 'No—I have a feeling that he is right here in this city. He is a marked man. With that face it would be difficult to go very far. The city of Calcutta is the safest hideout for him.'

Birenbabu said, 'So what is the plan of action now? I can only think of issuing notices with a description.'

Byomkesh continued to ruminate as he replied, 'That option is always open. But before that—if we could only get the number of the taxi . . .'

Putiram had arrived with the tea and was setting it out before Birenbabu. Byomkesh looked at him and said, 'Putiram, you need to learn English. I shall buy you a copy of the first book and Ajit will start teaching you from this very day.'

At this irrelevant digression, Birenbabu looked up at Byomkesh in surprise. Byomkesh said, 'If Putiram had known English, there would be no problem.' He explained what had happened and shook his head gloomily.

Putiram raised his fist to his mouth and coughed delicately. 'We—ll, sir . . .' he said.

'What is it?'

'Sir, I saw the number of the taski.'

'I know you did—but the problem is that you couldn't read it.'

'But sir, I did. Two fours with two zeros in between.'

The three of us stared at him in amazement. Finally Byomkesh said, 'You mean to say you can read English?'

'No sir.'

'Then how?'

'It was written in Bangla, sir—that's why I saw it.'

We continued to stare at him, wide-eyed. Suddenly Byomkesh guffawed loudly and said, 'I get it.' He patted Putiram on the back and said, 'Well done! Putiram, from this day your salary goes up by one rupee.'

Both delighted and abashed, Putiram said, 'You know sir, I was sitting in the yard when I saw the taski's number was in

Bangla. It was funny. That's why I remember it, sir.'

Birenbabu spoke up, 'But how is this possible? How did a taxi come to have a number-plate in Bangla?'

Byomkesh laughed and said, 'It was in English, not in Bangla. But by a stroke of luck it happened to make sense in Bangla too. Don't you understand? Actually the number was 8008, but Putiram read it as two zeros flanked by two fours, since the numeral four in Bangla looks the same as the numeral eight in English.'

'O—h,' Birenbabu's mouth and eyes remained rounded in an O shape for a few seconds.

Byomkesh said, 'In that case, let us get to work. Birenbabu, this is right up your alley. It's a blue taxi with a Sikh driver and the number is 8008—shouldn't be too difficult to locate. Why don't you start working on it—the sooner we get the information, the better.'

'I am on my way.' Birenbabu stood up and gulped down the remainder of the tea, saying, 'I am sure I shall have the information for you before evening.'

'Not just the information, but please round up the car, the driver and all. Meanwhile I shall inform the Commissioner of the events. He must be quite anxious.'

On his way out, Birenbabu asked, 'Would you be able to tell me anything about the criminal's name or previous identity?'

'I do not know yet if my guess is absolutely accurate, but . . .' Byomkesh scribbled a number on a piece of paper and handed it to him, saying, 'Perhaps if you looked up the record of this prisoner at Alipore Jail, it may tell you something.'

Birenbabu said, 'So the man has a criminal record?'

'Oh yes. Yesterday I had looked him up and got hold of the number, but I didn't have the time to read up his history. Since you are a government official, you will be able to do this much more easily, right?'

'Certainly.'

Birenbabu carefully folded the paper, put it in his pocket and left.

That evening, as we waited for Birenbabu to turn up,

Byomkesh was cleaning his revolver with a rag dipped in oil.

I said, 'Birenbabu is still not here.'

'He'll be here any minute now.' Byomkesh glanced at the clock.

I asked, 'Well, Byomkesh, what is the man's real name? I am sure you know it by now.'

'As I have told you, I cannot be certain.'

'But you must have surmised something?'

'Well, yes, that I have.'

'Who is he? I know him, right?'

'Not only do you know him, but he is an old friend of yours.'

'How is that possible?'

Byomkesh remained silent for a few minutes and then replied, 'I suppose you remember the name Kokanad Gupta from the letter. Doesn't that ring a bell for you?'

'How can it? Kokanad Gupta is an alias.'

'Which is precisely why it should reveal something to you. A person's real name usually has little to do with who he actually is; quite often the beggar is named Dhaniram. Just like your name, Ajit, or mine, Byomkesh, doesn't hold any clue as to who or what we are. But when a person assumes an alias, there is some purpose behind the name he chooses. Doesn't the word Kokanad remind you of something?'

I mulled over it and said, 'I don't know. Kokanad—that means "lotus", right?'

'Hmm. Anything else? Any phonetic correspondences?'

I thought it over and said, feeling a little foolish, 'The only thing that comes to mind is cocaine.'

Byomkesh laughed and said, 'And the resemblance between Kokanad and cocaine is stretching the limits of poetic licence, right? And so you are loath to consider it, but . . . Oh, here comes Birenbabu. And he has someone with him. Ajit, could you please switch on the lights, it is dark already.'

Birenbabu came in; accompanying him was a gigantic Sikh. He had an abundance of beard and moustache—a knot held much of it in place. His hair was braided.

Without further ado, Byomkesh began to interrogate the Sikh. He said that he clearly remembered his passenger of the morning. The man had boarded his taxi at about ten-thirty to go to Srirampore, where he had the car parked at a distance from the hospital and entered the building. He had returned soon enough and requested a return trip to Calcutta in great haste. On returning to the city the man had come to this house and, after picking up a few belongings, had got into the taxi again. He had gone to a place in Bowbazar, where he had finally left the taxi. He had tipped the driver two rupees over the required fare and so the Sikh had arrived at the conclusion that his passenger was a noble man.

Byomkesh asked, 'What did he do after he got off finally?'

The Sikh said that as far as he remembered, the man had hailed a porter to carry his bag and flask and gone on his way; the driver wasn't exactly sure which way that was.

Byomkesh said, 'You have brought your car. Could you drive us to the spot where you dropped the gentleman off?'

The Sikh said he certainly could.

The two of us got dressed and came downstairs. A blue taxi stood before the house—indeed the number was 8008. We got into the taxi and the driver drove off.

Sitting in the dark interiors of the taxi, Birenbabu said, 'We looked up your prisoner. It *is* him, beyond a doubt. He was released from prison about six months ago.'

Byomkesh said, 'Good, so that is certain now. How did he burn his face?'

'Since he was an educated gentleman and a man of science, he was assigned some chores in the prison laboratory. A couple of years ago a bottle of nitric acid broke and spilled on his face. It was almost fatal, but he survived.'

Nothing more was said. About fifteen minutes later the car reached a neighbourhood which made me burst out in surprise, 'Byomkesh, what is this! Isn't this our previous—' Many old memories flooded my head. It was in a boarding-house in this very neighbourhood that I had first met Byomkesh.

Byomkesh said, 'Yes. I should have guessed much sooner.' He asked the driver, 'Is this where he got off?'

The driver replied, 'Yes.'

Byomkesh ruminated for a few moments and then said, 'All right, now take us back.'

Birenbabu said, 'What? Won't you go in?'

'There's no need. We now know where our quarry is hiding.'

'But then we should arrest him immediately.'

Byomkesh turned towards Birenbabu and said, 'Would it be enough to arrest him? Don't you want the matchbox?'

'No—well, yes—we want that too, certainly. But what do you suggest we do?'

'I would like to be sure about the matchbox before we arrest him. Come, let us go back home and I'll tell you what we have to do.'

At about eight o'clock that night, Byomkesh, Birenbabu and I took up our positions, hidden inside a rented car parked in front of a dark alley. There was a garage at that spot, so our car was not likely to attract any attention.

We were nearly fifty yards away from our old mess. The house had not changed one bit in all these years—it was exactly the same. But there was no boarding-house on the first floor any longer. All the windows on that floor were unlit.

After waiting there for twenty minutes or so, I said, 'We may be laying siege, but what if he chooses not to appear tonight?'

Byomkesh replied, 'Of course he will. He would have to eat, wouldn't he?'

Another twenty minutes went by. Byomkesh had his eyes glued to the car window. Suddenly he exclaimed in a hushed tone, 'Now! He is leaving.' We peered out and saw a man coming out of the house, wrapped up in a shawl. He looked swiftly up and down the alley and then disappeared into the darkness.

The road was nearly deserted. After the man had vanished, we left the car and walked up to the house. The front door was locked. Byomkesh murmured, 'Come this way.'

The side entrance which led to the stairs was open; we entered through that door. A narrow corridor here connected the rooms downstairs to the stairs leading up. The door to the first room was locked. Byomkesh fished out a torch from his pocket and took a good look at this door. From long disuse, it was termite-ravaged and breakable. The lock cracked open under Byomkesh's hard grip. We entered the room.

Byomkesh shut the broken door and cast the torch-light around the room. The room hadn't been used in a long while; there was a thick layer of dust on the floor and cobwebs on the walls. Byomkesh said, 'Not this one; come this way.'

One of the doors in the room led inwards and we entered another room through there. This room was very familiar to us; it used to be the sitting room. We had passed several hours in conversation here. The light from the torch revealed that the room had been cleaned recently and a bed was fixed in one corner. In the centre of the room there was a desk and a chair. Byomkesh played the torch around and carefully looked the room over. Then he said, 'Yes, it is this one. Birenbabu, come—let us wait in the dark for the master of the house to return.'

Birenbabu whispered, 'Shouldn't we get the matchbox now?'

'Don't worry about that. Do you have the revolver and the handcuffs in your pocket?'

'Yes, I do.'

'Fine. Just remember that the man is not very submissive by nature.'

Birenbabu and I sat on the bed and Byomkesh took the chair. We began to wait silently in the dark.

We didn't have to wait very long. Scarcely half an hour had passed before we heard a click at the front door. We sat up straight and held our breath.

Soft footsteps advanced gradually and then suddenly, the lights in the room came on.

Byomkesh said cordially, 'Please do us the honour of joining us, Anukulbabu. Since we are old friends of yours, we have taken the liberty of coming in without your permission. I hope you don't mind.'

Anukulbabu—alias the second Byomkesh—stood with his

finger still on the light switch. For a while he remained silent. His lash-less eyes lingered on each one of us in turn. Then his pallid, hideous face was lit up by a terrible laugh; he spoke through gritted teeth, 'I see it is Byomkeshbabu, and you have brought the police along. What do you want? Cocaine?'

Byomkesh shook his head and smiled, 'Oh no, no, we wouldn't embarrass you by asking for something as valuable as that. We want a very ordinary object—a matchbox.'

Anukulbabu's eyes remained fixed on Byomkesh's face. With great deliberation, he said, 'A matchbox? What do you mean?'

'It means that I am looking for the box from which you had recently presented me with one matchstick. I want the rest of those sticks. I am afraid I shall not be able to pay the price that you have quoted for them in your advertisement, but I hope that in the light of our friendship, you will give them to me free of charge.'

'I am unable to understand what you are saying.'

'Not at all—you understand perfectly well. But I suggest you take your finger off that switch. If the room is suddenly plunged into darkness, there might be an accident. Perhaps you haven't noticed, but two revolvers are aimed right at your heart.'

Anukulbabu let go of the switch. His face twisted into a mask of naked fury. He screamed, 'You scoundrel, you have ruined my life. I shall—' I saw that he was foaming at the mouth.

Byomkesh gave a melancholy shake of his head, 'Doctor, I can see that the prison term has taken its toll on your language. So you won't give us the matchbox?'

'No, I shall not! I do not know where your bloody matchbox is. If you can, find it for yourself, you—'

Byomkesh sighed and stood up, saying, 'I shall have to get it myself, then. Birenbabu, please watch over him.'

Byomkesh went and stood at the head of the bed. A flask stood on a bedside table with a glass over its mouth. Byomkesh lifted the flask and flung it to the floor. It smashed into pieces; streams of water flew in every direction. From the broken pieces of the flask Byomkesh picked out an object wrapped in blue fabric and held it up against the light, saying, 'Waterproof, bottle, sealing wax, everything is in place—I see the bottle hasn't broken. Birenbabu, the matches are safe. Now you may arrest the thief.'

Byomkesh took a deep breath and said, 'The moral of this story is—luck works where wisdom and brute force fail. If Putiram hadn't been sitting in the yard and if the number of the taxi had not been 8008, how would we have found Anukulbabu?'

I asked, 'That is true, but how did you come to suspect that the matchbox thief may be Anukulbabu in the first place?'

Byomkesh replied, 'Of all the dreadful enemies that I have made in my entire life, only three are still alive. The first is Amir Khan who had refined the business of trafficking in women into an art. The court of law sentenced him to twelve years of prison term. He is still in jail. The second is the political pimp Kunjalal Sarkar, who used to steal classified information from the government and peddle them in the share-market. He was sentenced to seven years in prison about a couple of years ago. The third is our dear doctor. He was to serve ten years for trafficking in illegal drugs and for attempting to murder me. As per my calculations, he was the only one whose time could possibly be up. So who else could it be?'

'That's true. But did you know that this charred gentleman was Anukulbabu?'

'No. His gait seemed familiar, but I did not really suspect him. Then there was that letter from Kokanad Gupta—that too threw me in a quandary. The name Kokanad is so unusual that it was obviously an alias—and add to that "Gupta" or "covert". Perhaps you have noticed that whenever someone in this country assumes an alias, they tend to attach a Gupta at the end of the name. Hence when the second Byomkeshbabu failed to say with certainty that the letter was for him and yet took it back with him, I was left with an uneasy feeling. The name Kokanad sounds like "cocaine addict"—in fact, cocaine was what the name was supposed to remind me of—you got that right. But at the time I did not suspect the second Byomkeshbabu and so I pushed my doubts away. Then you told me that he came to see me in Srirampore. Suddenly all the clouds lifted and I could see the whole scheme. I realized that this Byomkesh was actually Anukulbabu, and it was he who was the matchbox thief.'

'But why did he assume the name Byomkesh and take up residence here?'

'I have told you before that the psychology of an avenger manifests itself in a strange fashion. He went to all this trouble in order to hand me that letter personally and see if I caught on to it or not. It was the same impulse that drove him to Srirampore to see my dead body. He knew that his face had changed so much that we would be unable to recognize him.'

After a few moments of silence, I asked again, 'Tell me something, how did you work out that the matches were hidden in the flask?'

Byomkesh explained, 'That is where Anukulbabu's genius comes into play. No one would ever guess that matchsticks can be hidden inside a flask, where they would surely get wet. So, if for some reason his room came to be searched, nobody would care to look inside the flask. My suspicion was first aroused when I heard that when Byomkesh Bose left the mess, he had taken with him a small bag and a flask. The bag I could understand, but why the flask? In the dead of winter, when the man didn't take his blanket or pillow with him, why would he carry a flask? Was that so important? Then, when the sealing wax and the waterproof came out of his box, everything became crystal clear. He had put the matchsticks inside a bottle, sealed it with wax and wrapped it in waterproof material before dropping it into the flask, so that the water would not cause them any harm. Anukulbabu was always intelligent—it's just that he used his brains to attain the wrong ends.'

Putiram came in to collect the empty teacups. Byomkesh looked at him and asked, 'Putiram, have you brought the first book?'

Sheepishly Putiram replied, 'Yes, sir.'

'Good. Ajit, let Putiram's higher education begin today. After all there is no guarantee that every time the culprit will use a taxi numbered 8008 for his getaway.'

Picture Imperfect

Satyaboti came and stood at Byomkesh's side with a cup of pomegranate juice. She said, 'Here, can you please drink this up?'

I glanced at the clock; it was exactly four o'clock. The clock could be set by Satyaboti and her ministrations.

Byomkesh was sitting in his easy chair reading a book. He stared gloomily at the proferred cup for a while and then said, 'Why do I have to drink pomegranate juice every day?'

Satyaboti said, 'Doctor's orders.'

Byomkesh grimaced and said, 'The doctor can go to the blazes. I don't like drinking that stuff. What good is it, anyway?'

Satyaboti said, 'It'll increase your blood count. Please, dear, drink it up.'

Byomkesh stole a quick glance at Satyaboti's face and asked, 'What's for dinner tonight?'

Satyaboti replied, 'Toast and chicken broth.'

The frown on Byomkesh's face deepened. He said, 'Hmm, broth. And who, pray, will eat the chicken?'

Satyaboti hid a smile as she said, 'Why, your dearest friend, I suppose.'

Hastily, I pitched in, 'Not all by himself. Your better half will also get her share.'

Byomkesh glared at me once and then screwed up his face and drank up the pomegranate juice.

It was a few days since we had arrived in this town, which was located on the western fringes of Bengal, for a change of air. Byomkesh had been afflicted by a serious illness in Calcutta and was bedridden for a while; it had taken Satyaboti and me two months of constant care to bring him back to health. The toll of nursing him had begun to tell on Satyaboti who had been reduced to skin and bones. I was not much better off either. So.

at the doctor's advice, we had set off in search of the rejuvenating climes of the Santhal district around the middle of December. The results of the change had been miraculous too. Not only had Satyaboti and I regained our health, but Byomkesh too was getting better by the day. His appetite was increasing rapidly as well. After the long indisposition, he had turned into something of an unreasonable child; he craved for food every waking minute of the day. The two of us were having a hard time restraining him.

We had thus far made the acquaintance of only two gentlemen in the town. The first was Professor Adinath Shome; it was the ground floor of his house that we had rented. The second was the local doctor, Ashwini Ghatok. Since we had arrived with a convalescing patient, the first thing we had done was to look up the nearest physician.

There were many other Bengalis in the town, but we hadn't had a chance yet to meet any of them. We hadn't been able to go out much in the past few days. It took a while to settle down into a new habitat. This was the first day we would have an opportunity to venture out—we had been invited to tea by a prominent Bengali gentleman of the town. Although we had tried to keep as low a profile as possible, the news of Byomkesh's arrival, like an unmistakable scent wafting in the air, had soon become common knowledge. Hence the invitation to tea.

We would rather not have taken Byomkesh out to a tea-party this soon. But Byomkesh, after being confined to the indoors for a long time, had grown quite restless. The doctor also gave us his permission. So it was decided that we would go.

Sitting in his easy chair and leafing through a book, Byomkesh was fidgeting and glancing at the clock at regular intervals. I was standing by the window and lazily puffing on a cigarette; the charming natural landscape of the Santhal district had me completely in its thrall. Here was an unique marriage of lushness and aridity, of abundance and dearth; human presence had not succeeded in reducing the rocky soil of the place into molten sludge.

Suddenly, Byomkesh asked, 'What time have you asked the rickshaw to come?'

I replied, 'Four-thirty.'

Byomkesh threw one more glance at the clock before lowering his eyes to the book again. I realized that the laggard pace of the clock's hands was making him impatient. I laughed and said, 'Patience, my friend, and the fruits will be—'

He snapped at me, 'Aren't you ashamed of yourself—brandishing your cigarette in front of me?'

I threw the half-smoked cigarette out of the window. Byomkesh was not yet allowed to smoke. Satyaboti had extracted a grave promise—if he smoked without her permission, he would see her dead. I too had stopped smoking in front of Byomkesh; there was no sin greater than tempting an addict who was bound by a pledge. But there were times when I would err.

Exactly at four-thirty, two cycle-rickshaws arrived at the main entrance. Byomkesh and I were dressed and ready; Satyaboti had also completed her toilette. So we set off at once.

The two storeys of the house we were staying in were not connected; the stairway to the first floor was set at the far end of the open veranda. In front of the house was an open courtyard and across it lay the main gate. When we came out of the house, we saw our landlord standing by the gate with exasperation writ large on his face.

Professor Shome was close to forty, but he didn't look much over thirty; his demeanour, too, didn't speak of his age at all. He was quite nimble and spirited in whatever he did. But if there was one difficulty that daunted the professor's life, it was his wife. Marital bliss was not something that Professor Shome had ever found.

He was dressed to go out. Seeing us, he gave a wan smile. We knew he was invited to the same party and so I asked, 'Why are you just standing there, aren't you coming?'

Professor Shome cast a telling look at the first floor of his house and said, 'I'll come. But the mistress hasn't finished with herself yet. You go on ahead.'

We got into the rickshaws. Byomkesh and Satyaboti took

one; I had the other one to myself. With a tinkle of bells, the man-driven, three-wheeled vehicles were on their way. A smile lit up Byomkesh's face. Satyaboti tenderly wrapped a shawl snugly around him, so that he wouldn't catch a chill.

As we travelled along the gravelled, hilly road, we had a good look at the town. The houses on either side of the road were not clustered together as in a city—they were few and far between. It was as though the town lay sprawled out over the uneven terrain, in a lazy droop; there was no cramping or jostling. Although the town was extensive in perimeter, its population wasn't large. However, most of the people who lived here were well-to-do. The prime reason for their affluence was the presence of a few mica mines in the area. We saw that there was a court and a bank in the town. We also noticed that nearly all the prosperous families in the area were Bengalis.

The gentleman who had invited us was named Mahidhar Choudhury. We had found out from Professor Shome that he was extremely wealthy. Although quite advanced in age, he was always up to something or the other—and very generous when it came to spending money. There was no dearth of activities like picnics, hunting and games under his patronage.

Within fifteen minutes, we arrived at Mr Choudhury's residence. It comprised nearly three acres of land enclosed by granite walls, giving the impression of a fortress rather than a home. Within the walls were a variety of trees, shrubs and seasonal flower-beds. Strewn across the irregular slopes were a fish-pond, a secluded willow-bower, and even a gymnasium. The embellished garden could suddenly be mistaken for wooded forestry. In other words, the grounds amply indicated the owner's wealth.

In front of the house lay the tennis court with its grass neatly cut. Tables and chairs had been set out upon it for the guests. The setting winter sun provided some warmth. The beautiful two-storeyed mansion formed a backdrop to this charming scene. On our arrival, Mahidharbabu welcomed us graciously. He was immense in stature and fair complexioned; the grey hair on his head was close-cropped, his clean-shaven jowls were like cantaloupes and his face was split by a broad grin.

The very sight of the man gave the impression of amiability and candour.

He introduced us to his daughter Rajani. She was about twenty years old, attractive, fair and cheerful; intelligence and merriment sparkled in her eyes. Mahidharbabu was a widower and Rajani was his sole companion and also the heiress to his fortune.

Within minutes, Rajani struck up a rapport with Satyaboti. They sat down on a sofa in a corner and began a tête-à-tête. We also took our seats. Of the other guests, only Dr Ghatok and another gentleman had arrived so far. We were introduced to the other gentleman. His name was Nakulesh Sarkar. He was a businessman of middling means and also ran his own photography shop in the town. The photography was just a hobby but it brought in some extra income; there was no other photographer in the town.

The conversation drifted casually. At one point Mahidharbabu glanced at Dr Ghatok and said, 'So Ghatok, you couldn't bring Byomkeshbabu back to health in all these days! I see you are nothing but a horse-doctor—a *ghotak*, that's all you are!' He laughed at his own joke.

Nakuleshbabu piped in with, 'How can he do anything except horse around? He's *ashwini* on the one hand and *ghotak* on the other! Both his names betray his horsiness!'

The doctor was much younger to both and he smilingly swallowed the barb. I noticed that a number of the guests quipped and jested with the doctor, but all of them were respectful of his medical prowess. There were a few other experienced medical practitioners in the town, but this youthful, good-natured doctor seemed to have acquired quite a name for himself in the three short years of his sojourn here.

Gradually the other guests began to trickle in. The first to arrive was Ushanath Ghosh, with his wife and son. Ushanathbabu was a government official in charge of the local treasury. Tall, dark and muscular, he was around thirty-five years of age, spoke in a sombre fashion with long pauses, and wore dark glasses. Even his smile was somewhat grim. His wife looked sickly, with an anxious look stamped permanently on her face. She continually stole nervous glances at her husband's face. The child was around five years old and he also looked as if he was constantly cringing from some unspoken apprehension. Perhaps Ushanathbabu kept his family under a tight rein and no one dared to speak up before him.

When Mahidharbabu introduced us, Ushanathbabu made a few noises deep down in his throat. These were probably meant to be words of greeting, but we were unable to decipher a single syllable. His eyes remained concealed behind dark glasses. I felt a little uneasy. One can never be quite comfortable with a man whose eyes one cannot see.

Then came Purandar Pandey, the DSP of Police. He was not a Bengali, but spoke the language fluently and liked the company of Bengalis. He was a handsome man; the police uniform sat well on him. He shook Byomkesh's hand and smiled, saying, 'You have come here, but such is our misfortune that we cannot even welcome you with a good mystery. There is a grave scarcity of mysteries in our part of the world, you see. Everything is out in the open. Not that there isn't the occasional robbery or theft, but there's scarcely any play of wits involved there.'

Byomkesh also laughed, and said, 'That, in fact, is good for me. My current diet forbids mysteries, among other things. Doctor's orders.'

At this point another guest made his appearance. This was the manager of the local bank, Amaresh Raha. He had a sparse figure and an inconspicuous countenance; perhaps this was why he wore a French-cut beard in an attempt to bring some distinction to his looks. His age could be anywhere between youth and middle age.

Mahidharbabu said, 'Amareshbabu, you were eager to make Byomkeshbabu's acquaintance—here he is.'

Amareshbabu joined his palms in greeting and said, with a smile, 'Who doesn't want to meet a famous man like Byomkeshbabu? None of you were any less eager, so don't point your fingers only at me.'

Mahidharbabu said, 'But today you are rather late. Everyone is here, except Professor Shome. He, of course, has a reason. Women take their time getting dressed. But you don't have that excuse. Didn't the bank close at three-thirty?'

Amaresh Raha said, 'I really wanted to come sooner. But Christmas is almost here and work pressure has mounted. The year-end is approaching. As soon as the new year arrives, all of you will throng to the bank to withdraw cash. I have got to make arrangements for that.'

In the meantime, some domestics were bringing out trays laden with various kinds of snacks and beverages and placing these on the table. Rajani rose and began to serve the food. Some people went and picked up plates on their own and started eating. Laughter and conversation continued unabated.

Smiling, Rajani stood before Byomkesh with a plate of sweets and said, 'Byomkeshbabu, some refreshments.'

Byomkesh looked quickly at Satyaboti and found that she was gazing at him steadily from a distance. He scratched the back of his neck and said, 'You'll have to excuse me. I am not allowed to have all this.'

Mahidharbabu was walking around and attending to the guests. He exclaimed, 'What's this! Absolutely nothing? A little something—? Hey, doctor, isn't your patient allowed to eat anything at all?'

The doctor was standing by the table helping himself to some edibles. He said, 'It's best if he doesn't.'

Byomkesh smiled wanly and said, 'There you are! Just give me a cup of tea. Don't worry, we shall come again. Today's visit is merely the prologue.'

Delighted, Mahidharbabu said, 'Every evening someone or the other does me the honour of visiting. If you stopped by from time to time, the evening sessions would really liven up.'

It was now that Professor Shome finally made his entry, accompanied by his wife. Shome wore a slightly abashed look. In fact, some embarrassment was called for. I have desisted so far from describing Shome's wife, Malati Devi, but it can be delayed no longer. She was about the same age as her husband; her dark and portly body was pudgy in shape, and her gawking eyes rolled proudly around in their sockets. It was impossible to find her countenance pleasing. To make matters worse, she had a tendency to overdress. Today, her well-adorned and bejewelled aspect was enough to put an *apsara* to shame. She was wearing a blazing scarlet South Indian silk sari and was bedecked with diamond and gold jewellery all over. This apparition, accompanied by Shome's hesitant, sheepish visage, was sufficient to cause the onlookers some discomfiture.

Quickly, Rajani went up to greet them, but Malati Devi's face held no smile. She glared first at Rajani, then at her husband, and proceeded towards a chair.

The conversation flowed as tea and snacks were consumed. Byomkesh wore a martyr's expression and sipped his tea silently. I had struck up a conversation with Nakuleshbabu over tea. Ushanathbabu was solemnly listening to Purandar Pandey speak, and nodding his head periodically. His son was walking up to the food-laden table covetously and then stepping back in apprehension. His mother held a plate of food in her hands and alternately threw nervous glances at her husband and her son.

Mahidharbabu raised his voice a little above the hubbub and said, 'Mr Pandey was saying a while ago that our town lacks the thrill of a mystery. Well, you can judge for yourselves whether that is true or not. Last night I had a burglar in my house.'

The hum of conversation ceased; all eyes were on Mahidharbabu. He stood there with a smile on his face, as if it was an amusing matter that he was narrating.

Amareshbabu asked, 'Was something stolen?'

Mahidharbabu replied, 'That, precisely, is the mystery. A framed photograph from the drawing room wall is missing. I didn't hear anything at night—in the morning they found the picture missing. One of the windows was open.'

Purandar Pandey walked up to him, saying, 'Picture! What picture?'

'A group photograph. It was taken by Nakuleshbabu when we went for a picnic last month.'

Pandey said, 'Hmm. Nothing else was taken? Were there any expensive items in the room?'

Mahidharbabu said, 'There were a few silver vases; besides

those, there were several silverware vessels in the next room. The burglar, instead of stealing any of these, just made off with the picture. Now you tell me if this is an intriguing mystery or not.'

Pandey said disdainfully, 'If you wish to call it intriguing, you may well do so. But I personally believe some Santhal found the window open and broke in. He probably found the golden frame attractive and made off with it.'

Mahidharbabu turned to Byomkesh and said, 'Byomkeshbabu, what do *you* think?'

Although Byomkesh was listening to their dialogue, his eyes had been wandering lazily around the room. Now he grew alert and said, 'I think Mr Pandey has put his finger on it. Nakuleshbabu, was it you who took the photo?'

Nakuleshbabu said, 'Yes. It was a good photograph. I had taken out three prints, of which Mahidharbabu had one—'

Ushanathbabu cleared his throat and said, 'I, too, had bought a copy.'

Byomkesh said, 'Yours is still in its place, right?'

Ushanathbabu said, 'I don't know, really. I had put it in the album and haven't really looked at it since. But I'm sure it's there.'

'And who took the third print, Nakuleshbabu?'

'Professor Shome.'

All of us turned to Shome. He had been sitting listlessly beside his wife and now, hearing his name spoken, looked up in surprise; his face began to redden slowly. There was no change of expression on Mrs Shome's face, however. She continued to sit stock-still, like a medusa carved in stone.

Byomkesh said, 'Your copy is still with you, I presume?'

With a burning face, Shome fumbled, 'Yes . . . well, I suppose . . . I don't really know . . .'

His behaviour was quite flabbergasting. It wasn't so grave an issue. Why was he getting so flustered?

It was Amareshbabu who rescued him from his discomfiture, saying, 'Well, so it's gone—so what! You can have another one. Nakuleshbabu, I want one too. I was also in the group.'

Nakuleshbabu scratched his head and said, 'That picture won't be available anymore. The negative is lost.'

'What! Where did the negative go?'

I noticed that Byomkesh was looking at Nakuleshbabu keenly. He replied, 'It was in my studio, along with the other negatives. I had gone to Calcutta for a couple of days, so the studio was closed. When I returned, I could no longer find that one.'

Pandey said, 'Please look carefully. I am sure it'll turn up—where could it go?'

There was no further talk on this matter. Dusk was approaching slowly. We started getting ready to take our leave because it wasn't good for Byomkesh to stay out after sunset.

At this point, we noticed a spectral figure who had slipped in and now stood beside Mahidharbabu, talking to him in an undertone. From his apparel, it was easy to tell that he wasn't one of the invitees. A scruffy dhoti and a cotton shirt hung on his tall, scrawny frame; his eyes and cheeks were sunken. In short, he looked like famine personified. Yet, it was obvious that he came of genteel stock.

Mahidharbabu was seated not far from me and bits of their conversation came to my ears. A little annoyed, Mahidharbabu said, 'What do you want now? Wasn't it only the other day that I gave you some money?'

In an anxious tone, the man said, 'No sir, it's not money I want. I have made a sketch of you and I wanted to show it to you.'

'A sketch!'

The man held a scroll of paper in his hands, which he unrolled and held out before Mahidharbabu.

Mahidharbabu looked at the picture in surprise. My curiosity was aroused as well, and I went and stood behind Mahidharbabu's chair.

The sketch was simply amazing. It was done in crayon on a white sheet of paper, and showed Mahidharbabu in profile. With a few strokes of a skilful and practised hand, a true-to-life image of Mahidharbabu had been captured on paper.

Following in my footsteps, Rajani also came and stood

behind her father's chair. She exclaimed in delight, 'Oh! What a lovely sketch!'

At that, several others joined us. The picture passed from hand to hand and there was a buzz of approbation. The emaciated artist stood at a distance and rubbed his hands in gratification.

Mahidharbabu said to him, 'You seem to have a talent for portraits. What is your name?'

The artist replied, 'Sir, my name is Phalguni Pal.'

Mahidharbabu fished out a ten-rupee note from his pocket and said in a pleased voice, 'Good, good. I am keeping the sketch. Here is your reward.'

Phalguni Pal reached out his claws like a crab, and immediately pocketed the note.

Purandar Pandey was scrutinizing the picture with a frown on his face. Now he looked up suddenly and asked Phalguni, 'How did you draw his portrait? From a photograph?'

Phalguni replied, 'No sir. I saw him once the other day—and so . . .'

'You saw him just once and you could sketch his portrait so accurately?'

Phalguni stammered and replied, 'Sir, well, I have that talent. If you give me the word, I shall do a sketch of you too.'

After a brief pause, Pandey said, 'All right. If you can sketch a portrait of me, I too will reward you with ten rupees.'

Phalguni Pal bent low to bid everyone farewell and left the room.

Pandey looked at Byomkesh and said, 'Let us see what he does. I was not in their picnic group.'

Byomkesh gave a nod of concurrence.

Thereafter the session broke up. Mahidharbabu's car reached us home. Mr and Mrs Shome came along with us.

At around eight o'clock that night, we were sitting in our room. There was still some time to go before dinner. Byomkesh was sitting in his easy chair, sipping the prescribed brandy. Satyaboti sat at his side, all wrapped up in a shawl. I sat across from them, periodically taking the cigarette case out from my pocket, only to put it back in. I had no intention of being rebuked by Byomkesh again. We were still discussing the tea-party.

I said, 'Phalguni Pal is living proof of just how much we value our art and artists. The man is truly brilliant and yet is impoverished enough to have to beg for his living.'

Byomkesh was a little absent-minded. He asked, 'How did you guess he is so impoverished that he has to beg for a living?'

I replied, 'It's not too difficult to come to that conclusion from his clothes and his countenance.'

Byomkesh smiled a little and said, 'Perhaps it is not too difficult, but you have reached the wrong conclusion. You are a writer yourself and it is only natural that the artist's condition would evoke your sympathy. But the reason for Phalguni Pal's destitute condition is not paucity of money. Actually, the man is more fond of his drink than his food.'

'You mean he is an alcoholic? But how could you tell?'

'First of all, from his lips. If you notice an alcoholic's lips, you'll find they are distinctive: a trifle moist, a little slack—I can't quite describe them, but I can identify them when I see them. Second, if Phalguni was famished, he would have looked at the food on the table yearningly; there was still quite a spread upon the table, you remember. But Phalguni did not even spare the food a second glance. Third, when he walked past me, I smelled alcohol on him. Not too strong, but alcohol nonetheless.'

Byomkesh picked up his glass of brandy and drained it in one gulp.

Satyaboti said, 'That's enough, I don't want to hear about the drunkard. But what is all this about the stolen picture, dear? I couldn't make head or tail of it. Why would someone do something as senseless as stealing a photograph?'

Almost as if he was speaking to himself, Byomkesh said, 'Perhaps Mr Pandey is on the right track. But—if that's not true, then there's cause for concern . . . The group photo was taken at the picnic. All the people who came to the tea-party today were at the picnic—with the exception of Pandey . . . There were three prints taken of that picture; one of them is stolen, and about the other two, we don't know—the negative also is lost.' After a brief pause, he suddenly pointed upwards and said, 'Wonder why *he* got so upset at the mention of the picture.'

After a few more moments of silence, I said, 'If somebody has removed the picture with a specific purpose in mind, what could that purpose be?'

Byomkesh said, 'Does there have to be a single motive, Ajit? It isn't so easy to say who might have what kind of an interest in something. The other day I was reading in an American magazine about this ape-couple that they have in a zoo. The male ape is so possessive, that whenever a male visitor comes near the cage, he grabs the female ape and hides her away.'

Satyaboti burst out laughing and said, 'You and your bizarre stories. Is it possible for an ape to be so smart?'

Byomkesh said, 'This isn't smartness, it's emotion; in simpler terms, it's sexual jealousy. And I hope you will not deny that this is a streak that runs in humans as well. It is certainly present in men, but perhaps even more so in women. If I were to get too close to Mahidharbabu's daughter, Rajani, you wouldn't like it, would you?'

Satyaboti lowered her glance and pressed a corner of her shawl to her lips, without saying another word. I said, 'But how is this jealousy linked to the theft of the picture?'

'Wherever there is a free interaction between men and women, this jealousy is bound to show up.' And Byomkesh raised his eyes to the ceiling.

I said, 'Doesn't seem like a strong enough motive to me. Could there be some other objective?'

'Certainly. The artist, Phalguni Pal, could be the burglar. His claim that he can sketch an exact replica of a person after seeing him just once might well be untrue. It is quite easy to make a copy from a photograph. Who knows, perhaps Phalguni is trying to impress everyone and earn more money.'

'Hmm. Any other possibilities?'

Byomkesh laughed and said, 'The photographer, Nakuleshbabu himself, could be behind the theft.'

'What would be his reason?'

208/ Saradindu Bandyopadhyay

'So that his photograph would sell more copies.' Byomkesh continued to chuckle.

'Do you really think that is possible?'

'Nothing is impossible for a businessman. In America, they burn their foodgrains to make the prices rise artificially.'

'All right. Anyone else?'

'Perhaps there is someone in that group there, who wants to erase all traces of his existence . . .'

'You mean someone with a criminal record?'

At this point, there was a soft knock on our door. I went and opened it. Professor Shome stood there, wearing a warm dressing gown. We received him cordially. Ever since our arrival here, he came down every evening at around this time to ask how we were doing. We would chat for a while; then he would go back, when it was time for dinner. His wife had also come down a couple of times. But she didn't seem too keen to get to know Satyaboti; the indifference was duly reciprocated by Satyaboti.

Shome came in and took a seat. I offered him a cigarette and lit one myself. This was my only chance of getting to smoke in Byomkesh's presence; he couldn't yell at me in front of a guest.

Shome asked us, 'So what did you think of our little party?'

Byomkesh replied, 'Quite nice. Interesting people, easy to get along with.'

Shome took a drag on his cigarette and said, 'It always seems like that from a distance. But you don't need *me* to tell you that. Mrs Bakshi, tell me, out of all the people that you met today, who did you like the most?'

Without a shred of hesitation, Satyaboti replied, 'Rajani. She has a sweet nature and I have really taken to her.'

A slight blush spread across Shome's face. Satyaboti didn't notice it and continued, 'She's as pretty as she's sweet. And she is very intelligent, too. Tell me, why is Mahidharbabu not doing anything to get his daughter married yet—he has enough money . . .'

Suddenly, a shrill voice shrieked out from the doorway, startling all of us. 'Widow! She's a widow! Which Hindu boy would marry a widow?'

None of us was aware that Malati Devi had come and stood at the door. The news was as unexpected as was the appearance of its bearer. Astounded, we all looked at Malati Devi. She swept her vicious eyes over us and spoke again, 'Don't you believe me? He knows, ask him. Everyone here knows about it. Only a widow who has lost all sense of decorum would go about pretending to be unmarried. But then, what would a brazen one like her know of shame? All her fancy airs—all meant to trap other men.' Malati Devi went back as suddenly as she had come in. The sound of her marching footsteps echoed on the stairs.

Professor Shome was affected the most by this unseemly exhibition. He was too mortified to meet our eyes. Silence hung in the room for a few minutes. Eventually, he raised harassed eyes and spoke in a low voice, 'I apologize to you all. Sometimes, I wish I could just run away somewhere . . .' His voice petered out into silence.

Calmly, Byomkesh asked, 'Is Rajani truly a widow?'

Shome answered, speaking slowly, 'Yes. She became one at fourteen years of age. Mahidharbabu had given his daughter in marriage to a brilliant student of the university. Two days after the wedding, he set off for England; Mahidharbabu sponsored his son-in-law's trip abroad. But the poor fellow did not make it to England; on the way, he died in an air crash. For all intents and purposes, you could say that Rajani is practically unmarried.'

For a while, no one said anything. I passed another cigarette to Shome and struck a match to light it. Shome lit his cigarette and said, 'My domestic circumstances are no secret to you all. The story of my life is, in many ways, similar to Mahidharbabu's son-in-law's. I was born in a poor family and was a bright student. After marriage, my father-in-law sponsored my studies abroad. But the rest of the story was different in my case. I completed my education and came back home to take up teaching. But I couldn't do it for very long. I quit my job and came and settled down here. Since then, I have been sitting idle—for seven years now. There is no dearth of creature comforts in my life—my wife has plenty of money.'

The bitterness within spilled into his words.

A little hesitantly, I asked, 'Why did you quit your job?'

Shome rose to leave and said, 'In shame! In the age of women's liberation, it wasn't possible to lock my wife into the house, and yet . . . Sometimes I wonder, how much more convenient it would have been for everyone if I had died in the air crash instead of Rajani's husband.'

Shome proceeded towards the door. Byomkesh called out, 'Professor Shome, if you don't mind, I have a question. Where is your copy of the group photograph that was taken at the picnic?'

Shome turned around and said, 'My wife tore it into bits. You see, I was standing beside Rajani in that picture.'

Dragging his footsteps, Shome went back upstairs.

There wasn't much conversation at dinner that night. At one point, Satyaboti suddenly said, 'Whatever anybody says, Rajani is a very nice girl. She was widowed in her childhood and I don't see anything wrong with her father wishing that she'd dress well like any young woman.'

Byomkesh looked at Satyaboti, and then, in an indifferent tone, he said, 'Today, at the tea-party, I observed something that both of you probably missed. When Mahidharbabu broached the subject of the theft, all eyes were on him. I noticed that Dr Ghatok was standing at a distance and Rajani sidled up to him and slipped a folded note into his pocket. They exchanged looks, and then Rajani moved away. I don't think anyone saw this little scene except me—not even Malati Devi.'

Five or six days went by.

By now, Byomkesh was well on his way to recovery. His allotted victuals had also seen an improvement. Furthermore, Satyaboti had given him permission to smoke two cigarettes a day. Due to the plentiful food, I was putting on weight rapidly; Satyaboti had gained some as well. We now went out for evening walks with Byomkesh every day, because this was a necessary part of his convalescence. Everyone was happy.

One day, we were going out for our walk when Professor

Shome joined us and said, 'Come, today I shall accompany you.'

Satyaboti showed some concern and said, 'Is Mrs Shome not . . .'

In a cheerful tone, Shome said, 'She has come down with a cold and is resting.'

Shome was a friendly soul; it was his wife's presence that sometimes enervated his spirits. We began to discuss various topics as we roamed the streets.

The subject of the picture's theft came up in the course of our conversation. Byomkesh said, 'Do tell me something—was there ever any mention of publishing that photo in a magazine or newspaper?'

Shome threw a startled glance at Byomkesh and then pondered over this, frowning. Finally he said, 'Well, no, not that I know of. But Nakuleshbabu did make a trip to Calcutta recently . . . But would he actually publish that photograph without consulting all of us? I don't think so. Particularly, if Ushanathbabu came to hear of it, he would be most displeased.'

'And why is that?'

'He is a peculiar kind of man. Although he is quite grim and sedate outwardly, deep inside he is rather timid. He is especially in awe of his superiors in the government. Perhaps the government wouldn't like it if a civil servant associated too freely with commoners. So Ushanathbabu is very reticent about having pictures taken with us. I remember, on the day of the picnic he was most reluctant to join the group when the photo was being taken. It took a lot of cajoling to finally get him to agree. If this picture was to make its way into the papers, Nakuleshbabu would be in for a rough time.'

I could tell from the look on Byomkesh's face that his interest was aroused. He asked, 'Does Ushanathbabu always wear dark glasses?'

Shome replied, 'Yes. It's been a year and a half since he has been transferred here and in all that time I have never seen him without his glasses. Perhaps he has a problem with his eyes, and cannot take bright sunlight.'

Byomkesh didn't ask any more questions about

Ushanathbabu. Instead, he inquired, 'What kind of a man is Nakuleshbabu, the photographer?'

Shome said, 'Shrewd businessman, and he is also intelligent. He tries to keep Mahidharbabu happy. I've heard that he owes him money.'

'Really! How much money?'

'I don't know. But I hear it is a fair amount.'

At this moment we heard the sounds of a motorcycle in the distance. As it drew near, we could see that the rider was DSP Purandar Pandey. He also spotted us and, stopping his vehicle, came forward smilingly to greet us.

After the usual formalities, Byomkesh asked, 'Has Phalguni Pal drawn your portrait yet?'

Pandey widened his eyes in wonder and said, 'Amazingly enough, the very next day he turned up with the portrait. And it was a very good one too. But there was no chance of his laying his hands on a photograph of mine. He truly is a talented artist. I had to shell out ten rupees.'

Byomkesh laughed and said, 'Where does this man live?'

Pandey said, 'That's a sad story. Such a talent, but he's a complete loser. A hardcore addict—liquor, grass, cocaine, nothing is beyond him. He has been here for a month now. On his arrival, he used to spend his nights here and there, sometimes on somebody's veranda, sometimes in a cattle-shed. Mahidharbabu took pity on him and gave him a place to stay. There's a tiny cottage within his compound where the man has been living for the past two days.'

Phalguni's fate was the same as many an unfortunate and dissolute artist's. Still, it was heartening to know that he had found asylum for a few days at least.

Pandey was revving up his motorcycle again when Shome asked, 'Where are you headed?'

Pandey said, 'I am on my way to Mahidharbabu's. I heard from Nakuleshbabu that he has suddenly taken ill. So I thought I would look him up on my way home.'

'What's he down with?'

'Just a common cold. But he is a chronic patient of asthma as well.'

Shome said, 'That's true. I should visit him as well; Mahidharbabu has been awfully kind to me—'

Pandey said, 'Fine, why don't you ride pillion with me? I shall drop you home on my way back.'

'That'll be nice indeed.' Shome mounted the rear seat of the motorcycle and held on to Pandey for support.

Byomkesh said, 'Please tell Mahidharbabu that we will drop in tomorrow.'

'All right. Goodbye.'

The motorcycle whizzed away with its pair of riders. We too headed back for home. I noticed that Byomkesh was smiling to himself.

Once we were back home, we sat down to a cup of tea. Byomkesh continued to be a little preoccupied. The door was open and, by and by, heavy footsteps sounded on the stairs. Byomkesh looked up, startled, and said to us in an undertone, 'If you have to answer any questions about where Professor Shome has gone, just say he has gone to Mr Pandey's house.'

Before we fully digested this information, the questioner had appeared before us. Malati Devi stood at the doorway. The cold had puffed up her face further and her eyes were bloodshot; she cast an inquiring glance around the room. Satyaboti stood up and said, 'Do come in, Mrs Shome.'

In a heavy, choked voice, Malati Devi said, 'Oh no, I am not feeling too well. My husband went out with you, I believe—so where is he?'

Byomkesh walked up to the door and replied smoothly, 'We met up with Mr Pandey on the way and he took Professor Shome with him to his house.'

Surprised, Malati Devi said, 'Mr Pandey of the police force? What would my husband have to do with him?'

Quite innocently, Byomkesh answered, 'That I didn't get to hear. Mr Pandey said, come on home with me and have a cup of tea. They must have something to discuss.'

Malati Devi scrutinized our faces one by one, heaved a deep sigh and went back upstairs without saying another word. We returned to our seats.

Byomkesh looked at us and smiled sheepishly, 'I had to tell

a blatant lie. But there was no other choice. It is best to avoid the possibility of marital strife.'

In a sarcastic tone, Satyaboti said, 'Your sympathies are always with the man. Mrs Shome's suspicions, in fact, are not entirely untrue.'

Byomkesh's tone grew heated, 'And your sympathies are always with the woman. Failing to win their husbands' love, women are torn by jealousy, and yet they have no sense of how they can make their husbands love them. Anyway, Ajit, you'll have to do something; keep a lookout from the front porch. We have to warn the professor the minute he gets in or the lie will be exposed. And that, of course, would spell disaster for Shome and trouble for all of us.'

I had no objections to this whatsoever. There was a chair on the front porch and I parked myself there, happily smoking one cigarette after another. It was a little cooler outside, but nothing that a shawl couldn't handle.

Shome returned nearly an hour later. Pandey's motorcycle halted at the front gate, dropped Shome off and went on its way. As Shome came up to the porch, I said, 'Please come this way—I have something to tell you.'

I led him inside. Byomkesh was sitting alone in the drawing room. Shome's face looked grave. Byomkesh asked, 'How is Mahidharbabu?'

Shome replied in a monosyllable, 'Fine.'

'Was anyone else there?'

'Just Dr Ghatok.'

Byomkesh then narrated the Malati episode to him. A glimmer of a smile appeared on Shome's solemn face and he said, 'Thank you.'

The following morning at breakfast I observed that marital strife was not unique to the upper storey of the house; it appeared to have drifted downstairs as well. Satyaboti's face was gloomy and there was a harshness to the tilt of Byomkesh's lips. I supposed marital discord was as contagious as the common cold.

The secret mysteries about the origin and decline of marital discord were beyond my understanding. But the phenomenon was not entirely unfamiliar. I had witnessed it several times in the three years that Byomkesh and Satyaboti had been married. Without fail, it would commence with the frills and fuss of a regular ceremony; then it would disappear just as suddenly as the morning mists upon the hills.

After breakfast, Byomkesh said, 'Come on Ajit, let's go for a walk.'

I said, 'Good idea. Let Satyaboti get dressed.'

Satyaboti made a face and said, 'I have work to do at home. I cannot afford to go traipsing round the place morning, noon and night like some others.'

Byomkesh rose and draped his shawl around himself, saying, 'My suggestion was for the two of us to go out. Come, there's no point in idling about the house.'

Satyaboti directed a glance at Byomkesh's feet and remarked, 'It would be desirable for someone who is convalescing to wear some socks before he goes out.' She left the room.

I could scarcely control my laughter and so I went out to the porch. Byomkesh joined me in a few minutes. His brows were knit in a scowl, but his feet were clad in socks.

We came out on to the street. I didn't know that Byomkesh had a specific destination in mind. I thought he was merely in the grip of a tourist's desire to take in some air. But after walking a short distance, he hailed a rickshaw and got into it. I, too, climbed in after him. Byomkesh said, 'Ushanathbabu's residence.'

As the rickshaw clambered on, I asked, 'Why Ushanathbabu, all of a sudden?'

Byomkesh replied, 'It's a Sunday, he would be at home. I need to ask him a couple of questions.'

After going about a half-mile or so, I asked, 'Byomkesh, I do believe you have started pondering over the theft of the picture. Does it really warrant any serious consideration?'

He replied, 'That is precisely what I am trying to find out.'

We arrived at Ushanathbabu's house after going another half a mile or so. The house was in the civil servants' colony which was surrounded by a wall. We asked the rickshaw-puller to wait at the gate. As we went in on foot, we noticed Purandar Pandey's motorcycle in a corner. Ushanathbabu and Mr Pandey stood at the main entrance. When he spotted us, Pandey said in a surprised voice, 'Well, hello! Look who's here.'

Byomkesh said, 'Since it's a Sunday, we thought we would pay Ushanathbabu a visit.'

Ushanathbabu gave an icy smile and said, 'You're welcome. Last night my house was robbed.'

'Really! What was stolen?'

Pandey said, 'We haven't figured it out yet. All of them sleep on the first floor at night; the ground floor is unguarded. The rooms are locked. Last night, someone broke into the office-room and tried to force open the locks on the almirah. He inserted a skeleton-key into the lock, but could not get it out again.'

'Well, really! And what does the almirah hold?'

Ushanathbabu said, 'There are some official documents and my wife's jewellery. The almirah is made of solid steel. You could almost call it an iron safe.'

Ushanathbabu had his dark glasses on and his eyes could not be seen. But in spite of that, his face suggested that he was considerably shaken. Byomkesh said, 'So the burglar was unable to get anything?'

Pandey said, 'We can't say until we open the almirah. We have sent for a locksmith.'

'Hmm. How did the thief enter the room?'

'He broke the glass on one the windows, reached inside and undid the latch. Come in and have a look.'

We entered Ushanathbabu's office. It was a medium-sized room with one table, a few chairs and a steel almirah. There was nothing else in it. Byomkesh examined the broken window; he tried turning the key in the lock of the almirah, but it wouldn't turn. Except for this key, the burglar had not left behind any clues about his identity. The drawing room was adjacent to the office. We went in there and sat down. Ushanathbabu offered us some tea but we declined.

The drawing room was furnished in a most ordinary manner. A radio stood in one corner. Some low end-tables were kept beside the chairs; some of them held brass flower-vases, some had photo albums on them—there was nothing valuable in the room.

Byomkesh said, 'I don't suppose the thief came in here.'

Ushanathbabu said, 'There is nothing worth stealing in this room.' As he spoke, he leaped up. Lifting his dark glasses for a moment, he stared at the radio intently. Then he replaced the glasses and said, 'My fairy! Where did the fairy go?'

In unison, we said, 'Fairy?'

Ushanathbabu walked up to the radio and began to look around as he said, 'A little figurine of a fairy, gilded with silver; the magistrate's wife had presented it to me—it always stood on top of this radio. I'm sure the thief has taken it.' We all went over and took a good look. On top of the radio, there was the mark of a little round spot, the size of a coin, where the figurine had stood.

Byomkesh said, 'Perhaps the thief didn't take it. Maybe your son took it to play with it. Why don't you ask him?'

Ushanathbabu scowled and said, 'My boy is well brought up, he doesn't touch anything without permission. Anyway, I shall go and check.'

He went upstairs. Byomkesh asked Pandey, 'Do you suspect anyone?'

Pandey said, 'Suspect—well, not really. But one of the orderlies says that last night, around seven-thirty, a crazy-looking man had come to meet Ushanathbabu. Ushanathbabu didn't want to meet him and the orderly sent him packing. The description that the orderly gave us seemed to indicate—'

'Phalguni Pal?'

'The same. I have sent a sub-inspector to look him up.'

Ushanathbabu came down and informed us that his wife and son knew nothing about the whereabouts of the figurine. He was sure that, thwarted in his attempts, the thief had mistaken the fairy for silver and taken it away.

Byomkesh was frowning. Suddenly, he looked up and said,

'By the way, did you check if you still have that photograph?'

'Which photograph?'

'The group photo that was mentioned at Mahidharbabu's place.'

'Oh—no, I didn't get around to looking for it. Why don't you take a look—it should be in that album, right next to you.'

Byomkesh picked up the album and began turning its pages. It contained photos of Ushanathbabu's father, mother, brother, sister, wife, son and even of Mahidharbabu and Rajani, but not the group photo in question.

Byomkesh said, 'I don't see it here.'

'But it should be there.' Ushanathbabu came up and began to look, but the photo was not found. He said, 'I don't know where it's gone. But this was not something valuable. If any of the documents or jewellery has been stolen from the almirah . . .'

Byomkesh rose to leave and said, 'Don't worry, the thief was not able to steal a thing. The jewellery is totally safe and the fairy too will turn up soon enough, I'm sure. We shall get going now. Mr Pandey, if the thief is tracked down, I hope you will keep me posted.'

Pandey smiled and nodded his head. We came out; Ushanathbabu accompanied us. Byomkesh took him aside to a corner of the veranda and conferred with him in whispers for a while. Then he returned and said, 'Let us go.'

The rickshaw-puller was waiting and we started back. Byomkesh remained lost in thought; at one point he said, 'Ajit, there was a moment there when Ushanathbabu raised his glasses. Did you notice anything then?'

'Why, no. What was there to notice?'

'Ushanathbabu's left eye is made of stone.'

'Really? So that's what the dark glasses are about?'

'Yes. Nearly three years ago he had a growth inside the eye and it had to be removed. He is always scared that the government would come to know of it and he would lose his job.'

'Talk about timidity! So was this the agenda for the secret conference?'

'Yes.'

I was not able to judge the weight of this piece of information. If Ushanathbabu had one eye instead of two, how would this affect anyone in any way?

Gradually, the rickshaw drew closer to home. Byomkesh said, 'Ajit, on our way there, you were asking if the matter of the picture-theft is serious enough. That question can now be answered. It *is* serious.'

'Really? How can you tell?'

Byomkesh did not reply; instead, he just flashed a quick smile at me.

In the afternoon we got ready to go and visit Mahidharbabu. Satyaboti said to me, 'Please do carry a torch. I'm sure it'll be dark before you return.'

I put the torch in my pocket, saying, 'So you aren't coming with us this time either?'

Satyaboti said, 'No. There's a poor woman lying sick in bed upstairs and she has no one to talk to. If I spend a few minutes with her, it might actually cheer her up.'

I said, 'I see that your sympathies for Malati Devi are on the upsurge.'

'And whyever not?'

I continued, 'Your sympathies for Rajani are ebbing with equal speed?'

'Certainly not. I have nothing against Rajani. She is not to blame in all of this. The blame lies squarely with the male species.'

I raised a finger in mock-warning, saying, 'Look here, don't bring "species" into it!'

Satyaboti crinkled her nose and marched into the kitchen.

When we reached Mahidharbabu's house it was still early evening, but the shadows were lengthening in the garden. There was no one at the gates. I presumed the gates stayed open at night.

The main door was open, but it didn't seem as though anyone was at home. After a few attempts at clearing our throats loudly, an aged domestic appeared at the doorway. He said, 'The master is resting upstairs. The little mistress is out in the garden. Please have a seat and I shall call her.'

Byomkesh said, 'No need for that. We'll find our way.' He headed straight for one specific corner of the garden. The trees and bushes made it difficult to see very far, but the tiny paths spread out under our feet like spiders' webs. I realized that Byomkesh was making for Phalguni's dwelling.

We reached the corner of the compound. A tiny hut stood there, with clay tiles for a roof; it looked like a shed to stock the gardening tools. Just beside it there was a huge draw-well.

The door to the hut lay open, but it was dark inside. I beamed my torch into the interiors. Someone was lying upon a pile of hay. As the light shone upon him, he got up and came outside. It was Phalguni Pal.

Today he was not in a good mood; his voice was full of injured pride. He said, 'Are you from the police too, come to search my room? Well, come on in and take a look. You won't find anything. I may be poor, but I am not a thief.'

Byomkesh said, 'We have not come to search. We just want to ask you a few questions. Why did you go to Ushanathbabu's house last night?'

Bitterly, Phalguni replied, 'I had done a sketch of him and I took it to show him. The watchman didn't let me in and sent me away. Fine, that suits me. But was it necessary to set the police on my heels?'

Byomkesh said, 'That was very unfair indeed. I shall tell the police; they will not trouble you again.'

'Thank you.' Phalguni went back into his dark hut. We retraced our steps.

Daylight was almost gone. We began to wander aimlessly in the garden, but did not see Rajani anywhere.

At the far end of the garden, there was a raised field house built with stones. It was encircled by a girdle of verdant moss. The field house was square in shape and resembled a pyramid. As we passed it, we suddenly heard voices raised in suppressed emotion, 'Picture, picture, picture! What's the use of the picture—I don't need it.'

'Shh! Someone may hear you.'

The voices were familiar; the first was Dr Ghatok's and the second Rajani's. We had found Dr Ghatok to be a mild-mannered, reserved person and it was difficult to imagine that such overt aggression could emanate from his voice. Rajani's voice too held a heightened note, but that wasn't so surprising.

When Dr Ghatok spoke again, his voice was relatively calmer, but there was still an excess of pent-up emotions in it. 'I want you—just you. It's not possible to quench a thirst for wine with the taste of water.'

Rajani said, 'And I? Do I not want you? But there is no other way.'

Ghatok said, 'There is a way, as I have told you.'

Rajani said, 'But Father—'

Ghatok said, 'You are not a minor. Your father cannot stop you.'

Rajani said, 'I know that. But—listen to me, please, Father is unwell right now. Let him get better and then . . .'

Ghatok said, 'No. I want to know this very moment whether you are with me or not.'

A pause. Then Rajani said, 'All right, I'll give you my answer today, but not right now. I need a little time. Meet me here at ten-thirty tonight; we can talk then. Perhaps people have come to the house now and if they don't see me . . .'

Silently, Byomkesh grabbed my hand and pulled me away.

We were tip-toeing away from the place, when we suddenly noticed another figure emerging from behind the pyramid and stealthily making his way in the opposite direction. But before I could identify him accurately, he vanished into the darkness.

After putting some distance between the pyramid and ourselves, Byomkesh said, 'Let's get back home; there's no need to visit today.'

We stepped out on the road. It was dark and there was no moon in the sky. The street was dimly lit. I turned the torch on from time to time and led the way back home.

Byomkesh was deep in thought. I guessed that he was trying to mentally map the path on which the two young lovers were about to venture. I did not disturb his contemplation.

When we were almost home, Byomkesh asked, 'Did you recognize the other man?'

I said, 'No. Who was it?'

Byomkesh said, 'It was our landlord, Professor Adinath Shome.'

'Really! Byomkesh, this case is growing too complicated for my taste. A missing photograph, a stolen figurine, a dipsomaniac artist, a one-eyed civil servant, a couple involved in illicit romance, an eavesdropping professor—I can't make any sense of it.'

'And you are not meant to either. You know that song—the strings are tangled up together, my harp can't play the tune? I'm in a similar dilemma.'

'Tell me, this matter of the doctor and Rajani—shouldn't we do something about it?'

In a resolute tone Byomkesh said, 'Nothing at all. We are like the audience at a cricket match—we may clap, we may boo, but it would be very indecent for us to get into the field and take matters into our own hands.'

We returned home to find Satyaboti knitting a woolen vest intently. I asked, 'How is your patient doing?'

Satyaboti did not reply and bent down upon her project instead, working the needles swiftly. I asked, 'What's the matter, don't you have anything to say? Did you go to visit Malati Devi?'

'I did.' Satyaboti did not look up, but a slow blush gradually crept into her face.

Byomkesh was standing at a distance, watching. Suddenly he burst into loud laughter and walked into the bedroom. Satyaboti started, as if pricked by a needle. She cast a wrathful glance at the bedroom door and then bent over her needles again.

I sat down beside her and asked, 'Will you please tell me what the matter is?'

'Nothing. Would you like some tea? I have put the water on the boil—I'll go and see . . .'

I stopped her and said, 'Oh no, first tell me what has happened. The tea can wait.'

Satyaboti burst out, 'It's nothing—it was just stupid of me to go and visit that scamp of a woman. Such a dirty mind—she tells me—no, I can't even say it. Someone with a filthy mind like that should rot in hell forever.'

Another volley of laughter greeted us from the bedroom. Satyaboti went away. The matter was clear to me. My face grew hot with indignation. I was aware that jealous, sceptical minds didn't think twice before jumping to conclusions; but if a person could make Satyaboti the subject of such atrocious comments, she had no right to live. Byomkesh could laugh all he wanted, but I was livid.

At night, when I went to bed, sleep eluded me. The events of the day had heated up my brain. The clock said ten. In these parts, in the month of December, ten o'clock was like midnight. Byomkesh and Satyaboti had gone to bed long ago. Lying sleepless in bed always made me crave for tobacco. I had to get up to satisfy the craving. Wrapping a shawl around myself, I lit a cigarette. But since smoking inside an enclosed room would pollute the air, I opened the window a little and stood by it as I smoked.

The window overlooked the main entrance. Right in front of my window was the main gate; across it lay the road, lit faintly by the light from a municipality lamp-post. I had been standing at the window for a couple of minutes when a sound outside alerted me. It sounded like someone coming down the stairway. I saw from the chink in the window that a shadow passed through the gate and crossed the road. As he passed the lamp-post, I recognized him—it was none other than Professor Shome, dressed in black. As if a bolt of lightning had hit me, I realized where he was headed at this time of the night. Tonight, at ten-thirty, Rajani and Dr Ghatok had a rendezvous in Mahidharbabu's garden; Shome would be present, uninvited, at the given spot. But why? What could be his objective?

Lost in my maze of bewildered thoughts, I was trying to get of the bottom of this matter when reasons for further astonishment presented themselves. I heard slight sounds of movement on the stairs again. This time, it was Malati Devi who emerged. It wasn't difficult to recognize her. There was the sound of a suppressed cough; then she disappeared in the same direction that Shome had gone.

The situation was quite obvious. The husband had set off on an assignation and the wife, unwell as she was on this winter night, had decided to follow him. Perhaps she wanted to catch him red-handed. Oh, the anguish of these mismatched lives! How terrible must be the ordeals of an uncaring husband and a distrustful wife! Surely divorce was a better option.

But what was I to do in the present situation? Should I wake Byomkesh and give him the news? No, that wasn't necessary—he was sleeping and should be spared this. But it did not look like I would be able to fall asleep soon. So I would sit by the window and keep a watch. We would see where all this led.

I lit another cigarette.

Five minutes, ten minutes. The light in the lamp-post flickered and went out.

A figure stepped in through the gates. Under the starlit sky, I could make out Malati Devi's heavy, stout shape. She made no attempts to conceal her footsteps. A muted sound emerged from her throat, and I couldn't tell whether it was a cough or a sob. She hastened upstairs.

The lady had returned, but there were no signs of the master. I deduced that she was not able to follow Shome for too long in the dark and soon lost sight of him. She must have looked around in vain for a while and then returned home.

Shome came back at eleven-thirty. He slinked in as silently as a bat.

In the morning, I narrated the events of the night before to Byomkesh. He listened quietly and made no comment.

A constable came in and handed him a note. Written at six the previous evening, it was from DSP Pandey and contained just a few lines:

Dear Byomkeshbabu,
The almirah has been opened and nothing is missing from within. You had said the figurine too would turn

up, but it still continues to be missing. There are no clues about the thief's identity either. Since you had wanted me to keep you posted, I am doing just that.

Yours truly,
Purandar Pandey.

Byomkesh put the letter in his pocket and said, 'This Pandey chap is truly a man of his word.'

Suddenly, Nakulesh Sarkar, the photographer, rushed into the room in great haste. After the party at Mahidharbabu's place, we had bumped into Nakuleshbabu a few times on the streets. With great agitation and excitement, he said, 'I was passing by and I thought I'd give you the news. I'm sure you haven't heard yet? Phalguni—you know, the fellow who used to paint—has been found drowned in Mahidharbabu's well.'

We were stupefied for a few moments. Then Byomkesh asked, 'When did this happen?'

Nakuleshbabu said, 'Most probably last night, but I'm not sure. He was a senseless boozer—I'm sure he lost his balance and fell into the well. This morning I had gone in to ask after Mahidharbabu's health and I found the gardeners dragging up the body.'

In silence, the two of us looked at one another. Apparently, the previous night had seen some very strange happenings in Mahidharbabu's garden.

'I'll be going—I have to go back there with the camera . . .' Nakuleshbabu made as if to leave.

'Oh no, do have a cup of tea before you go.'

Nakuleshbabu could not refuse the offer of tea and sat down again. Very soon, the tea arrived. After some pleasantries, Byomkesh asked, 'Did you search for the negative of that group photograph?'

'Which negative? Oh—yes, I have looked for it everywhere, but it didn't turn up. It's a real shame—I could easily have sold at least five more copies.'

'So, tell me, who were the ones present in the photograph?'

'Well, everyone who went to the picnic—let's see, Mahidharbabu, his daughter Rajani, Dr Ghatok, Professor

Shome and his wife, Ushanathbabu and his family and the bank manager, Amaresh Raha. All of them were in the picture. It turned out rather well, really—group photos seldom come out that well. Well, then, I'll be going now. I'll come again another day.'

Nakuleshbabu took his leave. The two of us sat there for some time. My heart was heavy, thinking of Phalguni. He may have been a hopeless drunkard, but he had been gifted with immense talent. But what use was the gift, if he was destined to die in this way?

Byomkesh heaved a sigh and stood up; he said, 'This possibility had never occurred to me. Come on, let's get going.'

'Where to?'

'To the bank. I need to withdraw some money.'

On our arrival in the town, we had deposited some money in the local bank; it was withdrawn from time to time for household expenses.

As we came out onto the veranda, Professor Shome was descending the stairs, clad in a dressing gown. His face bore a look of anxiety. Byomkesh greeted him, 'How are you doing?'

Shome said, 'Not too well. My wife has taken a turn for the worse—it's probably pneumonia. I think she is delirious at times.'

This wasn't surprising. She must have caught a chill on top of her cold last night. But perhaps Shome didn't know that. Byomkesh said, 'Have you informed Dr Ghatok?'

At the mention of the doctor's name, a shadow loomed over Shome's face. He said, 'I won't call Ghatok. I have sent for another doctor.'

Byomkesh threw him a sharp glance and asked, 'Why? Don't you have faith in Dr Ghatok any more? When I first arrived here, it was you who recommended the doctor to us.'

Shome pursed his lips and remained silent. Byomkesh said, 'Anyway! We just received information that Phalguni Pal has drowned in Mahidharbabu's draw-well last night and died.'

Shome did not seem interested. He said, 'Is that so? Perhaps he committed suicide. Artists are known to be a little unbalanced . . .'

Byomkesh fired the next question at him like a bullet out of a gun, 'Professor Shome, where were you at eleven o'clock last night?'

Shome looked stunned; his face went white. With visible lack of equanimity, he said, 'Me—I! Whoever said I went anywhere? I was just—'

Byomkesh raised his hand and said, 'There's no use lying. Professor Shome, you are to blame for the critical condition of your wife today. She followed you out into the streets last night. If she were to succumb to this illness—'

Eyes wide with terror, Shome said, 'My wife—Byomkeshbabu, believe me, I had no idea . . .'

Byomkesh raised his finger and said in a terribly severe tone, 'But we do. I am your well-wisher and so I am cautioning you. Please be careful. Come on, Ajit.'

Shome remained standing, quite petrified. After going some distance, Byomkesh said, 'I have really given Shome a scare.' Then he glanced at his watch and said, 'There's still some time before the bank opens. Come, let's pay a quick visit to Ghatok at his dispensary.'

The doctor's chamber was near the market. We were about to enter his office when we heard him saying to someone, 'Look, your son has typhoid; it is a time-consuming treatment. I cannot take on a case of such duration at this time. Why don't you go to Sridharbabu—he is an experienced doctor . . .'

We went inside as the other gentleman stepped out. The doctor greeted us with delight, 'Come in, come in. When the patient himself calls on the doctor, it's a sign that he is cured. The other day Mahidharbabu called me a horse-doctor. Now you tell me, are my patients human or not? Do you consider yourself a horse?' He laughed out loud. Ghatok's mood was jolly today; his eyes were bright with gaiety.

Byomkesh laughed and said, 'It's probably best for my own self-respect to agree that your patients are indeed human. How is Mahidharbabu?'

The doctor said, 'Much better. He is almost back to normal.'

Byomkesh said, 'Are you aware that Phalguni Pal is dead?'

The doctor looked startled. He said, 'The artist? What

happened to him?'

'Nothing. He drowned in a well last night.' Byomkesh briefly narrated all that he knew. Ghatok was a little perturbed for some time; then he said, 'I should go there once. Mahidharbabu is still weak and . . . Let me see if I can pay them a quick visit.' He stood up to leave.

Suddenly, Byomkesh asked, 'When are you going to Calcutta?'

There was a sudden change in the doctor's expression; he gazed steadily at Byomkesh for a few moments and then said, 'Who has told you that I am going to Calcutta?'

Byomkesh merely smiled a little. Ghatok said, 'Yes, I do have plans to make a trip shortly. Well then, I'll see you later. If I can, I'll drop in at your place in the evening.'

He got into his tiny car and drove away. We headed for the bank. On the way, I asked, 'How did you know the doctor is planning a trip to Calcutta? Have you also taken to the occult sciences these days?'

Byomkesh replied, 'No. But when a doctor says he doesn't wish to take on a case of lengthy duration, and it should be taken to another doctor, it may be safely deduced that he is planning a trip.'

'But how did you guess it would be to Calcutta?'

'That was from his general air of gaiety.'

The bank was very close to the doctor's chamber. When we arrived there, the doors had already opened. Two armed guards stood on duty.

The bank consisted of a large room divided into two sections with low dividers made of glass and steel. A row of windows lined these dividers. Business was conducted through these windows.

As Byomkesh stood outside one of these teller windows, writing out a cheque, I noticed the bank manager, Amaresh Raha, standing in a far corner, speaking to one of the clerks. Amareshbabu had also seen us and he came out to greet us with a smile. He said, 'Hello! Thank goodness I spotted you or you would have simply withdrawn the cash and left.'

Since the tea-party we had not encountered Amareshbabu again. He was apologetic about it; stroking his French-cut beard, he said, 'Every day I think of calling on you, but something or the other turns up. Working in a bank means twenty-four hours of drudgery.'

Byomkesh said, 'But such drudgery is pleasurable. You are handling money all the time.'

Amareshbabu made a wry face and said, 'Where is the pleasure, Byomkeshbabu? The bullock may carry the ingredients of a feast throughout the day, but at the end of it he gets to have just his fodder and water.'

When Byomkesh had cashed his cheque, Amareshbabu said, 'Come on, now that I have got hold of you, I won't let you go so easily. Let's go into my office and sit for awhile. I've read so much about your wonderful exploits in Ajitbabu's marvellous writings. It is a privilege to meet two such talented people.'

It was evident that the gentleman was not only an admirer of Byomkesh's, but also a connoisseur of literature. I felt some regret that we hadn't furthered our acquaintance the other day.

He took us inside the room. He had an entire office to himself; but as we reached its doorway, he said, 'No, not here. Let's go upstairs. There's a lot of disturbance and the hustle-bustle of work over here. Upstairs will be much more convivial.'

The door to the office lay open. I cast a glance within and saw that it held nothing more than ordinary chairs and tables, some accounting books and a few huge iron safes.

As we climbed the stairs, Byomkesh asked, 'Do you live upstairs?'

'Yes. It's convenient for the bank as well.'

'Your family—wife and children—they are all here?'

'I do not have a wife and children, Byomkeshbabu. I was blessed with some good sense and so I never married. Since I am alone, I live a decent life. If I had a family, I wouldn't have been able to make ends meet.'

The quarters upstairs were quite spacious for a single person. There were three or four rooms, which opened on to a huge terrace. Amareshbabu led us into the drawing room and offered us seats. It was a simple, unadorned room; there were no pictures on the walls or rugs on the floor. On one side, there was a single cot covered with a bedspread, a few armchairs and a bookshelf. Quite plain fare, but very pleasing. It was obvious that the occupant was a neat and orderly person.

'Do sit down while I fetch some tea.' Amareshbabu left the room.

The bookshelf was drawing me to it and I went up to take a look. Most of the books were fiction; there was also a dictionary and a collection of Tagore's poetry. I was delighted to find some of my books about Byomkesh's adventures.

Byomkesh also joined me. He pulled out one of the books and opened it; I realized that it wasn't written in Bangla but in some other Indian script. It looked a little like Hindi, but not quite.

At this moment Amareshbabu returned. Byomkesh asked, 'So you also know Gujarati?'

Amareshbabu made a clicking sound with his tongue and replied, 'Hardly. Once I tried to pick it up, but I couldn't make much progress. An average Bengali has enough on his plate learning his mother-tongue well, and then there is English. On top of that, if he has to learn a third language, it usually proves to be too much for him. But had I been able to pick up Gujarati, it would have stood me in good stead; in the banking profession, it helps if you know Gujarati.'

We returned to our seats. After some ordinary pleasantries, Byomkesh said, 'I guess you have heard that Phalguni Pal has died?'

Amareshbabu nearly fell off his chair. 'What! Phalguni Pal is dead?' he exclaimed. 'When—where—how did he die?'

Byomkesh narrated his tale about the demise of Phalguni Pal. Amareshbabu shook his head sorrowfully and said, 'The poor soul! He really was in dire straits. Yesterday he came to see me.'

Now it was our turn to be surprised. Byomkesh remarked, 'Yesterday? When?'

Amareshbabu said, 'In the morning. Yesterday being a

Sunday, the bank was closed. I had just taken the first sip of my morning tea when Phalguni landed up. He had made a sketch of me and he came to show it to me.'

'I see.'

The domestic came in with three cups of tea. He was in uniform; probably a peon from the bank who doubled as a servant. From the general appearance of things, I gathered that Amareshbabu was quite careful in his spending habits.

As he stirred his tea with the spoon, Byomkesh asked, 'So did you buy the sketch?'

With a doleful expression, Amareshbabu said, 'I had no choice. I wanted to give him five rupees but he wouldn't take anything less than ten. Had I known this before . . .'

Byomkesh took a sip from his cup and said, 'I would like very much to see the last work of the dead artist.'

'Certainly. It's quite a good likeness. Of course, I know nothing about art.'

He pulled out a thick, square sheet from the lower compartment of the bookshelf and held it up for us. Phalguni had done a good job; the inconspicuous countenance of Amareshbabu shone brightly in the sketch. Byomkesh was a good judge of art and considered the work with a crease in his brows.

Intially, Amareshbabu had been chatting quite jovially, but ever since we told him the news of Phalguni's death, he seemed to have grown inhibited. There was no further conversation as the tea was drunk. Amareshbabu put his cup down and spoke in a muted tone, 'Speaking of Phalguni, I just remembered, the other day at the tea-party something was said about a picture being stolen. Do you remember? I don't know if anything has turned up in that regard.'

Byomkesh was lost in his study of the sketch and didn't reply. Not knowing whether to speak or not, I too stared at Amareshbabu dumbly. He said, 'It's quite a trivial matter really, so I guess no one has bothered their heads about it.'

Byomkesh put the sketch down and heaved a sigh, saying, 'Wonderful sketch. If the man had lived, I too would have commissioned a portrait. Amareshbabu, do keep this sketch carefully. Today no one has heard of Phalguni Pal; but a day will come when his work will sell at a very high price indeed.'

Amareshbabu cheered up a little and said, 'Really! So you'd say the ten rupees weren't a complete waste? Is the sketch worth being framed and hung on the wall?'

'Certainly.'

We rose to leave. Amareshbabu said, 'We'll meet again. The year-end is almost here; I shall have to visit the head office during the New Year's holidays and confer with my bosses. This year it's a two-day holiday for the New Year.'

'Why is that so?'

'Thirty-first December is a Sunday, you see. If you count Saturday as a half-day, then you have a two-and-a-half days' holiday. You will still be here for a while, I hope?'

'We're here till the second of January.'

'All right then, goodbye.'

We took our leave. We didn't have to make our way back through the bank. There was a back door to the house, with stairs leading down. These brought us straight onto the main road. We were passing by the market when I suddenly remembered that we were out of cigarettes. I said, 'Come this way, I have to buy a tin of cigarettes.'

Byomkesh was a little preoccupied. Suddenly he came awake and said, 'Oh yes! I have to buy something as well.'

We entered a large variety store. I went in one direction to purchase the cigarettes and Byomkesh headed the other way. As I was buying my cigarettes, from the corner of my eye I saw Byomkesh buying a bottle of expensive perfume and putting it into his pocket.

I laughed to myself. I had no idea why these people fell out with each other and why they patched things up again. Conjugal life remained a comical enigma to me.

That afternoon, after lunch, I stretched out on the bed for a short nap. When I woke up, it was three-thirty.

There were murmurs coming from the direction of Byomkesh's room. I peeped in and saw that Byomkesh was sitting on a chair. Satyaboti stood behind it, with her arms around his neck, whispering softly in his ears. There were smiles on both their faces.

I moved aside and raised my voice, 'Hello there, love-birds—if you're going to take long, I guess I should look into getting us all some tea.'

Embarrassed, Satyaboti came out immediately, with her face partially covered by a corner of her sari. She hurried away into the kitchen. A little later, Byomkesh emerged, puffing on a cigarette. I was surprised, 'What's up? You're smoking like a chimney!'

Byomkesh gave a broad grin and said, 'I have been granted permission—as many as I want from this day on.'

I realized that in the marital equation, what mattered was not only the heart's workings, but the calculativeness of the brain as well.

After tea, I went upstairs to look in on our ailing landlady. Some social obligations were unavoidable.

Professor Shome looked worried. Malati Devi's condition had deteriorated, but it wasn't beyond all hope. Both the lungs were affected and oxygen was being administered externally. The fever was running pretty high and the patient was slipping into delirium periodically. A nurse had been employed to look after her.

As you make your bed, so shall you lie. I conveyed my sympathies and came back downstairs. A little while later, Dr Ghatok arrived.

The doctor's demeanour was different now. He was a little chary, a little suspicious and a little self-absorbed. From time to time he looked at Byomkesh as if the latter was becoming a cause for concern.

The conversation that ensued was commonplace. Ghatok had gone to Mahidharbabu's in the morning and taken a look at Phalguni's body. Byomkesh asked, 'What did you see? Is the cause of death known yet?'

After a brief pause, the doctor said, 'Until the autopsy results come in, nothing can be said for sure.'

Byomkesh said, 'But still, you being a doctor, couldn't you tell anything at all?'

He hesitated a little and then said, 'No.'

Byomkesh said, 'All right, let that be. How is Mahidharbabu? Last evening we had dropped in to look him up. But after much hollering and hailing, we didn't catch sight of anyone and so we came back.'

Warily, the doctor asked, 'What time was that?'

'Around five in the evening.'

The doctor was silent for a few moments and then said, 'I wouldn't know. I was also there in the evening, but I came back before five o'clock. Mahidharbabu is fine now. But after this incident in the house today—naturally he is in shock.'

Byomkesh said, 'And Rajani Devi—how is she?'

A slight tinge of colour appeared on Ghatok's cheeks. He spoke slowly, 'Rajani Devi is fine. I didn't hear anything about her being unwell. All right then, I shall take my leave today.'

The doctor stood up; we followed him out. At the door Byomkesh said, 'So your trip to Calcutta is all planned?'

The doctor whirled around; his eyes flashed. He gritted his teeth and said, 'Byomkeshbabu, you have come here to recuperate, not to play detective. Please do not stick your nose into matters that do not concern you.' He marched off through the door.

We came back inside and sat down. Byomkesh lit a cigarette and said, 'Dr Ghatok is quite a nice person, really. But if you step on his toes, he hisses like a snake.'

There was the sound of a motorcycle coming to a stop outside. Byomkesh jumped up and said, 'Well, Mr Pandey is here. That's good.'

Pandey entered the room. He gave a tired smile and said, 'Byomkeshbabu, your prophecy came true. We have found the figurine.'

Byomkesh offered him a chair and said, 'Please sit down. So where did the fairy turn up?'

'At the bottom of Mahidharbabu's draw-well. After retrieving Phalguni's body, we sent some men down the well and Ushanathbabu's fairy was dredged up.'

Byomkesh crinkled his eyes for some moments and then asked, 'Anything else?'

'Nothing else.'

'Has the post-mortem report come in?'

'Yes, it has. Phalguni did not drown to death. Death occurred before he fell into the water.'

'Hmm. So somebody must have murdered him last night. Then the body was thrown into the well. So it wasn't suicide.'

'That is how it seems to be. But who would stand to gain anything by killing a useless chap like Phalguni?'

'I am sure there is some gain somewhere, or why would he be killed? If a useless tramp came to know a terrible secret, then his being alive could pose a threat to someone. Phalguni may have been useless, but he wasn't senseless.'

Pandey pulled a wry face and said, 'That is true. But I am wondering how the figurine came to be in the well. Was it Phalguni, then, who stole it? Did he have a scuffle with the killer over that fairy-figurine? And then the killer pushed him into the well? But the figurine isn't even worth very much.'

Byomkesh said, 'By the way, were there any other wounds or marks on Phalguni's body?'

'No. But a substantial amount of opium was found in his stomach. It must have been mixed in the alcohol.'

Byomkesh said, 'I see. Look here, it is not very important to dwell on *how* Phalguni was killed. The real question is *why* it was done.'

Pandey looked at him in eager anticipation and asked, 'Have you figured something out in this regard, Byomkeshbabu?'

Byomkesh smiled softly and said, 'Perhaps I *have* figured out bits of it. There is a lot that I need to tell you. But would you have the time to listen to it all?'

Pandey took Byomkesh by his hand and began to drag him towards the door as he said, 'I'll show you whether I have time or not. Please come over to my house; you can have your dinner there.'

Pandey left with Byomkesh in tow.

Satyaboti and I played cards until nine-thirty in the night. When Byomkesh returned, I asked him, 'So, what do you have to report?'

236 / Saradindu Bandyopadhyay

He gave an angelic smile and said, 'The chicken was simply delicious!'

I chided him and said, 'Don't evade the issue. What all did you talk about?'

Byomkesh bit his tongue in mock shame and said, 'It wouldn't be right to reveal the secrets of the police. But I can say this much—nothing was said that you aren't already aware of.'

'And who, pray, killed Phalguni Pal?'

'Oh, that would be—the Jack of Hearts.'

Christmas was past, the new year was almost there. In this town there wasn't much revelry on these occasions—just some parties thrown by the government officials and their families.

There had been no new turn of events in the past few days. Malati Devi was well on her way to recovery. But when she regained consciousness and saw the young nurse in her room, the demon within her raised its ugly head again. She abused the nurse and threw her out. After this, her condition took a turn for the worse again and Professor Shome was at his wits' end, handling it all alone.

It was Saturday, the morning of the thirtieth of December. Byomkesh said, 'Come on then, let's take in some sun today.' We hailed a rickshaw and set off.

The first destination was Nakuleshbabu's photography studio. The shop was downstairs; he lived right above it. Nakuleshbabu was at home, and seemed a little perturbed to see us. It looked like he was in the process of doing some packing. Managing to paste a stiff smile onto his face, he said, 'Come in—do you wish to have a photo taken?'

Byomkesh said, 'No, not today. We were passing by and we thought we'd check out your place.'

Nakuleshbabu said, 'Oh well, that's nice. But I really do take good pictures. Everyone here has had their picture taken by me. Take a look.'

There were many photographs lining the walls; amongst them were the familiar faces of Mahidharbabu and Professor Shome. Byomkesh glanced at them and said, 'They're very good indeed. You seem to be a true artist.'

Nakuleshbabu was delighted with the compliment and said, 'Hey Lalu, go and get two cups of tea from the stall next door.'

'There's no need for tea, we have already had our breakfast. You seem to be preparing for a trip?'

Nakuleshbabu said, 'Yes, I am going to Calcutta for a couple of days. My wife and son are over there and I am going to fetch them.'

'All right then, we will leave you to your packing.'

Byomkesh got into the rickshaw again and said, 'Take us to the railway station.'

I said, 'What's the matter—everyone seems to be making a beeline for Calcutta?'

Byomkesh said, 'Calcutta holds a great attraction for visitors at this time of winter.'

We arrived at the railway station. It was a terminal stop on a branch line—quite a small one. The big junction was nearly twenty-five miles from here. From there one had to change to the main line. The junction was also accessible by road; those who owned cars preferred the roadway route.

But Byomkesh didn't get down at the station; he signalled to the rickshaw-puller and the man turned the vehicle around and headed the other way, towards the exit. I asked, 'What's the matter—don't you want to go in?'

Byomkesh said, 'Perhaps you didn't notice, Dr Ghatok was standing at the ticket counter purchasing tickets.'

'Really?' I began to bombard Byomkesh with questions, but he pretended not to hear.

As we were passing by the market we saw a motor car standing by the large variety store. Byomkesh stopped the rickshaw and went in; I followed him. I asked, 'What do you want now—more perfumes?'

He laughed and said, 'Oh no, no.'

'Some hair-oil then? Bangles?'

'Do come on in.'

We entered the shop and found Ushanathbabu in there. He was buying a leather suitcase. The words slipped out of my mouth involuntarily, 'Are you going to Calcutta too?'

Ushanathbabu looked up, startled, and said, 'Me? No, no, I am a treasury officer and there's no way I can leave the station. Who told you I was going to Calcutta?' His voice sounded quite rude.

Byomkesh intervened in a humouring tone and said, 'Nobody told us. Since you are buying a suitcase, Ajit thought . . . Anyway, I hope you have got your figurine back?'

'Yes, I have.' Rather brusquely he turned away and began talking to the salesman.

We returned to the rickshaw. I asked, 'What's up—why is his lordship angry with us?'

Byomkesh said, 'I don't know. Perhaps he would like to go to Calcutta but his superior won't allow it—so he is peeved. Or . . .'

The rickshaw-puller asked, 'Where to now, sir?'

Byomkesh said, 'To DSP Pandey's.'

Purandar Pandey worked from his home. He greeted us with a smile. Byomkesh asked, 'All set?'

Pandey said, 'All set.'

'What time is the train?'

'At ten-thirty. It will reach the junction at eleven-fifteen.'

'And at what time is the connecting train to Calcutta?'

'At a quarter to twelve.'

'And the mail heading west?'

'At thirty-five minutes past eleven.'

Byomkesh said, 'Good. In that case, I shall go to Mahidharbabu's at around five in the evening. You can come in at about five-thirty. Even if Mahidharbabu doesn't grant me my request, I am sure he wouldn't refuse to comply with the police.'

Pandey smiled gravely and said, 'I believe so too.'

This coded conversation made no sense to me. But I knew there was no use asking—Byomkesh would only bite his tongue and say, 'The secrets of the police.'

From Pandey's office we went to the bank. We needed some cash.

The bank was terribly crowded on account of the forthcoming holidays. Still, we managed to meet

Amareshbabu for a few moments. He said, 'Do withdraw whatever cash you may need for the following weekend. Tomorrow and the day after the bank will be closed.'

Byomkesh asked, 'When are you returning?'

'Day after tomorrow, by nightfall.'

It was a busy time and a clerk called him away. We withdrew money and were stepping outside when we saw Dr Ghatok entering the bank. He also spotted us, but looked right through us and strode up to one of the teller windows. Byomkesh looked at me and narrowed his eyes, which were brimming with laughter. Then he got into the rickshaw and said, 'Back home.'

Byomkesh and I arrived at Mahidharbabu's as the clock struck five. He was in the drawing room. It looked like the illness had taken its toll on him. The cantaloupe-smile was wan and the melon-shaped cheeks were sagging.

He said, 'Come in, do come in. Byomkeshbabu, you'll live a long time—I was just thinking of you. Your health seems to be restored. That's good, indeed.'

Byomkesh said, 'But your health doesn't look to be at its best.'

Mahidharbabu said, 'It was a little shaky sometime ago, but now I am all right. But Byomkeshbabu, something disturbing has happened.'

'What is it?'

'Rajani left for Calcutta last night.'

'What! Has she gone? Didn't she tell you before she left?'

'No, no, it's nothing like that. She has our trusted servant, Ramdin, accompanying her.'

'Then what's the cause for concern?'

Mahidharbabu was incapable of being secretive. He said candidly, 'Let me tell you the whole story then. An aunt of Rajani's stays in Calcutta. It is she who brought up the girl. Last night a telegram arrived from her husband, Rajani's uncle. He asked Rajani to come soon: her aunt had been taken ill. So I sent Rajani off by the evening train. She often undertakes this journey—it is only a matter of a few hours. I have received her telegram informing me that she has reached Calcutta this morning.

'So far so good. But now listen to this. Today I received two letters; one of these letters is from Rajani's aunt, dated yesterday. It contains ordinary news, but there is no mention of an illness.'

Mahidharbabu looked at Byomkesh with panic-stricken eyes. Byomkesh said, 'Isn't it possible that she suddenly fell ill after writing that letter?'

Mahidharbabu said, 'That is not entirely impossible. But I haven't yet told you about the other letter. It is an anonymous one. Here—read it.'

He handed Byomkesh an envelope. The postmark on the envelope indicated that the letter had been posted in this very town. Byomkesh took the letter out and began to read it. It was a few lines scrawled on a sheet of plain paper:

Unknown to you, a dissembling rascal is engaged in illicit romance with your daughter. If they happen to elope, there will be no end to the scandal. Beware! Do not place your trust in Dr Ghatok.

Byomkesh read the letter and handed it back. In a trembling voice, Mahidharbabu said, 'I do not know who has written this, but if it holds a grain of truth . . .'

Byomkesh said in a soothing tone, 'You know Dr Ghatok. Do you think he is capable of doing something like this?'

Mahidharbabu hesitated a little and said, 'I know the doctor to be a nice person; he comes in every now and then. But you never know what's within a man's heart. Tell me, is he in town at the moment?'

Byomkesh said, 'Yes. I saw him this very morning.'

Mahidharbabu heaved a sigh of relief and said, 'He *is* still here? Well then, perhaps someone has just sent a hoax letter.'

Byomkesh said, 'But the doctor is due to go to Calcutta tonight.'

Mahidharbabu got worked up again and said, 'Wha—t, he is going! So then . . .?'

In a firm voice, Byomkesh said, 'Mahidharbabu, please rest assured, there will be no scandal. You are worrying without cause.'

Mahidharbabu held Byomkesh's hands and said, 'Are you sure? But how do you know—you are just . . .'

Byomkesh said, 'There are a lot of things which I know and you don't. Please believe me when I say I am not doling out false assurances. Rajani Devi will be back in two days. She would not do anything to embarrass you.'

In a relieved and satisfied manner, Mahidharbabu said, 'Well then, that's all I ask. Thank you, Byomkeshbabu. You cannot imagine how much solace I have drawn from your words. I am not young any more and fate has cheated me once—so the slightest sign is enough to scare me.'

Byomkesh said, 'Forget about all that. But I have come to you with a request of my own.'

Eagerly, Mahidharbabu said, 'Please, anything.'

'We need your car for tonight, to go to the junction. There is some urgent work.'

'That is nothing at all. What time do you need it?'

'At nine.'

'Fine—at nine o'clock my car will be waiting before your house. Anything else?'

'No, nothing else.'

At this point Mr Pandey arrived. All of us had tea and plenty of snacks before returning home.

At nine o'clock sharp, Mahidharbabu's eight-cylinder motor car came to a stop in front of our house. Byomkesh, Mr Pandey and I got into it. The car started. A black police van was waiting; it began to follow our car.

The car left the town limits behind and set off on the long road to the junction. The road was lined with trees on either side; our car ripped a tunnel of light through the deep gloom and sped through it.

There wasn't much conversation on the way. The three of us sat in the car and puffed away at one cigarette after another.

At one point, Byomkesh remarked, 'Your culprit will buy a ticket for the first class.'

'Yes, I thought so too,' said Pandey. 'Whichever coach he gets into, Inspector Dubey will be in the next compartment.'

'How many in the police force know the real story?'

'Only Dubey and myself. We had to borrow Mahidharbabu's car to avoid a big fuss. Even the men in the van behind us do not know where we are going and why. There is always the possibility of information leaking out. Then there are those policemen who can be bribed. In any case, the police are notoriously bad at keeping a secret.'

Purandar Pandey was an honest man—he did not hesitate to criticize his own.

We reached the junction at ten. The station was brightly lit with several red and green lamps.

The police van contained two sub-inspectors and a few constables. Pandey posted them at various points both inside and outside the station. He then met the station-master and told him that he was expecting a message on the wireless and that he should be informed as soon as it arrived.

The three of us went into the first-class waiting room and sat down. Pandey was checking his watch frequently.

At ten-thirty, the station-master informed us that the wireless message had arrived. 'Everything fine—first class,' it said.

There were still forty-five minutes to go.

However long these forty-five minutes seemed, they did eventually elapse. The signal for the approaching train was sounded. We went and stood on the platform. We were all clad in overcoats and woolen caps and so it was unlikely that anyone would recognize us at first glance.

Finally, the much-awaited train arrived.

We stood at the spot where the first class compartment would come to a stop. The coach came and halted right before us. The wooden shutters on the windows were drawn and so the interior couldn't be seen. Soon, the door flew open. A coolie rushed in and came out with two large leather suitcases.

The coach contained one sole passenger, who now proceeded to detrain. He was a total stranger, dressed in a coat and trousers, clean-shaven, with a pair of shaded blue glasses perched on his nose. He was preparing to heave the suitcases on to the coolie's shoulders, when Byomkesh and Pandey walked up and flanked him on either side. In a mock-sorrowful tone, Byomkesh said, 'Amareshbabu, we can't let you go. You'll have to come with us.'

Amareshbabu! The bank manager, Amaresh Raha. I had completely failed to recognize him without his French-cut beard.

Amaresh Raha cast a swift glance to his left and to his right, then, like lightning, whipped out a pistol from his pocket, held it to his temple and pulled the trigger. There was a sharp, cracking sound.

A huge crowd gathered around the prostrate body. Pandey blew his whistle. At once, several policemen arrived at the spot, surrounded the body and dispersed the crowd. In a brisk tone, Pandey said, 'Inspector Dubey, these two suitcases are placed in your care.'

A man pushed through the crowd and made his way in. I recognized him—Dr Ghatok. He said, 'What's the matter? Who is this?'

Pandey said, 'Amaresh Raha. Please take a look and check if he is alive.'

Dr Ghatok knelt down and checked the pulse. He stood up and said, 'He is dead.'

From the deep caverns of the crowds, an inquisitive voice chimed in, 'What! What's going on? Amaresh Raha is dead—what! How did he die? And where is his beard, eh?'

It was Nakulesh Sarkar, the photographer.

Byomkesh addressed both Dr Ghatok and Nakuleshbabu and said, 'Your train is here. There's no time now, you can hear all about it on your return.'

Byomkesh said, 'I made a terrible mistake. Amaresh Raha was a bank manager; it never occurred to me that he could hold a licence for a pistol.'

Satyaboti said, 'Oh no, from the beginning, please.'

It was the second of January. We were on our way back to Calcutta. Purandar Pandey, Mahidharbabu and his daughter

Rajani had come to the station to see us off. But now, at last, we were alone.

Byomkesh said, 'Two things had got entangled—one, the theft of the photo and two, the secret romance between the doctor and Rajani. Although their love was clandestine, there was nothing shameful about it. They went to Calcutta and got married before a magistrate. Most probably Rajani's aunt and uncle knew about it, and nobody else—not even Mahidharbabu. As long as he is alive, they won't tell anyone. Mahidharbabu is not an orthodox man, but he hasn't yet shed his reservations about widow-remarriage. That is why they got married in secret and saved face all around.'

I asked, 'Did you get this information from the doctor?'

Byomkesh said, 'Oh no, I didn't broach the topic to the doctor at all. He was so prickly about this, that any mention of it would have made him bite my head off. I took Rajani aside and told her that I know everything. She asked, "Byomkeshbabu, do you think we have done anything wrong?" I said, "No. It goes to your credit that you have taken care not to hurt Mahidharbabu in the course of your rebellion. An aggressive mutiny is of no use, it only serves to rouse the opposing forces. Resistance has to be accompanied by tolerance. You will be happy together."'

Satyaboti said, 'Go on, tell us what happened next.'

Byomkesh picked up the threads of his narrative, 'If you were to look at the theft of the picture as a trivial matter, there could be many explanations for it. But if you were to attach any weight to it, there could be only one possible reason behind it—there was one person in that group who wished to keep his face concealed from the public eye.

'But what was the objective? One reason could be that there was a branded criminal in that group who did not want his photo to be circulated. But that theory didn't really hold water. None of the members of the group could be in hiding; they all had a public profile. So there wouldn't be any point in removing this one photograph.

'The possibility of a marked criminal had to be rejected. But if there was one individual in the group who was planning to become a criminal in the future, that is, planning to commit a serious crime and then abscond, then he too would like all records of his face to disappear. Ajit, you are a writer—can you possibly describe a man so accurately, just through the medium of language, that he would be recognized on sight? No, you can't—especially if his appearance was quite ordinary; it would be nearly impossible. But a photograph can record his exact likeness with great accuracy. That is why police files have photographs of marked criminals.

'So now we have the possibility that one member of the group was planning to commit a serious crime and disappear from the public eye. Now the question was: what was the nature of the impending crime and who was this individual?

'Let us consider each of the group members, one by one. Mahidharbabu could not abscond; he has a stupendous amount of immovable property and neither is his face one that you would forget in a hurry. Dr Ghatok could abscond with Rajani, but she is not a minor and eloping with her was not a legal offence. So why would he steal the photograph? Professor Shome could also be ruled out. If he had any plans of breaking his shackles and fleeing, stealing that one photograph would not have sufficed. There are other pictures of Shome. One of them hangs in Nakuleshbabu's shop, as we have seen. Let us now consider Nakuleshbabu. He was in the picnic group. He owed a large sum of money to Mahidharbabu and it was possible that he would want to disappear. But he had taken the picture and so his face was not in it. Hence, it would be pointless for him to steal the picture.

'The only two that remained, then, were Ushanathbabu and Amaresh Raha. One was in charge of the government treasury and the other was the manager of the bank. If anyone had anything to gain from absconding, it would be one of these two. Both had access to an immense amount of money that was not their own; the temptation to make off with some of it would always be there for both.

'Let us consider Ushanathbabu first. He has a wife and a child; his appearance is also such that even without a photograph, he could be identified quite easily. He wears dark glasses, but if those are taken off, he is blind in one eye. It would be impossible for him to elude the keen, searching eyes of the police. Moreover, such an act of defiance would also go against the grain of his nature.

'So the only one who remained was Amaresh Raha. Of course, suspicion was fixed on him only by a process of elimination. But then, if you observed him carefully, you would see that it could be no one else. His appearance was the most commonplace—there must be millions of people with his kind of undistinguished features. He had a French-cut beard. The advantage of this was that it could be shaved off and the face would look entirely different. Rather than wear a fake beard, growing a real one and then shaving it off is always a better and safer way to disguise yourself.

'Amareshbabu was a bachelor. He drew a reasonably decent salary and yet he griped about meagreness; he harboured a secret desire for untold riches. I believe he has been hatching this plan for a long time now. Do you remember seeing a book in Gujarati on his bookshelf? He was self-taught in that language; perhaps he intended to migrate to the Bombay region with the stolen money. There is a similarity in the physiognomy of Bengalis and Gujaratis and if he was fluent in the language, no one would be able to tell.

'He had thought out his plan to the last detail. But then, when the time came for him to turn his design into action, some unexpected hurdles came up. He had to have that picture taken at the picnic. There is no doubt that he was reluctant to be in the picture, but if he had protested too strongly, it would have raised suspicions. So he thought he would get around the problem by stealing the prints and the negative.

'So he stole the picture from Mahidharbabu's house. The following day we were present at the tea-party; the discussion that started there made Amareshbabu realize that he had made one mistake. He should not have stolen just the picture. So the next time, when he entered Ushanathbabu's house to steal his copy, he picked up the figurine for the lack of anything else to steal. Then he inserted the wrong key in the almirah to make it seem that the theft of the photo was by no means the thief's chief objective. There was no need to steal the copy that Professor Shome had, since Malati Devi had already torn it to bits. It is possible that he did go in to steal that copy, but found the picture was already destroyed.

'My arrival did not alarm Amareshbabu. His felony was still in the deep womb of the future. Everyone would come to know of his crime after he made off with the money. If I came to know of his misdemeanour at the same time, it would make no difference to him. But when the spectre of Phalguni Pal made its advent, Amareshbabu was truly disturbed. All his well-laid plans could now go awry. With Phalguni around, what was the use of stealing the photos? He would draw a sketch from memory in minutes.

'But there is something very exciting about the taste of forbidden fruit. Amareshbabu had already tasted the fruit; it was not possible for him to retreat after having come this far. So, on the day that Phalguni drew a sketch of him, he decided that the artist could not be allowed to live any longer. That night he mixed a sufficient amount of opium in a bottle of alcohol and went to Phalguni's hut. It was never difficult to get Phalguni to consume anything addictive. When Phalguni lost his senses, Amareshbabu picked him up and dropped him into the well. He had brought the stolen figurine with him and that too went into the well, so that the police would take Phalguni to be the thief. Most probably this incident took place after eleven o'clock at night, when the other conference, in another corner of the garden, was already over.

'The post-mortem report said that Phalguni died before he was drowned. But I think Amareshbabu had probably wanted him to be alive when he was dropped into the well, so that everyone would think that he had fallen into the well in an intoxicated state and drowned to death.

'Anyway, Amareshbabu's path was now clear. He could just destroy the sketch that he had shown us before leaving, and that would take care of everything—there would be no other way of identifying him.

'The moment I understood beyond a shadow of doubt that this was Amareshbabu's doing, I revealed everything to Mr

Pandey. He is a very intelligent man and he grasped the plot at once. Since then, there hasn't been a minute when Amareshbabu was not under police surveillance.'

Byomkesh lit a cigarette.

I asked, 'Tell me something, how did you know the exact day when Amaresh Raha would choose to make his escape? He could have chosen any other day.'

Byomkesh said, 'The advantage in absconding just before a long holiday is that you get some extra time. Two days later when the bank would open and the burglary would be discovered, the thief would be far away. Of course, he could have made his escape on the Christmas holiday as well; but from his end, he needed to do it on the New Year's weekend and none other. The bank which Amaresh Raha managed was a branch office of a reputed bank of Calcutta. At the end of every month a vast sum of money came into this branch from the head office, in order to meet the needs of the bank at the beginning of the month. In addition to the ordinary folks' needs, there are a few mines in this region and the workers there have to be paid on the first of the month. This time, that large sum of money came into the bank after the Christmas holiday. If he had escaped before Christmas, Amaresh Raha wouldn't have been able to take all of this cash with him. The two suitcases that he was carrying have yielded banknotes worth one lakh and eighty thousand rupees.'

Byomkesh stretched out in a supine position and said, 'Any further questions?'

'When did he shave his beard? In the train?'

'Yes. That's why he purchased tickets for the first class. There are less chances of having co-passengers in the first class.'

Satyaboti asked, 'Who sent the anonymous letter to Mahidharbabu?'

Byomkesh said, 'Professor Shome. But don't be too harsh on him. The man is educated and cultured, but his life is in ruins thanks to his battle-axe of a wife. It was this marital discord that made him feel attracted to Rajani. But that came to nothing either: he lost out to Dr Ghatok. Hence, the pangs of jealousy ... There is no baser instinct than jealousy. Of the seven deadly sins, the most fatal of all is envy.'

After a brief silence, he continued, 'Malati Devi's condition is still critical. One shouldn't wish anyone dead, but I for one won't be too unhappy if Malati Devi were to depart from Shome's life at this point.'

I couldn't have agreed with him more.